DEREK BATES

SHADOWS IN THE WALL

EDWARD,

GREAT PLEASURE

TO MEET & TALK.

Derek

Shadows in the Wall
2nd edition
© Derek Bates, Reflective Productions LLP, 2015.
Published by Reflective Productions LLP
ISBN 978-0-9560040-2-4

First edition published in 2012 by Reflective Productions LLP
ISBN 978-0-9560040-1-7

Front cover by Reflective Productions
Rear cover from an original painting by Paul Lake
Reflective Productions LLP.
Jindabyne
Moonhills Lane
Beaulieu,
Hants
SO42 7YW
derek@reflective-productions.com
www.reflective-productions.com

SHADOWS IN THE WALL

CHAPTER 1

Jake Dearsey put down the 'phone and returned to the silence in his office as he re-read the article his editor, George Salard had just criticised.

"Jake," he had said, "I fail to see why you write under different names."

"Does that matter? I make no secret of it."

"Of course it matters. Are you completely naive? When you write on economics in my paper and then you do an article with different signals for someone else under one of your other names readers are confused. Why? Because many of them know you are the same writer. I know as well as you that we can only get out of the mess we are in by growing the economy but your hair shirt readers in the Eco-Society magazine have somehow convinced themselves that abstinence is sustenance. Don't get me wrong, I do have sympathy with their 'sustainable futures' but I and, by the way, our readers cannot see how a policy of rapidly declining consumption will keep people fed and in work."

"If you read what I wrote in the last edition of Eco-Society, George, you will see that there is a way to reconcile the two aims."

"You know as well as I do, Jake, that we are just ciphers. I write what the readers want to hear and what my paymaster wants me to say. This article you've just emailed to me won't please anyone. Either leave out the paragraph on the way the greed of the West is directly causing starvation in parts of Africa or I will have to send you a rejection note." He waited for Jake to reply but, hearing nothing, continued. "It pains me to say this because I like you, Jake. You are one of the finest journalists I have worked with. I can think of at least five occasions when articles you have written have had an influence on government policy. Good for our circulation I know but, if you don't stick to the rules, we will have to part".

Jake wanted to continue but George had put the 'phone down. He meditated, as he looked over the article on the laptop in front of him. What George had said was not a surprise but it emphasised his disillusionment with the business of journalism which had given him a living for most of his adult life. Needing a change of scene, he closed the laptop, put a topcoat on and went out.

His spirit lifted as he pushed open the door of 'The Leda and Swan'. As he walked in, he smiled to himself as he remembered telling the landlord, a man with no literary pretensions, that the image of the swan hanging in front of his establishment was classical pornography rendered acceptable by depicting the god Zeus.

"Nothing to do with me, I'm just a tenant here." was the landlord's quizzical reply. But ever after he greeted Jake with a grin whenever he walked in.

The pub was quiet. No one he knew was there so Jake sat at the back sipping his pint of Old Peculier when the door opened and the stooping figure of fellow journalist, Martin Fluter, limped in. Near retirement, he still wore the suit, hat and the gaunt look of a sixties newspaper man.

"God, Jake, you look morose. What's happened? You've either been arguing with that woman you call your wife or... worse, you've had a rejection slip for something you've poured your delicate soul into." He puffed on the fag hanging from his lips as the dead ash fell to the floor..

Jake brightened at seeing Martin whose wit and humour never failed to elevate his mood. "The answer is 'yes' on both counts."

"Drink that muck down, I'll get you a double whisky. I'm celebrating."Martin grinned, "that series I told you about has been accepted and, wait for it - no, try to guess who d'you think bought it?"

"Not the FT."

"Right first time you clever young feller."

As they drank together, Jake looked at Martin's fingers holding the glass. They were blistered and yellow stained from years of nicotine. They and the laboured breathing of the older man were testament to a lifetime of smoking.

"Sorry to hear about the rejection, Jake but it happens. I could paper the walls of Buckingham Palace with mine." He said as the ash on his cigarette grew longer. "What about the wife, though? It doesn't take a mind reader to see she's not up to much."

Jake nodded, "It's a mad life we lead - that's the problem. I suppose that's what caused your break-up?"

Martin pondered as he drew on the cigarette and looked around at the other drinkers. "Not for married men and homemakers, is it? I've got to admit it's easier since Janey walked out. There were arguments every day. Twenty years now - but I still miss her in a strange way." He looked down at his clothes. "Ironing my own shirts is the thing I dread most."

"I wish I could say it was not obvious." Jake grinned, looking at Martin's dishevelled appearance.

Martin ignored him, went to the bar and ordered another whiskey for them both. When he had put the drinks on the table, he continued. "Journalism is complicated but I don't have to tell you that, do I"? He blew smoke into the air.

"Only the single minded make a go of it. It's not as though we work for only one newspaper and have a steady salary coming in each month. We freelancers have to turn our hands to any subject where there is a public interest and that means shutting out all distractions. I wouldn't have the time and energy for marriage. Never did if I'm honest what with travelling, meeting people and researching. It's a hectic lifestyle - puts pressure on a marriage and most break under the strain."

Jake nodded, "My first wife Bridie left me because she was alone too much. Stupidly, I hadn't realised there was a problem until once when I got home after travelling around Korea for a week. She was not at the airport to pick me up. There was no note when I got home. I phoned around to friends but they all said they hadn't seen her."

"You never told me about her." Martin said. "Then, I've only known you a few years and you've been married to Sabel all that time."

"After the divorce from Bridie was over, I went through a period revelling in single status having several flings. I even thought about looking up a girl I knew when I was doing research in Stratford years ago. Rhosa her name was, she had it all, brains, beauty and personality."

"She sounds right for you Jake, what happened?"

"Unlucky in love - that's my fate I suppose. She went for a better looking man." He took a drink. "I still miss her and, you know, I'm still convinced I will somehow take up with her again."

"Love is lovelier, the second time around," Martin sang the Sinatra song with his tobacco stained voice.

"Did anyone ever tell you that you could sing, Martin?"

"A few sycophants but I never believed them."

"I think you did the right thing." Jake grinned.

"Why didn't you contact this Helen of Troy?"

"I met Sabel, fifteen years younger than me. I suppose I was flattered that my greying hair could still attract a young woman. At first she excited me in a way that Bridie never did and a few months later we married." He watched Martin lighting another cigarette. "Sorry, you don't want to hear the story of my life do you?"

Jake guessed that his friend had been celebrating before he had reached the 'Leda'; the several drinks they'd had were instilling in Martin that love of humanity which comes from a surfeit of alcohol. "I'd like to hear your story, Jake." He leaned over and said. "You're as close as I've ever got to family, we didn't have any kids - Janey never wanted 'em. She's got two daughters now so it must have been that she just didn't want mine."

Jake took a drink from his whiskey before speaking. "Sabel and I had an intense honeymoon period in which we were happier than either of us had ever thought possible. A year went by before it came home to me that I had done what many men do and had married the same type of person as Bridie. As you say I can't change my workload or the lifestyle. One of the intoxicating things about

4

journalism is that we mix on equal terms with celebrities, Sabel doesn't like that - I get all the glamour that she craves. She suspects that because of the opportunities I get that I'm sleeping around. Bridie was the same."

"So was Janey - mind you there was some justification. You might not think so now but I was a bit of a catch when I was your age - caused a lot of arguments between Janey and me."

"Arguments with Sabel usually end in tears." Jake said. "Then she'll go out with an unhappily married girlfriend and they drown their sorrows together. Seems to have become a habit with her - drinking I mean. One evening when she was out with a friend, I made a salad and opened the cupboard to make a dressing for it. When I poured out what I thought was vinegar I smelt brandy."

"That might explain her difficult moods, Jake? You told me that she lashes out at you sometimes."

"You know when things aren't right. There's a distance, an irritation, a reluctance to smile which goes with a collapsing relationship. She stays up watching television long after I've gone to bed. I go downstairs and find her asleep in the chair, the television still on. I cover her with a blanket and go back to bed. For almost a year that's been her pattern. At other times if I wake in the night, I find her sleeping in the spare bedroom. 'Didn't want to wake you,' she says. I know it wasn't that she didn't want to waken me but that she did not want to be with me."

"When I'm round for a meal with you, I can sense that things aren't right." Martin held up his hand to the barman and ordered two beers. "I hadn't realised it had got to that stage."

They drank in silence. Jake looked at his watch and noticed the time. He walked back with Martin to make sure he got home without falling.

As he walked on from Martin's, he thought about his own life. It had become evident to him, shut away in his study absorbed in his writing that the marriage with Sabel was finished. Over dinner he and Sabel ate silently, the tension obvious to them both. They both needed to speak but neither one could muster the courage. Sabel ate slowly and, with exasperation threw down her knife and fork on the still half-filled plate.

He waited for her to speak; when she said nothing, he asked, "You're not eating, aren't you hungry?"

"No…I'm not hungry," she retorted sharply.

"Are you unwell?"

"That's right, I'm not well."

"What's wrong?"

"We are wrong!"

"How d'you mean?"

She glared at him. "You know exactly what I mean!" she said venomously. "Don't tell me you're not aware of the way things are. If you cannot see the obvious you must be blind."

Jake picked up the bottle of wine standing between them, filled his glass and drank while he considered what to say. "No, I'm not blind." He put his glass down purposively. "What are you suggesting?"

"It's over between us," she said defiantly staring into his eyes. "There's nothing left in this marriage. Marriage is not the right word anymore; we just exist in the same house. There is no pleasure in being together; you're so wrapped up in your writing that you make it obvious you have no interest in me."

"And you've got no interest in my work. You never have."

"I've never pretended that politics is my scene."

"Would things have been different if I had written for one of those fashion magazines you spend most of your time reading, is that it?"

"Fashion, what would you know about fashion?"

He was about to respond when he stopped himself. "No point in starting an argument. You're asking for a divorce, I suppose" he pursed his lips and took a heavy gulp before continuing. Finally he said "It's ok by me. The last year's been pretty empty for us both."

The decision, once it was made, was such a relief that Sabel took Jake's hand and said. "Sorry it has to end. Let's go out for dinner tomorrow and make some plans, shall we? We could go to my favourite restaurant in Stow on the Wold. You haven't been with me there for years. I only ever go with Julianna's group."

6

Jake smiled his agreement.

In the restaurant they each relaxed.

"Sabel," he said as the waiter cleared their plates, "I want to say that I know how you feel. I'm sorry I've not been the conventional caring husband you wanted."

"The same thought struck me. I suppose we were just never suited to each other. Now that we've decided, you can get on with your life without me being in the way."

He knew what she meant and allowed his mind to plan his future - something he had never been able to do either with Sabel or with Bridie.

For some years, he had been intending to write a book critical of political structures and the dominance of the people in power in Britain. He had tried many times to discuss with Sabel the injustice of the system which allows untrained politicians to control the lives of millions. He wanted her opinion on the interdependence of nations and the need for far more sophistication in politics, economics and capitalism. But when he told her, she merely made facile comments as she put more lipstick on.

Whenever he was at home, she wanted him to socialise with neighbours with whom he had nothing in common. The time he wanted to put aside for writing his book became consumed with trivial conversation and pointless gossip about the indiscretions of people whom he had never met.

The thought of having the freedom to concentrate on his work and the time to do research filled him with pleasure. Sabel was pleased when he told her of his plans to spend a few months in a hotel in Spain where there would be no distraction and he could concentrate on the book.

"Jake, I'm glad for you. There is nothing I'd want to do less but then it's obvious you and I are very different." She raised a glass which she had just filled with wine and said, "To you, Jake and to the book, whatever it turns out to be."

The wait for the divorce to be finalised was painful and took such a long time that Sabel forgot their peace treaty and returned to outbursts of verbal and sometimes even physical violence.

A while after they had decided to separate they were in Regent Street shopping for a dress for her for a reception they had been invited to. She had seen something she liked, tried it on and wanted it. Jake thought it was both ridiculously priced and unsophisticated and started to walk out of the shop. She rushed after him, shouting abuse. Incensed that he was ignoring her, she hit him on the back of the head with her handbag which contained a large book. Stepping over him as he fell, she stalked off without even stopping to see if he was all right. Jake, having been helped by the shop owner would have run after her but she had jumped on the first bus while it was pulling away. The shop owner gave him a glass of water to drink and tried to laugh the incident off as though it often happened to his customers.

Looking back he could see he had been thoughtless about the dress and if she had given him the chance, he would have apologised and forgotten the incident. But not Sabel. Whenever they met in lawyer's offices, she was always in an aggressively hostile mood. He noticed she had a small handbag and amused himself by wondering if the lawyers had suggested it because it would not hold a heavy book.

Jake's lawyer had advised him to sue for assault but he didn't want to. In spite of this, the lawyer brought up her attack in court and was triumphant that the settlement for Sabel was reduced. Jake found the whole procedure sordid and vowed that he would never go through marriage again.

The settlement left Sabel the Stow on the Wold house which they had bought together. Although the Cotwolds was breathtakingly beautiful and affluent from the residue of wealth from the woollen trade which had sustained Mediaeval England, it had never suited him, it was too much the domain of retired ex colonials. Their conversation bored him with their lawn problems and their complaints about the high cost of groceries and gardeners. So different from the colonies where you could get a man who would work his insides out for a few coins a day.

Sabel, conversely, had built up a circle of coffee mornings and reading groups and had no problem filling her days with idle chat.

London was the place where most of Jake's contacts were, so he loaded a few things into the car and drove to the city. On the journey, he thought with regret about the time he had wasted isolated from the excitement of the capital.

He took a hotel close to Chiswick with a room which looked onto the Thames. It was unpretentious and gave him time to re-assess his life. A nod and brief smile at breakfast was the only communication required of him. Between writing a series of articles which had been commissioned by 'Time Today', he would push his chair back to look at the river traffic and the people walking the Thames Path.

It struck him that he was watching a social microcosm in which there were three distinct periods of adult life - young couples, walking hand in hand; harassed and irritated young marrieds, pushing baby buggies, carrying children on their shoulders and shouting at their kids, and in between these were older couples holding each other's hands.

He mused on the idyll of new love followed by the stresses and financial pressures of child rearing. Some who survived the strains could find the love they had known in youth in late life.

He made comparisons with his own life. He had known the intoxication of new love many times but for him it had never lasted. He became depressed, thinking that he would always be condemned to live through failed relationships. His melancholy mood gave him an idea for an article on life patterns for 'Societies', a journal which concentrated on social relationships. The journal's editor had always welcomed his work in the past and he knew this piece would be no exception.

After starting the article he felt the need to walk and blow fresh air against his skin. In silence, he left the hotel and took the path along the Thames. Freedom from social pressures gave him time to think about what he was doing with his life and the mess he had made of two marriages. He walked for several hours, and went into a church to look at stained glass windows he'd read about. As he went to the front, he saw a young woman kneeling before the altar a few yards away from him; she looked up as she heard his footsteps and Jake was surprised to see that it was Bridie. He tried momentarily to connect with her and show concern, remorse and love in the same instant. She got up and ran past him as he called, "Bridie, please don't leave," but she ignored him. "You revolt me, I never want to see you again, ever!" she called over her shoulder as she ran out of the church.

He sat in the church and felt unutterable gloom as it came home to him that many years after they had separated, either Bridie was undergoing another separation, or she was still suffering from their own breakup. Seeing her praying alone in the church pained him. When they had married he'd hoped to give her a fulfilled life and instead she had been left with resentment.

Now that he was alone again, he found himself thinking more and more about his life. He went over his two marriages, aware that he could have done so much more to make them work. The more he thought about his past, the more his depression deepened.

As he walked into the hotel reception an older woman whom he had not seen before looked up at him as he asked for his key. She smiled but he was unable to respond. In his room, he closed and locked the door and fell on the bed, covering his head with a pillow, thinking about his thoughtlessness with Bridie and how he had repeated it with Sabel. He had loved them both in the early days of marriage and and convinced himself he was incapable of sustained, selfless love. He stayed in the foetal position for the rest of the day, not wanting to move even to get a drink. At night, he slept fitfully, tormented by a recurring dream in which Bridie, wearing a Venetian china mask had stood over him pointing a knife at his heart. He woke at five in the morning feeling unrested.

Unable to face the pleasantries and half smiles of the other guests, he rang reception and had breakfast brought to his room. As he picked at the cereal and drank the lukewarm tea, he determined to force himself to get back to normal by getting on with the pile of work in front of him.

Between writing he visited estate agents, who all assured him they had houses with the character he had asked them for. It became obvious after he had spent many futile days looking round unsuitable properties that none of them understood what he wanted.

The only estate agents who seemed to be in tune with his needs were in Barnes. Conveniently close to the hotel in Chiswick, it had the village atmosphere he was looking for, a duck pond and a quick rail journey to the centre of town. When the agent passed him details of a house close to the pond, he looked them over, nodded in appreciation, got directions and walked to look at the outside. What he saw was exactly what he was looking for.

The agent was a young South African with an over-familiar manner. "Firenze House has a history. We don't know the exact date when it was built but we know that parts of it are five hundred or more years old." While he spoke, he was watching Jake's response before continuing. "Been on the books for a few months; doesn't suit everyone of course. It's waiting for a particular type of person, someone like you to appreciate the atmosphere. You won't find one that fits the bill better. Originally small, it was extended by a merchant in the sixteenth century who did much of his business in Firenze. That's where it gets its name – it's what the Italians call Florence," he added in a tone which, to Jake in his sensitive state seemed to have a hint of condescension in it. "No one is living there; the owner has moved to be closer to his business, so I can give you the keys to look round. Don't do this with everyone you know," he said with a conspiratorial smile.

From the first moment he walked into Firenze House, Jake was captivated by its peace, silence, antiquity and its indefinable personality. It was larger than he wanted but still affordable. It had been modernised but many of its features had been retained. Although the front door opened on to the street it had a good rear garden, was close to the pond and a short walk to common land.

At the rear was what must have been the original building which was now a spacious kitchen and laundry. The lounge and the dining room had been large with tall ceilings and panelled walls.

"The place has been added to over the years. This room was divided in Victorian times," the agent said, noticing Jake's quizzical glance. "You told me you were a writer, Jake. You could make one of these rooms into a very smart library; you'll see that there are fine shelves with some nice old books left by previous owners. Mr. Iliver who's selling the place isn't what you'd call a literary man - told me the only things he ever read were the accounts of his business." He grinned.

He pushed open the door to another room. "We think this part of the house might have been a warehouse for textiles. That would have been before it was converted to be part of the home. What makes this place so attractive is the facing of Cotswold stone, added in the 1800s over what we think was probably a half-timbered structure. These unusually large rooms are a nice feature. Must have been hellishly cold in winter; the fire grates are still here but if you have ever lived in a house heated only by fires like I have, you'll know that they cook your front and leave your back cold. You won't need to worry of course, the house is centrally heated."

Jake admired the fire grates with their ornate wood carving and commented that they looked as though they were by Grinling Gibbons. The agent agreed but he "wasn't making any claims, you understand."

Jake made an offer and asked if he could know more of the history. The agent arranged for Jake to meet the owner who, he said, knew a fair amount about the house. A couple of days later they sat in the agent's office drinking over-brewed tea and eating digestive biscuits. Mr. Iliver, a short, stout man ran a fruit business, called Jake 'squire' and said if Jake needed anything, his selection of fruit was the best in London, "fresh from Covent Garden every day. I choose everything meself so I know it's good.

History ain't my line," he said, "but the foundation stone goes back more than five hundred years to 1486. Place was converted to a large home in the 1880s after it stood empty for ten years." He said he had photocopy pages from a book he had been given on old Barnes which had a bit about Firenze House.

The location was perfect for Jake, a short walk to open spaces, shops and transport. After the distress with Sabel he wanted to be alone. He relished the thought of walking on Barnes Common, Richmond Park and Wimbledon Common to give himself the thinking time he knew he needed.

He moved in while the house was still empty. Initially he slept on a mattress on the floor in one of the bedrooms while he looked around antique shops for furniture. He loved the place from the first but at night he found that what the agent had called 'atmosphere' was very pervasive. Firenze House had a personality that at times was friendly, but at others seemed possessed of moods of sadness which echoed his own feelings.

The heating system seemed to reflect the moods, the antiquated boiler was unpredictable and there were times when the house seemed always to be cold.

In his rational moments, Jake told himself it was simply that the house was partly stone which took a long time to warm up; but in periods of irrationality, which he found were occurring more often, he began to wonder if it was being perverse in remaining so cold. Plumbers came in to look at the boiler but said, as they proffered a bill. "Seems ok to me - sell you a new one if you want but they aren't as well made nowadays. Besides, we can service this one, these modern ones with all their fiddly controls break down and they forever want new bits."

The pleasure of having a house to himself lasted for only a few weeks before guilt about the divorce from Sabel and the memory of Bridie in the church filled his thoughts. To change his mood, he would force himself to think of happier things, imagining parties in which Firenze House must have rung with music and laughter. But his mind would always go back to times of suffering. He felt uneasy at what seemed to be an invasion by some presence in the house. His sleep became fitful and punctuated by dreams. Normally he would not have remembered them but these were so vivid that he found himself thinking of them during the day.

Once, when he was interviewing a young musician, he fell silent, staring into the distance.

"Are you all right, Jake?" she asked.

"Um, yes, sorry, I was distracted by what you just said," he lied.

"That music is like an addiction, completely satisfying but no way to earn a living. Is that what you mean?" she said, aware that he needed reminding.

Back to consciousness, he said. "I was just thinking that could be expanded into an article, Eleanor."

She nodded. "I now see that my father was right; I should have gone into his business as an architect and just been an amateur musician. Instead I am second violin, waiting for the old fellow who is first violin to decide he has had enough. That's another thing wrong with music, there is no retiring age. He's sixty five and could go on till he's over eighty, by which time I'll be forty and on the way to being as doddery as he is now."

"Sorry, Jake, I didn't mean that. It certainly doesn't apply to you." Jake grinned as he watched her put her hand over her mouth. "But…," she frowned, "there is something on your mind isn't there?"

He took a breath. "It's stupid, I know but…yes there is something."

"We've been around together for long enough, Jake, why don't you tell me."

"Firenze House."

"Lovely place, why?"

"Do you sense anything?"

"It's got a marvellous atmosphere, is that what you mean?"

"That's what I mean, yes." He nodded. "But it's more than that. One of the things I had always enjoyed was reading in bed."

"Same with me – so?"

"When I do I fall quickly asleep and then I dream so vividly that I wake up sweating." He saw a worried look on Eleanor's face. "You see the dreams follow a pattern; they are of trance-like scenes of injustices throughout history of religious persecution, famine, riots and the Plague which killed a third of Europe's population."

"And you're thinking too much about your dreams?" she asked. "Well, forget it. A house like yours must be full of memories and you're bound to think about them. You know as well as I that we live out our thoughts in our dreams."

Jake grinned at her but was still distracted and was not sorry when she said she would have to rush to rehearsal.

It was dusk when he said goodbye, shut the front door on her and decided he needed to go out to 'clear the cobwebs'.

He walked aimlessly, and found himself crossing the narrow and overgrown paths which traverse Barnes Common, and came upon a clearing which filled him with a sensation of menace. He tried to rationalise his mood but gave up and decided that since he had come without a torch, he should make his way home along the brightly lit streets, light the fire and spend the evening reading.

14

CHAPTER 2

Jacob D'Arcy pulled his cloak around him and moved closer to the fire burning in his grate. The wind blowing through the gaps around the doors and windows of Firenze House made the candles gutter, sending flickering shadows around the room. With an effort, he stood and walked slowly to the window to look out.

The few people in the streets were walking with their heads bowed against the freezing rain, their feet slipping on mud. The flaming torches placed on the walls of the houses to light the way were almost extinguished by the severity of the wind. Unsteadily Jacob returned to the fire, holding his hands out for warmth.

Memories of his wife dominated his thoughts. Added to the despair of bereavement, his early forties had brought the aches and pains of advancing age.

Since childhood, he had suffered from what he called his 'strangeness' which made him ill in body and mind, filling him with a sensation that life was passing from him. There were times when the affliction so weakened him that he would hear voices. His voices were benign but he knew that those heard by others caused them to commit acts of violence such as he had witnessed when he was a young boy.

The date, September 20th, 1518 would always remain in his memory. He had been visiting an elderly relative and was walking at dusk through an overgrown path in the darkening woods which led to his home in Barnes. His eyes often turned up to look at the tangled branches of leafless trees seeming to be watching him. Filled with dread, he recalled his mother's warning about wolves which could kill even a fully grown man. As he walked, he heard sounds in the nearby undergrowth. Afraid that it might be one of the few wolves still living in forests, he looked for a tree to climb. With surprise he heard the voice of a man shouting angrily. Slowly he crept closer until he came to the edge of a clearing and saw what would haunt him for the rest of his life.

A man wearing the black cassock of a priest stood looking down at a woman lying motionless on the ground. As Jacob's eyes grew accustomed to the dim light in the clearing, he saw that the woman's head was at an unnatural angle. The man was shouting oaths into the air and staring ahead with vacant eyes, unaware that he was being watched. Jacob had turned away to run home when he heard a woman's voice. He stopped, and looked back, unable to understand what he was seeing, the figure on the ground lay in the same crooked position. In the darkening light, he saw that the priest was moving sinuously acting out the attitude of a woman. From his mouth came the voice Jacob had thought was a woman's. Moments later, the man reverted to himself, cursing the body lying on the ground.

"Bitch." he screamed as he fell on his knees beside her body. "Harlot." he shouted as he grabbed her, shaking her lifeless body like a rag doll.

At the sight of this Jacob ran weeping from the scene. When he got home, his parents saw his distress. Afraid that he had seen something to frighten him, they asked him what was wrong but Jacob was unable to tell then anything.

He went to his bedroom, still haunted, knelt and prayed, his body shivering with emotion. "I don't understand," he said to the crucifix on the wall in front of him. "I must understand, my Lord, had that man killed the woman? Was he possessed by a devil?" Unable to speak any more, he broke down, burying his head in his hands.

Nearly thirty years had passed during which time his business, based in Firenze House, had prospered. He had so gained the respect of friends and neighbours that they would bring him their problems, knowing that he would find solutions. Most were without learning and were impressed by his ability to read and write.

His neighbours would watch his face as they related their troubles. What to do about a demanding landlord? How could they raise money to buy seed? What to do about a wayward daughter? He would listen to them, jot down some notes and tell them to return in a few days when he would have answers for them. Each evening, when his day's business was over he would sit with his wife Isabel by the light of a horn lamp and talk over neighbour' problems.

Isabel's health had always been delicate and when disease had spread from London and struck several nearby villages, he worried for her. When Isabel suffered an attack of vomiting, he knelt in his room and prayed. "Please Lord, do not let her suffer anymore, she is weak already."

When her illness seemed to go after a few days, he thanked God for her recovery.

For almost a week there had been no reported deaths but while out walking he had come across the body of a woman lying at an odd angle on waste ground. The memory of the murdered woman he had seen thirty years before came back to him. Unable to move, he stood transfixed as her body was taken away on a cart.

Distressed, he could go no farther and returned home. But his mood brightened when on opening the door, Isabel passed him a letter inviting him to meet an Italian merchant, Lorenzo Palloti, with whom he had done business some years earlier. He read that Palloti was coming to Dover wanting to buy a large consignment of cloth. At the time trade was quiet so he made the journey with a spirit of elation.

Lorenzo Palloti greeted him in a very friendly manner. They sat and ate looking over the sea which lapped the front of the Tavern where Lorenzo had booked rooms for them both.

The following morning Jacob passed over his samples of cloth and was gratified when the Italian smiled approvingly. They agreed a price, stood up, shook hands and embraced each other.

Jacob made the return journey on horsedrawn wagon, pleased at the terms he had negotiated with Palloti. He had drawn up a contract which would give him and his wife an income for many years. After an uncomfortable journey, he was deposited in the centre of London where he boarded another wagon to carry him home to Barnes.

Arriving in the early morning light, he walked the last half mile, picking his way carefully among the street dirt to avoid damaging the fine clothes he had worn to impress Palloti.

As he approached the house he was surprised to see that the door was gaping open. He and his wife had a strict rule of making the house secure against thieves and beggars. He pushed open the door and was surprised to see his physician in a dishevelled state asleep in a chair. Anxiety filled his mind as he rushed upstairs to his wife's room. She was in bed and at first he thought she was sleeping peacefully but as he drew closer he saw that her face was waxen and when he touched her flesh it was cold.

He heard himself screaming and took off his heavy cloak and put it over the bed, hoping that somehow the warmth of his body would revive her. Many minutes passed before he realised the futility of trying to bring her back. For more than an hour he sat beside her and talked to her as he had never done before, telling her of his love for her.

The finality of her death overwhelmed him. The emptiness she would leave in his life filled him with despair as he cursed the injustice that she should die from what the physician had told him was nothing more than a passing ailment for which he had prescribed liquorice and a tea made from dandelion roots.

As he knelt weeping silently beside Isabel's body, he heard a noise behind him, turned and saw the physician, Granby, "It is the fever, Jacob. I sat with her all night and watched her slip away."

Jacob turned his anguished face to the older man and asked, "Could you have saved her if I had been here to call you in?"

"No, Jacob, you must not blame yourself, she seemed to be better when you left. Her symptoms returned but they were much worse." He sat on the bed and put his arm around Jacob's shoulder. "Your assistant, Daniel, was working in the office, waiting for her to come to tell him what cloth to buy. When she did not come he went to her room and found her lying on the bed. He could not rouse her and ran to get me. When I came, Isabel was awake and was walking around the room but didn't look up and smile in the way I was used to." Too emotional to carry on, the physician stopped till he had recovered. "At first she seemed calm, looking out of the window at the garden but unaware that I was standing beside her. Suddenly she had an attack of shivering and almost fell as she put her hand to her head and cried out in pain. She fell on the bed and for a time was peaceful again. I sat with her thinking she was resting and would recover but then she became intensely hot and sweat poured from her. I raised her up and gave her a drink. When she had finished, she held her hands out for more and could not stop drinking. After a time, she became delirious, seeing demons in the room and screaming that they were trying to kill her. She was in such fever that I could hear her heartbeat. After shouting out, she fell back and slept, and I thought the crisis was over. I was pleased when her pulse gradually stopped racing but then it grew weaker and... she was gone."

"Why? Isabel, was so young and full of life and..." Jacob shook his head in disbelief.

"This disease is something none of us understands. I thought it was over but now I fear it is coming back to attack the village again." Granby said, through tears. When he had regained control of himself, he said. "Take care of yourself, Jacob. Stay away from the river, that's where the fever comes from, especially in the morning when mists rise. If you do have to go there, put a handkerchief filled with lavender over your mouth and nose and only breathe through that."

The physician left, saying that he would arrange things for Jacob.

Left alone, Jacob went to his room and knelt facing the crucifix.

"Help me to understand, why Lord," he said, "why did you take my Isabel?" His body shook. "We have lost so many people to disease. I have alchemy and my friends have medicine but we are still unable to prevent even one person dying." In anguish he beat his breast with his clenched fist. "Please, God, you must know how to stop the deaths. Tell me how..." Overcome, he could no longer speak and fell to the floor weeping before he returned to his wife's bedside.

The sun was setting and it was beginning to get dark when there was a knock at the door. Having sat for so long staring at his wife's side, his joints ached as he walked to the door.

Outside was a woman dressed in black, her face shrouded. He stared at her, not knowing what to say.

"I am Frances Riond." When Jacob did not reply, she said, "I am to mourn for you, Sir."

Jacob, still baffled stood silent.

"Your wife…she's dead," the woman said. "I will mourn for her." She repeated, annoyed that he did not seem to understand what she was saying. "The doctor said he would arrange things for you and asked me to come. I will mourn, it is what I do. You can go about your business."

Still unable to take in what she was saying, he stood with his mouth open. They stared at each other before his mind cleared. He fumbled in his cloak, took out a coin and gave it to her.

"You are kind, thank you" he said, "but I will mourn her myself."

"I'd help with other things as well."

"Thank you I…" he said hesitantly, "just want to be alone with her, nothing more."

The woman looked at the coin, put it into her pocket, shrugged her shoulders irritably and said. "You will be sorry, Mr. D'Arcy. I can be very useful." Turning, she walked away leaving Jacob wondering what she meant.

Back in his room, he knelt in front of the crucifix and wept, screaming to Heaven. "Why, Lord? She had done no-one any harm; there are so many wicked people, why not them? Why not the priest who has caused so many to suffer? Why not Lord Sartone who wants for nothing but allowed ten of his tenants to starve to death? Had she not suffered enough in her life that you need to punish her more? Why did you not take me instead of her?"

After the funeral, Jacob could not stay in the house and would wander aimlessly around the common, or lie for hours on the damp earth around her grave, sobbing and lamenting.

CHAPTER 3

After his wife's death, Jacob struggled to find a purpose for his life. He was unable to concentrate; nothing seemed to have any meaning and his only solace was sleep. He slept at least twelve hours every night and during the day. Even when awake, he counted the hours before he could go to bed again. He had no appetite and had lost so much weight that his friends found him almost unrecognisable. They would raise their hats to him as he shuffled by, eyes cast to the ground without seeing them. He was grateful that he was able to leave the running of the business to assistants.

The house which had always given him pleasure, depressed him so much that he would have to walk out into the streets, his cloaks dragging through putrid rubbish. He had frequently been irritated at Isabel's constant tidying up after him, but saw how necessary it was. He made efforts to put things away, but it was all an effort to him. It was only after he had fallen over on a heap of books which he had meant to move that it occurred to him that he would have to get someone to look after the house.

Time passed idly by; neighbours who visited him with problems to solve found him unable to talk about anything other than the unfairness of his wife's death, and would leave him, shaking their heads.

Eventually, he began to show interest in other people and their worries and even began to get some pleasure in conversation again.

By midsummer when there had been no rain for many weeks and the sun was searing the fields around Barnes, ponds were beginning to turn green and to stink, and some had dried up completely. Amongst the villagers, fear was growing that disease would return.

Jacob was trying to sort through letters and business papers which had piled up on his desk. Outside, the heat hammered on the roof and made the earth parchment dry so that deep cracks were forming. Jacob had opened every door and window to get as much benefit as he could from the shallow breeze which was too weak even to cause leaves to flutter on the trees.

Through the open door a tenant farmer, Jerkel Manter, who had been persuaded by friends to try to get Jacob to return to normal, came in, his boots striking the stone floor of the entrance hall and rising eddies of dust. Without being asked, he fell into a chair, sighed, mopped his face with a dirty rag and raised his arms away from his body, so that sweat would evaporate from his mud-stiffened clothes. Jacob offered him a drink of ale which he poured gratefully down his dry throat.

After he had wiped his mouth with the back of his hand, Jerkel said, "got a puzzle for you to get you a' thinkin'. I been wondering about dead and living things, Jacob."

"What brought that into your mind?" Jacob asked, his eyes brightening at a subject which interested him.

"My meat; it got me wonderin'."

"Your meat?"

"Before a week's out of me killing a sheep, it begins to live again."

"Live?" Jacob said looking puzzled.

"When I kill a animal it's only got one head thee knows."

"Yes, but why are you telling me?"

"In days it starts to have dozens of heads, tiny, wriggling things and the smell makes me heave. I seen it many times afore. I know 'tis because of this heat we're having, it do never happen when the snow be on the ground. I've seen it even when there's no sun but it do take longer. Canst thee tell why God wants dead meat to live again."

Jacob looked into the distance over the farmer's shoulder for inspiration. He stayed for so long motionless his mind enveloped with memories of his wife that he was not aware that Jerkel, tired of waiting, had stood up and left through the open door.

Wanting to share his thoughts with Isabel, he went out of the house through the blazing heat and into the churchyard where she was buried. She had died so suddenly that many wanted her buried in the lime pit with other fever victims. Jacob insisted that her body should be wrapped in thin lead sheet so that water could not reach her to spread the disease. In the churchyard, he knelt by her grave, laid his head on the earth and closed his eyes hoping to hear her voice through the dry earth. There was no sound, but just being near her was a comfort to him.

Kneeling made his knees ache, so he pushed himself up and let his eyes wander over Isabel's grave while he thought about what Jerkel had asked him.

He had seen what Jerkel described but had never thought much about it; indeed it seemed to make the meat more tender when it was cooked. He suspected that like rain and thunder there was no simple explanation and it might always remain a puzzle.

Into his mind came Ecclesiastes 3:1: 'To everything there is a season – A time to be born and a time to die.' There was a time for rain, a time for sun and perhaps there was a time for dead meat to be born again with a hundred heads.

"Can it be stopped?" he asked of the dead earth covering Isabel. The voices of his mind said, 'No more than you can send rain back to heaven, some things are ordained and are beyond man's reasoning,' but his scientific mind forced him to search for explanations.

For the next couple of weeks he found himself frequently thinking about the wriggling heads and the tiny white bodies which, although they looked the colour of death, must obviously be dead meat becoming alive, as Jerkel had said.

His business was out of season so he had time to meditate on the problem. Once, when he was in his study and his new housekeeper asked what he wanted to eat, his mind was so absorbed that he did not hear her and she went away. She had only been with him for a week and did not yet understand his habits. Thinking he was displeased with her, she had gone to her room and sat on her bed, wondering what she had done wrong.

When he returned to reality, Jacob was no nearer an explanation. The wriggling heads could not be new souls because the meat was from a dead animal and, the Church taught that only man had a soul, and then only one. He also knew that the wriggling things could be killed by soaking the meat in salt water or by hanging it up a smoking chimney.

The thought of smoked meat made him aware that he had not eaten. "Where is she?" he thought. "She should be cooking by now." He opened the door calling. "Mistress, where are you?" and was gratified to hear the sound of movement coming from the small room at the top of the stairs as she pushed open the door on its wooden hinges.

"Yes Mr. D'Arcy, sir."

He started to speak with his voice raised so that she would know that she was not doing what was expected of her. "What…" and then noticed in the dim candle light that she was wiping her eyes as she came down the stairs. "Is something wrong, Mistress?"

"No sir."

He stood aside to let her come in to the room and saw that her eyes were red.

"Are you not well?" he asked.

"I am well, sir."

"Then pray tell me why do you not have dinner ready?"

"Oh, sir, Mr. D'Arcy, I asked you a full hour since but you were not speaking to me."

"I am so sorry, Mistress, you will get to know that when I am in my thinking senses, or when my strangeness is upon me, I do not notice anyone outside of me." He stopped and looked at her, wondering if she could be trusted. "I… have…" he searched for words, "an ailment you see. When it affects me, I may seem not to be there…to be sleeping but with my eyes open. The ailment is in my mind alone so you need have no fear that you will be stricken. But the people out there," he waved his hand at the window, "if they knew, they would say that I am possessed. I want you to promise you will say nothing to anyone about this. Can I rely on you?"

"Sir, I am here as your servant. I do thank my maker for what I have in your house. I will not do nothin' that you don't want."

"Thank you, Mistress," he said. "You may find that I may just seem to be dreaming but when it strikes me severely I am told my ailment is not fit to be seen. I fall to the ground when I am like that."

"My man was like it, sir I know what to do for you. I would cover him and move everything away from him so that he do not hurt hisself."

"We must thank God that you were able to care for him and…" He hesitated, wondering if what he wanted to say would reveal the warmth he was beginning to feel for her. "Thank you, I am so pleased to have you here to look after things, Mistress. If you find me unable to speak and you want to tell me something but I can't hear you, leave me a note and when I get back to my ordinary sense, I will read it."

"I …canst not, Mr.D'Arcy." she said awkwardly. "I have only the little reading in me which the people in the last house I worked in did learn me, but I'd not be able to write so as you could read it." She wiped her hand on her apron, "If you are to eat soon, I will finish the cooking. 'Tis not far off ready, sir; I just have to build the fire up to heat it."

"Thank you, mistress; I shall be with my books until you call me."

He had been thinking a lot about her in the past few days. His mind went back to when she was one of many women who had wanted to keep house for him. She had seemed a scarecrow-like creature, ill cared-for in ragged clothes, underfed, looking suspiciously around her and with a strong odour about her body. But the other women were even less appealing. When she moved in to Firenze House, Jacob was surprised that she brought nothing with her apart from the clothes she stood in.

He chose her above the others because he sensed that she was more intelligent. Even beneath the dirt there was something which appealed to him and which also seemed vaguely familiar. He asked where she lived and she said "The streets, sir. Since my man did die, there weren't nobody to give me a roof."

He wondered about her man but felt he did not have the right to enquire. "Did you not think of going to a nunnery?" he asked.

"Sir, no, there were a woman who bin a nun; she did say to me that you wasn't let to speak, that you got up through the night praying and you did things all day that had no meanin'. She did run away from the nunnery. I am my own self. I don't want that life, t'would drive madness in me."

He nodded and returned to read his books while she cooked, but found he was unable to concentrate. His thoughts kept revolving around how much she had changed. The woman who looked after the linen had brought back several dresses and other garments which had belonged to Isabel. Jacob asked his new housekeeper if she had need of them. She was at first embarrassed but, when he insisted, she accepted gratefully. Washed and dressed in the new clothes, she looked comely to his eye and, he noted with pleasure that she was more confident. He also saw that her face was free of the pock marks which scarred the faces of many women.

He soon found that she learned quickly and would often understand what he needed even before he did. He smiled to himself with satisfaction that he had the good sense to recognise that she was not like the other women he had interviewed.

She was as awkward with him as he was with her but gradually their relationship became one that they were comfortable with.

"You may sit, you know." He said after she had been with him a few weeks when she stood waiting for instructions. He indicated the chair on the other side of the table. "No, sir, I should not sit in your room. The room upstairs is for me sitting in and 'tis very comfortable."

"I want you to know that while you are here in this house, you should forget that I am your master. Those things you didn't like about your life out there," he nodded indicating the street outside, "you should also forget about. Behave as though all those people who treated you badly do not exist anymore. In this house I want you to have a name. What are you called?"

"I'm not named. Them out there did never speak to me. 'Twas because of my man - he could do things no one understood and the priests didn't like 'im for it. They was afeard on him and didst say my man was from dark so like him I was dark called."

"Dark? Dark called? Then your name will be 'Dark call', Darkall, Mistress Darkall."

The newly named Mistress Darkall dropped her head in acquiescence. "As you wish, sir"

"No, it is not as I wish, it is for you to decide. Is it a good name for you?"

"If you wish it, sir."

"No, I don't want anything that has been imposed on you. Do you like it?"

Her gaze lifted and her eyes contacted his for an instant, before she looked down at the floor again.

"I like that name Darkall, it do sound well."

He put his hands on her shoulders and guided her to sit in the chair. When she was seated, he said. "Now, Mistress Darkall, I have to ask something of you even more important than being silent about my illness"

"Yes, Mr. D'Arcy. What must I do?"

He could see fear in her eyes and guessed that she suspected that he meant that she should pleasure him.

Jacob saw the look in her eyes and quickly said, "no, Mistress, not what I want you to do, but what I want you not to do."

She nodded but looked puzzled. "Tell me, sir."

"I am interested in scientifical things."

"I don't know what they are, sir."

"No, not many people do. It means trying to discover new things and then to make use of them. There are a few friends that I have, who meet in this house, in this very room," he said, waving his hand in the air so that her eyes followed as they would a fluttering bird. It was a trick he used when he wanted to add illusion to his speech.

"We have decided to use the word scientifical because no one else that we know uses it. Our group meets to learn. We learn from each other, we talk and we carry out what we call 'experiments'. We are seeking knowledge, and understanding of how the earth is made, how we are made, how plants grow, what makes rain, all these things and many others."

He stopped to make sure that she understood. "We also want to discover a secret cypher," again he paused and seeing that she appeared to understand, continued. "We call it, the stone of the philosophers. If we find it, it is said that it will have magic powers, able to change base metal into gold."

"I'm sorry, Mr. D'Arcy, all that you are saying is outside my knowin'."

"While you are here we will talk about many things; some of them will be difficult but with the mind you have I am sure you will understand.

"Sir, I would like if you can explain," Her eyes wandered and she looked out of the window. Jacob guessed that she was thinking of the time before she started as his housekeeper. "I only learnt things when I met my man. He was clever, he talked like you, sir, told me many things of wonder which got me athinkin'." She stopped and looked up awkwardly, wondering if she had spoken out of turn.

Noticing her consternation and wanting to reassure her of the value of her opinion, Jacob said "Do go on Mistress; tell me what you spoke about with your man."

She took a few moments before she spoke cautiously. "People said he was strange and at first he was so to me. Would stare into the sky at night for hours - many times he talked about God – said he could see him in the stars and in the things round him. He picked up a big round pebble one day, chucked it for me to catch and did say. 'Look at that Silda,' – that was a funny name he give to me – 'God is in that stone you have in your hands. Feel his presence.' And I did too, it felt warm to me. He said, "God is in everything around us. 'tis how he knows everything we do.'

I only started to live after I met him." Overcome with her memories, her head fell forward. "I will never go back to the streets, sir. I ver' near died afore I met my man and I'd as soon died the day they killed him."

"You must tell me more about your man later. But what happened to you is now all behind you and you will never again suffer such things as long as I am around," he touched her arm, sensing a momentary excitement from the intimacy growing between them. "I will be pleased to teach you anything you want. First we will build on the things that you know and then go on to things new to you," he looked sternly at her, "but I must ask you again not to tell anyone about what you learn and what we do here. There are important people who say that learning is an evil thing for ordinary people."

"I swear I would not, sir but what're you afeard on?"

"I am a Catholic believer but in these troubling times, I worship only in friend's houses. We believe that the Catholic religion is the only true one but we want it to become more human. As things are, anyone with new ideas would be punished by the Church."

"I be not in danger then, sir."

Jacob laughed with her, pleased to see that she could make jokes about herself and suddenly aware that he had not laughed for a long time. Isabel had not liked frivolity.

When he stopped laughing, he said, "There was a man called Daniel of Morley; he brought back new ideas from Toledo, but anyone who was found reading his writings could be excommunicated. Another man called Roger Bacon - was imprisoned for doing scientifical things." He stopped to think.

"Let me explain, Mistress," he said. "We are blessed by having a brain," he touched his head, "it makes us different from beasts. We are able to think and to reason in a way that no beast can and our minds need knowledge like the body needs food. There is much to be discovered by my Group. I am convinced that there are inventions which can make life easier for the poor people we see out there." He pointed out of the window.

She nodded her head. "I know, I seen people dying from nothing to eat. So many did die same time as your wife; some died from no food to eat but most was from the sickness. Bodies would lie many sunsets before the carts did come and carry them off.

"Near where I was they dug a big hole, put white stuff in it and chucked the people in it, some on 'em weren't dead but they were from the streets and nobody did care about them. I was in fear I'd get thrown in as well. I seen that happen when a man walked by that they didn't like the look of, they picked him up and pushed him into the pit."

"Three friends, good men, clever men were taken." Jacob said. "One of them, Quarly his name was, was working on an elixir which he said would cure the sickness. Whatever it was, it died with him. We need more scholars like him who understand medicines.

"We don't have nearly enough in England. Much of what we know is from clever men who came from Greece and Arab countries many hundreds of years ago. There is a physician was Paracelsus who believes that there must be a balance of chemicals in the body. He treats people with his potions and cures many. He also believes that some illnesses are caused by the mind."

"I do think that too, I've seen people die because they didn't want to live. What did other Arab people do?" She asked.

"They gave to the world many subjects such as how to make plants grow, music, law, money management, navigation, books, science and much more. This was while we in this country were fighting each other with primitive weapons and we had no real scientifical knowledge. Only now are we beginning to catch up, but very slowly, because the Church's doctrine limits us."

She nodded slowly. "My man did talk like you, sir but what he did say were sometimes beyond my reason." She smiled. "T'ain't difficult, I never had to do much reasonin'."

Jacob smiled with her. "What did he look like, your man?"

"He had a bent body and when he walked he had a funny leg." She dragged her leg and hunched her back, laughing as she did. "Like that but he was such a man as never before'd I met."

Her humour was infectious and Jacob laughed aloud at her comic walk.

When she had finished clowing, his face lightened. "Did your man have a stall where he sold rabbit skins to make coats?"

"He did, sir, I used to clean the skins for him. He were called Benjy," she said with tenderness in her voice.

"Then I knew him, not well but I did meet him, once when I was at his stall to buy fur for Isabel and once when we passed each other in the street. We spoke, not for long but enough for me to see that he was not an ordinary man. I was going to ask him to come to one of our meetings if I had seen him again."

"He did tell me he met you," she said. "He was a ugly little man, all the women would laugh at him and at me 'cause I stayed with him. But, when we was alone every night when the light went, we'd sit in the dark and he would talk of everything in the world. He had music in his head which would make him dance in a awkward way. There were times when I could not make much out but the way he spake made him most lovely. He did say he met you, sir when you bought the fur collar for your wife. He did want to come to talk a' you," her eyes flickered in the light and emotion revealed itself with a solitary tear on her cheek.

"Sometimes he'd ask me," she continued animatedly, "'why do we breathe, why can't we breathe in water?' He tried with a dried stem of Queen Anne's Lace he laid hisself back in water and put it in his mouth. He could breathe with it underwater if the stem did stick up in the air." Suddenly a sadness came over her. "He did sell seeds of Queen Anne's Lace 'cause they would stop women falling with child. The priest said such things were of the devil. They got him – drowned him. But 'twas only because he was clever and told stories and made things which no one'd ever seen afore. Because he did magic, they made 'im out as evil."

Knowing now that he had met her man, Jacob said, "I know what happened to him. I saw a man of the Church, goading the villagers into frenzy to make them believe that your harmless man with his bent back was wicked and hated by his maker. I heard the priest telling the people that your man was responsible for their misfortunes and saw them tie him to a board on a tree trunk like a seesaw. When he went under the water the crowd cheered because they could see him drowning, proving to them that he was guilty." Momentarily a thought struck him. "I remember now that is why you looked familiar to me when you first came here; it was there that I saw you, trying to reach your man and weeping hysterically as the crowd stood in my way."

Mistress Darkall was overcome with the memory but said, "I wanted to hold him but a woman like a witch shouted at me 'Serves 'im right, my son died las' week. It was 'im,' " Mistress Darkall pointed and pulled a face. " 'im what done it. 'im with 'is magic. Thinks 'isself clever. Look at 'im now. 'is magic don't save 'im do it?'"

"Yes, I was there, Mistress. I prayed that your man would survive so that I could have him brought here to this house where he could have stayed away from those creatures. Those people have the bodies of humans but they are demons in the flesh. We shouldn't blame them; it is not their fault they are like they are. The Church has filled them with hatred and if your man had not been there, they were in such a mood that they would have turned on someone else. The crowd tried to drag you off when your man had been cut from the board," Jacob said. "I saw that you could not get past the hands holding you back."

"I stayed long enough to see them take him off to bury him. At least they weren't like other crowds I have seen who would tear off limbs, burn them or worse, feed them to the dogs."

Jacob wanted to comfort the young woman whom he could see was breathing deeply with emotion at the memory.

Mistress Darkall sighed deeply and buried her head in her hands. Her grief caused her to lose herself but within minutes she sat up with her hands folded in her lap. Jacob stretched his hand forward to comfort her and continued. "The trial by water which they gave your man is just superstitious nonsense and proves nothing."

She was still distressed and to distract her, pointed at the floor, "Something I must tell you, Mistress. You may wonder why I cover this floor. Sometimes I fall to the ground and could hit my head. The sheepskins are to soften my fall." he said, reaching down to touch the skins. "From what you told me, it sounds like he might have had the same ailment as I have. If they did to me what they did to him, I too would die but more quickly than your man because I am older and less strong.

There is one other ailment I must tell you about, Mistress, it is called melancholia; I have had it since I was a child."

"Melancholia, sir?"

"A sadness which afflicts me; I find that when it is upon me, there is nothing that interests me, I sit passive, I cannot talk to anyone. Oft times I have to go to my bed and stay there without light." He looked to see if she had understood and when she nodded her head, continued. "I am not alone in this; some of my friends also have the affliction. It seems that when I think a lot, my mind uses up its strength and needs a period of somnolence to become fortified. With me it lasts for no more than a day or two. You will think I am aggrieved as you did when you couldn't rouse me for dinner. But with you that will never be so, I am indeed pleased with what you do for me."

"My man – he was the same. He would be quiet and he would say he needed to be alone and sleep. I'd await and always he'd return and would laugh and talk, sometimes 'twould be days."

She seemed to be regaining her peace but he sensed that it was a great effort for her and he suspected that she did not want to speak much. "I will read for a while, Mistress."

She went into the kitchen and closed the door of this room behind her. Sitting down, he opened his book but found he could not direct his thoughts away from the woman who had just left. The wind outside murmured mournfully and throughout the house it caused the tapers to flutter and the fire in the grate to flare its light around the room. He heard a sound and became aware that he was not alone, and turning saw his housekeeper standing at the door.

"You startled me, Mistress. Is there something you need?"

"Sir, I only want to say," She hesitated, "my sorrow that your lady died."

"Thank you." A look of sadness came over his face. "Do sit here," he said, indicating a chair. Hesitantly she sat down and waited for him to speak. With some awkwardness, he gathered his thoughts and when he spoke, his voice was restrained. "My wife and I…well…we did not share a great love, we married not because we chose each other but because the families wanted to join their businesses. But we grew together and became used to each other." Overcome, he was unable to speak. While she waited for him to recover a look of concern came over her face. When he spoke again there was a break in his voice. "Her going seemed so pointless and only afterwards did I realise how much she meant to me. I cursed God that he had taken her away before I'd had the sense to tell her of my love and that I had grown used to her not wanting physical contact."

"Did you not go to other women, sir?"

34

"No, I know many men do but for me that was always distasteful."

To clear his mind of the memory of his wife, he stood up and went to look over the books on his shelves before returning to his seat and continuing. "For some time after she died, I did not want to go on and it seemed that my life had ended with her going. But gradually, the pain lessened and now I can see that I would have been wrong if I had decided not to continue with what she and I had built together." He looked up at Mistress Darkall; "You have suffered too, and in a horrifying way. To see your man in the full flood of life killed in front of your eyes must have torn you apart."

She lifted her apron to her eyes. "Why did they want my man dead, he never done no harm?"

"There are people in the Church who want us all to live in fear."

He could not gauge her thoughts from her facial expression and she surprised him when she said, "I know what you mean, sir."

"We are not allowed to think for ourselves, and it has been so for centuries." He spoke slowly. "We are ruled by Monarchs, wealthy land owners and are told that the Church is supreme and that, like all God's works, is perfect. Most of their congregation do not understand because the clergy speak only in Latin. 'Nulla salus extra ecclesiam' they say. Do you know what that means?"

She shook her head. "No sir, I don't."

"It means, 'Outside the church there is no salvation'", he said.

"What do they be meaning sir?"

"They are saying that unless you believe what the church tells you and stay within its laws, you will not be saved. They tell you that you will suffer hellfire and damnation. The Church organisation that we have exists not for the people or to glorify God, but to feed greedy and powerful men, for the men of the Church and to keep us suppressed. The Church tells us the myth that we shall go to Hell if we do not obey its laws. Would a merciful and forgiving God expect that from us? Why should we keep these lazy people in idleness?

You should know that I do not agree with much of what the priests say. Your man was not evil, even though the so-called men of

35

faith called him that. These self-serving men have bent the message of Christianity to their own ends. They were afraid that what your Benjy had to say would cause people to question their system and order."

"I always worried when he went to talk out on the common. Many people come to listen and cheer him. 'e would shout loud as 'e could and they who was listening would cheer. Last time, four big men pushed 'im off 'is stool and kicked his bent back and 'is face. The crowd turned on the men and they ran off. We carried Benjy back to the hut where we lived. But men had set the place alight. We put the fire out with buckets of water from the river, but the place did stink of smoke ever after." She wiped her eyes again. "Benjy weren't down, he just laughed when I cleaned 'is face and did say, 'all these things make us stronger' I put my arms round him and blood got on my clothes but I minded not." Benjy laughed. 'Trying to destroy my looks. They got the wrong man. I couldn't look any uglier, could I?" As Mistress Darkall told the story she was trying to smile.

"I am sorry I did not hear him speak." Jacob said. "One of our Scientificals, Josephus told me he had heard a bent man speak on the common and had been astonished at the things he was saying. He told me of the cheers of the people who listened and that he had many followers. I was going to go to hear him but they killed him before I was able to." A thought struck Jacob, and he said, "Imagine if we could rouse the people, we could shake off the chains the priests use to hold us and become free."

"Free, sir?"

"Free to think our own thoughts, free to use our own English language in religion and to find our own God. We have our own language but we are told that it is crude. Did anyone say to you 'Oft ic wig seo, frofre ne wene'

She looked down at her feet. "No sir them words are foreign to me."

"No need to feel disappointed, Mistress. Our language has been so corrupted by Latin and French that we have been persuaded to think of Old English as a peasant way of speaking that only an untaught man would use. But there has been much written in Old English that the Church wants forgotten. It is what we call a conspiracy." He saw that she was frowning. "By that I mean 'a trick';

a trick to keep us in order. Your man transgressed and they killed him in that trial by water."

"But if he was without sin, he would have lived. Is't not so?"

"No, mistress, you see how, even you; you who have suffered much, have been so persuaded by them that you believe he was guilty of something. No, no, no! Mistress," Jacob shook his head decidedly. "I have already said that his death proved only that he was not a strong man in his body. His only sin was that he was challenging the self-righteous orders of the Church and our rulers. "

"That is just what our group of thinking people wants to do. Amongst other things, we want to get English back to replace Latin in services."

He saw her still frowning. "Let me explain. I told you that there was a Cardinal who said 'The Church is the work of God and cannot be changed because it is perfect.' He and many others say this so that they can live in comfort, never to suffer as you have. Never to have fear as you have, never to be hungry as you have been hungry. Do you see what I mean?"

When she spoke her gentle voice drifted around the room so that even in the silence, he had difficulty in hearing her. But he was pleased that her voice had a tone of confidence that had not existed before. "You have told me we have God in our hearts, why do we need a church. Is't not like Benjy said 'God is in everything. Is he not in the air, in the sky, on the wind and in the sun and the rain?'" She raised her head as though in surprise at what she was saying.

Jacob noticed with pleasure that there was a change in her voice when she talked with him. Whereas when she was working, she lapsed back into street vernacular.

"You have told me you want to learn new things?" he asked.

She fumbled with her hands, smoothing her dress before she replied awkwardly.

"I do but don't you just want me to cook and clean and to serve you?"

"Yes, I do need you to take care of the house and the cooking because that is something you do well but which is beyond me. I do not want you to 'obey' me. No one has the right to dominate another person. There is great pleasure in learning and I would like to teach you."

She looked so pleased that he wanted to touch her hand but instead said. "Do you know what I think, Mistress?"

"No, sir, I don't."

"I think there is music in you waiting to be played."

"D'you mean singing, Mr. D'Arcy?"

"I do like to hear you singing in your room," he said, "but no, what I mean is that, when we think, we form patterns like music."

"I want to learn, sir." She fumbled with her apron. "When my man did talk I liked the sound and his talk did mostly make meaning to me but not always."

"Does my talk make sense to you?"

"Sir, I likes to hear your voice but I don't always know the sense."

"You know why that is?" He looked into her eyes. "It's like when I used those old English words and they meant nothing to you. Your ear has not yet been trained."

She remained quiet, her eyes cast down on the floor before she said, with hesitation, "Wil't be hard, sir?"

"If I tried to teach you by rote, it would be, but I do not believe that is the right way. I will just tell you of mysteries and when you have learned how to write, you will be able to write them down. At first it will all seem difficult but slowly things will stay in your mind. You will have seen small snowballs being rolled downhill, as they roll they get bigger; that is what will happen. But we have talked enough."

"I must clear away," she said, moving things off the table and carrying them into the kitchen.

Jacob stood up with great effort, staggered slightly and steadied himself by clutching the table.

She saw how unsteady he was, put down the things and went to support him. "Thank you, Mistress. I have not been feeling well for two days. I will sleep here tonight if you wouldn't mind getting the bedclothes for me," he said as she helped him onto the couch.

CHAPTER 4

It was six in the evening and already the light was fading; the day had been cold and grey with a tumultuous wind and rain. Jake had returned from an interview and, instead of walking as he would normally, took a taxi from the station. On the way, he chatted with the driver, a Jamaican man who had recently arrived in England. He told Jake he had been in the Caribbean when a hurricane had struck the island."Started just like this; strong gusty wind but overnight it turned violent. Frightening it was. Trees down, roofs blown off, twenty nine people killed including my neighbour and his kids. Wife had left him and was going to live with a white man in Florida. I never found out if she was ok - hurricane was going in her direction so she might have joined him in heaven." He grinned at Jake as he pulled up outside in front of the pond and looked at the large oak beside the house. "Watch that tree, wind's blowing at your house, could smash it to pieces. You sleeping there tonight? If I was you I'd go to a hotel, man. I've seen what the wind can do." Jake thanked him and with some trepidation went into the house.

He went to bed early, slept fitfully and was woken by the cold biting into the house. The central heating had gone off even though he had left it on to run continuously. The wind had dropped and had left a stillness which contrasted dramatically with the ferocity of the night before. There was no traffic noise from the road outside. As he roused himself, he remembered that it was Sunday morning and too early for people to be collecting newspapers, jogging, driving to the golf club or the many other ways of filling rest days which non-churchgoers indulge in.

Even though he had assured himself that the silence was normal, he still felt uneasy, as though something had happened through the night while he had been asleep. He had had a powerful dream which had made him feel as though he had inhabited another body and even more puzzling, in the dream there had been a woman whom he had found attractive.

He dismissed this as nothing more than another one of the vivid dreams he had been having in the house since he had moved in. He switched on the electric blanket and took himself downstairs to turn on the central heating again. As he went back up to bed to wait for the house to warm he passed the library and saw that his desk had been tidied while he had been away. His thoughts turned to his cleaning lady, Kate, and realised he knew very little about her except that she was doing an Open University degree in history. To help her he had suggested she borrow books from his library. Once, while sitting at his desk, he had put something in the waste bin and saw beside it a screwed up envelope. He spread it out, expecting it to have his name on it. It was addressed to Mrs. Kate Beadle, in a street he remembered thinking was in a nice part of Putney. He recalled that she had told him that she lived in a large house which had been the family home of her late husband.

Jake wondered why she should be doing a menial job when she was obviously intelligent, well informed and capable of holding down something more demanding than housework. He mused that there were times when she appeared to be making overtures to him. She had come to him as a cleaner and that was how he saw her but suspected that in another situation she would have been the sort of woman he would have been attracted to.

After two failed marriages, he had become wary of women and had reached a period in his life where he did not want any other serious entanglements, at least until he had sorted himself out.

Firenze House seemed to be able to sap his energy and when he was working on an article, he found he had to force himself to write. The book on political reform which he had promised himself he would concentrate on when he became free of marriage was still only an outline.

The initial euphoria he had felt following the divorce had diminished. He often thought that he was alone too much but it was what Noel Coward would have called bitter-sweet. He enjoyed the freedom to go wherever he wanted, play loud music, meet his own friends and please himself what time he went to bed and got up but, when he arrived home from a noisy meeting with laughter ringing in his ears, he found the silence of Firenze House oppressive. As he closed the front door behind him, his footsteps on the stone floors

41

would echo around the empty rooms. He would try to cheer himself by lighting the fire and putting music on to bring life into the place. Sometimes it worked but at other times it had the opposite effect and he became mesmerised as the flames flickered, like the shadows of the many people who had lived in the house.

The personality of the house was not one that he could easily describe; at times he was convinced it was trying to tell him something. Once, he thought he heard voices but told himself that it was just his vivid imagination playing tricks on him.

One evening when he came home late he made himself a hot drink to take to bed while he read. Without knowing why, he felt impelled to go into the library even though the novel he was reading was upstairs on the bedside table.

At random he took a few books from the shelves and noticed that behind it there was a panel at the back of the book case. He took out several other books and saw that behind the panel was a recess filled with dust, cobwebs and dead insects. He brought a torch from his desk and discovered a leather bound book in the recess. With some trepidation - he did not like spiders - he eased the book out after wrapping his hand in his handkerchief. As he dragged it into the light, he saw with amazement that it was a copy of a Tyndale bible, the first Latin to English translation produced after the introduction of printing. He turned over the pages and saw that it was a complete translation. Tyndale had been executed in 1536 before finishing his work and the date 1538 on the inside cover meant that it must have been the work of others as well as Tyndale. Holding the book excited him so much that his hands started to perspire.

Transfixed by the atmosphere in the darkened room and with the emanations from the book, he sat down and picked it up and seemed to see a tunnel in front of him at the end of which was a man dressed in mediaeval clothes. He supposed that it must be Tyndale, sitting at a desk writing what Jake thought to be the bible. The writer looked anguished as though suffering at the hands of the Church. He was aware that he could be hallucinating, sensing two realities, one imaginary and the other from his rational mind. In the dim light of a flickering candle flame a woman sat beside the man, her hands in her lap listening in an enquiring manner. Although he knew the scene could only be an illusion Jake could not escape a sensation of foreboding.

Putting the book down, he walked into the kitchen and picked up his drink, which had gone cold. He looked at the clock on the wall and was surprised to see the time was 11 o'clock. He had made the drink at 10 and could not imagine where the hour had gone; he wondered if he could have dozed in the library, even though he had no memory of sleeping.

He reheated the drink, drank it and with an effort went upstairs to read the novel but could not rid his mind of the images of the man and the woman. He looked at the small desk in his room, which was screwed to the floor and had been in the house when he moved in, and realised that this same desk had been in the images he had just seen.

Jake considered himself to be agnostic but at that moment he felt the need to communicate with some being. Without thinking, he knelt down at the desk and bowed his head. As he did so, a sensation of peace came over him.

"What have I seen? Am I just tired or am I seeing shadows of people who have lived here before?" He stopped as though waiting for a reply. Then another thought struck him. "Are the images telling me something?" He spoke quietly, as though in a church, and as he did, he remembered the time he had seen Bridie kneeling in prayer. "How thoughtless I was with Bridie, and with Sabel," he said aloud, "Why did we marry, was it no more than desire?" He looked up at the ceiling as he thought about the questions he had posed himself. "Bridie, you meant so much to me." He shook his head. "It was never only lust. I loved you and wherever I was, you were in my thoughts. I am sorry for the way I treated you. And you, Sabel, was it I who drove you to find solace in alcohol?" He placed his hands on the wall with his head still bowed and was overcome by images of desperate poverty and suffering which the walls had seen.

CHAPTER 5

Often Jake would take his breakfast to eat in bed. Normally, he would listen to the news on the radio but today it seemed to him that the house wanted to be quiet so he ate silently, listening only to the sounds in his head.

He sat in the window, looking out onto the green and the pond outside. It was one of those days of inactivity when the sky was grey and the wind was breathless. For the previous few weeks he found he was often thinking critically of the life he was leading and what if anything he was achieving.

As he stared at the ducks on the pond and heard the cacophony they were making, he wondered if their lives were content. Were they aware and afraid of the foxes frequently stalking around the pond, catching and killing them, leaving only piles of feathers to mark their departure from the world? Or were they so lacking in imagination that they thought only about the present. As he looked at them, moving on the surface of the pond apparently aimlessly, he meditated on the size of their brain, and if it controlled them, or if they only reacted to impulses from the wind and currents, or the nourishing smell of pond weed.

These small creatures with equally small ambitions were obviously inferior to humans in brain power. But has intellect and the wealth and comfort it provides given us anything like the contentment these ducks seemed to enjoy? He turned from the window and surveyed the room and the antique furniture he had bought, perhaps never to be used. Downstairs the shelves in the library were filled with books which he would never have time to read. The house was far bigger than he would need even if he had had a wife and four children. Why had he chosen it, he pondered as he got up and walked around the place, trying to see it with new eyes? Was it simply that it gave him pleasure to bring friends and clients so that they would admire him for his taste?

While mankind strove to be surrounded with more than was necessary, ducks were content with just their waterproof feather shelters. As he watched, he saw that two male ducks were courting one female and at that moment the edifice of contentment he had constructed, collapsed as the two mallards fought. He smiled ironically, realising that, in the ultimate, competition drives ducks as much as it drives humans. The difference being that civilised mankind needed more provocation. While the fighting was going on, the female paddled around, eating weeds and appearing to be completely unconcerned. It intrigued him that there were only differences in degree between humans and these birds. Freud was right about the motivating power of sex; the house onto which he had grafted his own personality followed the same behaviour pattern as the preening, displaying and mating ritual of the birds.

But animals and birds would not derive pleasure from accumulating knowledge for its own sake and with no commercial outlet. He went downstairs to the book case, took out the bible and opened it.

Holding the Tyndale, he sat and thought about the few who were strong enough to protest and risk the torture meted out to dissidents. In the early 16th century, Martin Luther by nailing his ninety five propositions to the door of the Wittenberg church had been an instrument of the Reformation. He attacked Papal abuses, the sale of indulgences and the rejection of the disciplines that a true religion should have imposed.

A strange feeling came over him as he looked around the room. It seemed darker and dirtier and had an unpleasant odour of human bodies and he felt that he was not alone. Without knowing why, he placed his hands on the opened pages of the bible. He seemed to see hazy shapes in the darkness. Shadows formed people, a man and a younger woman going out of the house, looking around cautiously. Outside there was noise and crowds of people watching actors on a canopied wagon performing a miracle play.

He recognised that what he was seeing was illusory but it gripped him as though he was part of the crowd watching an allegory on virtue and its reward. Almost as though he had fallen asleep, his hands dropped away from the bible and the image of the play faded.

He reached for his notebook and wrote down all he could remember and then went to the bookshelves and took out a book on history. Inside he found notes which he had written for his doctorate on the social inequality of that period. He had written on the effects of the Black Death and the shortage of labour afterwards. Landowners had to increase wages to retain the surviving farm workers who lived well. But over the next century the balance between labour and wages returned and a day's work would only buy him half as much. Working only two days in three and then only when the weather was good enough, the farm worker could barely survive.

Some labourers who lived on farms could be paid in kind and a percentage of the crops they produced. In 1500 it could be one tenth but, at the end of the century he would receive as little as one fifteenth of the produce of his labour.

It was not possible for a labourer to provide for illness, injury or old age and the burden would fall on their children who could then suffer starvation. But landowners did not starve. In one paragraph, he had written about William Paley who at around the end of the 18th century had commented, 'In a field, undernourished pigeons are building a hillock of corn. At the top of the hillock sits an overweight family of pigeons who attack any of the working pigeons who attempt to eat from the hillock or who do not constantly add to it. Would we not find such behaviour incomprehensible in pigeons? Yet that is normal in human society.'

This gave him an idea for an article. He saw that in the modern world, the same ills were present but masquerading now in different clothing. Power hungry individuals still manipulated society, exploiting communities for their own benefit, preaching humanitarianism while ignoring the evils around them, mouthing phrases like 'If they worked as hard as me, they wouldn't be in the mess they're in'. These same exploiters receive plaudits and honours from others in power in a self-supporting cosy coterie.

Jake became depressed as he realised that the use of overt violence had been replaced by the written word of journalists such as himself.

He picked up a pen and in his notebook wrote:

I have seen the world divided in
The hearts of evil men
I have walked the streets and wondered
When will they smile again
Is this all they have to offer
Just the comfort of themselves
While the emptiness and loneleness
Rings time on distant bells
And the futile lives the others lead
Cause ripple tiny swells
On the rivers of the dead
So tell me are you ready
To begin this time again
And give to those unsteady
With a future yet unknown
Who sit alone in solitude
With clocks that tick in silent rooms

CHAPTER 6

Mistress Darkall came into the house, carrying a wrapped package. Jacob rose to greet her but stopped in horror. Her hands and her apron were blood stained.

"What has happened to you? Are you hurt?"

"No I ain't. That butcher on the stall, he've been trouble to me before. He did sell me bad meat today. I told him it was not good. He changed it and wrapped up another piece but he threw it at me." She looked down at her apron. "This is beef blood." She hurried away. "I will wash my hands and put this apron to wash."

When she returned she was wearing a clean apron and her hands had been washed.

"That butcher has been difficult for a while." Jacob said. "And yet he used to be quite a nice person. I know that he is having a lot of difficulties. His wife disappeared and left him with six young children to care for. When his meat went off before that he used to make it into stew and sell it cheaply. I suspect he can't afford to do that now." He looked up at the ceiling. "I've been thinking. There is a lady called Marita Segola, she came from Italy when she married an English sailor. He died before they were able to start a family. I know she loves children. I wonder if she would be able to look after the butcher's brood for him."

"That'd be good." She laughed. "Perhaps he'd stop selling us bad meat. But he's always been difficult to me," she said, "can't see him changing."

"I don't agree. If the circumstances of our lives change, we become different. Are you the self you were when you were born? You're not and I'm not. Look outside there at the people walking by," Jacob pointed out of the window. "Some of those people are old, some wearied by toil, some young, but not one of them is free. They've all been patterned by so many things. Often it is the Church telling us about Heaven and the punishment we will receive in Hell.

48

We believe what they say, but nobody has seen, touched or listened to Heaven or Hell."

"You did tell me about people who saw visions of Heaven though."

"That is only in the mind, you see, Mistress; we make our own reality. Every day we receive impressions. Sometimes we see them as helpful and when our mood is changed we can see them as threats which terrify us. I know that if a man is starving, he can experience visions which to him will seem to be real."

"The priest talked to us in the streets and said he seen Hell which was a flaming pit and we would all end there if we didn't learn to fear God and obey his laws," she said.

"These stories have their real purpose to frighten us so that we stop using our own minds and become passive and controlled. By doing that they are patterning us."

She still frowned. "Sir, that is new to me. What you do be saying about patterning, but I am not sure of the meanin'."

"Let me explain what I mean by patterning." he said, pulling a chair out from the table for her. She sat hesitantly, not knowing what to expect. "You see that horse going by with a rider on its back. The horse is obedient and does what its rider wants even though it is contrary to its nature which would be wild and uncontrollable. But patterning by man has so changed it that it is now of a docile nature. We are the same, we copy what we are taught by those around us and are not what we would be if we had been left alone without contact with others.

Out there you see tradesmen selling their wares, carriages going by and people wearing clothes which follow fashion. All these things happen because of what I call patterning which you can think of as a teacher sitting quietly inside us. Some people are wealthy and do not need to work, others are carpenters, tailors, shepherds or wool merchants like me. All of those patterns are good and if we did not have them and thought only of ourselves, we would starve."

"Oft times I have starved and there were nothing I could do to change things, but someone'd share bits of food with me." she said.

Impressed, Jacob continued. "We survive because we all help each other. I buy goods from William Stumpe who weaves cloth in Osney Abbey. I do it because it gives me a living. Some would criticise me for profiting from the work of others but if no one ever bought and sold cloth, the shepherd would not work and he would then not be able to buy the food and shelter he and his family needs. It goes on throughout communities. That dress you are wearing was made by Mrs Stalpeter and she charged me more than it cost her to make. If she didn't she would starve. I call all this 'constructive patterning' and it is a necessary part of all of us. But there is 'destructive patterning'."

"Can you explain?" she interrupted.

"What I mean is that if we are prevented from using our talents because of taxes and conventions imposed on us such as by Barons and Kings. Because we are made poorer we do not discover things like cures for the fever which killed my wife".

"We could do so much more to help each other. We become wiser when we have problems and find answers. But we are told that the only answers are in the scriptures and we must not question these."

"Is't not stupid, many people do die?", she queried.

"That is exactly what we think in the Scientificals. We must progress or we will never find answers. Let me give you an example".

"I was taught in a church school and my lessons were all in Latin. I used Latin figures, not the simpler figures which the Arabs use and I did no calculations because to use Latin figures is very difficult. Later when I took on the business, I employed clever men who came from the East and taught me how to calculate. The Arabs love learning and I suspect it may be because their faith does not seem to stop them."

"Dost use Arab calculations?"

"Without arithmetic and Arab numbers, I would have been unable properly to run the business. My family did not know much about arithmetic; the business was almost destroyed partly for that reason. So, even as a boy I asked myself why was I only taught the scriptures, religion and obedience to God in Latin?"

"After I left school, I continued my studies and I learnt that even four hundred years before Christ was born, Aristophanes was able to put on plays in Greece which ridiculed people in power. We cannot do that now. If I criticise those in power, I could be put to death just as your man was. So, nearly two thousand years have passed and men are less free than they were then."

"Ain't there a way to change things? I'd like to help."

"To change things is what the Scientificals want," he smiled with pleasure at her question. "I would like you to help if you feel you can but I must tell you that it is a dangerous thing to do."

Jacob saw that she wanted to know more.

"I need to explain more about what I mean," he said, "but before you do, why don't you get us both some of that honey drink you bought last week."

When she returned with the drinks and sat down again, he continued. "Let me tell you about Wycliffe, a very clever man whom we Scientificals have been talking about only last week. He was admitted to Oxford University very young. He also translated the Bible from Latin to English. The Church objected and many of his followers who took the name of 'Lollards', were tortured and killed. An Act of Parliament was passed which forbade the reading of the bible in English. Can you imagine why?"

"Is't what you said, sir - they want to stop us learning?"

"Exactly," he said, "and that is the very reason, they destroyed Wycliffe. He died a broken man. Twenty years after his death, his remains were dug up and burned in public view by orders of Church leaders. But there was such a demand for his bible that there are still many copies around, even though some years ago the church had a bonfire of all books which they had decided were heretical." He turned his eyes away from her for a moment. "Do you see what I am saying? I am talking about the way our leaders treat people who try to think for themselves."

She nodded her head, but slowly, making him think that he had not been clear in what he was saying.

"Let me tell you about William Tyndale, another clever man who was treated badly for translating the bible into English. His followers called themselves 'Christian Brethren'. Like your own man, Benjy and like Wycliffe, Tyndale was destroyed by the Church. That is why I say that anything I and my friends do and talk about in this house must never be repeated outside these walls." He looked at her intently. "We want to continue the work of people like Wycliffe and Tyndale, so that we shall be able to use our own language in religion, government and the law. Priests mumble their way through services because often they cannot understand Latin themselves. They are part of a trick that suppresses the people so that the lives of the clergy can be comfortable and secure, yet many of them are so badly taught that they cannot even tell you the Ten Commandments."

He saw that his words distressed her and let her stay quiet, staring ahead with her hands folded on her lap. Finally, she spoke, but in a whisper, so that he had to lean forward to hear her.

"There was a woman, sir, Anne Askew was 'er name, she did give me comfort when my man died; she was the only one who cared," she wiped her eyes with her apron. "Like my man they got 'er, sir; she were Protestant. They did put 'er in the Tower to make 'er change. She dursn't for the love of her Church."

"I have heard about her," Jacob said, "she was burned at the stake as a heretic."

Mistress Darkall frowned in pain at the memory. To distract her, Jacob filled the silence by talking.

"So many people have been destroyed. Marsilius of Padua in Italy risked his life by writing that the state does not need a Pope or a Church and that if a ruler is evil his subjects should overthrow him. He said that priests should be servants and have no more rights than the people."

She stood up. "I must get logs, sir, 'tis chilling in here and the fire's low."

Jacob enjoyed being able to pass on knowledge to her receptive mind, and felt momentary disappointment as she left the room. Soon she returned carrying logs in an old wicker basket. Jacob picked up the book in front of him while she poked the embers into life. He looked at her back view as she knelt to brush the hearth and realised again how comely she was in one of Isabel's unused dresses.

When she had tended the fire and settled, she said, "Canst thee tell me more, sir?"

"I am so glad to hear you ask. There will be some things which are difficult." he said, turning towards her with a smile. "But I can see that you want to learn."

"I do knowst that there is much which I must learn. Like that Marsillius you just told be about. I never heard tell of him before."

Jacob smiled with pleasure that she had remembered the name of Marsillius. "I want to talk to you about unfairness and the way some men succeed and others fail. When I look out of the window and see the wealthy cosseted and the poor often near to starving, I am driven to wonder why the Lord allows this to happen." He looked up and was gratified to see her nod her understanding. "Men have always been cruel to each other and we have always had those at the top exploiting those beneath them.

Laws should be impartial and be administered exactly the same for the poor as for the king and the wealthy people who surround them, but they are not. Two thousand years ago, Hammurabi, the first King of the Babylonian empire laid down laws which favoured the wealthy. If a man put out an eye of a noble man in a fight, he would have his own eye torn out, but if a nobleman put out the eye of a commoner, the noble would only have to pay a fine; the same ideas apply even now."

"I seen it, men who are well off treat their workers like animals and, because I am a woman, I have been spat on in the street."

"Many men are afraid of women because of lies they hear. We are told that women are the Devil's gateway and that wickedness with women is worse than all other sins committed by men. A monk has a duty to fight the forces of evil in his body and to scorn pleasures as filth. Of course, many monks ignore this and there has been a great deal of corruption and sexual laxity in monasteries. That was one reason King Henry used to justify destroying them and taking their wealth. Before he did that, there were a thousand monasteries in England; many are gone, but even now the Church is very wealthy"

"But how can that be, sir?"

"They convinced people that if they want to be sure that they or a dead relative would go to heaven, they must pay so that prayers can be offered to God.

"We are told that the Pope is incapable of making a wrong decision. A long time ago, one Pope called Urban declared that Knights should free Jerusalem from the infidel. In the battles, many guiltless people lost their lives. Is it right for the Pope to teach us to hate people we do not know or understand?" Seeing that she was quiet, he asked. "Those things I have just said..."

"Yes sir?"

"Do you know what I mean?"

She looked down at her apron and brushed away some dirt left from the logs she had just carried in. "I did, sir; as far back as I can think I wanted to read and to write and learn. My man talked about some of the same things."

"Indeed." Jacob raised his eyebrows, "It is a great sadness to me that I never got to know him. I would have enjoyed talking with him."

The fire in the grate began to blaze and sparks flew into the room. She rose and brushed soots from the floor as he looked for things to tell her from the book he was reading.

"Sir," she said, looking as she bent over to clean the hearth. "You said that there was something you want me to do. What was that?"

"Oh, yes, I almost forgot and yet it is very important," he said, looking up from his reading at her kneeling figure. "I told you about my interest in scientifical things."

"Yes, sir, I remember, and also am thinking what you told me about the Church."

Jacob glanced in her eyes and felt a momentary sense of fear as though there was a threat in her voice but the look on her face reassured him.

"If you want to know more of what we do, will you mind swearing an oath to me and the other people you will meet here? We can then get you to help.

"In my dealings with women, I have observed that they have great understanding. When, as so often happens, we are faced with problems, we should listen to opinions of both men and women." He thought for a while. "I would like to tell you everything we talk about in the Group. But before I do, we have a strict rule that anyone we talk to must swear on the bible. Are you ready to do that?"

"Do there be a bible here, sir?"

"I have Tymdale's work hidden in a panel in one of the walls in this house. I will get it but you must never speak of it to anyone else."

"I already knowed you did not want me to talk to anyone about what you said, because there is people outside here who would tell the priest about you. If that is what you wanted to warn me about, I don't need no bible. I do have no friends out of this house and I am no friend of them what drowned my man."

"Thank you, Mistress Darkall, I was sure I could trust you." He turned to a drawer and took out some papers and read a few lines. "There are other things that you should know."

"Yes, sir," she said apprehensively.

"I have told you about my strangeness, there will also be times when you may see me as though I am in a dream. At those times you should not try to waken me." He looked up at the crumbling lime washed ceiling above him, waiting to decide what to say. "There are mushrooms which when I eat them, make me see things, magic, mysterious things in amazing colours and shapes so that I see things more clearly than without them."

"My man did too and what he saw he told me about. He told me about colours brighter than anything he had seen before. He wanted me to eat the mushrooms too."

Intrigued, Jacob asked. "And did you?"

"No, sir; I was too afeard."

"I understand, but they do have the power to open the imagination." Jacob looked at her. "Mistress, I want to say something which is quite complicated - I would not talk if I did not feel that your mind is ready though."

"What be you saying, sir?" she asked, looking worried.

He turned to look out of the window. "Look out there again, what do you see?"

She stood up and looked.

"I don't know what you do mean, sir. Men are walking by, carts are being pulled. Over there's a man selling apples. The street mud be wet from the rain. Why, sir, I see much else but what dost mean me to see."

"I want you to use your mind in a different way."

"What means that, sir...?" she said hesitantly.

"I'll give you an example, I speak and read Latin but not Greek but if I spent enough time I would learn it. So that part of my mind which not able to speak Greek is not used, but it is there waiting." He watched to see her reaction, "I would like to open your mind so you can see the glory in the world out there. But be aware that what your mind lets you see will be different from what I see."

She looked confused.

"Let me explain." He pointed out of the window. "You see a man selling apples but do you not know that behind his smile he is thinking of his ailing wife and a deformed child, dying from want of a cure? A cure that I am sure we could find if we were allowed to."

"What stops you, sir?"

"We are told it is the will of God which causes that man's wife to fall ill and their child to be deformed."

"Is there anythin' you can do?"

"For the mother? Yes, there could be but it is not easy to get her to listen and that is because of what she has been told. The Priest has told the mother that her child's deformity is punishment for the wrongs she has done."

"What have she done that could be that serious?"

"Nothing, Mistress, nothing more than any of us has done."

Jacob returned to his seat and indicated again that she should sit.

"The priest visits her and tells her that he prays for her soul so that she can be released from her misery."

"The priest tried to do that for my man as well."

56

"That was the same priest. He does not want her well and he did not want your man well. He wants souls and tells everyone that they will find happiness in heaven."

"Is't not true?"

"That is what I am saying, Mistress. You are saying only what has been forced on you by…" he looked into her eyes waiting for her reply.

"The Church?"

He nodded; glad to see she had followed what he was saying.

"I wonder why the mushroom makes me see a better world."

"I cannot say, sir unless it is like when you dream."

"You may be right." Jacob said with surprise. "It must change the way our senses work and just like in dreams, we see everything differently."

"Is't possible? I have ate mushrooms which I took from the common but I was the same after."

"They are not the mushrooms that sailors discovered. There are many new things that they found in foreign lands. The place was called Tenochtitlan, but now they call it Mexico. Your man must have got his mushrooms from sailors returning from that country."

"Mexico?" she frowned, "never did hear I of such place."

A slight smile played around Jacob's lips at her words. "Mistress," he said. "You use words in your own way, a wrong way but it is like poetry. I don't want you to lose your poetry but there are other ways of speaking."

"Sir, that would I like. I do want to speak like you."

"No, I will not teach you to speak like me but I'll show you how to use words. It will seem as though I criticise you but it is only to help," he said and was pleased to see her nod in agreement.

"And the mushrooms, sir?" she bowed her head and he saw that she smiled to herself.

"Like a magic spell, the mushroom can make that drab and dirty village out there like burnished gold." He thought to himself for a moment and nodded at the window. "Perhaps what we can see out there is not real, it is the only way our eyes work and it is the mushroom that lets me look at what is really there."

"Can you tell me what you mean, sir," she said.

He pondered, took off his glasses and passed them to her. "These are a new invention, awkward to get used to but they will be made better. Clumsy as they are, they allow me to read. Without them I can see very little, when I look at you without them, your face and this room are as though in fog. Try them on and you will see what I mean."

A gasp of horror escaped from her lips as she put them on. "Sir, it makes I feel sick, when I look round the room, it do move."

"That's what I mean, Mistress. What is our reality? Mine is when I look through the glasses. Yours is when you don't. But there are many other realities. When the sun shines, we see things differently from when it is cold, raining or snowing. We like people we know one day and at other times we dislike them."

"I've not thought that."

"Think about what you see, about what I see and what those people out there see. Each will be different and not one is the right view; there never is only one truth." He took his glasses back. "Now that I have my glasses on and can look at you, I could say 'you look beautiful'. There are many ways that could affect you. You might be pleased. You might think I was just saying it to make you feel better'."

At his words, her face glowed. "Sir, I would not think such."

"You might think many different things but tell me," he turned his eyes to her to catch her response, "what would you think if I said that?"

"What'd I think?" she bent her head and spoke so quietly it seemed she did not want him to hear. "I do be happy at what you said first off," she coloured and looked away.

"Well, Mistress...I do mean it, you are beautiful."

Aware that this was a change in their relationship, she turned her eyes back to him and held his gaze for several moments before she looked down.

"I am happy." She spoke with her eyes looking down. "You have ways of saying things which are lovely to me. I want to speak in that way." She turned her gaze back to him. "Then you'd say I pleased you, sir."

It was his turn to be overcome. He opened his book to wait for words and then said. "Mistress Darkall, you do please me in many ways." They sat in silence, each wondering what to say next. He picked up his book and turned the pages.

Looking under his brows, he saw her shoulders shaking as she lowered her head. Abruptly, she got up and left. Jacob thought he could hear her weeping in the other room and for a long time he sat still, waiting. He had had so little experience with the emotions of women and was afraid she was shocked and annoyed at what he had said and worried that she would not want to stay in the house.

After a while she returned, her eyes reddened. Cautiously, she sat in the seat beside him again.

"I did not mean to upset you, Mistress," he said, noticing that she was still breathing heavily. In spite of his concern he saw with pleasure the fullness of her bosom rising and falling with her breathing.

When she spoke, her voice shook with emotion. "I... I...don't have words, sir but it is just ...I'm happy..." She stopped, wondering if she could say what was in her mind." I am happy to be here with... you."

Jacob was also lost for a response.

"I ..." his heart was pounding and his throat so tight that he could say nothing except a mumbled "thank you." They were both silent and he said the first thing that came into his head. "I was saying that things like those special mushrooms or my glasses change what we see. Sometimes and for some people, the feeling is bad, even terrifying. But sometimes, it is like heaven must be."

"How is that, sir? Nobody never told me about it."

Jacob thought for a while and then said carefully. "Did you lie with your man?"

She nodded awkwardly but said nothing.

"And, at the end there is a feeling of intense pleasure?" he asked.

Again she nodded.

"For some that is heaven," he said.

"I was happier than with anyone else. Is it then my heaven?"

"I think it is God showing us what heaven is like. And it's like that with the mushroom."

"I have drunk mead with my man sir and that did make me feel light like a bird. Do the mushrooms make you feel the same?"

"No, it is very different. With mead and with wine or ale, you lose control. You stagger and then you can fall. With the mushroom, you still seem to be in control but looking at things which have changed." Closing his book, he said. "Nothing else has the same effect; when I have eaten the mushrooms I see and taste music and hear colours."

She looked down at her hands, folded in her lap, then said, quietly. "Can I... try your mushroom?"

"I have none here and they are difficult to get. I think there will be a ship in next week if the weather is good at sea. I will try to see if I can get some from the seamen."

"What of money, sir? You can take it out of my wage."

"No, mistress, you must save your money; you will need it to buy yourself a home one day when I am no longer here."

"Where will you go, sir?" she asked, her eyes still looking down.

"Go?" he looked away feeling awkward, "I am here now but I cannot say for how long. I have the same illness that my father had and he died at an age not much older than I am now."

She looked concerned. "But you will not go, sir. I will be sure of that. My man had a illness but, when he was in pain from his bent back, he told me about the bark of the tree which would make him better. I know the tree and I know more like 'un. I will cut some of the bark and will keep it to make a drink for when you need it."

"Thank you, Mistress. If it makes you happy, we will exchange the mushroom for some bark."

Her smile lit up her face. "My man too did keep dried berries which he did eat every day. He'd say that there was something in the berries which kept away fevers. I will get some of 'em too. They're bitter so none do like 'em but he ate 'em and so do I. They will make you live, sir, I want you to live for a long time."

"Dear Mistress, I am indeed lucky to have found you." Outside, the bell in the church chimed the hour. "It's late, now I must go out," he stood up, reluctantly.

"Yes sir." She became still and he could see that she wanted to say something to him, so he waited. After a while, she looked over at the books on his shelf and said. "I would like to read these, sir. You see," she paused. "I do think about things my man told me. Oft times he'd tell me a puzzle because he said, with my woman's mind I could see things different."

It was Jacob's turn to be silent as he weighed up his thoughts. "I would like you to think about something which puzzles me. I have not yet told the Scientificals because we are thinking on other things but listen to this.

Do you ever wonder what things are made of, what we are made of, what keeps us together, why we don't just fall into a pile of dust?" Jacob waited to see if she had understood him.

"My man didst talk to me 'bout that."

"Did he tell you about Democritus?"

"Never did I hear that word."

"The Ancient Greeks whose writings we can now read thought a lot about the world around us. There were many thinking men such as Aristotle, Plato, Socrates but the one I'd like to tell you about is Democritus it was he who decided that all things are made of atoms."

"Atoms, sir, what're they?" She leaned forward so that she could hear better.

Jacob picked up a knife and an apple. "If I cut this apple into half and then half again and again and again and kept on cutting, I would reach a stage where I could not cut any smaller. What I would be left with would be atoms. Democritus said that all atoms could not be the same. There were atoms of hair, olives, tallow and so on. They all had different shapes with hooks to join them together. That is why he thought we do not fall into a heap of dust. Another philosopher, Anaxamenes, thought that everything was made from air and that water is also made from the air around us, you can see why he thought that because when it rains it comes out of the air.

"Sometimes these men agreed but more often they disagreed with each other."

"You told me about Thales Miletus who thought that water was the beginning." She said.

"I had almost forgotten I had talked about him."Jacob said. "He saw clouds around mountains and decided that they were making them. When he climbed the mountains he found sea shells on them, which showed that they had been made from water in which sea creatures lived. He also observed that water was turned to earth in the bottom of rivers. Empedocles thought that matter was composed of earth, fire and water. He said the human eye is also composed of earth, fire and water. I think he was wrong but I don't yet know why, and that is one of the things my friends want to reason out. I have done some experiments and I have seen something which I cannot reason.

"When I put a pan of cold water over a flame, the pan first becomes covered underneath with a liquid on its underside. I have tasted that liquid and I am sure it is water so there must be water in fire. Now here is something very odd which I would like you to think about, if I pour water on to the flame, the flame goes out."

"That I have seen with these my eyes, sir. When they set fire to my man's house, the men made a line and from the river, passed water in leather buckets and they put the fire out. But if water is made by fire, why do it put fire out?" she asked.

Pleased and impressed by the quickness of her mind, he said. "Take some time to think about the scientifical of it and tell me what you think but tell no one else. If the people out there, any of them, get to hear what we are doing, it could be the end. I am not fearful about that because I know that we will all die but I want to stay alive long enough to complete my learning and to be able to pass it on to others who are not yet in our group, and also to you, Mistress."

"If I can help your scientifical work, I will want that."

She stood up, picked up a log in her hand and held it as though it were a weapon. "I do not fear for myself, either. My man has gone and part of me went with him," she said. "I was accused with my man but he told them that I was just simple so I was set free."

"You were lucky, Mistress."

"No, I b'aint lucky," she said and he could see her sadness, "without my man, I did not want to live. I would've died with him 'cept he did tell them I was no more than a fool. I don't want to be a fool no more. Inside this house, I want to do the scientifical things you do. But outside, I shall be a simple fool as they think I am. I don't mind when they laugh at me, I allus keep my feelings to myself."

Jacob, overcome by her attitude could think of nothing to say except, "thank you." He said, aware that she had come to him without learning but was quickly becoming a kindred spirit.

Without saying anything more, she took things into the kitchen. Soon, he heard clattering as she started preparing food.

"I must go out." Jacob said, "I didn't notice the time going by and I have to see a friend to deliver a book to him. I will be back before the food is cooked."

When he returned, carrying two new books under his arm, she was still cooking.

"Mistress," he called, standing outside the open kitchen door. "When I said we are interested in scientifical things, I meant anything which has no explanation and which we need to find meaning for. Many things we can't understand, so as you've noticed I keep reading.

Jacob opened one of the books he had brought in. "These books are from the friend I've told you about, Josephus Dorman, one of our thinkers. We call ourselves philosophers; it means that we are lovers of wisdom. Like me, Josephus is an Alchemist, searching for the stone which I told you about, an old man now, over eighty years of age but he has remarkable learning and can talk about anything. When you see him here, you will not find him pretty to look at but he is inspirational and says we should all be free to say what we believe in. He criticised the Church openly in a public square. Less than a day later, villains came to his house, dragged him in front of an altar in a house of God. They slit his nose and branded his face with the sign of the cross. That is what the servants of the Pope do to those who disagree with them. It was a long time before he recovered but when he joined us again and saw that we were all shocked by his appearance, he simply said, 'It isfortunate my fires have died down and I no longer covet a woman because I know none would want to be with me. I have had my wife and my children and now, the way I look is of no import'. His brain was not hurt and he still amazes us all with what he knows and understands."

"Sir, I've sin him – the man with his nose cut and he do frit me."

"It is a sorrow to me that we look on faces as showing the soul behind. The truth is that the soul remains the same even though the face ages or becomes ugly. He says he is not concerned but I know he finds his face repulsive. Like you, when I look at him I am shocked but I know that Josephus still has a wondrous soul. He never seems to be bitter and I have only once seen him weep and that was when his beloved wife was forced to leave him."

Mistress Darkall saw that Jacob was distressed and waited silently for him to regain his composure. Eventually he said. "His wife, Estrella, was the dearest woman. She gave everything she could to ease suffering of others and was asked by Lord Bikton if she could help his wife who seemed never to be happy. Estrella spent weeks in the big house, cooking special foods, praying for Lady Bikton that she would get well. Instead she got worse, became insane and was locked in a special room for her own safety.

"Lord Bikton claimed that it was one of the potions which Estrella had made and he denounced her as a witch. Josephus could see that her life was in danger and sent her to Holland where she had been born. I saw Josephus on the day she left. He knew if he ever visited her, he would be followed and so would never see her again. That was the first and only time I saw him in distress, I did all I could but it was more than a week before he got back to his old self. He sent me a note which said 'Jacob, they will not rest till I am dead. But when that happens, be sure that I died happy. They can kill me but my work will go on through you.'

"Nothing will change him. He seems to remember everything, if he reads a thing once, he never forgets it." Jacob went to the shelves, took out a book which he held up so that she could see. "I wrote this down after I heard him say it, it is from Nicomachean Ethics of Aristotle I find it impossible to recall but it is one of the many things that he remembers. I have looked at the original and it is just the same - 'If there is some end of the things we do, which we desire for its own sake, this must be the good and the chief good. Will not the knowledge of it then have a great influence on life? Shall we not, like archers who have a mark to aim at, be more likely to hit upon what is right?'"

"Sir, he do say difficult things," she called over her shoulder as she stirred the food in a pan on the fire and mopped the sweat from her brow.

"Indeed he does, we all know there is wisdom in what he says but we don't always know what he means."

"No more do I sir."

Jacob frowned to himself, "I must tell you that I am worried about him."

"Sir?"

"A messenger brought a note from him yesterday. I read it and put it on the fire."

She stopped her cooking, turned and waited for him to continue.

"We thought he'd been punished enough by the Church and they would leave him alone." Jacob's face clouded with anguish. "His note told us he will not come here anymore. He wouldn't say that if he didn't know that the Church is threatening him again."

"Threatening?"

"His life I mean. He has criticised some of the injustices he sees every day. He has been watched. He does have some friends who have warned him that there are people who want to silence him. " Jacob looked grave. " He knows that he may be subjected to torture and a painful death."

Obviously moved, he turned to look out of the window. When he spoke, his voice shook slightly. "He is such a kind man, even when his life is in danger, he thinks of us; he is afraid that if he comes here we may also be in danger.

In his note, he asked to see me; there is something he wants to talk about. He doesn't want me to go to his home because I could be spied on. He has another house which few people know about where we can meet."

"Can you look out my clothes, Mistress?"

"You will not want to be seen, so I will put out your old things for you to wear."

"Did you not say you were going to give them away?"

"When it came to, I thought they might come in for something so they are upstairs in your room."

With a bemused smile, Jacob dressed in raiment which he had thought he would never have seen again. As a precaution, Mistress had also put out his sword and his dagger. When he saw them, he nodded approvingly.

On the journey there, Jacob walked around in many different directions, ambling as though out for pleasure and looking behind him several times. When he knew he was not being watched, he walked through the woods to the house. Overgrown and showing signs of neglect, the roof had begun to collapse on one part of the building where timbers had suffered from beetle infestation.

Josephus was sitting outside catching the sun and waved to Jacob, who had had to use his old sword to cut back overgrown vegetation. The walk from Firenze House had been tortuous and he was grateful when, after greetings, Josephus offered him bread, cheese and ale.

"I am sorry that you had to come here, dear friend, but as I said in my letter, it would have been too much of a risk for you to meet at my home. I want to tell you what I will be doing." He waited while his man Mortenson unpacked the meal he had carried to the house.

When Mortenson went back into the house, Jacob's eyes looked questioningly at his retreating figure. Josephus, picking up the inference, said. "You need have no fear about that man. He would lay down his life for me. He hates what the Church has become as much as you and I do. He had a house in which he was planning a family. It was on Church grounds and was in the way of a building the priest wanted for his own private pleasures. Mortenson was evicted, which is to my advantage but not to his. He came to me to see if I knew anywhere he could live and he has been with me for over five years."

Jacob nodded and looking worried, said. "But tell me about yourself. Have you been threatened?"

Josephus smiled in an effort to alleviate Jacob's concerns. "I am used to threats." He pointed to his torn nostrils. "The priests' henchmen did this to stop me criticising them.

I am going to stand in my usual spot and tell the people I have learned of another plot. But you must not be there because the Church knows that you and I are friends. If you know nothing, you will not be able to say anything if they question you."

"I am aware that I face danger. But what of you, if you stand on the Common and speak to the people, they are in such a mood that they may riot. If they do, your enemies will seek you out."

"Jacob, thank you for your concern, I am near the end of my life." He smiled disarmingly. "Look at my face; I know that people turn away in disgust when they see me. I can put up with it but..." He cast his eyes around what was left of the garden and then looked up at the sky. "I am ready to go to my God."

"I understand what you are saying, Josephus, if the people rise up against their masters, I will be with them even though I lose all I have. We cannot go on living in this storm of deceit."

Josephus leaned forward and embraced his visitor. The two men ate and drank in silence.

CHAPTER 7

Jacob saw concern on Mistress Darkall's face and sensed that she wanted to talk to him.

"You look worried, Mistress. What is going through your mind?"

"I..." she said as she struggled to find words, "want to go to the mystic in Putney. I must hear how Benjy is but...I never done this afore - don't know what happens?"

Jacob did not want her to go, for several reasons, one of which was that he was disappointed that she needed comfort when he had thought that she would have felt sufficiently cared for by him. Another reason was that he was convinced that the woman in Putney was a fraud and would take what little money she had, but he didn't want to dissuade her, so said "Julius Redwooll, one of the men in the group died suddenly in the fever. His wife was in terrible distress. We all tried to help but she was inconsolable. Eventually she went to the mystic many times. Each time she talked to Julius and always felt better afterwards."

"I would prefer for you not to go, Mistress but if you must then go with my blessing but be careful, the journey is dangerous; there are robbers waiting to attack travellers." Seeing her concern, he said. "If you are worried, I will come with you."

"Benjy'd want me on my own, I think."

"But are you not afraid?"

"I shall be all right, sir. I just want to talk to my Benjy," she said.

She set off in the afternoon, planning to be back before dark. The ground beneath her feet was sodden and she slipped several times falling heavily into briars which tore at her clothing. Several times she lost her way but finally came upon an old man who with his stick pointed to where the mystic could be found.

The mystic's house was dark and had a deep odour of incense which did not conceal the smell of the hut and the mystic's body as Mistress Darkall went into the dingy room where the old woman lived, slept and ate. She sat in a chair in the darkened room where one tallow candle glowed, giving out a dim light and casting grotesque shadows on the wizened face of the mystic. For many minutes the mystic remained with her head bowed, seeming to be unaware of the younger woman who had entered the room and who was shaking with fright.

Hanging beside the woman was a dead rabbit, its entrails had been torn out and laid beside her on the table. Her hands were red and steaming from the blood.

The mystic saw her visitor's eyes looking at the blood on her hands.

"What you looking at, the blood?" she glared. "'tis from the sacrifice that I do so that the spirits will listen." She grunted. "B'aint no spirits without sacrifice, learn ya'."

Slowly the mystic breathed deeply, her head bowed and a croaking sound came from her at first unintelligible but gradually words formed. "You come to talk to someone you lost."

"You know?" Mistress Darkall asked in surprise. "My man - yes, they drownded him."

"The priests?"

"Yes but he done nothin'."

"I know."

"How?"

"He has been through and told me."

"You have spoke to him?"

The old woman's head moved slowly up and down and she grinned, showing a toothless mouth.

"You must first put one groat in this bowl to show your faith."

Her visitor put a coin in the bowl and the mystic's gnarled hands picked it up, examined it and then buried her head in her hands.

The next voice which came from her was a man's.

"You are missing me?"

"I am, Benjy, I bin sad wi'out you. Wanted to die with you." Without thinking, she had reverted to her street voice.

"But you must not, you are my beautiful lady, I still live through you."

"No one calls me Silda any more like you done."

"That was just my name for you, Silda, no one else must use it."

"I am a housekeeper for a man. He bist good to me and he did call me Mistress Darkall because I told him that they said you were from the dark."

"Mistress Darkall; I like that name for you. He must be a good man."

"I were near dyin' when he did take me in. I have food; a room I can sleep in and he do give me clothes from his wife. She be dead. I do the cleanin', tidyin', cookin'."

"Are you happy?"

"He have made me happy, yes."

"I am glad to know you are looked after. Goodbye." The last words were said in the woman's voice.

"I do have things to say - don't go Benjy." Mistress Darkall called out in distress.

"He can stay no longer. You must know that it tires me and it is very painful for me to talk with the other side. You must come again and bring more money, I will see if he can talk more to you, Mistress Darkall." She touched the younger hands on the table in front of her and caressed them slowly, leaving still moist blood on them.

"You know my new name?"

"Your man, Benjy told me."

Her visitor stood up and said "My thanks to you," turned and ran from the house in tears. Outside it was raining and growing dark; three times she got lost and had to turn back, crossing and re-crossing the many paths.

The walk back from the mystic's house took more than two hours. She was bruised from several falls in the dark, shaking with cold and distressed from talking to Benjy. When she returned to Firenze House it was late evening. The strain had been hard and when she went into the house, she stood shivering with her back leaning against the door in the entrance. Jacob heard her arrive tired and cold and said. "My dear girl, you look worn out, you should go straight up to sleep. I have a stone on the hearth; take it to warm the bed for you."

"Can I sit by the fire for a bit?"

"Of course, take my seat; I'll put another log on. I'll put on some small sticks, they will blaze up quickly. I moved the stew you made on the fire here to keep warm. You were away so long and I fell asleep; when I woke up the fire was out, the man o' the fire passed the house with a flaming torch and I was able to get him to light the wood again."

He stood up and put logs on the flickering flames in the grate and moved the stew closer to the flames. "Were you pleased with your visit, did you speak with Benjy?"

Instead of taking a chair, she sat on the floor and watched the flames as she held her hand out to warm them.

"Whatever did the mystic say? It seems to have upset you."

Her body shook as she replied. "I talked with my man," she wiped her eyes and moved back from the heat of the fire, "he did say he was happy that I am here in your house."

"And you?"

"Sir, I thank my God for the time when I did meet you. I was ver'near dyin' - wanted to die 'cos if I did I thought I'd meet my man agin'. Now I am more happy than anybody should be."

Jacob pulled his chair closer to her and placed his hand on her shoulder. Without thinking, she laid her cheek on his hand and looked up at him with tear filled eyes.

In that moment, he experienced the first physical contact with a woman that he had had since Isabel had died.

"You still miss your man, Mistress?"

"He was such a good man. 'cept for Anne Askew he was the only kind thing I knowed till you." Suddenly wanting to tell him what she was thinking, she raised her head, "My heart did die...till you."

Looking into the flickering fire, she said in a voice he could hardly hear, "I do feel much better than I did when I came in and it is time I served the stew. I would like it if you talked to me, sir like you said you would. I need talking to. I was afeard of the mystic. Her hands were bloody from pulling the guts out of a rabbit."

While she went for dishes, Jacob looked around the room trying to think of something to say to take her mind off her experience. When she came back with dishes and spoons and laid them in front of the fire, he wanted to get her thinking about other things and said. "The time we live in is one of greater change than we have ever seen before. There are many new inventions which would give us all better lives. Only the very wealthy are permitted to have new ideas because the Pope allows his friends and supporters to do what we, the ordinary people would be punished for."

He leaned over the fire beside her and with a spoon, took a little of the stew to taste. Finding it was hot enough he filled the dishes. He felt gratified to see her eating hungrily. When she had finished, she looked up at him smiling and said. "Sir..."

"Yes?" Jacob asked.

She hesitated, "Thank you, sir, that have never happened to me afore."

He had been pleased to take care of her. "To be served your food? Then we must make sure it is not the last time."

"Warmer I am now..., but...tell me more."

"One of the most amazing inventions I have seen is in the Tivoli Gardens in Rome. I was taken there while I was on business. The garden was not completed but it was astonishing – figures carved from wood were wearing clothes made from wool and silk and they moved almost like real people, they played instruments, other figures were doing things like making wine in casks and there was even a butcher killing a calf. They have an ingenious device called a cam which is a piece of shaped wood which lifts levers and a cylinder which has pegs which raises hammers to strike bells and pluck strings to make music. It is all for amusement but I am sure that the machinery which operates it and is driven just by water falling from a hill could be used in ways to make things for all of us. I am looking at how we can use this power in spinning and making cloth in my business. The Church I am sure would have objected to the Tivoli Gardens, saying that it was playing with God's will but it was built for the son of Lucrezia Borgia." He saw her frowning. "The Borgias are a very wealthy Italian family, known I am afraid for their corruption, murder of their enemies and even incest."

She looked up and said, "What is that?"

Slightly embarrassed, he turned his head away. "It is having sexual congress with your parents, siblings or your children. You might not think that is a sin because you do not have a family."

Unperturbed, she stood up to give another stir to the pan on the fire and refilled their dishes while Jacob continued talking.

"Pope Alexander, who was a Borgia, was said to be an evil person. If a wealthy man committed a murder, he could buy an indulgence from the Catholic Church which would remove his guilt and he could walk free. It is happening now and people still pay the Church to hold masses for the souls of their dead and as I have told you that is one of the ways that the Church has become very wealthy."

"But that ain't right, out in the streets where I lived, if I done anythin' wrong, they would punish me," she said.

"Which is the way it should be...," suddenly her meaning struck him, "what you have said is very interesting and is something I have seen. In poor communities, there is an understanding and an acceptance of right and wrong. With rich people, corruption brings wealth and to sustain their living standards they become more corrupt."

He saw a worried look on her face. "Are you not happy with what I have said?"

"Sir, be you not rich?"

"My Lord, no; these people of whom I speak would not even notice me. To them I would be as insignificant as a flea on the back of a horse; they would pass me by in the street as someone not worthy of notice. What I have provides for my own needs. I must have a reserve to keep my business going in times of difficulty. I keep money in case my business becomes quiet. We have cloth to sell and the nature of things is that, when these are sometimes over-produced, the price drops and many people who have not made provision lose their businesses. If I have any left over after keeping a reserve, it goes to poor people. That is my duty."

Mistress Darkall had been listening intently to what he was saying when she realised that the stew was beginning to spoil, hastily, she stood up and said, "the soup will burn unless I move it from the flames." She lifted the pan with a cloth around the handle and carried it to the kitchen. When she returned, she brought with her a pitcher of ale, another of water, and cups. She filled the cups with water. Jacob looked into the cup and saw that the water was cloudy. "I sometimes think that the cloudiness of the water may be bad for us. Perhaps even one of the reasons we have so many ailments." He passed the cup to her. "You see, there are small bits of dirt in it, they are not always there. I don't know where they come from but, sometimes when I am ill, I think back and I remember that the water which I had drunk the day before was like this. I talked about this once when I went to the Scientificals meeting and many of them thought drinking of dirty water was followed by illness. When they are travelling they think they were caused to become unwell from water. I have told them that when my water is dirty I pour it through sand and only drink it after it has bubbled on the fire."

Let us try something, we will pour it through a fine cloth and take these bits out and then put it on the fire in a pan. I've also noticed that when it begins to bubble, it tastes better. I wonder what has happened. There is a horrible torture which is to put people in large pots, fill them with water and put them over a fire. Even before the bubbles rise, the people are dead. It may be that the particles which I see in water are alive and heating the water kills them."

"And wine?"

"Apart from the drunkenness which accompanies too much wine or ale, I do not feel it is bad for us."

He moved his books off the table and put them on the floor while she laid out bowls of stew. "While we eat, I'd like to tell you more about what the Scientificals are interested in." He drank from the ale she had served him. "You will know how much I love books. We have learned so much about Greek civilisation through them." He turned and picked up a book from a pile beside him.

"We have to thank a man called Aldus Manutius, who was a printer in the Italian city of Venice. He got scholars to translate ancient books and then printed the writings of all the Greek thinkers. He made them cheaply and in a size that would go into a pocket. I have them all and read them often." He put the book back on the pile. "When the weather is good, I take them down to the river with me. Some of my happiest moments are spent there. I find great pleasure in learning, Mistress." He pointed to the books beside him and said, "I have a great love of these and you will often find me reading so deeply that I forget where I am."

He ate the second helping of stew she had served him, nodding appreciatively. When he had finished, he picked up another book, read from it and said. "This book is about travel. Sailors from many nations have travelled to parts of the world we had never even thought existed, places like Mexico where the mushroom comes from. These travellers have brought tales of the strange way people live their lives." He turned the pages and read a paragraph to himself.

"I am reading about conflicts in times past." he put the book down and looked at her, "There has always been hostility between different religions. An example is the persecution of Jews caused by nothing more than jealousy of their remarkable ability with money. I know how clever they are because I have worked with many of them. Something in man makes us capable of love for our own but hate for anyone different so we inflict wars, torture and violence on people we disagree with and on other countries, religions, and races. All these things are destructive and against God's will. You would think that man would realise how much progress could be made if we all got together and worked for our common benefit. When I was in Florence..." Jacob stopped, disappointed to see her gaze turning towards the kitchen.

"I must go to the fire in the kitchen. I am cooking a nice apple droff which I made yester and put on the fire to warm just now," she said as she stood up and walked to the kitchen, "but I like you to talk more, sir." As she tended to the food, she called over her shoulder. "You been there, sir, to… Florence, I do mean, can you tell me."

"It is a city of such civilisation," he said, his voice raised as he walked to where she was working, "I first went when I was a boy with my uncle, who was a merchant like me. He took over English wool and cloths to trade for the silk the Florentines and Venetians bring in from the East. While my uncle was at his business, his agent's wife took me to see the work of some of the artists. We have so little here but there they are common - statues carved in marble which are so lifelike you think that you see a human body living and breathing.

They are in the open in squares where people stand and talk to each other and others give speeches. I could not speak much Italian then but just listening to their voices and their language, which sounds like poetry, entranced me. In the evenings they had music and singing." He saw that she was ready to serve the droff and returned to sit at the table.

She brought the steaming pudding from the kitchen. "I do want to hear about Florence, sir," she said as she served the pudding, "can you tell me more?"

"I will but first let me try this," he said starting to eat. "Until you came, I had never heard of a droff and now it is a favourite of mine."

"Tis from the streets where I used to live; when the apples fall, they do get bruised and rough and all 'cept starving folks find they makes 'un sick. So we'd cook droff with honey if we were lucky to find a hive."

He stopped eating, put his place aside and pointing to a small table close to her, he said. "Would you pass me that pile of paper?"

Mistress Darkall turned and picked them up. "They be heavy, sir."

Jacob turned over the pages. "This is a drawing I did of one of the magnificent churches," he passed the drawing to her. "I sent it to my family when I wrote about what I saw and the people I met. Such interesting people those Florentines, more cultured than the English. But they are very violent; three people I met over the years have been murdered because they stood in the way of powerful men."

She looked at his drawing. "That is mag…" she said, hesitating over a word she had heard him use before.

"Magnificent," he said, completing the word for her as she stood beside him. "I'm glad you like it. Building that dome on the Cathedral must have been a wondrous achievement. We could not build it in England. I am sad to say that in this country we still have a lot we must learn. We are fortunate that people from Italy, France, Spain and other countries come to England to live. Many say that the foreigners take work from us but, in truth, they are doing work of a quality that the English would not have been able to master and by being here, they train us to do it.

King Edward in the last century invited Flemish weavers to come to this country; if that hadn't happened, my own business as a cloth merchant would probably not have been possible." He turned and waved his hand at the window. "And all that I have would not exist. In other countries there is learning which is all new to us. I have travelled and seen wonders. Giovanni de Dondi, many years ago, made a machine with a spring which would tell the movement of the stars."

As he finished eating, he picked up a drawing. "I will just talk and you can ask me questions." He said, raising his voice as she returned to her kitchen. When she came back to the table, he put his hand on her arm and said. "I am pleased that you are better than when you came home." She smiled her agreement. "I have said before that I think it is wrong for you to eat alone. I do not like eating on my own either. From today, will you eat with me whenever I am at home? I am glad of your company. You came in exhausted this evening and we've eaten together and we must continue to do that."

"Sir," she said, her face tinged with pleasure.

"You must forget the stupid rules we have where people are considered superior and others inferior simply because of their birth or wealth. I could have been born of a poor family and lived in the streets as you did and you could have been born a lady and lived in a big house. We sit here as man and servant but, if things had been different, you could be sitting here while I acted as your servant."

"No sir that could not be. You are different, you are a gentleman. I do not have learning like you. I don't know behaving."

"You will though."

He talked for an hour more before he saw that she had fallen asleep. Carefully he picked her up and part carried her to her room. She was not heavy but the weight of even her light body brought on pains in his arms and legs. Upstairs, he laid her on the bed, covered her with a blanket and looked down at her with a tenderness he had thought he would never experience. He leaned over, kissed her forehead and left her to sleep.

The following day when she told him food was cooked, he said he was not hungry and would like to leave eating till the evening.

"But, sir, 'twill be spoiled."

In truth, he was not feeling well and the thought of food made him feel worse but seeing her concern, said. "You are right, mistress. We will eat together."

When she had put the steaming food on the table, Jacob stood up and placed the chair at the table behind her. He could see that she wanted to join him but needed encouragement.

"I will eat here and you can eat with me. I won't sit down unless you join me like you did last night when you came back cold."

Reluctantly she nodded but he was glad to see a smile of pleasure playing around her lips.

She looked apprehensively at Jacob but, wiping the table down, she did as he asked. He heard the clatter as she put out the food on wooden plates and brought them, steaming, to the table. Quietly they ate together, both feeling odd about being in each other's presence and so close together. He tried to behave normally but the proximity of this young woman was causing his heart to race.

While he ate, she watched his movements closely and copied them. When he picked up a knife and fork and cut the meat, she followed his actions, eating at the same speed and even wiping her mouth when he did.

"You are right, Mistress, this meal is too good, it would have been sad if we had allowed it to burn and be wasted. My wife was a moderately good cook but you are better. I've eaten all round Europe in some splendid eating houses, one I remember in Florence, was particularly good but this meal you have cooked for me is as good as

I've had anywhere." He wondered if he should also say, 'partly because of having your company,' but was afraid she might be embarrassed.

He wiped his plate with a piece of bread which he ate slowly. As he finished, he stood up to look out of the window and, turning back said. "We are to work together but there is one thing I want you to do."

With difficulty, she looked up at him as he stood in front of her.

Seeing the look of concern on her face, he said. "No, mistress, I have said before, I am not the sort of man you may be thinking. It is mental, not physical. What I want you to do is to forget."

"Forget, sir?"

"Yes, forget. I want you to forget wrong things you have learned. Forget those people out there with their suspicions and hatreds." he turned round and pointed through the window. "They cannot use their minds because they've been taught not to."

"They need a teacher like you."she grinned.

Jacob laughed with pleasure and satisfaction at her joking appreciation of his teaching. He sat down and, still smiling, shook his head.

"People are expected to stay in their places. If they are stallholders, they stay as stallholders. If they are road menders, they stay as road menders. If they are servants, they stay that way - but why? Many of them will have brains many times better than those who consider themselves to be superior and yet they do not have chance to use them. It is a tragedy to live with a talent and then to die never having discovered it. I would like people to be free to use what they have and I want you to do the same. In many ways you are my equal and in some ways you are better, it is just that you have not realised it."

"Sir, I never had training till now."

"I don't mean going to school and sitting in front of a teacher as I did. No, your training came just from the people around you. You already told me they thought you were simple and that made you think of yourself as useless. But in this house, I want you to use those talents that I see inside you." He raised his eyes to hers and saw that tears were beginning to run down her face. He put his hand out and touched her and saw with some pleasure that she did not pull away. "Do not be unhappy ever. I shall never want you to do anything you do not want."

"Sir, I am not unhappy. I am thinking why I should be lucky when those out there," she nodded at the window, "have nothing."

"I want to see a world where they will have better lives. It may not be in my lifetime but I want to do all I can to make it happen."

She wiped her eyes on the back of her hand and smiled at him tearfully.

"We live in a cruel world, mistress, but it will change." He stopped and thought as he heard two cats fighting outside the house. "From my travels, I am aware that we in England are a backward people. As I said, we import from other countries skilled men to tell us how to do things, stonemasons from Italy and France, glass makers from France. We have no copper smelting and I know that there are moves afoot to bring skilled people from Germany to show us how to do it. It might not seem like that to you until you have travelled and seen the learning in Florence and Venice and the fashions in Paris. I am filled with sorrow for this nation which does not have the same love of beautiful things. Not many years since, hat makers were brought in from France. In Norwich weaving is carried on from those Flemish people I told you about and at Glastonbury Abbey a group of weavers from Flanders was encouraged to settle. We are learning but we need to do so much more.

"There are thinkers like my friends who want to change things but they are so filled with foreboding that we will be treated like your man was that we are cautious about being the first to move. There is so much we have to learn about curing the sick, about the way our minds work and about what the worship of God should be like and about leadership."

"I don't know what you mean by that, sir. Tell me."

"Yes, I will." He said, marvelling for a moment that this woman wanted to listen to his musings. He pursed his lips, thought for a moment, took in a breath and asked. "What makes us different from the animals?"

"We change things, you have told me." She frowned and then said. "Smilin', sir? We smile... sometimes."

Jacob clapped his hands. "Yes, we do, don't we? But that was not what I was thinking of. What raises us above the animals is that we think and we also wonder," he pointed to his head, "we have this amazing thing. Animals must have brains which tell them when to eat, drink, sleep and perform other actions. But the remarkable thing for us which makes us so different from animals is that we imagine things." He stared into the air while he thought about what to say next. "No one I've ever spoken to understands how we can do it. Some people think God must be in our heads controlling us. Some even think it may be the devil because we do so many evil things. Another puzzle is what happens when we eat our food. It becomes digested and keeps us alive but we have no idea how we do it, it's as though we are machines which are controlled by another being.

"Something else that is strange is that sometimes when I am with a friend, I seem to know his thoughts. I begin to wonder if that means that our minds are linked and perhaps joined with other minds like the strands in a fishnet." He pointed out of the window. "Look, there you see horses pulling carriages, you see water flowing where we want it to flow - that man who has just got out and is walking towards us with his servant following him," he nodded so that she would follow his gaze, "he is wearing very expensive clothes and silver jewellery so we know he is rich and he and his servant carry jewelled swords and daggers for protection. I know that man; he is walking home to a house which is filled with everything money can buy, carpets, velvet hangings, paintings and many other things. He has many scientific instruments on which he carries out experiments but he doesn't trust people and will not tell me what he does to earn his wealth."

As the man walked by, he raised his hat to Jacob, who bowed in acknowledgement then turned back into the room. "Let me explain what I mean. We are creatures of fear and suspicion simply because we lack understanding of what we see around us. What makes the wind blow? What makes the sun shine? What makes it rain? What do our crops need to make them grow and why do they sometimes fail to produce what we need and some of us starve? We don't know these things so we fall back on crude 'logic'." He smiled to himself as a thought struck him. "It would be better called 'illogic' because often we are wrong in our interpretation. I have been to some countries where they sacrifice people and animals to please their Gods so that they would have good harvests and win battles.

"We no longer do that in this country but God's laws come to us from the Church and instead of people and animals we sacrifice ideas and freedoms." He saw that she seemed to be asleep and touched her arm. Immediately her eyes opened. "I am sorry Mistress. I was forgetting that you need to sleep."

"Sir, I am not tired, I was closin' my eyes so that I could listen more carefully" she said. "But I will clear away." She stood up, collected things from the table and took them out. After a while she returned and sat down beside him. "Sir, I am ready to listen."

"If you are sure, mistress, I will continue," Jacob said. "I will talk about other ways the Church takes our freedoms. If you and your man had decided to get married you would have to pay them. If you had a child and then had it christened, you would pay; you even have to pay to bury a relative in consecrated ground and if you don't, you will be told that the soul will go to Hell and damnation. By such means the Church has grown rich while being surrounded by poverty."

She shook her head. "That is puzzling is't not; last week you read the bible to me, what Jesus said in Matthew 19:21 'go, sell what you possess and give to the poor.' And the bible in Luke 14:12-14 'when you give a feast, invite the poor, the crippled, the lame, the blind."

Jacob's mouth fell open as she spoke. "You remembered what I read and even what part of the bible it came from. I am amazed."

Mistress Darkall beamed with pleasure. "You told me you could be killed for what you think but they tell us God loves us all. If he does, he wouldn't want us to be killed, so why should they think that killing would please God?"

"Those are my thoughts as well. Those with power have different ways of seeing things. Their spectacles distort their vision as my spectacles did with you."

"How is that, sir?"

"I mean the truth in their eyes is not the truth as we see it. If they sold everything and gave to the poor, the comfortable life they live would be gone," he said. "Then there is the puzzle of why we are here – do we have to behave in certain ways to please God? Different countries and different religions try to make sense of the world in their own ways. Some people believe our lives are controlled, some believe in demons, some believe there are many Gods. Some even worship animals." Jacob watched Mistress Darkall's reaction. "I have been told that in India they believe that we are born over and over again, we start existence as things like trees, then, when we die we are reborn as animals, next time we are born as humans and the next time we become better humans"

As he spoke, Mistress Darkall shivered and then turned to the fire and was about to put on another log when Jacob said. "It is becoming cold, the fire is getting low and we have little tallow left for light. I have become tired as I am sure you are as well. I need to go to bed."

As they both climbed the stairs, Jacob stopped and said, "I am worried about my friend Josephus. His servant came to me and said he has not seen his master for two days. He is a man of regular habits and he has never before been away without telling his servant where he was going. I am going to pray to God that he is well but I am fearful for him, there is much violence in his enemies."

CHAPTER 8

Although his ex-wife would probably have disagreed, Jake felt himself to be a fairly stable person. But there were times when he knew he was not being rational. Who had put the bible behind the panel, how long ago, under what circumstances and why had the books in front of it seemed to have moved? He began subconsciously to create stories around it, wondering if Tyndale had lived in Firenze House at a time when he had been in terror of his life unable to light a fire for fear of attracting attention. Tyndale could not have put the bible there because this copy had been printed after his death, but perhaps it was a follower of Tyndale. A Tyndale bible in the house was incredible, but he could not explain why when he had found it he had been overcome with a sense of dread. It struck him suddenly that the house had been sold at a very reasonable price. He had been told that the owner wanted to be near his business but Jake had seen his warehouse only a few miles from Barnes and began to wonder if the house had been sold because of the shadows in the house.

Sometimes, when he was particularly apprehensive, he would put on a record of Chopin Etudes, hoping to chase away the unexplained sensation. If that didn't work he would try to distract himself by watching the endless drivel that passed for television entertainment. The anodyne programmes failed to direct his thoughts away from a growing conviction that he was picking up shadows of events which had happened in Firenze House centuries before.

One night, the atmosphere was so pervasive that he felt he could not stay in the house any longer. Dressed against the cold outside, he walked to the local pub to relax and, surrounded by a crowd of people he hardly knew, talk about nothing. He looked at his watch and saw that it was still only seven. It had been a day of snow and as he cautiously stepped out into the streets, he slipped on a patch of ice. It struck him that walking on such a night like was stupid. Slipping often on the frozen pavements, he made his way to 'The Rod of Iron'. As he pushed open the door, a swell of warm air, laden with alcohol saturated breath surrounded him. Faces looked up as he walked to the bar, some smiled; some waved between gulps of beer and yelled out, "mine's a pint, Jake mate."

Jake smiled back when suddenly he stopped in his tracks. As he looked in the mirror hanging behind the bar he saw a reflection that took him back ten years. Sitting alone at a table close behind him was Rhosa Cowen, whom he had seen only once since he had last been in Stratford doing research for an article. She smiled at his reflection in the mirror and as she stood up quietly said, "Can I buy you a drink, Jake?"

He turned to face her as she came towards him. When he looked surprised, she said. "I'm celebrating tonight."

"Rhosa," he said. "Is it really you?"

"It is."

"I'm so glad to see you," he said and as he looked at her the anxiety he had felt in the house was forgotten, "You're celebrating, what for?"

"Nothing much," she said with a coquettish smile, "I just landed the part I always wanted."

"Portia in the Merchant of Venice?"

"No, idiot, I'm not that good…yet…but the next best."

"Nerissa?"

She nodded quickly. "the same."

"Then it's my turn to buy you a drink."

"I'm already pretty far gone. I'll just have a strong, black coffee. I start rehearsals in a couple of days. The Merchant opens in a month."

During the ten years since they had parted in Stratford, Jake saw occasional press reports about Rhosa but had no more contact until he had seen her in a bookshop in Oxford Street. She was in front of him and, although she had filled out very slightly, still had the distinctive and elegant walk that he had found captivating.

One of Jake's beliefs was that we emanate vibrations so he was not surprised when, before he caught up with her, something made her turn round. She recognised him, even though in the intervening years, he knew he had aged a lot. She looked around at the other shoppers and with what seemed to him a worried voice, said, "I'm ready for a coffee if you've got time," just like that, none of the normal 'how nice to see you' greetings.

He looked at his watch, explained that he had to dash off to a meeting but would be glad to share a coffee with her.

"Oxford Street has so many cafes all with exotic named drinks at stupid prices." Rhosa said, "they make the best coffee and also it's fairly empty." She smiled with pleasure at seeing him but he thought he detected sadness in her smile and noticed that her eyes were constantly looking around at the other customers.

In Shakespeare's Stratford, there had always been an easy flow of conversation between Jake and Rhosa but in the coffee bar, she was very diffident. He found her pre-occupied and sensed that she was talking to fill the silence.

In the Rod of Iron, she was back to her old self. "God, Rhosa, it's amazing to see you again," he said after greeting her with the conventional kiss on the cheek. "After that awkward meeting in Oxford Street and you didn't 'phone soon' as you said you would, I thought that was the last I would see of you." He picked up coffee at the bar and passed it to her. He was inclined to tell her that seeing her had dispelled the eeriness he had felt in Firenze House but resisted.

"I want to apologise for the way I was when we met in that coffee bar." She said as they sat at a vacant table. "I think I was almost off my head with worry."

"Your husband?"

She nodded, "He'd been hounding me, had been for weeks. You may have noticed I put on my sunglasses - I didn't want anyone to see me with you. I was so scared that he or one of his buddies was snooping on me," she shuddered. "I'm sorry, Jake, I was so happy to see you. When you left I almost burst into tears in the café; I even had to stop myself running after you. Why didn't I contact you afterwards? That must have seemed like a brush off but there was a reason. The divorce process was awful, filled every spare minute and I got so depressed. " She looked up at him plaintively. "Can you forgive me?"

Jake shrugged. "You're here and," he smiled, "it feels as though it could be Stratford again. It's all over with your husband now isn't it? I read about it in the papers."

"All settled, thank God." Her face beamed with pleasure. "I pray I never ever have to see him again."

"Let's not talk about him then. Tell me about the Merchant. You always wanted the part even when we were in Stratford ten years ago."

He looked at her, dressed in jeans and a sloppy shirt which did not flatter her figure but she still looked as devastating as she had when he had first met her. Sitting around a cramped table, he could feel the warmth of her body as their legs touched and she didn't pull away.

"You asked if I had the part of Portia," her smile broadened. "I'm actually understudying the lead. If she falls ill, I get the best female part in the English language."

"Some would encourage fate," he put his hand on her arm and said conspiratorially, "I have a formula somewhere for a laxative which I'm told can put a full grown man out for days."

"Don't tempt me, it wouldn't take much. She's a great actress but a hateful cow and people are saying she is too old."

"You're not being ageist, are you?" He grinned.

"I couldn't." Rhosa laughed at Jake's quizzical look. "She's only five years my senior."

"But she looks much older," he said and it was true; perhaps it was the dim light, but Rhosa was still the same nineteen year old woman he remembered. The only thing that seemed to have changed was that she was more confident.

"So glad you said that. If you hadn't I probably would never have spoken to you again," she laughed, "Thanks for my coffee, I needed it, I've probably had a bit too much wine waiting here."

He wondered whether to say something clichéd like 'I'd buy you a million coffees for these few moments with you' but anything he thought of seemed hackneyed so he let the chance go by. "How is it you are in my local tonight, you've never been here any other time I've been in and I drop in most nights when I'm at home?"

She drank and looked at him through steam rising from the cup. "Why do you think?"

He shrugged, genuinely baffled.

"I've read all your articles; those you write as Jake Dearsey and those under your other pen names."

"Only three others."

"Matthew Sarby, Maurice Digman, Bruce Willerby. Who are you tonight?"

"Whoever you want me to be."

"You know who I want you to be?"

He shook his head and raised his eyebrows.

"I want you to be Jake. The man who writes sometimes with an acrid pen and sometimes with one dipped in the inkwell of humanity. I want you to be Jake who can write more about life than I ever could; I want you to be Jake, the man I used to know in Stratford." She turned away, looking around the room at the other drinkers laughing at their private jokes. Quietly she said, almost to herself. "That's why I am here. In Stratford, you were the most exciting man I had ever met. Looking back over those lost years," she looked up at his reflection in the mirror behind the bar and in almost a whisper said, "I still feel the same."

"Even about husbands?" he asked.

"I'll tell you later. I am too happy to talk about that sort of thing now."

As she spoke, the jazz group which had been warming up started to play Alexander's Rag Time Band. "Forget your drink, come and dance," she pulled him to his feet and dragged him to the tiny dance area. No one else amongst the drinking crowd seemed in the least bit interested in dancing and they were the only couple on the floor. The excitement of being with Rhosa overcame his reluctance to be on the dance floor while so many eyes were watching them.

"Amazing they're playing the song we danced to at that pub in Stratford," he yelled above the music. It wasn't until much later that she admitted that while he had gone to the bar, she had slipped the group a note and requested the tune when she gave them a sign.

She had always been a good dancer but, it was obvious by the way she responded to the rhythm that the level of alcohol in her blood had freed both her mind and her body.

Several of the customers gathered around them and encouraged them by clapping in time with the music. The more they clapped and the more the group increased the tempo, the more feverishly Rhosa danced. When the music stopped they collapsed into each other's arms, laughing to the cheers from the watchers. "Go on, get in there, Jake, boy," yelled one.

His heart was pounding as they walked back to their table. He glanced at Rhosa, her breasts rising and falling as she breathed heavily from the exertion.

"Come on," Rhosa said grabbing his arm. "Let's get you that drink I promised you."

As they threaded their way to the bar, the group started playing again but without the life of the first piece. Inspired by Rhosa, many couples remained dancing after she had left the floor. The leader of the band caught Rhosa's eye, smiled and gave her a thumbs-up sign, a few of the customers whom he had met before came up, patted him on the back and said. "Great dancing - who's the lady?"

When she had bought him a drink, they sat in a corner, communicating but wordlessly.

When the music stopped for the band to drink their beers, Rhosa said, "Amazing how music affects us, isn't it? Why do we need it?"

"How do you mean?"

"What I mean is, it's not like food, water and shelter which are obviously necessary but music doesn't have a function in survival."

"Stop all music and life would still go on you mean?" Jake asked. As he spoke he realised how much he had missed talking to her. She had very little small talk but almost everything she said, made him think. Even as a nineteen year old, she had a mind which absorbed information and never stopped learning. Rhosa nodded as the band, having slaked their thirsts struck up with 'The Saints'.

"What's happening with you these days, Jake?" Rhosa asked, almost shouting over the sound of the music.

"The same as usual, 'a bit of this and a bit of that'."

"No, don't fob me off. You were always uncommunicative but I'm asking because I really want to know."

"Thanks." He said as a thought struck him. "You're more confident than the Rhosa you were."

"I'm beginning to sort myself out. And I'm older and wiser than I was then."

When he had first met Rhosa he was doing research for the article on his belief that Freud's theories had been influenced by Shakespeare. Jake had gone to Stratford at the invitation of the producer, Jonathan Rhyl, whom he had known at university. Jonathan had organised someone to look after him and show him around. The guide was Rhosa, at nineteen, still in drama school. She knew her Shakespeare and, while they sat in the pub over a pint, would deliver whole passages, changing her voice to suit the characters.

He had been under pressure from an editor to come back with a convincing story that could be used as the basis for a book and a radio programme. Even with Rhosa, he was guarded about the purposes of his research because he didn't want his ideas to be used by other journalists. He told her that he was there to learn more about the life of Shakespeare. Before long he got the impression that she suspected his real purpose.

She had often talked about the way Shakespeare could express in a few lines the suffering of mankind. She had quoted Polonius's speech 'To thine ownself be true and it must follow as the night the day that thou canst not then be false to any man.' She so inspired him that he told her the real purpose of being in Stratford.

She smiled one of her provocative smiles which always stole his heart. "I somehow guessed that." she said.

"How could you?"

"Well - you remember when we were in the bar of the Traveller's Rest and you went to the toilet."

He nodded. "You didn't read my notebook?" He asked as he recalled that he had been puzzled that it had seemed to have been moved."

"You were gone a long time and you'd left it open at the first page turned slightly towards me. I thought you had done it deliberately and that you wouldn't mind."

"If it had been anyone else I would have minded."

"But not with me?" she smiled coquettishly.

"I guess not," he said, "but can it be a secret between us? Until I have it published it must remain between me and my publisher," he grinned, "and you, of course."

"You're writing a book?"

"Maybe it'll become a book, but it might only be an article," he said. "A radio programme is planned."

"I won't say anything to anyone." She put one finger against her lips, "I think Shakespeare has incredible understanding of the way the mind works. Freud wrote well and got us all thinking about what motivates us. But the Bard did it all so much more poetically.

"What about the sex drive which so interested Freud?"

"That as well," he smiled.

Over the following few weeks, they saw a lot of each other. She would visit him in the room he had rented which overlooked the Avon. They would talk until late at night. He had gone overboard with Rhosa and was thinking more about her than his work. He was sure that she felt the same until one day she turned up with the actor, Jed Stapleworth, on her arm. He was good looking and charming in a vapid way and was about the same age as Rhosa. From the way she looked at him it was obvious that this was more than a passing friendship. The ten year gap between Jake and Rhosa suddenly seemed to divide them. Jake was hurt so much that he left Stratford the next day without saying goodbye. He heard later that Rhosa had married Jed but as Jake had suspected, found him empty and self-interested. The marriage had ended when Jed had been offered a television series. With so many women fluttering round him, he had wandered too many times and they had divorced after only a matter of months.

During the time they had spent together at Stratford, she had told him that Sheana was her real name, given her by her mother Vruska, who had been brought up by her Romany mother Sybilant, who with her daughter had fled her turbulent country leaving her morose husband behind in Moscow. She had wound up in Alexandria with very little money. She survived in the new land by dancing in the wild manner of the gypsies she had grown up with. Freed from the restrictions of marriage her dancing was highly erotic and she found she could get work in Westernised night clubs which had tired of belly dancing. She soon developed an international reputation. Her work took Sybilant away from home for long periods of time and Vruska was left alone even as a young girl. Sybilant felt that she had done enough for Vruska by keeping her in comfort in a house with servants to care for her. Her success even though she could hardly read convinced her that there was no advantage in educating Vruska.

With an undisciplined but enquiring mind, Vruska found a library where she could read voraciously. In the English literature section she met a retired English professor, Thomas Shorning who, although ageing and bent, was still possessed of an active mind. He taught her to speak and to read English and guided her choice of books.

By this time, Sybilant had become known internationally and was making a lot of money travelling throughout Egypt, but more often in other countries. She sent money wrapped in a scribbled note, but never attempted to enquire about Vruska's wellbeing.

Rhosa had shown Jake photographs of her mother when she was young. He had commented that she was attractive and he could see where Rhosa had got her looks from. Inevitably Vruska had been admired by many men and one day, responded to the pleas of a traveller passing through Egypt, who never came again but left Vruska pregnant with Rhosa. Professor Shorning arranged for her to be cared for by a doctor friend and when Vruska went into labour, she was assisted by some of the other mothers in the locality. One day an illiterate woman saw the baby and was reminded of her own dead child, Ana, in faltering words she said, "She Ana."

Vruska liked the sound and gave her baby the name Sheana which from her reading she knew was a Celtic name. She brought up Sheana on her own and passed on to her daughter all that she had learned from her reading. Professor Shorning became both tutor and a father figure to the child. When Sheana was eight, Thomas Shorning died suddenly. He had given Vruska and her daughter a romantic vision of the England of Dickens and, distraught at the death of her mentor, she decided to go to London, the city he had spoken so much about. The Professor had told her about the British Library and the books which were there and she pictured herself spending days doing nothing more than reading.

Sybilant had become feted around Europe and had been persuaded by her lover, an Italian Count, to start a dance academy in Milan. She was sending her daughter large amounts of money and Vruska was able to buy a small house in Richmond on the outskirts of London. Regretting her own lack of a formal education, she found a good school for Sheana near to her house, but her strong Egyptian accent and stumbling English marked the ten year old as an oddity to the girls in her school, and she suffered constant ridicule.

Vruska developed an interest in the history of her adopted country and spent much of her leisure time reading in the British Library. She always sat at the same table which was also used by historian Herbert Cowen. Intrigued by this attractive Egyptian, he invited her to lunch. Vruska was charmed by this austere man of letters and when after a few lunches, he proposed marriage she was overcome with the romantic idea of becoming the wife of a professor. After a short courtship she accepted his proposal, overjoyed that her status as the wife of an academic who had a reputation gave her an immediate entree into London Society.

Sheana found her step father a self-opinionated bore. For him, Sheana was an irritation and her manners were a constant source of complaint. His attitude began to sour Vruska's opinion of her daughter and the bond which had existed between them weakened. Sheana despised her stepfather for the estrangement with her mother and found it hard to be in the same room with him, and would spend most of her time in her bedroom reading.

To get her out of the house for longer, Herbert Cowen paid for his stepdaughter to go to a more expensive school much farther away. She had learned to cope with the criticism of the other pupils at the first school but was pleased to be moved and determined to use the opportunity to get rid of her accent. When she found

Shakespeare's 'Merchant of Venice' in a junk shop it gave her a new interest and she would shut herself away in her attic room, listening to tapes of Shakespeare's plays and copying the voices of the actors onto another tape recorder.

When she had rehearsed all of Shakespeare's works, she would read any book she could find in English and dictate it onto a recorder so that she could listen again.

She became so familiar with much of English literature that her teachers started to respect her literary knowledge and the other girls brought their essays for her to read and correct.

She made a few friends but saw little of them because most of her spare time would be spent reading and recording. Her room in the attic was so remote from the living rooms in the dark Victorian house that she was able to act out violent scenes without anyone hearing. She became so enthralled by the characters of plays that her room became a focus for her imagination. Only when she shut the door on the world behind her would she come to life. After an evening acting all the parts in King Lear, she collapsed into bed exhausted, her mind in turmoil with the emotions of the play. For many days she had dreams in which her stepfather was King Lear. Shakespeare's plot would become intertwined with her feelings about the man her mother had married. Sometimes she would wake up in torment. During the day following, her mind would be numbed and, if she saw her stepfather, she would see him as Lear with herself as the disinherited Cordelia.

At the age of sixteen, she decided she had to leave home and go to drama school, and told her mother that she wanted to become an actress. Her stepfather gladly paid for his difficult step daughter to study with the condition that she should find somewhere to live and leave home for good. On the evening that she left, he arranged to be out of the house attending a lecture. He insisted on Vruska coming with him even though she was almost hysterical with grief at Rhosa's leaving home and would not normally have gone with him.

Rhosa took a room with her stepfather's sister who became both aunt and mother to her and also helped with expenses. At drama school, Rhosa was seen as a fine but un-disciplined actress and, after a couple of years, the head recommended that she should go to Stratford to immerse herself in the craft of acting.

She often thought about how events had taken control of her; Vruska's moving to England, meeting and marrying Professor Cowen had stimulated her desire to read and learn. One afternoon Rhosa talked with Jake about the slender chances on which our lives are based and the statistical improbability of our being conceived. If the two people who had been responsible for our births had not visited a shop, a dance or dinner party and met but had not felt inclined to make love at the very instant they did, none of us would exist.

She wondered if six million Jews would have lived their lives and procreated if Hitler's parents had not looked into each other's eyes with that hidden message which says come to bed. All our lives would have been different if they had chosen another occasion instead of the very day and minute when everything conspired to bring Hitler into the world.

In his turn, Jake often thought about the chance meeting with Rhosa in Oxford St. While they drank coffee, Jake sensed her preoccupation and wondered if the passing years had so changed them both that their conversation was now like two people talking into the air.

He tried several topics and she responded after a fashion but nothing clicked. While he gathered his thoughts for his meeting and stood up, she implied she wanted to see him again with the inevitable "I'll 'phone you soon."

A few months passed since he read that the divorce had gone through but she had not rung him. Then one evening after a tense business meeting, he walked into a pub in Islington and there she was, singing with a group of hack musicians. The way she sang 'Summertime' was so moving that if he had been an over emotional man, he would have wept from nostalgia, lost love, desire for her or some other emotion which he couldn't define. When she finished singing, she went and sat at a table with a man, who put his arm round her shoulder but something about their body language told him he was only a passing fancy. Jake remained in the background so that she would not see him and left after a quick drink.

He looked at her as she sat with him in the pub and knew that this time it was completely different from the way it had been when they had met in Oxford Street.

When the band was having another beer break, Jake asked her about Jed.

"It was such a short time in my life that I've almost forgotten him. To build up grounds for divorce, Jed made up stories about me and other men. By that time I cared little about him and did not deny the lies. It wasn't until the settlement came through that I found out how little money I was left with," she said. "For a long time I loved being on my own. I might still be enjoying it if I hadn't met Martin at a party. My girlfriends were envious because they knew he was something in the city, very successful and making pots of money.

He wasn't much of a looker, just the opposite of Jed. I had suffered during marriage to him and I guess I wanted someone who would not always be chasing other women. To start with he was interesting and very attentive - all that Jed was not. I always wanted to live surrounded by flowers and he made sure that I did. Showered me with the roses I love. At the time I was convinced it was very thoughtful of him. He was so well off he told me that he could buy anything I wanted."

"Did you feel very spoilt?"

"I did; which was what he wanted me to feel. The facade began to collapse when I found a bill from a flower club – one of those where you pay your money, tell 'em how often to send flowers, pick at least twenty messages from their catalogue and they do the rest.

"He deposited a large amount of money in my name." With a wry smile, she added. "To avoid taxation, of course." she shrugged. "I later found that he had ensured that it would revert to him if we parted. We'd been married for just over a year but for me, it was finished after a week. He was a strange mixture. In business tough and very successful but in his private life he was insecure and very conscious of his lack of education. He constantly wanted me to read to him."

"Shakespeare?" Jake asked quizzically.

"Who else?" she said, "he said he loved the sound of my voice. I must have spent endless hours reading to him. Don't think he got much out of it."

"Probably helped you with your acting though?"

"D'you know I think you're right. I got through all the well-known plays and many of the sonnets." She looked at Jake for a few moments as though weighing him up. "It kept him away from me too."

"Violence, you mean?"

"I seem to be able to pick 'em," her voiced drifted away. "But he was worse, far worse than Jed…"

She was happy and in a celebratory mood. From her speech it was obvious that she had had rather too many drinks. He noticed by the car keys clipped to her handbag on the table that she must have driven to the pub. "You are in no fit state to drive," he said, "I walked here so I'll drive you back in your car when you're ready to leave, the pavements are icy but the road seems fairly clear."

She looked at him for a long time. With most people, he would have been forced to look away but the communion in their eyes seemed to him to be in itself almost an act of love.

"Where is back?" she asked.

"You live somewhere, don't you?"

She continued to study his face. It was obvious that she was near to dropping so he decided to take her to Firenze House. She was asleep by the time he got there. With an effort, he lifted her and slipping on the pavement, managed to carry her into the house and up to a spare bedroom.

The next morning, he took her a cup of tea, put it beside her bed, gave her a light kiss and started back to his room. The floorboards creaking from his weight woke her. With a murmured "thank you," she picked up her drink, slipped out of bed and followed him into his room. She stood for some time by the window looking out at the dawning sun before she spoke.

"Didst thou but know the only touch of love.

Thou wouldst as soon go kindle fire with snow

97

As seek to quench the fire of love with words."

She turned back and said as she looked at him with penetrating eyes, "Down on your knees and fasting for a good man's love." She came to the foot of the bed and knelt. "Cupid is a knavish lad, thus to make poor females mad." She slid under the bed cover at the bottom of the bed, came up beside him and said. "For love is heaven and heaven love."

"That's not Shakespeare."

"Scott. I don't only read Shakespeare you know."

Picking up her mood, he said: "Sorry am I, dear maid. Do never descend me as you did your husband and just read 'til sleep o'ercame desire."

She punched him. "You pig, to bring that up. Did I tell you about reading to my ex-husband last night? I was pretty far gone. Wish I hadn't told you now." She pouted, buried her head in his shoulder and, with her voice muffled said. "You know I could never think of you as a dependent person, don't you?" When he didn't reply, she put her arms round him and asked again. "Don't you?"

By now he was enjoying the tempting and teasing between them. "Do I?"

"Of course you do. You must know that I was charmed by you and your mind from those first Stratford days."

"When you turned up with that handsome young actor, Jed, weren't you saying that you had had enough and that I should depart?"

"Stupid fool, did you really think that? When you left without even a goodbye, I was lost. Jed was dishy and we did have something going but it was pale shadow, nothing more. After you left without even telling me your phone number, I turned to him for comfort. I was young then and to both of us, it seemed like love. But pale shadows disappear when the sky clouds over."

"Has the sun ever come out again?"

"Sometimes but not for long after you left." she said. "Jed and Martin were just substitutes for you."

"Thank you," Jake said, smiling. "Rhosa, what you said about the sky clouding over is poetry; you should write it down."

She smiled, "I have of course, I am quoting from a poem I wrote soon after Jed and I got married."

"Can I read it?"

"Wouldst thou but read the private thoughts of feminine youth?" She laughed. "Not sure where I put the things I wrote at that time. They were my therapy, a way of trying to understand what was happening." She got out of bed walked softly out of the room and returned with a note book from her handbag. "I woke in the night, I often do and sometimes I find if I scribble my thoughts down, it helps me sleep again." She passed him the notebook. He was pleased to see that she had written about their meeting in the pub.

The mirror looked back
As ten years passed
Again in Stratford with you
With Shakespeare in the air I breathed
My thought in all directions
But always back to you.
Midsummer Night's Dream
Just for you
You were my Romeo, my Bassanio
My living and my death
For dead I was when you left.

The poem held him so that he was unable to say anything. Rhosa, sensing his mood, spoke to break the silence.

"This is a lovely room," she said as she sat cross legged on the bed, resting her head on her hands and looked around. "Are those paintings real?"

"If you mean are they copies, no, they are originals, fixed permanently I'm told - came with the house. This used to be a sitting room, downstairs was an office, that's why they are here. Painted in the sixteenth century - there is a covenant on them so they can't be taken from the house."

"Are you sure they're permanently fixed. They look to me like paintings on canvas; they've got frames around them and glass over them, haven't they?"

"All I know is what the lawyer told me. The previous owner was a business man so I expect he would have moved them and sold them if he had been able to."

"And who is the striking man?" She nodded at the painting on the left.

"They told this was his home and a warehouse for cloth. I'm told that it was his father who built the place and the man in the painting extended it and gave it the name 'Firenze House'."

"What's his name?" she asked.

"They tell me he was called Jacob D'Arcy."

"That's a coincidence."

"Why?"

"That's almost your name."

"And what's even more intriguing is…" He waited while he thought. "I bought this house…"

"Because of the name of the first owner, is that what you're going to say?"

"Not because of his name. Something else…"

"Yes…?"

"It seemed like home."

"Why shouldn't it feel like home?"

"No, I haven't explained myself very well. I've lived all over the world, little houses, medium houses, in two of them I lived as a married man. In Romania I had six months in a pretty big palace with servants and every possible luxury when I was commissioned to write a book about the transitions which occurred as the country replaced Communism."

"Good for you, but what are you saying?"

"This place affected me like nowhere else. Nothing seemed as much like home to me ever before. It almost seemed as if I didn't have a choice." He looked away from her. "I've never had a feeling like that before, almost as though the house locked its arms around me - that's what I'm saying. As soon as I walked in through the door of this house; no, it was before that - it even happened when I read the advert for the place in the agent's window. I knew it was to be the place where I would live."

"Say that again."

"Yes, you heard me right. I knew it was home. The place drew me to itself."

"What does that say about free will?"

He laughed. "I remember you and your free will and how important it is to you."

"What is life without it?" she bit his shoulder playfully.

"Mm," he pondered. "Yes, I'm not saying I did not come of my own free will. It's just that I was drawn here by..." he sought for the right word, knowing that she would analyse whatever he said, "harmony."

"Harmony," she mused. "Yes, looking back, I know what you mean. I've never lived anywhere with harmony. The life my mother and step father led was like an orchestra playing with the sheet music upside down. Cacophony started at the breakfast table and was listened to at every meal. I hated it when they fought but it made me search for peace after I had left home. I want to say something but I don't know how to put it into words." She looked into his eyes and said, hesitantly. "I think it is here with you, Jake."

"Peace d'you mean?" he asked with raised eyebrows.

She pursed her lips. "Not peace, at least not completely; I don't think I am intended to be at peace."

"Doesn't that sound as though you're not in control?"

"You got me that time, Jake Dearsey" she said, laughing. "I try to believe in freedom but if I am completely honest, at heart I am a fatalist."

"Your destiny is decided?"

"I fool myself it isn't."

"But...?" he started to ask.

She sighed. "I can't stop myself thinking that it is. I try hard but nothing makes me feel any different."

"You can't change your personality so, better to stop thinking about it."

She sat up put her arms round her legs and her head on her knees again and stared at the portrait of Jacob D'Arcy. "We are machines you know. Our souls drive the machines, sometimes well, sometimes badly but the machine is unchangeable. I have been given a fatalistic machine which I try to drive in an optimistic manner but in my sub-conscious, I know I shall fail."

"Yes," he said, sitting up beside her, "and…"

"I try to drive it with as much freedom as possible."

"You have control?"

"A bit but if you are born with a tractor, you can't drive it like a sports car."

"It comes off the road?"

She nodded pensively and said. "Let's talk about that man there." She looked towards the painting. "He's staring at me from what I guess is more than four hundred years ago but I would prefer him not to be looking at me like a voyeur. What was he like I wonder? He looks interesting; the sort of man I'd like to spend an evening with."

"Just an evening?"

She pushed him with her open palm so hard that he almost fell out of bed.

"Don't talk like a crude man! There are other things than body meeting body."

"Like mind meeting mind?"

"That's what I meant, typical male."

He grinned. "I take that as a compliment."

"It wasn't meant like that," she said, still looking at the portrait. "D'you know," her gaze turned from Jake to the painting, "I think he even looks a bit like you."

"I can't see any resemblance. He looks quite ugly to me."

"Well…"she said turning and looking him in the face a smile flickering on her lips.

He grimaced.

"There are handsome faces which destroy the character of the owner. That was Jed's problem, he didn't bother about interesting conversation – didn't need to." She shuddered slightly at the memory of her first marriage. "There are interesting faces and those are the ones I prefer," she said.

"Can I take that as a compliment, then?"

"Idiot. Why do you need compliments? They are so easily given and rarely truthful."

"Now I am a soul lost."

"Like in Dante's Inferno do you mean?" she said, deliberately overacting. She turned back to the painting. "What do you know about him?"

"Almost nothing; I'm told he was a wool merchant, comfortably off. That's about all I know and even that is estate agent's talk and you know how they embellish."

"I want to get to know him."

"Not me."

"I already know you," she said; then, seeing him feigning disappointment, continued. "But of course, I would like to know more."

"I have tried to find out about D'Arcy," Jake nodded at the painting, "I've been to the library, waded through books on the history of this village of Barnes."

"And."

"Just one Jacob D'Arcy."

"Really, what did you find about him?"

"Born 1894."

"He must have had a father - where was he born and his father and the father before him."

"No good, I'm afraid. The 1894 man was born in Salem before he came to live here."

"Is that Salem, Carolina?"

"The same."

"Then you need to look there. Go back through the generations of Salem folk. Probably his family emigrated from Europe. Find out where they came from. I wouldn't mind betting his family came from this part of England. Jake," she said with a smile. "I even bet they came from this house." She turned and looked accusingly at him. "How can you lie there looking like a slob?"

"Must be my slob looking day," he grinned. "But all I am doing is looking at you."

"Ok, I've taken the bait, Mr. Dearsey. What do you see?"

"What do I see?" he supported his chin on his fist and kept her waiting for a reply.

As the seconds passed, she interrupted. "Come on Jay, don't be a sod. You've got me hooked now."

"I see you at nineteen the young woman whom I found delightful and I see you now, not showing the torment you have been through."

"The 'now' interests me most. What do you see now?"

"Well, I've travelled the world's art galleries, fashion centres, interviewed many so called beautiful women. And here I am in a bedroom with no heating, feeling slightly cold and even more than a bit hungry…"

She raised her voice, "Jake! Don't keep me waiting."

"Ok, I see the loveliest creature."

"Cut out the crap. Now I know you are lying. I look in the mirror every day. I know what I look like."

"Don't believe me if you don't want to but I've never meant anything so much before. Ok. So you're not Helen of Troy. But, who wants icy perfection, you are so much more. I'm looking behind that tough shell which I think you try to cover yourself with."

"Tough shell – is that what you see?" she frowned, "then what do you see beneath?"

"A woman..." he weighed up his words before continuing, "vulnerable and therefore precious and with honesty, sincerity and humour. A woman I would like to spend time with."

She looked away, obviously overcome so he waited till she turned back.

"Thank you, Jake. For me that could be more inspiring than anything else in English literature," she said, trying to conceal her emotion with humour.

"Let me make you some breakfast." Jake said flinging his legs over the side of the bed.

"No," she said. "I'll make it for you. What do you have in the kitchen?"

"Some stale bread which you'll have to toast, jam and cereal, I keep all that sort of thing in the tall cupboard beside the fridge."

He lay back in bed, and read the Daily Telegraph which Rhosa brought up to him and hearing with satisfaction to the clinking of crockery as she busied herself. While he listened, he read the editorial in the Telegraph on the fragility of global economics. Normally the subject would have depressed him but the sound from the crockery and the coffee odour coming up the stairs so cheered him that he saw a positive side to the article.

He put the paper down as Rhosa pushed open the bedroom door, carrying a tray. "You seem to be out of butter but there is something that looks like marg."

"That's my stuff. I don't eat butter."

"Not a bit of a food crank are you?" she asked as she put the tray on his knees.

"A bit," he grinned, "comes from having an overprotective mother. She read an article on butter and cholesterol when I was a small child and I've had substitutes ever since and prefer it to butter."

"Vile stuff but I suppose if it's smothered with jam you almost lose the taste." She passed the tray to him, climbed into bed, passed him a plate and, spread margarine and jam on a slice of toast and put it on his plate.

"I've been in the company of other women but I've always been alone even when they were sitting beside me as you are... Rhosa, I've missed you."

"But we haven't seen each other for ten years except that once in Oxford St. when I was feeling totally, hellishly depressed." she replied.

"Ten years have passed as though they didn't happen. I don't mean I missed you in the conventional way. I missed the memory of you."

"You mean I am an idea, not a reality?" she joked.

"Difficult to put into words so I won't try but I'm sure you understand what I mean. This is so nice. Two wives and they always wanted me to bring them breakfasts in bed, never the reverse."

"Well, I'm different, I like the caring role."

"Do you mean that?"

She let out a breath. "Funny, I didn't mean to say that at all."

"Why did you say it, then?"

"Perhaps it's my sub-conscious taking over," she said with an ironic smile, as she ate her toast spread with jam but, he noticed, without the margarine. Her body touched his when she leaned across to take her dish of cereal. As they made contact, a jolt passed through him.

Rhosa saw the effect she had on him. "Jake," she said between mouthfuls, "I was quite drunk last night wasn't I?"

"Let's put it this way," he said as he put down his drink, "I didn't think you should drive."

"Did I persuade you to bring me here?"

"Not directly but, when I asked where your home was, I got the feeling you were saying you didn't have a home."

"God, I must have been far gone. I don't remember that and I don't recall how I got here and into bed."

"I put you in one of the spare rooms. But, when I came up to my room, you had moved into my bed. You said something about feeling cold, so I put the electric blanket on in the spare bed and carried you back."

106

"Jake." she stopped eating. "Did... did anything happen?"

He thought to savour the moment by topping up his cup from the coffee pot and then, to keep her waiting, drank a couple of mouthfuls.

"Jake, did you hear what I asked?"

"Oh, sorry I was miles away, thinking of Jacob D'Arcy, there," he teased, nodding at the painting on the wall.

"Well, answer me now."

"I am not a pervert, Rhosa. You were sound asleep."

"And you didn't take advantage of the situation?"

"You've heard the phrase 'consenting adults'?"

She nodded. He could see she was agitated so he continued. "That's the only way with me."

She took his opened hand and kissed it for so long that he began to feel aroused. Sensing the effect she was having, she pulled away. "Sorry, Jake, I shouldn't have done that."

"Why did you, then?" he asked feeling confused.

"I don't know, I suppose I was just grateful."

"Grateful?"

"You...behaved like a gentleman."

"Is it so important?"

"It is..."

The silence which followed was strangely awkward until she slid her hand into his and said. "I need to explain."

He nodded, "but only if you want to."

"I do want to," she said pursing her lips, "but..."

He busied himself tidying crockery on the tray which he'd put on the floor while she made several attempts to speak. When finally she spoke it was as though confessing to a crime. "You see, I'm – well – unable to...I'm...." She hesitated and then blurted out, "in a man you would call me impotent. But it is more than that, impotent means lack of desire. Desire has left me completely and been replaced by... terror. I am afraid that if I had to have sex, I would scream out in pain. It is not you, darling Jake, something that happened made me

107

like this but don't ask me to tell you." She looked away and he saw that she was fighting back tears. "I can't."

He said nothing while her words sank in, pushing his mind at one moment into shock, another into disappointment and another into sympathy. He said nothing because he thought that if he had spoken too soon he could easily cause her distress.

"Did you hear me?" she asked.

He collected her breakfast things, put them on the tray on the floor and pulled her down into the bed beside him.

"Jake, please tell me," she said, raising her head from the pillow. "How does that make you feel?"

"How about ...relieved?"

"Relieved? How do you mean, relieved?"

"I mean I never liked to do the conventional thing and I'm relieved that you do not expect me to chase you till you succumb. I would far sooner cherish you than ravish you."

She sat up in bed, smiling through her tears. "That's the most disarming chat up line I've ever heard and I've heard a few," she said, "d'you mean it?"

"Do I ever say anything to you I don't mean?" he replied with a smile.

"Ok, joker." She raised herself on one arm, thought for a while, then said. "But it was such a nice thing to say."

"You make it sound as though you didn't trust me," he said, "have you been so hurt by men"

She looked at him quizzically.

"Do you have a fear of men, Rhosa?" he asked.

"I have no fear of men but 'man', singular, his intentions and coarseness...yes man singular fills me with apprehension."

"That bad experiences?"

She nodded, slid back on the bed, looking up at the ceiling and stayed silent, wanting to speak but unable to find words. When at last she spoke almost in a whispering voice, she said. "If only you had not left Stratford and that nineteen year old girl." Her hand slid down and found his. "I would not have lost ten years of love? When you left, April was the cruellest month - If T.S.Elliot will allow me a paraphrase." She became silent again. "It was like bereavement...I never knew that I could suffer such emptiness. You were there one day and the next you were gone and the only thing I was certain of was that I loved you. Loved you so much that nothing else meant anything and, dear man, everything else since has been a distraction, an attempt to find you in other men. I have loved you every day of those ten years and I never stopped looking for you. Even while I was on stage I would look at the audience. And when the play was over and we were taking a curtain call I would hold my hand over my forehead to screen out the lights and look to see if you were there. But you never were." She wiped her eye with the back of her hand. "Why were you never there, Jake?" She hesitated. "Sorry, this is foolish of me; I'm probably still a bit hung-over and shouldn't have said all that." When she spoke again he was surprised at the change which had come over her, her voice had become confident. "We seem to have eaten all the toast there was but I feel like another coffee, can you pass my cup," she said casually. "I'll make us some more. Then I must shower and go." She jumped from the bed, the pyjama tousers Jake had put her in the night before slipped down and revealed part of her naked backside. Laughing, as she dragged them up, she said. "Can't say I like wearing pyjamas - even though they're yours."

"I had nothing else and I didn't feel you'd want to sleep with nothing on. But you do look good in them."

"Sweet of you," she pulled up the pyjama bottom higher and went down the stairs. "Thanks," she called back.

He heard her in the bathroom and sat in bed reading the paper for ten minutes.

"Fresh coffee's on the kitchen cabinet, beside the sink," she yelled up the stairs. He put on a dressing gown and went down. She had washed the dishes, showered and dressed and was just putting on her top coat.

"Do you have to go?" he asked, picking up a cup. Rhosa poured out the fresh coffee for him and he went to the bar to drink it.

"Do you want me to stay forever?" she said teasingly, "no, I have to go to a rehearsal," she started to look around, "my car keys?"

"On the hook behind you, they're next to mine."

She turned. "How tidy you are, Jake. I'm afraid that's something I can never be." She picked up her keys, blew him a kiss and was walking down the passageway.

"Rhosa," he called after her, "is that it 'is that all there is'?" he said, quoting Peggy Lee's song.

"What d'you mean?"

"Wilt thou leave me so unsatisfied? - Are you leaving my life as well as my kitchen?"

She skipped back along the tiled floor, kissed him on the forehead and sang, "Oh no, John, no, John, no John, no."

"Then…what?"

"If that is an invitation to return, I shall be a bit late this evening, about 7.30, we've got a difficult scene to do but I could cook you dinner if you don't mind it being rushed. You won't have noticed yet but I have already written my 'phone number on your 'things to do' notice board."

"Come back here, then. I'm working on an article so I don't have to go out. We'll have roast swan, shall we."

She laughed. "From the pond there," she pointed through the window.

"That baby swan would be tender, wouldn't it?" He grinned.

"I'd sooner starve."

"Ok, I'll open a tin, then."

"You can get tinned roast swan, can you?" she smiled, kissed him on the forehead again and ran off. "I'll 'phone when we've finished," she called out as she opened the door and dashed off into the cold morning.

That day, the article he was writing took him forever. Every sentence he dredged out of his brain was punctuated by memories of her. At nineteen he thought he would never find anyone so intriguing. Now, at twenty nine she had matured and not just her looks, her attraction was the way she used herself, her mind, her body and her language.

When she didn't 'phone as she had said she would in the evening, he was devastated. Eventually, she turned up at 9.30, apologising and looking harassed.

"It was the producer. He insisted on taking me out for a drink or two to celebrate what I had achieved."

"Why not?" Jake said, trying not to show his irritation. "All you had to do was ring me." Although he felt let down, most of his distress was tempered by his pleasure at seeing her again.

"Jay, I'm sorry, that was thoughtless," she said, her speech slightly slurred. "But that's me. I get so excited when a scene goes well that everything goes out of my head."

He had been let down by other women so many times and knew this was a decisive moment. If he did not make a stand, Rhosa would think him weak and, if he did, it would be a presumption in a relationship too young to have imposed any responsibility on either of them.

"Another time, if there is another time, just ring me." he said, feeling that that would not make an issue but would show he was not pleased at being stood up. "I've done a cold supper, so it's not come to any harm," he said. "You haven't eaten, have you?"

"No." he noticed her hesitation. "Not much."

He had laid the table with candles to give an atmosphere but it seemed contrived to light them. When they sat down and he started putting food out, she said, "candles, how nice, aren't you going to light them, Jay?" he noticed that she had called him Jay a few times, it was a name nobody else had used and to him it was like a bond between them.

Lighting the candles was symbolic, changing the atmosphere in the room. She put her hand on his and said. "I know that forgetting to ring you was unforgivable."

"Don't worry about it."

"But I do worry. I don't know what comes over me. I just forget everything when I'm in my acting mode."

"I'll remember that," he said with a laugh which broke the ice. "Is he interesting?"

"Who?"

"Your producer, I mean?"

"D'you know I didn't even think about it. He's a person with whom I have to work, a cipher almost. Only through him will things happen." She shrugged her shoulders and sensing his concern said, "That's all. There's nothing more."

She was obviously tired so, when they had finished eating, he asked if she wanted him to take her home. He felt elated when she shook her head and said. "Can I stay here?" He showed her into the spare room and left her to sleep.

The next morning, when he woke, she was sleeping beside him.

CHAPTER 9

"So many things puzzle us in this life of ours." Jacob said, getting out of bed and putting on his day clothes. Mistress Darkall was tidying up his bedroom which had become disarranged while he had spent several days in bed recovering from a recurring illness. "People get frightened about what they do not understand. I'm sure that, in time we would reason out things if we were all free to think." He started to help her by picking up books which had fallen to the floor. "What is happening when we have storms and the sky flashes with a noise that frightens us. And why does milk go sour when we have thunder?"

"Methinks you are saying that it is all God's will, Sir," She picked up her cleaning brushes and put them under her arm. "'tis tidier in the room now, I will go down and look at the cooking," she said as she turned to go down the stairs.

"You may be right, but I don't think that is all God's will." Slowly he followed her carrying some of his books, put them on the table and pulled his chair into the kitchen close to the fire and watched as she stirred the stew. "Something which is puzzling me is what a farmer friend said about his meat. You may also have seen the same thing when, after some days, little white things appear on the meat."

"Yes sir, I've seen 'em many times. I've also seen the same wriggling things on dead people when they do lie in the streets for days."

"Have you indeed! I'd never noticed that they also come on dead bodies. I suppose you've seen many people dead."

"Many people do die of starving. I've seen 'em fighting each other with knives over a crust. I saw a man kill a dog with his knife. Before he could cut it up there were a dozen tearing at it. The man who killed the dog got trampled on. When they had all gone, he just lay there. He never got up again" she said, adding salt to the pan cooking on the fire. "Once when I was very sick, I slept for days in the street and when I come round, the man next to me was dead, must've been days afore, because he had them white things, same as you get on meat. He smelled and it made me spew so bad."

"I know that smell on meat, it is so bad, it is impossible to eat."

"Been so hungry at times, I've had to cook and eat meat like that."

"Ugh!" he shuddered "how could you."

"When you are starving, you'll eat anything. Spring and summer was the worst, fruit don't grow and if the winter have been long even people in houses have run out. A lot of people do die when the sun is shining. So you eat even rotten meat. With herbs and garlic which grow wild it don't taste too bad if 'tis cooked over a fire for a long time."

She turned to him, stopped stirring the vegetables and said. "Them white things, I saw them grow wings and fly off. I've seen 'em stop on the mouth of a new born baby and go inside his mouth."

Jacob raised his eyebrows in amazement. "Mistress, that may be the answer; they are souls and have to find a baby as a home," he stood up and put his arm on her shoulder. "Thank you. I don't think I would ever have thought of that," he said. "Always tell me things like that or if you see anything that puzzles you. If they are souls, it means we may not have one soul but many." He stood up in silent thought. "Where does that leave the Church?"

"Do the Church say we have one soul only?" she asked

He nodded.

"But I can't see a soul."

"It requires faith to believe that we have a soul," he said. "But it is that which makes us live."

"I think I will not please you that way, sir. When my man did get killed, I tried to die as well. I went without eating for days. A woman, a friend of Anne Askew, found me near dying, took me to where she lived with a lot of other kind people and made me eat. She saved me but there weren't enough room for everyone so one night, I left and went back to the streets."

"I can understand you wanting to die after losing your man. I felt the same when my wife died. Somehow you and I found strength and we are here still." Jacob looked at the floor and said almost to himself, "I'm glad you're here," he looked back again as she stirred the pot and said, "It must mean that you are a survivor."

"Can you tell me what you mean, sir?"

"I mean that you have learned how to stay alive when others have died. One of the things we admire in our Group is the ability to learn how to overcome." He looked at her as a thought struck him. "Have you been taught by anyone?"

"When I worked for another family. The grandfather, he were nice to me like you are. He would read to me and taught me some words." she said.

"But you were on the street when you came to me." Jacob looked puzzled.

"The family were not like you."

"Why...what happened?"

"They turned me out."

"But why? You do everything anyone could expect. You work hard. The house is cleaner and tidier than it has ever been."

"There were a baby."

"Yours?"

She shook her head. "The Mistress...she was brought to bed. I did have to bring hot water and clean things for her."

"I'm sure you would have done everything they could have wanted. What happened?"

He noticed that she was distressed and waited for her to speak.

"The...baby...it did die." She could not say any more for several minutes. "They said it was my fault because I had an ugly man who did magic. That same day they turned me out. Until I come here, I never had another home since."

"That is very like what happened to the wife of my friend Josephus, she now lives apart from him in another country."

115

Jacob knelt down in front of her, put his arms around her and held her as she shook with emotion. "You did not marry your man?"

She shook her head.

"And what age are you now?"

"I have seen sixteen summers I think, sir."

"That is late to be unmarried. I married my wife when she was fourteen."

"My man, sir, he didn't want marriage nor anything to do with laws made by them in charge of us."

"I understand," Jacob said, nodding, "and children?"

"No, sir, my man said it was not fair to bring children into life when there is so much evil."

"But…"

"He was a careful man, sir," she said, understanding his meaning and continuing with her cooking.

Jacob walked back to his desk and tried to read again but his mind was distracted by what she had said. As he sat silently, he became aware that she was standing in the doorway.

"Yes, Mistress," he said, raising his eyes.

"The meal be soon ready, sir." she said, wiping her hands on her apron as she stood in the doorway, "When can we do what you said," seeing his enquiring look she said, "learnin' is my meaning…"

"I am just reading something which I think would interest you. Would you like to come and sit at the desk here?"

"The meal will soon be ready."

"It matters not, the food will keep. I will read you just a little."

Cautiously, she took a seat beside his desk, so close that he was aware of the cooking odours on her hands and the warmth of her body.

Looking down the book, he realised that the words would be foreign to her. He closed the cover and turned to her "I will not read from this; there are a lot of words you will not yet have heard. Tomorrow, my friend Michael Dalgett is coming to see me. I have

116

told him about you and he asked if he could meet you. He has spent a lot of time on the writing of the Ancient Greeks and the rebirth of thought and can tell you more than I can."

The following day there was a loud knock on the door. Jacob himself went to open it and in came a short rotund man dressed in velvet with lace at his cuffs and collar. The sun was shining through the window of Jacob's study and reflecting a red glow onto the walls from Michael Dalgett's clothes.

He sat down and Jacob called Mistress Darkall into the room.

Overcome by meeting a new man and with exuberant energy, she remained silent.

Seeing that she was daunted, the visitor stood up, performed an elaborate bow and said. "Hello, hello, hello. You are the young lady Jacob has told me about. I see you seem to be shy of me. I don't want you to be like that. You will soon see that I am what my friends call a buffoon which means I enjoy a joke and a laugh. What would life be if we could not make fools of ourselves?"

She looked from the noisy visitor to Jacob as though wanting permission to reply and was surprised to see that the normally serious Mr. D'Arcy was laughing uproariously with his guest.

"Michael, you old fool, can't you see that you are making so much noise that neither she nor I can think."

"So sorry," he turned to Mistress Darkall. "I live alone with only a servant whom I suspect was born in a graveyard and would want to spend his time meditating on death - such a relief to fly away from him." He smiled broadly and flapped his arms like the wings of a bird. "You will no doubt be thinking, 'why do I not get rid of him?' And you would be right to ask. But, you see, I have a certain affection for him and he is so competent. Each morning, I am wakened with breakfast and a hot drink, he ministers to me if I am ever unwell and, as you can see," he stood up and rotated so that they could admire his clothes, "I am always well groomed so I am often complimented on my style of dress - which pleases me." He bowed with exaggerated grace. "But I do crave humour and when I get away from him, I need the relief of being able to act foolishly. So if you don't mind I will do just that, even though I will speak and laugh louder than is seemly." He let out a roar and said. "When I do that at home, which is rarely I

117

might say, I am sure that my servant Gastoban - a man from France as you can tell by his name, would like to tell me that I might wake the dead. His dead of course, not mine." He laughed long and hard. "Now, my dear, let's get formalities over. I am Michael Dalgett, Jacob may have told you about me but possibly not - he talks so little he is what you might call 'a thinking man' and I am sure he would never refer to himself as a buffoon as I do of myself. But I know he would be a better man for it." His laugh resonated around the room.

Michael sat and motioned for Mistress Darkall to sit beside him. "Don't think I am just a fool, though. I and a few others meet here to talk about what Jacob refers to as 'Scientificals'. That is what you might call a sheltering word under which we include many subjects. Our purpose is to increase our knowledge and to seek to improve the lives of less fortunate people. You will know that there are many of them. Jacob has told me that you were amongst them."

"And would be now if not for Mr. D'Arcy, or I would be dead."

"We all count ourselves fortunate to know Jacob." Michael Dalgett said. "How do we try to achieve our purpose you may ask? We do it through subterfuge even though that might sound contrary to you. We want to spread the message that we are all human beings and that none of us should suffer neglect. We particularly want our leaders to treat people as equals." Taking this as a cue, Jacob guided Mistress to sit on a chair by the table. "That's better," Michael said. "How could you be an equal if we expect you to stand while we make ourselves comfortable? So, in furtherance of that, you will call me Michael and I will call you Darkall. I don't like formal titles." He stopped, looked concerned, momentarily and said. "I am doing what I always do and talking too much and I notice it is making me a little parched." Turning to Jacob, he said. "Do you have some of that excellent wine you bring in from Italy?"

When Jacob had filled glasses Michael said. "Do you know, I think I would be better left with Darkall so we can talk freely, don't you think?"

"I suspected you would not want me around." Jacob said smiling at his guest's lack of formality. I will go and see Josephus and I will take him some of the wine which you seem to like so much."

When they were alone, Michael said. "You may think this is unusual, a man being left alone with a young woman but I will tell you that you are completely safe. I do know many women but they remain only as friends. I don't indulge in the tempestuous love affairs that I hear about and I must say that I find them all very boring."

He stood up and lifted his chair closer to the table so that he would be nearer to her.

"Jacob has told me you want to learn about the Greeks. I won't read the book to you because it goes into tedious detail. I'll give you just a summary of it." He said. "Have you heard of the word Riniscita or Renascent?"

"My man did use that word but he never told me what it meant."

"Renascent is a French word. It means re-birth." He looked at her to be sure that she understood.

"Re-birth? How is't possible?" she asked.

"It means re-birth not of people but of knowledge. It started with the discovery of the writings of Aristotle; he developed a way of learning difficult subjects. When Aristotle's works were found, they caused people to think in ways which were new to them. That is the re-birth I talk about." She was so close now that he could tell from her breath that she had tasted the food she had been cooking.

Florence, in Italy, is the place where the European re-birth started, but we now know that it began earlier in Arabia. Scholars discovered ancient books of writings. They were almost too late because invading Heathens destroyed many books in the past but a lot survived and from them we can now read what the ancients thought." He picked up the book on the table and held it reverentially in the air. "This is a marvel; it has done more to change the world than anything else. I don't mean just this book of course; I mean the invention of printing in Europe." He put the book carefully down and opened it to a picture. "You might say to me 'No, Michael, wars have had more influence. And if you did say that, I might get a little cross and tell you that you were mistaken. Printing puts knowledge into the hands of everyone. Jacob has told me, Darkall, that you have not yet read a book but Jacob has and so have I. He tells me that you learn quickly. You will learn more quickly when we tell you about things that we have read." He took a drink and refilled his glass. "This wine is good, Darkall, you should get Jacob to take you to Florence where it comes from. There you will see astonishingly beautiful painting and sculpture. Ask him to take you to see Michelangelo's statue of David. The beauty of that body, the muscles and the way he stands so proudly is very exciting. I am sure that it will never be equalled in a thousand years.

Let me tell you of the Italian scholar Petrarch, who discovered the letters of Cicero. Probably it was he who started the Riniscita and deeply influenced Italian language culture and thought. Including new things like perspective." Michael waved his hand theatrically towards the window. "You see the way that building in the distance gets smaller the farther it is away from us? If you don't paint with perspective, nothing looks real." Suddenly he yawned. "I'm sorry, my dear lady. I seem to have drunk most of this flagon of wine and have made myself sleepy. Would you mind if I leaned back in that chair by the fireplace and caught up with Morpheus for just a few moments, I assure you?"

"Oh, no, sir," she hesitated, "...Michael. I will go to the kitchen while you sleep, I do have a stew cooking slow." she said. "But what you have told me is wondrous; would that I could see that David you told me of."

"As I say, Jacob should take you." He moved to the chair by the fire." I shall fall asleep quickly Darkall but one thing I would like to say which I am sure you have already realised is that your Jacob is a most marvellous man. He would not tell you himself because he is a modest person but he is very clever with a mind that can analyse situations quicker than any of us. We all take our problems to him and you can be sure that he will find an answer. I will go so far as to say that I would not be here today if it hadn't been for Jacob. You see I went into business with a man who was not honest. He took a lot of my money and would have had it all if Jacob had not warned me against him and also found a way for me to get out of the contract. I owe your master a lot as I am sure you do." He stopped for a moment. "And, as I am sure you know, he is a very caring man. It was he who started the Scientifical Group; we want the poor and needy to be cared for. There are a lot of people who want to stop us but in many small ways and because of the inspiration of Jacob, we have been able to ease the suffering of many hungry people."

"I know what a good man he is. I thank God that I work in his house." She said and was about to say how lucky she was when heavy breathing from the fireplace told her that the guest was asleep. He remained where he was for many hours. When he woke, he had some of the stew cooking over the fire before he danced out of the house as Jacob returned.

When he had gone, Jacob said, "I have a deep affection for Michael. He is our jester and our sage. I hope he did not make you feel uncomfortable, I know that he embarrasses some people."

"No man I met was ever like him. He did not make me feel uncomfortable. He made me laugh and he would've taught me new things but the wine got to him."

"It pleases me that you liked him. He will come back again to tell you more, you can be sure."

CHAPTER 10

Jacob was reading the book by Zosimos of Panopolis which treated alchemy as a spiritual discipline and compared the separating of elements to the cleansing of the soul – the divine spirit from the flesh. But Jacob was finding the book particularly difficult and had dropped off to sleep.

A knock roused him.

After a moment, Mistress Darkall came to his room. "Sir, there is a man at the door to see you."

"A man?" In the moment of wakening, a sense of foreboding filled his mind. Cautiously, he put the book under the cushion on his chair. "Who is he?"

"He would say nothing."

"What does he look like?"

"I casn't say, sir, he wears a cloak with a hood which covers his face."

"Well," he said, slowly recovering his consciousness, "you'd better let him in." He stood to greet the unknown visitor.

A few moments later the cloaked figure entered the room, bringing with him an odour of incense. The figure took the seat indicated by Jacob but in spite of the cold outside and the welcoming warmth from the fire he did not attempt to pull back the hood of his cloak.

"Are you cold, sir? Come to the fire." Jacob said, moving his chair to one side.

The cloaked man raised his hand to indicate that he would stay where he was and Jacob saw on the fingers of the hand, many heavy rings; the biggest having a pentacle of gold inlaid in a precious stone.

"May I offer you a drink sir? I have a good wine, just imported from France."

"Thank you, no, I have just eaten," the figure turned to see Mistress Darkall who was standing, waiting for instructions. "We must talk alone." Jacob noticed that the man had a strong Italian accent and since he was fluent in Italian wondered if he should suggest not talking in English. But on reflection, thought it better not to reveal his ability.

"We are alone, sir. My servant can be relied on for complete discretion."

"Then, we cannot speak. What I have to say must be to you alone and to no other ears."

"Thank you, Mistress there will be nothing more." Jacob said with some reluctance and a look of apology to his maid, "please would you shut the door."

When she had left, the cloaked figure stood, went to the door, opened it, looked round and then, closing it firmly returned to sit down again. His hood fell back a little but not enough for Jacob to see his face.

"You are Jacob D'Arcy."

Jacob nodded. "Is anything wrong?"

"There is a lot wrong but it is not to do with you. I will talk a little with you about certain matters but I must insist again - what I am to say is for your ears alone." He waited while Jacob nodded his acquiescence. "I want you to understand that if any word of what I tell you is repeated, you will be dead - not by my hand but there are others. Do you understand?"

Jacob frowned but said, "I know what you are saying but can't say I understand."

The hooded figure looked down, his head resting on his hand. When he looked up he said.

"You know of Savonarola."

"I do."

"You know that he declared that Pope Alexander was an infidel and a heretic?" the dark figure asked.

"Yes, I have been in the square in Florence where the Pope ordered him to be hanged and burned in the Piazza della Signoria."

"Although I have no respect for Savonarola, he was a man tormented by ill-conceived ideas of right and wrong and he caused much suffering, there are those who still have sympathy with what he said all those years ago," the voice was muffled by the hood which gaped open slightly. Jacob remained silent, looking into the folds of cloth surrounding the face but unable to make out any features.

"Do you understand what I am saying, Mr. D'Arcy?"

Hesitant to reply and commit himself, Jacob simply nodded.

"But why do you not speak, Mr. D'Arcy?"

"I do not know you. I don't know why you are here and I must know what you want from me."

"Then tell me. What are your opinions about the Papacy?"

"My opinions are between myself and the Lord God."

The hooded figure remained silent and then said. "Come, Mr. D'Arcy, we are playing games with each other."

"The game is yours, sir. The rules are yours." Jacob said. "Tell me why you are here."

"I am here because we need someone we can trust."

"I can say only that I can see that there is a need for moderation. If this is your intention and you need someone whom you can trust in that endeavour, then I am that man and I will do all I can to make change happen. Until I hear what you and your friends are planning, I have nothing to say."

The figure stood up, held out his hand and said. "Thank you, Mr. D'Arcy that is what I have come for. I can say no more at this moment but I will arrange to meet again."

Jacob raised the proffered hand to his lips, grazing them slightly against the large rings. He bowed and followed his visitor to the door of the house.

CHAPTER 11

The sun shining through the bedroom window woke him. He had slept well and had dreamt long and well. The dream was about Mistress Darkall but their roles were reversed; she the house owner and he the servant. Instead of feeling apprehension, he had, in a perverse way, enjoyed the experience. He had become aware that, during his waking hours, his thoughts were often of his housekeeper and now even his sleeping time was being invaded. Although she was softer and had more understanding of his needs than his late wife, in some ways they were similar - instinctively able to take over duties without needing to be instructed.

She had heard him moving and when he went down stairs, his breakfast of bread and cheese with a flagon of beer was laid ready for him.

"Mistress Darkall." he called as he sat down to eat. "Thank you for my breakfast." She came to the door when she heard him. "I've been thinking it is time you came and sat with me always instead of only sometimes? I have suggested this before," he said as he ate what she had put in front of him.

She looked shocked. "Oh no, sir, that'd not be right. You must be master of the house."

As she spoke, he started to shake his head. "No, mistress, you are wrong to think of me as your master. I know that in the eyes of the people out there," he nodded in the direction of the window, "I am your master; but in these walls, I want you to feel that I am a friend and..." his voice became quiet, "as well as looking after things, I would like you to be a companion... Can you do that?"

"Sir, there is too much separatin' us."

"What do you mean?

"I mean, sir. You're a gentleman, a man from good family; and me – I canst not recall the time when I had a family. As long back as I can remember, sir, I been alone. Not till I come here did I have clean clothes and water to use and to wash in. You always had these things because you're from family."

"You are wrong, mistress. Our birth puts us in different positions but the way we run our lives can make us equals. I have seen qualities in you which you won't know yourself yet but they are there and I want to see them grow."

She stayed quiet for a moment and then, with her eyes still looking down, said. "I like it when you talk to me, sir, my man'd say things but he didn't have the words like you. Now I'm gettin' to know much more and I want to learn everythin' I can."

"I've had enough to eat, thank you." He pushed his plate to one side. "If you will make yourself comfortable, I would like to tell you more about Martin Luther."

She collected up the things, took them into the kitchen and began to wash them. He went to the kitchen door. She turned her head as she heard his step. "Don't think I never heard of Martin Luther, sir, does he live hereabouts?" she called over her shoulder.

"I have mentioned his name before. No, he was from a country hundreds of miles away. You have to go across the sea to a town called Wurttemberg." He thought for a moment and then said, "Mistress, do you mind if I sit here while you work. I find that for me it's peaceful."

"Peace?" she said, turning her head to look at him. "Mind I not 'bout you being near but I wonder at your needing peace, sir."

"Does it sound silly to you? That I, a man with comfort and a life without want should not have found peace."

"Indeed it do, sir," she said as she poured water from a jug over the dishes. "For me, I knew no peace until I came to you and this house," she said, wiping the dishes with a cloth and stacking them on shelves. "Now I have peace."

"I am so glad to hear you say that, Mistress," he said. "But peace, for me is difficult. It will sound strange to you but with ease, comes remorse."

"Remorse? Not a word I've used, sir. What is it?"

"It may be difficult to understand but when you had nothing. Anything which came your way like food or clothes, were yours alone

126

to enjoy. No one could deny that you deserved them. But when you have all one can need as I have, there is a guilt which seeps into your life. I wonder if you can understand what I mean."

"Sort of, sir. Please say more." She started to stack the plates in the cupboard.

"Guilt is like when you bite into a rotten apple - it spoils the taste."

"When I were in the streets, I never had an apple 'cept it were rotten, sir. I saw piles of good uns' in the market but they were for people with money."

"Like me do you mean?" he joked.

She nodded slightly.

"When I say apple, I mean it to represent life. I feel that there is rottenness in much that I do." He walked into the kitchen and there being no chair, sat down on the floor, his legs bent and his head resting in his cupped hands.

"But why, sir? You're a good man, you have took me in, I've had kindness from you and you have never struck me nor 'ave shouted at me. I did sometimes work for other men and they be like devils. It do not matter how hard I work, they would want more."

"Mind and body do you mean?" he said looking up at her eyes and, when she nodded. "You can be sure that will never again happen. Anything you do for me I would like you to do because you want to. I don't intend ever to ask you for anything that you do not want to give willingly."

She said nothing but looked with what seemed to him to be affection then turned away and lifted her apron to her eye.

He stood up and went to her, placing his hand carefully on her shoulder. "Are you sad, mistress?"

"No, sir, I be not sad."

"What is upsetting you, then?" He asked, moving so that his arm was closer around her.

Sensing his closeness, she moved away slightly and said. "I must get doing my cleaning, sir."

Her words disturbed him, as though she was rejecting him. He stood up and walked slowly into his room and quietly shut the door.

A feeling of emptiness came over him and he stood motionless, wondering what to do, whether to walk in on her and tell her his feelings or to turn away and wait. As he sat at the table, he reflected that he had reached an age when many of his friends had died. But he had never before felt such depth of affection for anyone. He and his wife Isabel had never declared their love. They had been friends but there was never intimacy, never the sharing of the secret parts of the mind wherein the real person lies. And never did they have shared humour. Jacob had not complained and neither had Isabel. Their combined businesses provided enough to satisfy all their needs. Even during times of difficulty when other businesses were failing, theirs remained profitable. They both accepted the inevitability of the events that had brought them together when in a severe epidemic of ague, both his and her parents died. Neither of them had thought of love as something they should seek. Love of God was natural but love between man and woman was not inevitable.

Isabel had been a very supportive wife. His meals were always ready. She had clothes made for him which would impress his customers but she had made him aware that she did not want children and suffered his advances in silence.

Emotions that were new to him filled his mind when he thought about Mistress Darkall. A woman, lacking the education of his wife but who, nevertheless interested him and roused him more.

Often, when he was out meeting customers, he would find his mind wandering and thinking about her and how long it would be before he could return to his home. He struggled for a way to tell her but although he tried many times he always felt tongue tied in her presence.

CHAPTER 12

"Why are we so different from other creatures," Jacob said.

She looked up from her sewing. "I don't 'stand your meaning, sir."

He got up from his chair, put another log on the fire and sat down before he realised that this was the first time he had tended to the fire, a job which would have been done by this woman who had grown so necessary that she now sat with him in the same room each evening after she had finished her work.

He looked over at her and saw that she also had noted his action but she was acquiescing in it and had made no attempt to stop him.

"What I mean is..." the flickering flame rising from the log lit his face. "Let's start with this fire. No other animal use fire to keep itself warm."

"Do not dragons, sir?"

"Dragons? Are there such things? I've never seen one and never met anyone who said that they have caught a glimpse of one." He looked up, smiling to himself. "Do you know what I think?" he asked and, not waiting for a reply said. "I think that dragons and the fires of hell are myths, created just to frighten us."

"Why do you think that, sir?"

"A frightened person is easier to control," he saw that she needed more explanation so continued, "these people with great wealth; Kings, Lords and Ladies, the Pope and his Cardinals, live in terror that their wealth and power will be taken from them. So, they frighten us and tell us of demons and dragons, Purgatory and the fires of Hell, witches and wizards."

She still looked puzzled. "Why?"

"So that we remain passive and look to them to protect us." He leaned over and poked the fire. "Let me explain, Mistress, and, I'm sorry if I say things that will upset you."

She nodded.

"Why do you think the mob killed your man?"

"That is a thing I did never know, sir." She grimaced at the memory of the Priest and his goading of the crowd.

"Fright, Mistress, terrible fright. Not for any sensible reason though, because your man had not attacked them. Those people who govern us sow this fear amongst uneducated people; they destroy the object of fear which in this case was your man." He watched for her reaction. "I have seen animals in enclosed spaces. They graze happily without anger and only fight when they are seeking a mate and want to copulate." As he said the word, he felt a slight pleasure as he looked out of the corner of his eye at the woman sitting across the room bent over her work.

"Sir, also do I see these things."

"And marvel at them?"

"I do not use that word but I do be peace-like looking at them."

"'Peace-like', that sounds nice," he said but as he spoke, she saw that he was trembling and then his eyes rolled.

Jacob was having one of his 'strangenesses'. She went to him, held his head against her breast and enclosed him with her arms, her head resting against his.

Quietly, she said. "There, my lover, I am here, I will care for thee. Do be peace-like for me." She began to rock and sing softly, repeating the same phrase again and again. Minutes passed as she sang and then, as suddenly as he had drifted away, he returned. Fearfully, she laid his head back on the chair, hastened to her seat and picked up her work.

When he spoke, his speech was slurred. "Mistress Darkall, I am recovering, did you care for me while I was gone?"

"Sir, I were sad for you."

"Yes, I knew I was going. Sometimes it is bad. Was it this time?"

"You were peace-like, sir."

He nodded. "My peace came from you, I think. When I came back, I saw you were close to me."

"Sir, I am sorrow but you needed care."

"Thank you." He said and reached over to her and touched her hand. He saw that, although she did not react, she did not move away. He wanted to talk with her about his growing feelings for her but judged that the moment was not right and he was also overcome with tiredness.

"I...," he sighed, "I must sleep."

"Your bed is ready, sir, I will put the hot stone in for you, 'tis warming ready."

"Thank you Mistress." As he went through the door, he turned and said. "You have given me new life and I am so pleased."

With her head down, he saw that she was smiling to herself. As he put on his sleeping clothes and got into bed, he recalled her smile of pleasure. "Mistress Darkall," he called. She came to the door but no farther while he was in bed. "Although I am tired, I do need to read before I sleep. I wonder would you mind fetching my book. It is open on my study table."

A few moments later she returned, this time coming into the room. As he took the book from her, their hands touched momentarily. He noticed that she was shaking slightly. "Are you well, Mistress," he asked.

"Sir, I am well."

"And ... happy?"

She stood looking uneasy before she spoke. "I never thought to be happy, sir," her voice became quiet, "but now I know I am."

He reached out and put his hand on hers but touching only the back in the manner of a friend.

"Do you want more, sir."

He looked in her eyes and with disappointment, saw that she meant worldly things. "You have put me some ale, so I have all I need," he said "you go to your bed as well."

"Sir," she said, lowering her head and curtseying slightly. As she turned and left his room, she closed the door behind her.

Normally, he could read easily and fall to sleep over a page but, he noticed that he kept reading the same paragraph without any understanding even though it was a book by Aristotle which he wanted to study. It had been printed on a Caxton press and had been lent to him by Josephus Dorman. Josephus was spending more of his time experimenting in search of the Philosopher's Stone although he was not interested in what the Stone could do for, like Jacob, he believed that extreme wealth bred a corrupted mind. His pleasure was in the searching and Jacob suspected that if he ever found the Stone, it would be an anti-climax for him.

He turned in his bed, the book falling from his hands as sleep overtook him.

The next morning, he awoke earlier than his normal time, even before it had become light. Sleep had rejuvenated him and the aches which often racked his body felt easier.

He got out of bed and noiselessly went downstairs, meaning to light the fire and warm the house for when Mistress Darkall came down. At the door, he stopped and looked in amazement. She was standing unclothed, washing in front of the already lit fire, her back to him. Hastily, he turned and on tiptoe started to walk to his bedroom, thinking she had not heard him. He was startled to hear her gasp as his footsteps made the stairs creak.

Hurriedly he hastened to his room. As he began to dress, the memory of her delicately shaped back filled his mind.

He heard her footsteps as her figure, now clothed, rushed past his still open door.

"I woke early, mistress," he called after her.

"I will get your breakfast, Mr. D'Arcy" she called back.

She cooked over the fire in the kitchen as he drank the water she had drawn and boiled for him. Neither spoke but, as he looked at her back, so recently naked in front of him, his mind was a whirlwind of desire. He wanted to go to her but instead, shifted noisily on his chair.

When she turned to him, her face was flushed. He wondered if it was just from the warmth of the fire or that she was also in a state of excitement.

"Your bread is toasted, Mr. D'Arcy." She said as she placed it on the wooden plate in front of him, carefully averting her gaze. "And I gotten some o' that berry jam you liked."

"From the market?"

"The farmer's wife did come with it."

"To the door?"

She nodded. "She did so."

"Her man Magnus has asked me to see her, we are worried about her, she looks so unwell. I wish I had been here when she came."

"On the morrow, she will be again here."

"With more of her produce?" he smiled at her but she did not return his smile.

"She do have a thing called ginger and said you like it."

"I do but is it not expensive?"

"She got it from a sailor changed for eggs she give him. She wants no money for it."

"That is uncommonly good of her, but why?"

She turned back to the fire to put on another log. "She says you are kind to her and have helped her."

"I did nothing. She was getting very thin so I gave her some wormseed, sometimes we have things inside our stomachs and I know that wormseed seems to stop them. I was told about it by a learned man in Florence, it came from that very clever physician, Paracelsus that I told you about. I have observed that it can cure people of other ailments."

"She told me to say to you she do feel better."

"I am so glad. She is the third person I have given it to and each time they have improved."

"When I was with my man, he would give me plants to eat when I was sick."

"There is so much we have to learn. Paracelsus knew a lot about cures from plants and herbs which have magic powers."

"Could there be something for your strangenesses?"

"I hope there is. I have tried many herbs. Sometimes they seem to help and I think I have been a good deal better for many years. When I was very bad, my strangeness caused me to throw myself around. Many times, I would draw blood. Now, when it comes on me I think I am quiet, am I not?"

"You seem so, Mr. D'Arcy"

"There is a poppy which in Latin is called papaver somniferum. You cut open the seed case and a juice comes out which is very calming for me. It gives a feeling of contentment. "

"Tell me where you keep it and I will give you some when your strangenesses do come on."

"I have been told that it would not be possible to give me anything when I am in one of those states."

"I know, sir from when my man was like it."

"And what did you do?"

"I took my arms round him," she said awkwardly.

"Like you did with me?"

She coloured and turned back to tend the fire. "I tried but to help, Mr. D'Arcy."

"And you did, Mistress Darkall." He stood up and put his hand on her shoulder. "And I want to thank you again for your kindness."

She looked up, her face showing pleasure but tinged with apprehension.

He caught her look and tried to hold her gaze but she quickly turned away.

"Shall I do 'e more toast, Mr. D'Arcy," she said, looking into the fire.

He noticed with pleasure that her voice had become softer and she was now using his name instead of calling him 'sir'. He struggled with himself, looking for words which would bring them closer. Instead, he could only say, "thank you that would be nice." Then he returned to the table where he busied himself with his breakfast.

"It is raining again today," he said.

"Yes, I seen rain coming in at the roof in the little bedroom. Should I get Tom Carpenter to do some work to stop it?"

"If you would, please," he said, looking up at her, "and, Mistress." She turned and came to stand by his table. Again, he waited for words to come to express his feelings but said only. "I am so glad that you look after things, each day you seem to take on more when I had always thought I would have to do them myself. You see I am not a very practical person."

"'Tis not hard to do things for you."

"Will you sit, mistress?" he said, indicating the other chair standing empty beside the table. "Please, I want to say something."

She sat and waited for him to continue.

"I know that you are intelligent and understanding."

For several moments, he moved things around on the table and then looked out of the window again. "For me, there was nothing to live for after my wife died. Without her, all that we had worked for became meaningless. I brought and sold cloth as I always did but she was not there and there was no one to share with." He looked up. "Do you understand, Mistress?"

"I would like to know more about your business if you could tell me."

"It's not my work that I am talking about."

"No," she said quietly. Jacob waited while she gathered her thoughts. "It's about you and me is't not."

His eyes met hers fleetingly and she saw his smile of relief that she had made it easier for him. "Yes, Mistress, it is about you and me." He raised his hand from the table, wanting to communicate by touching her. Slowly his hand fell back as the awkwardness of the moment overcame him.

His action prompted her to ask, "Mr. D'Arcy, shall I clean up?"

"Thank you, no, mistress...there is more I want to say."

As if in obedience, her hands fell to her lap and she sat quietly waiting for him.

"I…" he said. "I…" he stood up and walked to the window, staring out at the driving rain. "I want to say, mistress, that you have given me a purpose and… great happiness."

"I, Mr. D'Arcy, nothing have I done special. I care for things in the house, 'tis all."

"And I am one of those things, am I not."

She nodded and then added, "You are, sir."

"That's something I have to tell you." With a sudden desire to be close to her he said. "Come here, if you would."

She moved to the window and stood beside him. He turned and, as he did so, her breast touched his arm. He felt a stirring in his body such as had not happened for years. He looked intently out of the small panes in the window and resisted the urge to put his arms round her and pull her close.

As if recognising his mood, she moved so near that her skirt folded around his leg.

"I thank God that you came to this house, without you here I don't think I would live." He said, placing his hand on her shoulder.

"I've knelt and given my thanks in prayer many times, Mr.D'Arcy."

They both remained silent, waiting for the other to speak.

Jacob broke the silence. "Tell me, mistress, what does that storm look like to you?" He pointed to the violent rain and wind.

"It do frighten me sometimes."

"Yes," he said "that is one of the things I want to say. Sometimes I am in torment like that."

She turned from the window and looked up at him. "Sir?" she said questioningly.

"I am not a simple man." He hesitated before continuing. "You may think I have become 'possessed'."

"How?"

"I walk around and shout out things. I am not always sure what I say." His brow wrinkled with anxiety.

"But why, Mr. D'Arcy?"

"I don't know. There is something in me which takes over my thoughts. I have seen that some things can make men lose their senses," he said. "Sometimes when men eat old bread which has gone mouldy they seem to go out of their minds."

"I seen that, sir. When we had that long winter, last year, we had to eat bread that was going funny colours; it seemed to make some people go off their heads. A young 'un I knew jumped off a bridge as tho' he could fly like a bird. He was dead when they found 'im. Nice boy he were."

"I was there when he did it. I shall not forget the smile on his face as he jumped from the bridge. It seemed to me that he thought he was in heaven."

"You were there? I saw you not."

"I was in a carriage going to visit a customer with samples of cloth. The driver stopped when he saw the boy on the bridge wearing a white smock which made him seem like an angel and I thought he flew for a few moments. I can see it in my mind's eye even now."

He turned away from the window and, taking her by the arm, led her to his shelves and took out a large folio. "This is my drawing book," He said, turning over the pages, "When I was in Holland, I saw paintings by Hieronymus Bosch," he placed the book on the table and pointing out a page. "He depicted every day images in a unique and peculiar way. His images are the weird inventions of what most people would call a disordered mind."

"Mad, do that mean?"

"No, Mistress, to me it means creativity, a preference for anything new." He thought for a moment and then said. "When a man lies with a woman, you know what drives them to couple with each other?"

"To begat children."

"They want to – they are driven to it by their natures. But afterwards when they are at peace there is still a want to create something besides children. In my mind it is the same obsession. We are driven to reproduce our bodies and some of us are driven to reproduce our minds, by that I mean our thoughts."

She frowned.

"We are restless beings, always wanting to change things. It is not just the English, all nations want to. The Chinese I am told are very creative. They have many inventions and had for many centuries, a device which makes a loud explosion and sends missiles into the air, far exceeding what a man could do with his arms or with a crossbow. They smash through walls. And with such things, they have conquered other nations. We have weapons in England which are similar but they are not as developed as the Chinese ones."

"The man who did these," she looked down at the Bosch paintings. "He do frighten me, they're so weird."

"He and that boy who tried to fly off the bridge may have thought they had found divine inspiration. Maybe they saw visions from eating mouldy bread."

"Some of what you tell makes me get to thinking what you mean by it all?" She said. " 'tis nice when you talk about strange things."

"I am puzzled about what makes me shout out. We have another man in our group. He raises his voice almost to screaming and people gather to listen to him and become excited even though what he says often cannot be understood," he said, "I can be like that in my strangeness. Do you know what I mean?"

"I do, sir. My man was like that. I did look a'times at him, shouting and waving his arms but he weren't there to listen to me when I aspoke. He'd come back after a bit and then he'd sleep in my arms. Thrice times or more I have seen you like that."

"I only know the one time. I don't remember any other times. Are you sure?"

"That I am, Mr. D'Arcy" she murmured.

"Then I must thank you again, Mistress."

She inclined her head and with a smile said, "I do have things I must do upstairs," slowly and with what Jacob thought was reluctance, she left the room.

"Now I feel well, I will go to my office and walk around the warehouse to inspect some new cloth which has just arrived back from the dyers," he called to her as he left.

In the evening when he returned, she was quiet. He wondered why and to break the silence, he said. "The weather has been dreadful today, there has been flooding in the streets near the river where it has broken its banks. John Salin's house is under a foot of water and a lot of his produce is ruined.

"It is things like that which bring out the best in people. All his neighbours are helping and he is staying with a friend till the water recedes."

He stared out of the window at the dark, glowering storm and was about to sit down when there was a sudden hammering on the door.

Without waiting for Mistress Darkall, he walked quickly to the front of the house, anxious to discover who was knocking. Before he got there, a terrifying wailing came from the other side of the door.

As he opened the door, a sodden figure fell into the hall and collapsed on the floor.

In the dim light, Jacob could not recognise the man but, when he leant down to pull him to his feet; he saw that the figure was Mortenson, the servant of Josephus. Jacob tried to help him to stand but only managed to get him to sit up leaning against the wall. Mistress Darkall, hearing the noise came and tried also to lift the man up.

Seeing her, Mortenson tried to calm himself and between wails said "It's him, sir, my master. I went out looking for him."

"Where is he?"

"In the forest."

"Is he all right?" Jacob asked but seeing that Mortenson was too distraught to speak, said, "Take me to him." He told Mistress Darkall that he was going out and that she should bolt the door and let no one in until he returned. "There may be great danger for us all."

It was dark as they stepped outside and the heavy rain on the paths had turned the earth into mud so that Jacob slipped many times and had to hold on to Mortenson.

They were too preoccupied to notice the many beggars who held out their hands. They walked past an Inn where drunken voices were singing coarse songs. A man staggered out of the doorway, his hands caked with dirt, his face covered with pock marks and pustules. He tried to drag the two men in but Jacob and Mortenson pulled themselves away from the threatening man.

When they were out of the town Mortenson stopped, rooted to the spot. "Sir, I... I can't go to him, it is horrible to see," He said, pointing with his finger at a large tree on which was a dark shape.

Jacob sat Mortenson down on a fallen branch and unsteadily made his way to the dark figure. For a while he saw nothing but as his eyes became accustomed to the poor light under the trees, he saw a torn cloak flapping in the wind. Facing him was Josephus, hanging as though crucified; his hands tied to the branches of an oak tree, his head slumped against his chest.

Distraught, Jacob fell to his knees, raised his arms to the skies and cried out. "My God, my God, how could this happen." He fell forward into the rain sodden earth and wailed his despair. Prostrate as though in worship in front of his dead friend he screamed his anger and beat this fists into the ground for so long that his clothes were soaked. Stiff with cold, he staggered to his feet, trying not to look at the body in the tree.

"Mortenson," he cried, "bring your dagger!"

Whoever had hung Josephus had placed the trunk of a fallen tree against the oak to act as a ladder. Jacob climbed along the thick branches and with the dagger cut through the ropes. As the body of Josephus fell face down with arms outstretched, fixed in the position in which they had been tied, the air in his lungs escaped with a sigh.

Jacob jumped to the ground and tried to lift the swollen hands of his friend but cold and wet from the rain they slipped from his grasp.

"Mortenson," Jacob called, "run quickly and get help, call Jes Browen and his brother to bring their cart. I will stay with him till you return. Take the torch with you. And for God's love, come back quickly."

He pulled a log over so that he could sit beside Josephus. When Mortenson had gone and the light from the torch had left him alone and in the dark with the corpse of his friend, his mind became possessed with the image of this man who in life had inspired them all. He looked up the branches above his head as the wind tore at them making them groan as though suffering with Jacob for the loss of this beloved man. "This man loved you, my Lord, how could you let this happen to him?" he wailed at the sky. There was just enough light for Jacob to see the once handsome face now grossly disfigured, the result of prejudice and hate.

Tears filled his eyes and distorted his vision so that he saw shapes amongst the undergrowth. As he did, he recalled the body of the dead woman and the priest standing above her and was fearful as he had been as a child. All his reason told him to run as he had done then but at that moment, in the distance he heard the muffled voice of Jes Browen as the three men came towards him pushing the cart over the sodden earth.

Even with four of them, the effort to lift the huge body was almost too much, but finally they managed to raise him on the cart, his face looking up at the sky. The flickering torch light across his face made him seem as though speaking but with a silent voice.

CHAPTER 13

The death of his friend so unhinged Jacob that he fell ill with melancholy which kept him in bed for many days, unable to write replies to letters from cloth merchants asking for his goods. He was grateful for several helpers who came in to work at the warehouse whenever he needed them.

The soaking he had had on the freezing ground had given him such pain that he was convinced he would have died if Mistress Darkall had not looked after him and made him drink the bitter tree bark potion which she had prepared.

"This always helped my man, Benjy, when he was sick," she said when Jacob shuddered at the unpleasant tasting liquid.

The mixture seemed to take away the pain in his limbs so that for the first time he was able to sleep soundly.

The following morning he woke as Mistress Darkall brought him a light breakfast. "I slept well, Mistress and in my sleep a dream came to me which I often have."

"Tell me," she said as she helped him to sit up.

"I dreamt of a time when there is no unfairness, where man cares for man and the weak are supported by the strong just as you have cared for me while I have been unwell." He began to drink the honey sweetened curdled milk she had brought him. "It can happen and I am sure it will, perhaps it is too late for my lifetime but maybe it will come to pass in yours."

"I would like it to be soon."

"In my dream, so many things became sorted out. You know we have rowdy behaviour in the streets out there and it is dangerous for a woman to walk at night for fear of being molested. There is so much violence in men and they have no outlet in this country.

In Italy, where I go often, they have a method which I think works. A hundred or more men go into a pitch and play a game with a ball. When one of the men breaks the rules, fights start out. It goes on till they are all worn out. But it lets the animal spirit find an exit. We should have that here."

As the days passed, he began to feel improved but with legs weakened by lack of exercise, was only able to stagger around the house. His appetite returned and he began to eat the broths Mistress Darkall prepared from rabbits caught in the fields.

When he felt better, Jacob was so grateful that he sought for ways of thanking her for her care. An idea occurred to him; he would hire a carriage and take her to Hampton Court on the following Sunday. There they would walk together as equals; it amused him that people might confuse them as being man and wife.

When he suggested it to her, she was obviously delighted but asked, "what should I wear, I've only the clothes I work in?"

He pulled himself up from his chair and with difficulty slowly led her up the stairs to Isabel's bedroom. Since his wife passed away, he had been in the room only once to get the few clothes for Mistress Darkall. As he pushed open the door, he faltered as the memory of the last time he had seen his wife returned to him.

She saw him lean against the door post and said, "Are you still not well, Mr. D'Arcy?"

"Just the illness, it has made me weak," he lied to conceal his distress at entering the room of his dead wife.

He opened the door to the wardrobe. Isabel had shared his love of textiles and had had many dresses made from samples which had been left over from customer's orders which were too short in length to sell on.

"You choose something, Mistress. I have suddenly become tired. I need to rest in my room for a while." She saw how weary he looked and walked with him to his room. "I shall feel better shortly," he said. "You see if any of those clothes suit you."

She helped him onto his bed and for an hour tried clothes on while he lay in his room trying to forget the unutterable sadness which had overcome him.

On the following Sunday, when Mistresss Darkall came down the stairs Jacob gasped at the transformation of this once dowdy creature. She had chosen a yellow and blue silk dress which had been made for a celebration at the Guildhall which had been cancelled because of an outbreak of fever. The dress had never before been worn. On her head Mistress Darkall had a broad brimmed hat in a matching yellow.

He wondered if he should tell her how beautiful she looked but was interrupted when the carriage drew up outside the house.

With a feeling of pride, he helped the transformed young woman climb the steps. When they reached the road around Hampton Court they descended from the carriage, this time helped by the driver who treated Mistress Darkall deferentially, calling her 'my lady'.

The pleasure at seeing how the clothes had made her into a lady made him feel young again. When they went along the Long Walk, skirted back and continued along the Thames he was without pain. On their way, they passed other couples parading in their elegant clothes. Jacob was delighted to be beside her, noticing with pleasure the admiring glances at this young aristocratic looking woman wearing her obviously expensive dress and her hat with a large feather in matching yellow. He looked down at his own clothes and saw that they were drab in comparison. At that moment, he determined to get his tailor to make him another outfit.

He wanted to link his arm in hers as he would have done with his wife after they had obtained permission to do the walk but she always walked slightly behind him.

"Mistress," his voice faltered, "I want to..." he could find no words to express his pleasure at being with her. Her youth filled his mind and he recalled his interest in his youth in the opposite sex which had always been un-requited.

"Yes, Mr. D'Arcy?"

"I find being with you in that dress which suits you so well is a wonderful experience."

For just a moment, she slipped her arm in his but pulled it out when she realised what she had done. They stopped walking to look over the river at a boat filled with people singing religious music and praying.

As they listened to the music, he picked a berry and threw it into the river to watch the ducks racing towards it. Together they laughed at the squabbling birds.

"It is such a lovely day and not the time to talk about things you want to learn. We should all be free of the chains that prevent us from doing what we want. When we are at home, we will talk about the way to free the mind from those patterns I told you about that stop you thinking freely. For now, we will walk to that house there." He pointed through the trees hanging over the river. "We have been a long time walking; it is very hot and I'm sure you are ready for a drink. They serve a very nice pressed apple drink in the garden and we can get something to eat. The way you have looked after me has made me much better and the walk has made me quite hungry," he smiled.

"I have never before felt so needed as when I look after you." She bowed her head to a passer by who had acknowledged her by raising his hat. "You are so much better. Walking with you is a pleasure, Mr. D'Arcy."

As they pushed open the gate into the garden, Jacob noticed several young men sitting with older women. The men looked up appreciatively at the lovely creature in her yellow dress. He felt a pride and he had to admit it, a growing love for this woman who in her elegant clothes had grown noticeably in confidence.

It was late in the evening when the carriage dropped them back at Firenze House.

Jacob unlocked the door to let her in and saw that her body was shaking.

"Are you unhappy, Mistress?"

"Not unhappy," she said, drying her eyes. "When we came back, we passed the street where I did sleep before I come to you. Those times I wanted just to die but now I want to live and…," she hesitated, "take care of you always."

Jacob started to tell her of his own happiness but he was afraid that emotion would take him over as well. Instead, he took her hand, brought it to his lips and just said "Thank you."

"Today has been a time I will never forget as long as I live. Thank you, Mr. D'Arcy."

"I have never had a day like today and I do not want it to end."He bowed his head in fatigue. "I am sorry, we have had a day of idyl but now I am tired as I am sure are you."

Wordlessly, they turned from each other and went to their rooms.

CHAPTER 14

It was one of those cold, grey days and so miserable that Jake had put the heating on and lit the fire.

Bad weather always made him feel dejected and he was glad when Rhosa 'phoned, saying that she was also feeling miserable and wanted to drop round. He had asked her several times to move in with him but she said her independence was too important.

When she arrived, Jake saw that she must have planned to come. She was carrying a round tin which she laid on the dining room table. With obvious pride, she opened the tin and took out a cake.

"You never cook, Rhosa, have you changed career?" he joked.

"When I'm feeling low and the weather is like this, I have found that cooking is like a therapy for me."

"It's like drudgery for me." Jake said grinning.

She laid everything out, served cake and said. "I had another motive; I also wanted to read my lines to you."

In between slices of cake, she began reading the script to him. When she got to the end of the scene, with a sigh of satisfaction, she looked up at the ceiling.

"That was perfect, Rhosa," Jake said. "You almost had me in tears."

"Still needs a bit of polishing – that speech always eluded me but your rehearsing it with me last week was a great help. I could say the words and get the expression in that the director needed but I never really understood the way the character was feeling." She smiled with satisfaction. "Now I know."

"If you use a word as it was in Shakespeare's time and not as we use it now, the meaning becomes clear?" Jake said. "The beauty of language is that it is always changing. A blatant example is that 'gay' always meant happy. It is a mystery how it came to mean homosexual because not all of them are gay, some are sad and depressed.

Shakespeare used the word hour which would have raised a laugh in his day because it sounded like whore. It's lost on the modern ear because of our different pronunciation." He grinned to himself as a thought struck him. "In theory, words should change less now because we have dictionaries which fix the meaning. We have Frederick Furnivall to thank for his work on the dictionary of English" as he said the name he could not avoid laughing."

"What is it?" she said looking puzzled. "Why are you laughing?"

"Sorry, Furnivall was one of the Victorian eccentrics; very erudite but consumed by sex. He 'befriended' attractive, full bosomed waitresses from the cafe run by the Aerated Bread Company and took them to the river where he taught them to row so he could be physically close to them. He constantly bought them presents. He married a young woman, Elizabeth Dalziel but left her when he got bored and went off with his 21 year old secretary. He was 58 and the archetypal 'dirty old man.'"

"Every older man's dream," Rhosa laughed.

"His friend Arthur Munby was even more odd - preferred his women coarse and unclean. He married his servant, Hannah Cullwick and liked her to clean the chimney naked before their sexual liaisons."

Rhosa laughed, walked over to his desk and picked up some papers.

"Tell me about this article you are writing, Jay," she said, "and this time I don't want to hear that it's 'just another topical issue' because I know it isn't and I don't like being fobbed off with an empty phrase."

He looked up at the portrait of Jacob D'Arcy and the unknown woman beside him. Even though he'd been told that the paintings could not be moved Rhosa had found that by taking off the oak panel from the wall to which they were attached by secret screws, they could be freed. Jake had then hung the pictures in the lounge where they looked better. "You remember when you talked about how Jacob D'Arcy looked like me? It made me feel close to him and got me thinking about the oppression people suffered when he was alive. At first, I thought what a dreadful time it must have been. The lack of freedom, the inability to say what one thought, the fear which

148

pervaded every action, you know what I mean don't you - mendacity, self-interest, corruption, the dominance of the power seekers."

"Are we so very different now?"

"Exactly, that's what struck me. It crystallised what I have been thinking for many years but had never put into words. We are constantly told we live in a 'free society' but is this just one of those delusions foisted on us? Our freedom has very rigid boundaries."

"Go on, Jay, I'm listening, you're talking my language." she stood up and went to the window, "I hate hypocrisy and I see it all round me." She looked out at the sky. "The rain has stopped. I need some air. Shall we go on the common? You can continue while we walk."

A weak sun was breaking through hazy clouds when they got outside. "Just the day for a walk now that the air has been washed clean." Rhosa said, linking her arm in his, "This is lovely, you're so lucky to live with this on your doorstep. I wish I'd looked here rather than Acton but at the time I just wanted a place I could call my own. I've got over that now."

For a while they walked in silence while he wondered if what she meant was that she would sooner live with him. For a moment he became apprehensive because he had also discovered how much he valued his own freedom. He found her fascinating but was doubtful if they were ready for a long term relationship. The irritation when Rhosa had not turned up on the night when he had prepared a meal for her and other times when she had let him down was fading. But he harboured an irrational fear that her unreliability was evidence that she was seeing another man.

"You're thinking." She pulled his arm closer to her side. "I can feel it. What is it about?"

Again he wondered if there was a meaning behind her words but he took the easy route and said. "I'm just thinking through what we were talking about back at the house."

"I've been waiting for you to tell me more." She pointed to a fallen tree. "Come and sit for a bit, we can look at the view while you think," she said. "I know you don't like talking about yourself but I want to hear what's going on in that head of yours. You have a face you present to the world but I see behind it..." She turned his face with her hands to look at him. "Jay love, you're not happy are you?"

She saw that he was reluctant to reply as he took off his coat and spread it on the rain covered trunk. She sat beside him and said "Do tell me, Jay - I don't like you bottling things up inside."

"I suppose in a way I've reached a minor crisis point," he said hesitantly.

"Oh, dear," she put her hand on his, "self-doubt?"

"Not so much self-doubt as self-realisation," he looked around, absently watching the wind shifting the trees. "What am I doing, Rhosa?" he asked, turning back to her.

"You're a journalist, what you write is having an effect on so many of your readers," she said, "why do you ask yourself what you are doing." A gust of wind blew the chiffon scarf across her face taking his mind momentarily to the marble sculptures in the National Portrait Gallery of female figures covered in diaphanous fabric.

"I know what the job is, I've done it for so long that I think I could write my thousand words a day in my sleep. It's not so much self-doubt; it's the morality that I find I can't take. When I have to comment on topical issues I must find an angle and make it different. Then I have to extend the situation. You know 'Women are afraid to go out after dark in spite of all the extra police being deployed to tackle crime' the result is that women are afraid to go out at night even though the statistics don't support their fears."

"You need honesty but are forced to be dishonest?"

"I wouldn't put it quite so black and white but I want to write what I know is the truth. Our streets are much safer than they were in times gone by but if I said all is well, go to bed and sleep happily, that would not sell newspapers. The need is to exaggerate, criticise and instil fear."

"You hate it?"

"Journalism?" he screwed up his face and nodded slowly. "When I was younger, I just accepted that I was in a gutsy business and the dishonesty was a way of life. Now... yes, I've started to find it intolerable."

"Why do it? Give it up. Do something else."

"Do what? What could keep me as well as journalism?"

She stood up and walked around the tree as though she were on stage. "I could, Jay," she said with her effervescent laugh. "If this Merchant of Venice has a long run, and then they do what they want to and turn it into a film, I shall be pretty well off, you know."

He stood up, walked a few steps and looked at the view. "Thank you, it's a nice thought, Rhosa and I appreciate it a lot. But just like you I couldn't take a comfortable life with no challenge, I would get bored if I became a kept man."

Coming up behind him, she put her arms round his waist and laid her head on his back. In that moment he was filled with conflict, pleased at what she had suggested but unable to shake off the sensation of depression that came from Rhosa putting into words what had been nagging him for years. He began to wonder if there was anything he had done with his life which he was proud of. He'd always made a fast and easy 'buck' because he had an ability to sense the tide of popular feeling before it became apparent to other writers. Editors wanted him because his articles were usually ahead of other journalists who just followed trends.

"You are brilliant at seeing problems before they occur, Jay. I know that what you have written on the way we are damaging this world has done a lot of good. Doesn't that help - doesn't it make any difference?"

"I do get a buzz from it sometimes." He nodded weakly. "In a way you are right."

"I remember reading an article you wrote on the fact that the earth and the atmosphere which surrounds it is carefully balanced and precisely right for our survival but we're doing everything we can to upset it," Rhosa said. "You made me aware that for at least a billion years after the big bang, the atmosphere was poisonous. Then bacteria made oxygen available for life to begin. Billions of years later, humans took over. But as you said, we can't last much longer if we keep destroying what we have been fortunate enough to inherit."

Jake nodded. "More and more people are realising that we cannot sustain the standard of living we have."

"That's what I mean but in spite of being able to do that sort of pioneering work, you're not happy, Jake," she stated, taking his hand in hers, sitting on the tree and pulling him close beside her.

She laid her head against his shoulder and, in a voice muffled by his clothes said. "You're not, are you?"

"Why do you say that?"

"It's in your body – you're tense. It's in your voice - it's strained.

Sometimes I see it in your smile which at times is only a facial movement with nothing behind it. And what's worse, it's in your thoughts."

"How do you know my thoughts?"

"I can't explain." She raised her head. "I just do. Perhaps it's my Shakespeare; some of his sagacity has rubbed off on me. When we met in Stratford, you said he understood the human psyche three hundred years before Freud and had much better poetry. I believe that as much as you do."

He looked surprised. "Can you go back to what I said when we met all those years ago?" He smiled with satisfaction. "And are you saying that Shakespeare helped you to understand what I am thinking?"

"I can see you're very often depressed and it's the worst sort – irrational - because there is no reason for it. You are successful and respected but you are plagued by illogical fears. Even when you are in bed, I can feel your body tense. Once you talked in your sleep about a woman who had died from the Plague...you called her your wife. It's that sort of thing that shows me things are going on in your mind which you don't express."

Jake's mouth dropped open. "Did I really say that? Firenze House must be affecting me and I was dreaming about something that must have happened in the past."

Rhosa nodded. "You often say things in your sleep. It's as thought there is a tumult in your mind."

They had been sitting for so long that the hard bark of the tree began to be painful so he stood up, put his coat down onto the grass and pulled her down with him so that she settled in his lap.

152

"You're so often right about things, Rhosa. And, yes, at this moment, I am in a tumult. I can write what I feel about the environment but I have to be cautious and consider the editor's interests when I am writing about politicians."

"You're afraid to write what you think because up to now you've only rocked the boat but never attempted to sink it, and it's the sinking of it that you want?"

"My income comes from writing. If I sink the boat, I will go down with it."

"I don't think you will. There is widespread disillusionment with things as they are. Politicians are despised, bankers are despised. The entire democratic process is a sham. Write what you feel, I'm sure you'll be amazed at the response. Whatever you do, I'll support you. I know how you admire Zac Goldsmith's 'The Constant Economy', let's work together on a book on Democracy... or as things are, the lack of it."

He knew she was right and, as they walked back to get out of the cold and to burn toast in front of the fire, he came to a decision. He would write only what he knew to be honest and would be more critical of the decadence he saw around him.

As they walked back, Jake said, "We have the dilemma scenario in politics."

"How do you mean?"

"Implicit in a politician's brief is the dilemma that unpopular but often critically necessary actions are avoided because an MP wants to be re-elected. So we have the economies of nations manipulated so that before elections, everything gets better."

That afternoon brought them closer; from then on they met as often as they could. Whenever they had free time, they would spend at least part of the day together. If he had to be in central London, he would catch her in between rehearsals and listen as she went through her dialogues in one of the quiet rooms where the props were stored. It was at these sessions that he discovered his enjoyment in acting which would otherwise have lain dormant. Shakespeare's language became like a mantra taking them into a euphoric state and they would set an alarm to ring when they had reached the end of the lunch break.

Used to clandestine love affairs, the cast suspected that they were taking themselves off to indulge in physical pleasures. When Rhosa returned to continue her rehearsals with the other members of the cast, they would cheer and, in their nudging way, make crude remarks on Jake's ability to keep going for an hour. Rhosa and Jake took the banter because they were so pleased at being together. Rhosa, because of her sexual inhibition, was delighted that their closeness exceeded any physical liaison.

Eventually, the predictable comments from the cast became tedious and they ceased their one to one rehearsals and took to sharing lunch with the others. Initially, their allusions about Jake's supposed loss of virility became equally tiresome but gradually, his presence amongst them ceased to excite comment. On one occasion, one of the actors had fallen ill and Rhosa suggested that Jake should stand in for him.

After the speeches between Jake and Rhosa, which by now they both knew by heart, the cast remained silent before bursting into applause. The actor whom Jake had stood in for had been unable to understand what was needed of him and had constantly disappointed the director who took Jake aside during the break. In a conspiratorial voice, he asked if he was interested in taking over the role. In earlier years Jake had toyed with the idea of an acting career but, the more he saw of it, the more he recognised it as a life to be endured rather than enjoyed. He thanked the director for his compliment but declined.

From then on, Rhosa and Jake met sometimes at her house but more often at Firenze House, because of what Rhosa said was the 'atmosphere'.

"Don't you feel that this place is trying to talk to us, Jay?" she said when they were alone in his house one afternoon. "There is a story it wants to tell us. Aren't you aware of it?"

He didn't want to influence her attitude to the house and thereby make her feel uneasy in the place so, nodding his agreement, he said. "Friendly story too, isn't it?"

She nodded but it seemed to him that it was with a lack of conviction.

The early start for rehearsals became unnecessary as time went on and the actors had learned their parts. Rehearsals now started in the middle of the afternoon. Jake and Rhosa were able to have time together most days. Sometimes during her rehearsals or when Jake was writing an article, Rhosa would read what he had written and make suggestions. Her understanding of complex matters such as economics, or politics surprised him. He seemed only to need to give her brief details and she would be able to fill in the gaps and even give him advice. They worked together on what started out as an article but because of the complexity of the issues, soon became large enough for a short book. Partly this was because Jake had a friend who was in publishing who needed a serious book to fill a gap in his programme and made an advance to cover research.

The common perception is that when a man and woman are together, to find fulfilment, there must be sexual attraction. When Rhosa sat beside him reading and jotting down notes for his book, the experience of two minds working together was almost erotic to him. Whenever she found anything interesting, she would put her hand on his thigh and squeeze. The sexual frigidity which had filled her with despair was of no importance when they shared their love of learning.

At home together one evening, Rhosa who was reading his notes said, "Jake, when I was having a drink in the library café I met a young woman, Lilyana, who had been born and spent her early years in Nigeria. She was one of those attractive young women who command attention. We got talking about the Enlightenment." Rhosa put her hand on his. "It had always been in the back of my mind but talking to her, I realised I didn't know much about it, certainly not as much as she did. She thinks the time we live in is so threatened that we need a revolution as profound as we had in the eighteenth century." She nodded at the painting on the wall. "I'm sure Mr. D'Arcy would have been pleased that as reasoning replaced blind faith, all conventions were being questioned."

"I had wondered about drawing on the Enlightenment in Chapter five. It was a time when women were still subservient but there were a lot of women who made major contributions."

Rhosa nodded. "Fascinating time for men and women but I don't suppose I'd agree with everything that happened. Lilyana told me something I didn't know about Rousseau; he said that the education of women should be centred on the needs of men. This thinker, renowned even today, had many children with his mistress but refused to acknowledge them and put them into foundling hospitals" She grimaced. "Can you imaging that. Nowadays it would be publicised on the web and he would be seen as a selfish monster."

"That's new for me; I've always assumed that he was a man of humanity. Intriguing that a chance meeting with your Lilyana will alter our book. What did she say about Nigeria?"

"Pretty scathing, I asked her about violence by men against women and told her about you, the kindest man I had ever known." Rhosa said slightly jokingly, smiling at the effect it had on him. "I wondered how her country compared with Egypt which is still male dominated. She said there is constant violence against women in Nigeria but it is difficult to get facts. Sometimes a victim sees aggression to be an integral part of male supremacy and normal in marriage. I didn't tell her about Egypt but Rousseau would feel at home there, I'm sure. I love my country of origin but I couldn't live there."

"Can I meet this intriguing young woman?"

"Jake, sometimes you are so transparent." Rhosa teased, sensing his interest.

"Just that she might have a new angle on the Enlightenment which we could use in the book and we might get to know her."

"*Ménage à trois* sort of thing - is that what you mean?" she joked, punching him on the shoulder.

"You just make her sound interesting, that's all." Jake said defensively

"Ok. Yes she is your type, Jake, very intelligent, voluptuous with a beautiful cream coffee skin. Lovely smile and a great sense of humour...And..." She looked up at the ceiling. "Have I said enough?"

"Hmm." he said pensively.

The following week end, they were together in his study; she behind him with her arm resting on his shoulder and peering at the computer screen. She pinched his ear to attract his attention. "You know what I think?" she asked.

"No. I don't ever know what you think, lady of mystery. Why?"

"There is something in this place."

"Are you still thinking about it?"

He felt her head nod against his cheek. "Yes, I'm trying to put my finger on it." She moved to lean against the desk so that she would be looking towards him. "I've been trying to think what it is that I feel and it's just struck me." She folded her arms. "I think it's him."

"Him?" he asked with a frown, "who is him?"

"Jake, are you being deliberately obtuse?" she said, "D'Arcy, the man in the painting, that's who I mean."

His mind was still on his writing and he did not take in what she was saying. When he said nothing, she continued. "Don't you sense it as well?"

"Maybe, in a way but, if you are saying that he is here, I have to disagree. That way lies insanity."

"Pretty strong word, Jay; I'm not saying your Jacob is here in physical presence – that would be extreme even for me - but that he has left his memory and the shadows he cast."

"Sort of still haunting the place? Ok, that I can accept" he said, turning from the desk. "I felt it myself when I was shown around this place by the estate agent. It seemed to be communicating with me – still does. What do you think he is trying to tell us, dear lady of illusion?"

Rhosa pursed her lips thoughtfully. "Have you changed in the time you've lived here?"

"About the way I think, do you mean?"

Rhosa nodded as Jake remained silent while he thought. He looked around the room and then said. "The only thing I've noticed is that I've become much more critical of what I am doing and of the iniquities I see around me."

"That's what I mean. Is it that you are more critical of yourself, or of what you are doing or is it just your dislike of politics?"

Her questioning attitude set him back but he saw what she meant. "Yes," he pondered, "I know that I must do more to bring about change and I can't do it through mendacious journalism."

"Journalism - mendacious?" she raised her eyebrows in mock surprise.

"Yes, that about sums it up; I know I've said all this before but I'm more aware that I am peddling distress. We take an ordinary story and inflate it to the state where readers will be incensed." A cloud crept over his eyes as he spoke. "People don't just get annoyed or irritated – 'FURY AT FAILURES IN THE HEALTH SERVICE'. Headlines designed to inflame and grab attention when the story was thought up only a few hours before and had no real substance."

Rhosa sensed his mood and to cheer him said. "Don't blame yourself, Jay."

"But I'm part of it; I've known for years but never put it into words until that day we were walking on the Common. Just seems to me that everything I've done up to now has been contrived, empty or pointless; motivated solely by what it would earn me and, in the final analysis disappointing and, yes, dishonest."

"Hell, Mr. Dearsey, that's a lot to take in at one go. What brought all that on? Did the world just collapse around you?" she joked, trying to inject humour into the situation and raise his spirits. He sensed what she was trying to do and laughed with her but Rhosa saw that it was forced. "Come on Jay love, you need cheering up," she said. "Let's go for a walk along the Thames, I do that if ever I am feeling low. There's a pub I know where the beer is as enjoyable as the clientele. You meet all sorts there, poets - beats - drop outs – artists – musicians, even actors. The only thing you don't get there is boring people. Are you up for that?"

"Sounds good to me," he said, jumping to his feet to get their coats.

A storm the night before had polished the air to crystal. Birds swooped low over the Thames and fish leapt at flies. The wind brought fresh breath to them with every step they took. He knew that she would be looking forward to a drink but was concerned about her weakness for alcohol. As they got near the pub he began to feel a sense of dread. Once she started on alcohol, especially in the company of other drinkers, the barriers would often fall and she would want a second, a third and then more. Jake would see her descend into a coarse version of herself, laughing at any suggestive joke. To see her enjoying the humour of lewd men was more than he could take, especially when she had told him of her disinterest in sex. On one occasion – perhaps he had also had more than he should have – he became so overwrought that he felt physically sick.

Along the river where they were walking, there was a good restaurant which he had been to once with Sabel before they had broken up. It overlooked the river where Sabel and he had watched the swans haughtily sailing by and they had given each one a name.

"I'm hungry, Rhosa," he lied, "there's a lovely place just round the bend in the river, great Italian food. Let's stop there and grab something to eat."

"If that's what you want and if it'll lift your spirits, I'm happy."

"Lovely view of the river too; we're quite late, the crowd will have gone so we'll get a table near a window or on the terrace."

"Good, I'm not particularly hungry but you know me, I can always eat."

"And never put on weight." he said eyeing her figure provocatively.

Seeing his gaze she pushed him hard on the shoulder. "Behave; we're just going to have something to eat."

"Sorry, I was distracted," he said, happy that his ploy had worked. "When we get back, we'll work on the book together."

"Seems to me that all that's wrong with you is that you needed food," she teased, "low blood sugar, perhaps."

"If only life were that simple. Packet of toffees and the worries go." he said.

They took a table on the terrace and as they sat, the sun came out from the cluds and warmed them. He ordered veal; Rhosa just wanted olives and salad. When his meal came it was huge so they shared it between them. Rhosa wanted to reinforce Jake's changed mood so she raised the topic of society's interdependence and suggested he could deal with it in his book.

"Tell me what you mean," he asked.

"In nineteen sixty five, when a badly set fuse blew in a power station in the States, eight hundred thousand people suffered, some stranded in lifts and subways. People died in hospitals, businesses suffered and some were bankrupted. My mother has a cousin in New York who'd had no physical contact with her husband for years and they were going through a divorce. That night of complete darkness when the shops were either sold out or looted, meant that they could not even buy candles; all they could do was to go to bed. That one night of enforced contact transformed them. Now in old age, they are still together and still look at each other with eyes that communicate the memory of that night.

"When I was in a play on Broadway a few years ago, I went to see them; they prepared me a marvellous meal with all the things my mother told them I liked. They sat close together and I saw them secretly holding hands under the dinner table. People were frightened in that blackout. Some died, some were conceived, others parted but Auntie Helen and Uncle Gresten began a new life together. All those things happened because someone had incorrectly set an alarm system. Can you imagine what that means, Jake, millions of lives altered by the negligence of just one person - isn't that terrifying?"

"A fatalist would tend to think it's all about birth, life and periods filled with pleasure and pain before death. Things go wrong and things go right. Some people are dealt a good hand, some get only low number cards and wind up hating their lives."

"Sounds a bit like Schopenhauer, Jake." She ate a few forkfuls of Jake's meal as she watched the rowers on the river. When she spoke, her voice seemed to drift over the water. "Being with them convinced me that there was more to life than waiting. I loved seeing them, loved being in New York and being able to please myself but when I came back to London, nothing had changed for me; I was still in my terrible marriage."

"I knew I had to get away; I found a part time philosophy course. I read many of the Greeks but we are so much more sophisticated now that I often saw them as searching for answers to problems which we have resolved. Do we enhance our lives by being told by Aristotle that a horse has both form and substance, the form is the shape that we all recognise and the substance is what is inside the form? Does that advance your appreciation of horses or life or people?" She looked over her wine glass at Jake, "I always had trouble with philosophers labouring over the precise meaning of words." She smiled to herself. "Maybe it would have helped if philosophers had a more developed sense of humour." Suddenly she was overcome by a fit of laughter.

"What's got into you, now?" Jake asked, unable to stop himself smiling with her.

"I was just remembering the Monty Python sketch about the philosophers playing football. The start was delayed because they couldn't decide if the ball existed or not." Both she and Jake burst into laughter.

When they stopped, Rhosa continued, "D'you see what I'm getting at. That fuse blowing in 1965 or whenever it was, influenced me, decades after it had happened." She looked at Jake intently. "That's what I mean about interdependence. We should have a chapter on the interrelation of people, politics and society. 9/11 changed everyone's lives. We now accept that we are watched and listened to wherever we go. Even buy a packet of crisps in the corner shop in a town and the chances are that pretty soon your action will be recorded and kept to be referred to if someone thinks it might be useful."

Jake put down his fork on his plate. "What about Aristotle's horse, didn't that persuade you to study something else?"

"I was getting pretty disillusioned, but against my better judgement, I carried on. I just wanted to block out the awful reality of the marriage and partly because I hoped it would open a bank of knowledge that would help me understand and accept my own life."

"Isn't that the constant problem with philosophy? It talks a lot but delivers little." Jake turned in his seat to look over his shoulder at the river. "Let's take a philosopher's view of the swans there. Would we not say they are regal? But what is the regalness of swans? Are they born with this special quality or do they acquire it? Is it even part of them or is it thrust upon them? Are there swans, cowering in shame in dark recesses of rivers because they are not regal?

"What about those beautiful horses," Rhosa smiled as she looked into the field behind her at horses grazing, raising their heads and tossing their manes.

"Yes, of course, horses. But that must be a different kind of regalness so we have to consider that of horses as well as that of swans."

"And what of kings and queens - do they not have regalness?" Rhosa said, entering into the absurdity.

Jake sat quietly before saying. "I've been going over in my mind the kings and queens of the world and I have to say that I know of no heads of state with the quality possessed by those swans. So in Aristotelian speak, we must conclude that it is possessed only in the animal kingdom. If we think of it as a syllogism we can say 'Regalness is peculiar to animals, this creature is regal, and therefore it is not human'. Wouldn't life be easy if we could solve all our problems with syllogisms?"

"If only," Rhosa said. "Probably would have helped me with 'thinking about thinking'. I couldn't get my head round theories which should be accepted and not analysed. I was fortunate, I happened to hear 'In Our Time' on BBC talking about Logical Positivism. That cleared my mind when I learned that what philosophers claimed to be deep, religious and mystical was actually meaningless; a hypothesis is only tenable if it could be proved or disproved."

"No God, then."

"Can't be proved or disproved so he's not tenable." Rhosa nodded and then said out of the blue. "Jake this is heaven. I love being with you. I don't get to play verbal games with other people."

"Can't say that I do either."

"So many men rave on about sport over lunch. I find myself hiding yawns behind garlic bread. With you it's real life and unlike my football mad friends we can't argue over who won because there is no arbiter, Kant did not score more goals than Rousseau. Well, when I say he didn't, I have no proof of that because no one bothered to be referee."

After he had watched the sun glinting on the river and talked about the regalness of swans, Jake felt more at ease with himself. His mood change was partly because his subterfuge had worked better than he could have wished; they'd had only one glass of wine each and a jug of water to drink.

They stayed reading newspapers and talking until late afternoon.

As they walked the opposite way along the river, Rhosa brought the conversation back to him.

"I want you to do something for me, Jay," she said, pulling his arm round her waist.

"You know I'd do anything", he joked

"Well then, write all the books living in your head and play down the journalism. It is oppressing you too much. As I said, I've seen times when you are down."

They crossed the river over a bridge and stopped to look at the water flowing under it. Rhosa picked up a twig and let it fall into the water, ran to the other side of the bridge and called with joy when she saw it come from under the bridge.

"Playing Pooh sticks at your age?" Jake said with a smile.

"Is that meant to be rude?" she looked at him quizzically.

"Did you not read that children's story when you were a little girl?"

"What, in Egypt! I read Egyptian fairy tales," she pouted, "I didn't read about Pooh sticks, whatever they are."

"How much education you've missed then."

She pushed against him. "Ok Mr Literary, did you ever read Rhodopis."

"No I didn't - never even heard the name."

"Well I'm sure you did," she teased.

"How do you know I did?"

"Rhodopis had her shoe taken by a bird that dropped it in the lap of the Pharoah. He determined to find the owner of the shoe and when he did he married her." Rhosa smiled. "Ring any bells?"

For a moment he looked puzzled and then his brow cleared. "Cinderella?"

"Cinderella indeed and from five hundred BC. At that time, you dear Englishman, would have been carrying a cudgel and grunting."

"Never! my hands would not have been strong enough to hold a cudgel; I would have been a scribe." After thinking, he said, "You are so English, Rhosa that it's impossible to imagine you growing up in Egypt. Have you ever gone back?"

"I always thought I'd moved on from being an Arab and that I never would have wanted to go backwards."

"But?"

"But I hadn't metamorphosed totally," she smiled as she said the cumbersome word. "When I got into trouble after my first marriage, I felt empty. There was something missing in this country. One morning I got up, rang my agent, packed a suitcase and just went. I travelled by sea because I wanted a gradual evolution. I wanted the journey to last and to absorb Middle Eastern culture slowly."

"Go on," Jake said expectantly. "Sounds like a journey I would have enjoyed."

"You were with me all the time, Jake." Rhosa said with humour, "I had that photograph I took of you the day you enticed me away from Stratford and took me to London. You know, when we were in the National Portrait Gallery looking at the painting of Thomas Moore. I took that photograph with me everywhere. Each night I would get it out of my bag and put it beside my bed or sleeping bag. If I happened to be in the open I was always fearful that I would wake up and some creature would have eaten it so I had it put into a metal sleeve.

Egypt was like an explosion. Suddenly I had found my spiritual home. I walked those grimy streets, carpeted with donkey dung and hordes of flies and Jake, I discovered my soul. For three months I wandered arid countries, sometimes staying in hotels, sometimes sleeping in tents. Sometimes I stayed awake all night in front of a camp fire, just looking at the stars. One of the bus journeys took me to Jericho."

"Looking for the destruction wrought by Joshua's trumpet?"

"You can't imagine the effect that ruined ten thousand year old cradle of civilisation had on me. The accident that changed grass seed into wheat turned man from nomad to farmer. Without that, you and I might still have met but we would be driving our goat herds in different directions, looking for grazing.

You know, the most moving moment of that journey was when I held a brick which had been made when Jericho was built and it still held the fingerprints of the man who had made it. I put my fingers into the same holes, it was as though in them was his memory telling me about the changes he would have seen in his lifetime."

She halted. "You know what, Jay? I get that same sensation when I am in Firenze House."

"Past events still communicating with us you mean?" he asked. "You never told me this before?"

"You know 'Pathfinders', that book by Jim Al-Khalili I've been reading over the last few weeks. Even though I grew up in the Middle East, I still believed that the West led the world in sciences. In his book, he made it obvious to me what a huge debt we owe to Arab scholars. I wish I'd had it with me when I wandered. I didn't even know about the astonishing centre of learning that Baghdad had been.

When I did a journey in the desert with a tribe of Bedouin I didn't know then that Al-Buruni had travelled that way centuries before. The journey would have had even more meaning for me if I'd known when he was also trying to find himself." Quickly, she looked up at him. "Sorry, Jake I'm on one of what you call my mind flights."

"Don't stop."

"One of the other moving visits was to the ruins in Sumeria, just about the beginning of civilisation. By damming the river to create a head of water, they were able irrigate the land with canals. Because crops grew so profusely, few labourers were needed on the land so communities developed as people moved to cities and lived in great affluence because they were able to export their produce."

"Why did the civilisation collapse though?"

"A lesson for our own time, Jake and we could use this in the book. What they didn't know was that over use of irrigation meant that the water table rose and as it did it brought salts to the surface which poisoned the land."

"Paralleling our use of oil and the increase in carbon dioxide in the atmosphere?"

"You and I would be more careful though, wouldn't we, Jake," Rhosa laughed as she pulled up the collar of her topcoat and said. "It's getting cold. Let's go home and light the fire."

They laughed together and, swinging their locked hands, walked in silence back across the bridge.

"D'you ever think about how music can transport us. I listened to Barbra Streisand singing 'It's Over' a few months ago and I was back in Stratford after you left. I had played that record over and over, thinking about you and the times we had together. It made me cry then and it did when I heard it again. You know how the mind hears echoes of times passed, Jay; the other day I was in a café having a drink and they had on a record of a jazz pianist. Immediately I was back listening to you playing Scott Joplin in the pub in Stratford. You didn't know I was listening but I was entranced. I sat motionless because I wanted to keep that time with me forever," she said jumping over a big puddle at the end of the bridge. She hummed the tune and held out her hands to guide Jake as he jumped and landed beside her.

"When you were in that pub it seemed you were playing just to me. No one else was in the room - you must have thought you were alone. I knew that if I moved you would hear me and stop. You always hated playing to an audience, didn't you?

"You're the same as me, Jay, in need of contact but wanting solitude. I've spent a lifetime looking for a kindred spirit who could feel things as deeply as I do but it eluded me…," she squeezed his hand, "except with you. I talk about the sensations - music, theatre, literature, a glimpse of a familiar in a restaurant. I try to explain to whoever I am with but they respond only with a nod of the head and a polite smile. It is why I love acting. From a small idea, an event happens; typewritten words on a page cause people to talk, walk and have a life." She squeezed his arm. "That's why I enjoy your writing so much. You make me aware of things below the superficial."

By the time they were back in Firenze House, he had mulled over what Rhosa had said and he had more or less decided on the layout of the book he had been working on, its title and how long he would need to write it.

CHAPTER 15

"I am to clean your room, sir," she said, looking at the papers strewn on the floor.

"I am sorry, Mistress, I had forgotten it is your day for cleaning this room. I am doing the accounts for the business." He knelt down and began collecting the papers together.

"The accounts tell me that my business selling and buying wool and cloth is going well. I manage to run it with very few helpers."

"I know that you are a clever man, Mr. D'Arcy."

"Thank you for that. It wasn't always so with my family. The business goes back a long way. Nearly one hundred years ago, it was very large, we employed eighty people and had warehouses filled with wool of the finest quality, we sold English cloth to many merchants throughout Europe. Our biggest sales were in that beautiful city of Florence which I have told you about. Customers in Italy were very demanding and almost all of our wool went there. It is a long and complicated story but there was one bank, owned by the Medici family, we depended on for finance to keep the business running. The bank was very powerful and for a long time, it lent money out to many people at reasonable rates and everyone it dealt with was pleased with them. But Cosimo, the man running it, died in 1464 and the bank was then run by his son Piero di Cosimo de' Medici. He was much more demanding than his father and when he looked at the accounts and knew what he and the Medici family needed, he recalled many of the loans, forcing a lot of merchants to go bankrupt. By doing that he created many enemies.

Our King Edward was greatly in debt to the Medici bank and when they asked him to repay what he owed them he sought to punish them. He stopped the export of wool to Florence where the bank was based. So, my family were without their biggest customers. They lost a lot of money and were forced to close. Even sadder, the business had to get rid of their workers who then fell into poverty.

Many of them had been friends and they were made so poor that they could not even feed themselves properly. My family did all they could for them but they could not do much. Warehouses which were filled with wool had to be sold, often at less than cost."

"But, if they lost everything, how did they survive? Did they have money to keep the business going?" She looked around at the room. "And... how can you live here now in this nice house?"

"It was a lesson to my family. We never let the business grow so big again. Now I can manage to run it myself with just a few people to help. Some of the warehouses that we once owned were sold and if we need space, we have to rent it. It was unfortunate but in a way it has been good for us."

"Can you tell me how that is, Sir?"

"If you'd like to hear, I will tell you, Mistress." He indicated a chair and, when she was seated, opened a drawer, took out a large book and placed it on the desk. "I buy wool, have it dyed and made into cloth. Trade is sometimes good but at other times it can be very bad, so I have to keep money aside for the hard times." He turned the pages of the book. "This is the accounts book for the business just before it almost collapsed after the Medici bank recalled my family's loan. Look there," he pointed to the bottom of a page. "Do you see that figure?"

She looked awkward.

"I'm sorry, Mistress. I have not shown you how to read these figures yet; they are Roman numerals. When you can do figures, you will see that the amount at the bottom of this page which was drawn up before the Medici bank asked for its loan back is more than ten times what my business makes today. I was told by my father that the way my ancestors lived was luxurious. I have read letters which were written between the members of the family and I have seen that they were letters of envy."

"I am not understanding."

"These people had everything they could want, big houses, jewels, fine clothes, all the food they could eat and many servants to take care of them."

"They were blessed."

"No, I don't think they were blessed, I think they were cursed."

"Why?" she frowned.

"It is my belief that money beyond a certain amount begins to fester unless it is made to work."

"Made to work? You showed me some money but how does it work?" She thought for a moment. "I think what you are saying is that it is not the money but the people who own it who have to make it work."

"It's clever of you to see that." Jacob said with a broad smile of pleasure. Taking a small slate board from a drawer, he said, "sit closer and I will tell you a little about what is called mathematics and I'll show you how important it is in business and in my business." "You see this?" With a piece of chalk, he drew on the slate. "This is a letter 'C' and this is a letter 'X'."

She nodded.

"In the Roman system of counting, 'X' stands for ten," he held up his fingers for her to look at and as he opened and closed them, ten times. As he did so, she copied him. "What we've done is to multiply X ten times. That will make one hundred which is what the letter 'C' stands for. Then there are other letters such as 'M' and 'L' which I will tell you about later."

Again she nodded.

"So you have to remember a lot of different letters to add and subtract and it's very easy to make mistakes, which was one of the reasons the family's business failed."

"Can you explain what you mean?"

"I will, you see they thought they made so much money that they became lazy. With Roman numerals if you make a mistake once it is easy to repeat and multiply those mistakes but you may not notice. So my family never knew how much money they had and when they were asked to pay back what they owed to the Bank, they did not have enough money to do it."

"But the figures you've got down there, they are not Roman." She said as she pointed to another book. "Is it easier to know what money you got?"

"Exactly! I will explain." He smiled with satisfaction at her understanding. "The Arab nations taught us a much simpler system of calculation. That is what I use and is one of the reasons I can run the business almost on my own." He held up one finger, "that is written as 1," he scratched on a slate with a piece of chalk. "Now, instead of having to remember lots of letters for different numbers, you have only to remember ten. If you put a nought after a 1, you make 10 and if you add another, it becomes 100 and another nought it becomes 1000. I will stop there and let you think about this revolution which has made my work and many, many other's much simpler."

"The Arabic nations have given us so much and we must be grateful to them. I always find it very difficult when I go to visit my clients in Italy; they have slaves, many of them captured from Arab nations and my clients consider them inferior people. They are treated like animals – no, often they are treated worse than animals."

"The Church also has slaves, although it tries to conceal this. They tell us that the chains worn by slaves to prevent them running away will not chain their souls and therefore they are still free. They are also trapped by marks cut into their faces. "

"Some years ago, Pope Innocent VIII accepted the gift of 100 slaves from Ferdinand II of Aragon. Slaves have no rights - can you imagine that? The Church used them in an inhuman manner simply so its leaders were able to luxuriate while the slaves worked. No lasting good comes of idleness, indeed, it brings discontent."

"I have seen nothing like it so I can't even imagine it."

"Do you ever think about money?"

"I never had money to think on." She smiled at him.

"I want to increase the money I pay you so that you can save your coins in the big jar in your room. Just think about the discovery of coinage by King Croesus of Lydia, who transformed commerce. If I wanted to buy cloth without money, I would have to carry goods. I'd need a cart load of apples for a bolt of even low quality cloth. With coins, I carry a few in a bag or I can even carry a promissory note which, because it is a piece of paper is even easier to carry. It can be said that because Emperor Alexander's coins were accepted all over the world, his city of Alexandria, in Egypt, became the centre of trade for the world. That was three hundred years before the birth of our

Lord Christ. Now we use Florins which come from Florence and I can carry them to buy things anywhere."

"This is an amazing time we live in. In our Group we are learning all the time but there are so many things we do not understand and people ask me to help." He glanced at her before continuing.

"Let me give you an example. A man who has a mine, asked why pumps cannot suck up water for more than thirty two feet. That started me wondering if the reason could be that air is heavy and pushes down on water and what we are doing is making use of that weight. If air has weight, we must be carrying it on our head all the time but how can we do that and still stand up?" He waved his hand slowly in the air. "When I do that it is obvious that air is soft and not very strong. But that is not always true because in storms it moves very fast and trees are blown down and houses can be destroyed."

"If air is heavy, Mr. D'Arcy, inside us must be the same heaviness otherwise it would make us squash."

Jacob looked at her in astonishment. "That is amazing, mistress and of course, you must be right. I had never thought about that." He stood up, went to a cupboard and from a shelf, took out a piece of stone. "Now here is something which has puzzled me and other people in our group. This stone seems like magic as though it has a life force." He placed it on the table and rotated it. "It is called a Lodestone. Do you notice how it moved back to the position it was in before I pushed it. I have tried it in other houses and other parts of the town and even in other countries and it always settles pointing in the same direction. Does it live and have a memory, do you think?"

She looked surprised, moved the stone and smiled at its resistance.

"Is't magic?"

"I don't think it is magic, I think it is something we shall understand one day." He picked up the stone and then said, "Let me ask you something else. Do you ever think about people Mistress, how far ahead of all other creatures we are? And how this thing up here," he touched his head, "never rests. When we seem to be silent the mind is still thinking and even when we sleep, we dream. Think of how we pass on our skills. In monasteries books can be copied.

Books are one way by which knowledge is passed from those who have knowledge to those who do not have it. Letters and books are carried by pack horses, fast messenger or wagons to other monasteries. They are then moved on to other monasteries and to scholars all over a country and over Europe. The Romans, who were amazing administrators, owed a lot of their success in governing their empire to the clever way they were able to get messages to their legions.

It is the same with money. There are people I use whom I can trust who carry goods and money for me. So, when I sell something, I can still run my business because I do not have to travel long distances to the customer. The trusted messengers do it for me.

Just like you do things I can't do and I do things you can't do, we all depend on each other. The Medici family is very rich but it is a sad fact that their money has filled them with greed for more. They are cruel people and I have been told that they will kill or destroy anyone who stands in their way. That is what I meant by the destruction which comes from having too much. I do not envy their power because I fear I would become as corrupted as they are. The Church has become corrupted and so your man lies dead. Do you understand, Mistress?"

"I think so, Sir. You're saying God is not what is wrong, it is the men who are evil."

Jacob looked up surprised, he had never gone so far as to use the word 'evil' but now that she had used the word, he realised that it was his opinion also, "You are right, that is what I am saying." he nodded his agreement. "The Church along with Barons, landowners and the King, and all those who have command over those beneath them are obsessed with power. When it is challenged, they strike out."

CHAPTER 16

The next morning was Sunday and when Jake woke, Rhosa was sitting up in bed looking at photographs.

"You're looking thoughtful today," he said blearily.

Rhosa sighed wordlessly. "Ever think that when we wake each morning we are different people?" Rhosa asked.

"Go on, tell me what you mean by that," he said, intrigued.

"We have left Saturday Jake, and today there is a Sunday Jake."

He looked quizzically at her and sensing his confusion she said. "Each day we experience new things, we meet new people or we talk to friends who may surprise us by behaving out of character. All of these things change us." She looked at Jake and saw his continuing confusion.

"What would I be if my mother had not wanted to come to England to find a husband or if my grandmother had not been able to earn a lot with her dancing? Probably I'd be a gutter woman in Cairo like many of the friends I used to play with. You see what I mean – everything that happens is a modifier. Sometimes it is only slight but at other times dramatic. Like changing my name from Sheana Zaros; if I hadn't read a book with the character Rhosa in it, the Rhosa you have sitting up in bed beside you would never have existed."

"Can't say it's something I've ever considered. Besides which, you are forgetting the brain architecture we were born with which drives us to overcome adversity." He leaned over to her and ruffled her hair. "What made you think about it anyway; odd thing to say first thing in the morning."

"I haven't just thought it; it often occurs to me how vulnerable we are. Perhaps it's just that I woke in one of those early morning states of unreality, convinced I had left behind the Rhosa I put to bed and must now decide what I shall be this day. Will I be nice Rhosa or difficult Rhosa."

Momentarily, he wondered if he should bring her down to earth but before he could, she was talking again.

"And if I'm right, the ether must be filled with all our yester personalities which means twelve thousand different Rhosas somewhere out there," she continued.

"Going to be hellishly crowded then." Jake said and with a laugh as he sat up in bed beside her. "Because of my age there are going to be thousands more of me jostling for space."

"It isn't just me?" she said, sliding her hand beneath the bedclothes to hold his. "Have you read Kierkegaard on the difficulty of staying with anyone when that person would be different from day to day; he even broke off his engagement to a young woman because of it."

"A bit like Plato."

"Tell me more. What did he say?"

"He asked in 'The Republic' how we could understand things like trees when they change from day to day."

"Almost the same idea; what else did he say?"

"Some time since I read him but I seem to remember him saying something like things are like shadows."

"That's how I feel about this house. It's filled with shadows from the lights of the flickering fires of the past. People who have lived here have left their memories behind. I sense they are still trying to reach us."

"Can't all be trying, there must be scores of people who have lived here. Dreadful cacophony if they were all at it."

"What about television and radio."

"What do you mean?" Rhosa looked puzzled. "That they wouldn't have had television?"

Jake walked to the radio turned it on and bowed knowingly as an announcer started talking.

"Sorry Jake, I've lost you."

For answer, he tuned to a different station and a woman's voice was speaking in French.

Rhosa shook her head. Expecting her to understand, Jake said nothing. When she stared at him with a look almost of irritation, he explained. "The air in this room is full of thoughts and music yet we are unaware of it until I tune the radio and pick up speech and music from all around the world."

"So."

"I can tune this radio so it can reproduce all the sounds in the room which we would otherwise not be able to hear. What I am saying is that perhaps you and I just happen to be tuned to the shadow of Jacob D'Arcy."

"How clever you are, Jake." Rhosa said with a note of sarcasm. "Or could it be that we didn't 'happen' to be tuned."

"Now you need to explain."

"Jacob left his memory for you. You remember how you felt when you first came here – almost as though the place had chosen you."

Jake pursed his lips and, after a moment, said. "I find that a bit…"

"'Disturbing' or 'frightening', are those the words you wanted?"

"Well yes. I've gone along with your Logical Positivists - if it can't be proven it isn't true. But I keep having dreams and… I've never said anything before but, when I first found that bible behind the bookcase," he stopped meditatively. "I had a sort of vision of a man and woman in mediaeval clothes. I was pretty tired and I put it down to being nothing more than a day dream. But this place…? I'm sure it's affecting my thinking."

With an effort, she said, "did Plato talk about people changing?"

"Can't recall that he did." he said.

She squeezed his hand under the bedclothes. "You know, I've never told anyone else about waking up as a different person every day. They'd probably think I was off my head."

"Isn't that one of your qualities?"

"Being off my head, you mean?" she laughed.

"No, I meant seeing things differently. Probably comes from your acting so many different parts." he said and then, as a thought struck him, added. "Or perhaps it's the other way round and you were born to be an actress."

"Probably," she said distantly. "No, what got me thinking was talking to a friend, Katherine Crawley."

"You told me how bright she was?"

"Yes. Remarkable mind, you can talk to her about any subject. We were thinking about self-knowledge; she says the mind is like an orchestra which we conduct. Sometimes it is dominated by the strings, sometimes the woodwind, sometimes the percussion and on good days, they all play in harmony."

"Is she a psychologist?"

"Don't think so, she's just perceptive. She seems to me to be a complete orchestra. Talk about art, psychology, media, the Bloomsbury set and their literature and she's ahead of you."

"Did you sound her out on your idea that we are different every day?"

"I would have done but she couldn't stay long, I wanted to hear what she thought about Eastern philosophy and the intellectual games played by Brahmin priests."

"Don't think I know about that," Jake frowned.

"Well, that's because, European man that you are, you only think about Western philosophers, you probably think Eastern thinkers were dabblers." She looked at the trees outside and for a moment was distracted by their beauty. "Brahmin priests were not good on physical sport; their pleasure came from mental games. They would deny themselves food then have a yoga session and when physically tired, one of them would give his interpretation of god or life. The other priest would contradict. They would go on using ideas as tennis balls until one of the priests was reduced to a state of mental emptiness and unable to respond. At that silent, wordless moment they knew they were in the presence of Brahmin the sublime and ultimate reality and they would remain silent, allowing only the meditation of Brahmin to fill their minds."

"One of the different routes we use to survive." Jake said as Rhosa started to leaf through her album of photographs. "What have you got there?"

She nodded. "This one, almost the first photograph I took in this city, I must have been twelve, I suppose. A tiny church spire of old London raises its finger above drab concrete buildings. The power of photography is to freeze a moment forever. Another thing that intrigues me is how our origins and our experiences are written on our faces."

She turned a page and pointed at a photograph. "See this woman. I managed to get her with a long distance lens. Even if she had noticed me, she would have thought I was taking a picture of the building in the background. She was sitting alone in a square in Paris where I'd gone on a whim to get away from Jed. I guess she was a refugee. Can you see the lines of suffering on her face? The residue of hardship in her eyes, the sadness, the yearning - they're all there. I wanted to speak to her when she looked up as I walked past her and I did try but we had no common language. Made me wonder why we divide ourselves with language. So often it bars contact. That's why I like taking photographs. Every time I look at her face I want to try talking to her again." She passed the album to Jake. "She made me think about what defines us when I saw her in a culture which would have been very different from her own."

"What do you mean 'what defines us'?" Jake asked

"What makes us what we are? So many things form us, parents are the most obvious. Even now, I sometimes wake fearful that my stepfather will be standing over me, angry as usual at something I've done or not done."

"But it's much more than parents. They had parents themselves who formed them and who in turn were formed by their parents. We are shaped by our history." She looked up at the ceiling as she leaned back on the pillows. "You and I don't have a religion but our moral standards will have reached us by a circuitous route. It's all there, parents, teachers, religion and culture. If I had been born not in Egypt but in Germany I would be so different from the Rhosa I am now?" She frowned, "Am I me or am I a chiselled and polished version of the embryo which started life in my mother's womb. Am I

178

just hanging like a fish on a line, able to thrash around a bit but not to get off the hook?"

Jake was thinking about what she had said when she took the album back and said.

"That woman was sad but look at this face," she turned a couple of pages and passed the album back to Jake. "That man; he was outside the theatre when we did 'King Lear' in Moscow. You see the open sack on his back. He would dance - such a pathetic dance which had all his sorrow in it - a sort of ballet but like nothing you've ever seen before. People would throw coins and he would leap to catch them in the open top of the sack. I tried to photograph him when he was leaping but the light was not good enough."

"I suppose, like the refugee woman, you weren't able to speak to him?"

"He heard me speaking English and came over to me. I was so embarrassed when he bowed to me as though I was someone important. He spoke English, with hardly an accent."

"Probably he thought it would encourage you to give him money."

"Don't be such a cynic, Jay it wasn't like that at all. Look at his face – don't you see majesty about it."

"Don't know about 'majesty' but he certainly looks to be a man with character. What was he doing dancing in the streets?"

Rhosa looked at the photo intently. "So sad, this man's family had been wealthy. His grandfather was a count who had servants and a grand house. The revolution destroyed them. Their home was burned to the ground by a mob. Gregory's father had been carried out as a child in a basket covered with wet towels."

"You're sure he wasn't just spinning a story?"

"With some people, you can tell, can't you? No, this man was genuine. I took him for a drink in a bar; he told me about his life, so much suffering, it almost brought me to tears. I was so moved that I put into the bag on his back all that I had on me. I had been paid in roubles for my performance that night. When I gave it to him, he cried. It was all I could do not to cry with him."

"Did you think he might have been outside of the theatre because it was a place to meet English women who had money to give him?"

"You know what? It wouldn't have mattered to me if he had. I would have paid just to talk to him." She took the album back to look at the photograph again. "You'll never guess what he did with the money?"

"Booze I shouldn't wonder, the Russians are great vodka drinkers."

"Well you're wrong. He asked me to go to dinner with him."

"You accepted! Weren't you afraid you'd get involved in something nasty?"

"It never crossed my mind. We arranged to meet at the Godunov restaurant. You haven't been but if you get the chance you must go, it's near the Bolshoi Theatre, close to where I was staying at the Metropole Hotel – you must go there as well, steeped in history. People like Tolstoy, Rachmaninov and Chaliapin used to stay there. The Gudonov restaurant is magnificent, used to be a monastery; murals on the walls, carved wooden chairs and tables, that sort of thing. I got there a bit after him. When I walked in, he was sitting in the reception, dressed in a smart suit and looking like the Count he should have been."

"So he was a conman after all, had a house where he would change into scruffy clothes to attract well off women."

"Don't keep being cynical, Jay. He told me he lived in a tiny room in the home of an impoverished aristocratic woman. His evening clothes were a bit crumpled and old fashioned but in the dim light they looked good. I suspect he had kept them as a reminder of his previous life. He had washed, and trimmed his beard." She turned the page of her album. "This is a photograph taken by one of the diners for me. See the restaurant; it reminded me of photographs I'd seen of the Katarina Palace."

Jake studied the scene - ornate rococo room with waiters hovering around with fixed ingratiating smiles. There at the table was Rhosa, looking very young and with the distinguished 'Count' Gregory sitting beside her.

"What age was he, Rhosa; he looks as though he is over seventy at a guess? Much older than you."

"I would have been in my early twenties then. I never asked his age. I could have but it didn't even occur to me. I was even more of a romantic then than I am now and I didn't even think about the age difference. There was a dignity about him and, when I saw him in the dress suit, he looked like the cultured aristocrat he should have been." She stopped as a thought struck her. "Interesting isn't it that just the clothes changed him from beggar to aristocrat." She shrugged, "Didn't even notice the lined face which you can see in this photograph, I saw a man with a young mind, cultured and interesting. I was completely captivated, overcome by his charm. He called me his countess - don't suppose that'll ever happen to me again.

I saw him put a note in the head waiter's hand and whisper in his ear. The waiter put the money in his pocket without looking at it and beckoned to the other waiters obviously signalling them to look after us."

Jake looked at the photograph. "I know what you mean; it's hard to believe he was a beggar."

"An aristocrat at heart, though. That man was so cultured," she said, "I had an unforgettable meal with him; we talked of ballet, Rachmaninoff, Tolstoy, Dickens and of course, my Shakespeare as well as his particular interest, the Pre-Raphaelites. It felt that we talked all of literature and art that evening. He told me about a man, Sergei Shchukin, whom his parents knew and who had bought so many of the French Impressionists that he was said to have the biggest collection in the world. He bought many of Matisse's paintings and was probably responsible for making the painter well known. The collection was stolen by Lenin and then in 1941, packed up and put in cellars in Siberia. In 1953 there was an exhibition of thirty six of Picasso's paintings. They had belonged to Shchukin, Count Gregory said." Unable to speak, she stopped and wiped her eyes with the back of her hand. "I learned so much in a short time with him.

"In 1914, his grandfather had been at the state visit to Moscow of the Tsar and his family. The people worshipped Tsar Nicholas and thought that he could do anything for them and what he could not do, God would do. He and the Tsarina were there with their beautiful daughters, followed by their ailing child Alexis being carried in the arms of a Cossack. The crowd was cheering. When the Tsar reached the platform, an old man shakily walked forward and knelt down with a large pile of papers in his hand which he held up to the Tsar who ignored him. The strong arm men caught hold of the old man and carried him off. The people around Gregory's grandfather whispered that the peasant would be taken to prison - the punishment for preparing a petition. People think that oppression started after the Communist uprising of 1917 but Gregory told me it was always there," Rhosa said, as she stared at the picture of the old man.

"The family saw the 1917 Revolution coming, sold everything and fled to England, taking enough with them to live comfortably. Count Gregory had been born in affluence but the money ran out and the life he was forced into was one of loneliness. When we talked, the suppressed memories of his lost years poured out of him." She turned the page to look at the first picture of Gregory. "Jake, this man who had been begging a few hours before," she hesitated, "captivated me that night."

"You mean…?"

She nodded. "He came back to my hotel. I offered him my bath, you see. The first he had had for many years I suspect. When he had finished, he splashed cologne on his body and I gave him a pair of my pyjamas. Only then did I see how small he was; even my pyjamas looked big on him," she smiled at her memory and turned to look at Jake. "Unusual experience, you know, making love to someone in your own clothes."

"I'll bet it was," Jake said, wondering why he was never shocked at anything Rhosa told him. "Interesting that you should be so attracted to him physically when there was such a difference in age."

"I've often thought that there is a 'real' in which convention governs and there is a 'dreamreal' in which all those conventions disappear and behaviour becomes free. It wasn't so much physical as a feeling that his mind was entering mine, all his experience and suffering went through me. The lined face in this picture didn't exist for me." She looked at Jake and saw the shadow of consternation.

"It was before my husband had destroyed my ability to enjoy sex," she said, to defuse what she suspected he was thinking. "I remember seeing Gregory leaning on his elbow, looking down at me as though I were an aristocrat of his class; he said he had found a woman whom he had been looking for but she had never lived until that moment. I'd had a pretty full life but I remember thinking my real life began on that night. I looked up into his eyes and there was such love passing between us. As our bodies connected, I lived his life from his birth, saw him as he grew to be a man and the suffering of his lost destiny. The wealth he would have known had it not been torn from his family by the 1917 Revolution. They would have stayed in England if it had not been for their love of Russia and the promise by the Communist Party that they would have their old life back and be given a position in the Party. It was all lies though; the Party just wanted to make sure they could get them to return for propaganda purposes. After some years when their propaganda value had dimished, the adults were imprisoned for treason. Gregory was spared because he was too young. All those things passed through my mind as I fell asleep that night."

With sadness in her voice, she continued. "That was the last time I saw him."

"Took the money and ran you mean?"

She punched him playfully. "No he didn't, sceptic. He must have spent everything he had on the meal and the tip he gave the head waiter. You should have seen the way the staff in the restaurant bowed to him. I had to smile to myself at the thought of how they would have behaved if they had known that a few hours before he was begging on the streets."

"What did you mean by 'the last time you saw him'?"

"He was not there when I woke so cold without him beside me. On the bedside table he had left a pile of roubles. He spent the money I had given him on the meal and must have put everything he had left beside my bed.

He left a little book about his family's history; inside was a note, thanking me for the loan of the money and for being his countess for one night. I still have that book and his note. It goes wherever I go, along with the photograph of you."

"But what happened to your aristocrat?"

She could not speak for several minutes as the memory flooded her mind. "It was terribly cold." Her voice quavered and she waited till she had recovered. "I couldn't believe the earth could be as cold as it was that day. That morning when I was walking to the theatre, I saw people looking at a frost covered figure. They moved off as they saw me." Rhosa's body shook and Jake pulled her to him and she laid her head on his shoulder. When she could finally speak she said in a whisper, "it was him, still wearing the same suit but rigid and frozen."

"What had happened?"

"In the note he left in my room, he said no night could be like the night we had had together and that his life was complete. I don't know what could have happened, perhaps he had slipped down in the street and the frost had killed him – or...," she stopped to wipe her eyes, "I've been told that it is easy to end one's life when it is so cold, you just lie down and hardly feel anything." As she spoke she got out of bed went to the window and looking out, said. "So sad, Jay, that lovely man ending his life as nothing more than a shape in the snow," she turned back from the window, wiping her eyes on her sleeve, "I need to think of something else. I'll make us some breakfast."

Jake was still looking at the photographs when she called from the kitchen. He put on his dressing gown and went down to find her in tears.

"What is it Rhosa?" he asked, going to her and putting his arms round her.

"That poor, poor man - no one mourned him".

"I managed after enormous effort to organize for him to be buried. You can't imagine how anyone could get through the bureaucracy in Moscow. After two days of trying, I met an official with a spark of humanity who told me that there was a cemetery near the centre of the city where Gregory's family vault was. I arranged for him to be buried still wearing the same suit he wore to the restaurant."

"No doubt it would have been much easier if you had had a big wallet."

She was unable to reply. Jake sat her down and after a while she had regained control and continued. "Apart from the people who were doing the burying, I was the only one at the funeral except for one solitary man who took a photograph as I watched the coffin being dropped into the vault, I assume he was a journalist. Can you imagine, in this country where we have so much freedom to be what we want, Gregory would probably have been a diplomat, a writer. I don't know - whatever - he would have made a success with a brain like his but he lies in that cold stone vault and no one knows he is there."

"Except for that man who photographed you."

"What do you mean?" She frowned.

"Did it not occur to you who he was?" Jake asked. "No doubt your details and your photograph are held in a police record somewhere. Have you been back to Russia since?"

"Twice and each time I've gone and put flowers on his grave."

"Did anyone see you?"

"Come on, Jake – it's not like that nowadays, nobody would have…" she stopped in mid-sentence and put her hand to her mouth.

"What's wrong?" he asked.

"I just remembered – the last time I was in Moscow and went to his grave, there were two people I didn't know standing around. It was pouring with rain and as I walked to the vault, I suddenly knew I was not alone. As I stood beside Gregory's grave, there was a woman and a man wearing long coats holding umbrellas. The woman seemed quite young but I couldn't be sure because she and the man she was with were wearing sunglasses. The day was grey and I remember thinking at the time that it was strange to be wearing sunglasses. I would have spoken to them if I had any Russian because they didn't look like mourners."

She and Jake were sitting down at the breakfast bar and as they ate, looked out across the green outside. Normally words poured from her while he, the more silent, would listen to her. But today, even though he tried to rouse her interest in other things, she was abnormally quiet. She had cleared the breakfast things and was washing up while he dried the dishes before she spoke.

"Don't mind telling you, Jake, I feel weird." She put her hand over her mouth in nature's way of holding back the reaction to vomit. "Could I have a criminal record in Russia and be watched from the time I walked through customs at the airport? "

"It could have been that the man you thought was being helpful in getting the vault opened for Gregory's body reported you." Jake said.

She finished the washing up, emptied the bowl and went to sit down. "I need to get out and wander round the common where only the trees watch me."

"With your looks and your reputation as an actress, I don't imagine you can go anywhere without people watching," he said light-heartedly attempting to lift her spirits. "D'you want to go out on your own?"

"No, if you can break yourself away from work, I'd like you to come with me, but first I need to get myself clean, wash away this feeling in the shower."

"Go ahead, I'll finish tidying up. As soon as you are ready, we can go out."

Before she went to shower, she took his hands, wrapped them around her body and put her head on his shoulder. When she looked up, she said with a tearful smile. "I've always needed someone stable like you, Jake, a man with broad shoulders."

As they walked, a light breeze fluttered the leaves on the trees. The air was still cold but seemed to have on it the scent of blossom. The walk took them nearly an hour and fetched up at Jake's favourite pub, 'The Rod of Iron' where they had danced together. By the time they sat down in the familiar surroundings, Rhosa was nearly back to normal. As she drank a glass of her favourite burgundy, she looked around at the other people sitting at tables scattered around the room.

"I like coming to places like this," she said as her eyes wandered round the room. "It's full of people leading ordinary lives."

As she spoke, a sports car drew up and from it jumped a middle aged man with hair carefully styled. The collar of his jacket was turned up. Between his lips was a part smoked cigarette which jutted out aggressively and pronounced him a 'go-getter'. Carefully and with a look of slight irritation, he ground it out under his foot as he stood in the doorway. He had a leather briefcase slung over his shoulder which swung in as he walked purposefully. Jake had not seen him before but saw that he must have been a regular because as he sat down at a table, his eyes met those of the girl behind the bar who, without his asking, poured him a drink and took it to him. He nodded cursorily at her as he opened his brief case and with a frown and a shake of the head, started to read from a pile of papers and to write on a foolscap pad of paper.

"We all wear badges that tell people what we are don't we Jake? See what badges that man wears," Rhosa said, lowering her voice.

"Mm," Jake nodded, "what do his badges say to you?"

"The same things they say to you I should think. 'I am an important man, you can tell by the haste with which I came in and immediately started work. You can tell by the way I walk. I have parked my expensive Jaguar sports car where you can all see it. When I drive it I smoke my cigarette which juts out like an erect penis. I have no trouble with the opposite sex, they all love the way I look and the way I wear my clothes which are casually expensive. My hair style - guaranteed to attract females but I have so many that I am a little bored with them. I give my custom to this place because it is nearby but I am really too busy to stop work for long even on a Sunday when the rest of you are behaving in a leisurely manner, I am only here because I've had an exhausting morning and I need a drink'."

"You know, Rhosa, I'm aware of all that but only on a sub-conscious level. I wonder why it wasn't obvious to me." Jake nodded his head. "Partly comes from your acting I suppose and partly from having grown up in a different culture which makes you more analytical of people in your adopted country."

As he spoke, the outer door was pushed open and about a dozen men and women came in, anoraked in readiness for bad weather. Their heavy walking boots scratched the stone floor as they took seats, dragging chairs to the table they had selected and with hushed voices, decided who should sit next to whom.

Jake leaned close to Rhosa and said, "A lot of badges there."

With a studiously averted gaze, she listened to their voices as they talked amongst themselves laughing constantly as convention demands when numbers of people group together.

"Office outing, I think. Judging by the way the others cluck round him and laugh every time he says anything mildly amusing, the big man with white hair is the boss."

The barmaid went over to them and they began to order sandwiches until the big man decided he would like a cooked meal whereupon several others changed their minds with, "that sounds good, I think I'll join you," and had what he had ordered.

"Big-white-hair is casting his influence," Jake said quietly.

"Quite tribal," Rhosa observed. "You notice the women are also deferential to the boss's wife. It's the youngest couple I feel sorry for, probably newcomers to the group; the wife is very attractive and you see the older men sneaking lascivious glances at her cleavage when their own wives are talking to the boss or his wife. The husband is sending messages to her to flirt with the boss but only mildly. On the surface you'd think they were a relaxed group of walkers - a loose-knit community but it's actually very structured."

He smiled at her comments and said, "I'm waiting for you to write your Harold Pinter play."

"If I ever write a play, it will be about Gregory and his life. You can't help wondering why we build these hierarchies." She took another drink while she collected her thoughts and then, looking over at the group, now free of their anoraks, said with a slight smile: "You see it in microcosm over there don't you; the false obeisance to big-white-hair."

When she got up to go to the toilet, Jake, amused at Rhosa's analysis idly watched the group, assigning positions in the hierarchy.

When she returned, she sat down and said, "Is man ever free, Jay? Didn't Karl Marx have an expression?"

"You mean Rousseau, don't you? His 'Social Contract', 'Man is born free but everywhere is in chains'."

188

She nodded. "That's what I mean," she said picking up her glass. "Why do we do it? Why do we build systems which limit our freedom?"

"I'll have to introduce you to Haig Skarn, if his ideas become accepted, and I think they will, we shall have real democracy," he said, then realising that he was opening up one of her favourite topics, said "We ought to get back." He sensed that they were close to one of her Socratic diatribes. "Quick drink in a pub before we return isn't the right time to discuss the mechanics of the State," he said as he stood up and helped Rhosa into her coat, "but we will later."

Rhosa remained quiet as they walked to the house. When they got back, she went into the kitchen and took a long time washing her hands as Jake lit the fire. While they watched the flames in the fire growing, Jake said. "You've really been thrown by this Russian thing haven't you?"

She nodded gravely, "Don't mind telling you it has made me think just how much we are watched and how dominant the state is in our lives. Our governments are supposed to act for us but they are self-seeking and self-perpetuating entities. They preach so called 'welfare of their people' and take that as justification for oppression. As we walked back I was thinking about the terrible killing that took place in the French Revolution and then the Russian Revolution."

"I noticed how quiet you were," he said, "Yes, not difficult to see why every now and then the masses rise against authority. The way we are allowed to elect our politicians is all wrong. I had always known it but it was not until I met Haig Skarn, the university lecturer I told you about, that I realised it after I heard one of his speeches."

"Tell me again what he is proposing."

"He is a quiet revolutionary. We are told we live in a democracy but all we have is a 'sham' to use your word. Once every five years, we are allowed to vote for people whom we have little respect for and who act in their own best interests. Skarn says we should vote for policies not for parties and those policies should be administered by people who are trained. Education by educators, manufacturing policy by economists who have worked for manufacturers, health by trained medical people, and these managers could be sacked if they don't perform. They will manage the business of the nation just as large companies are managed. When Haig talks in public, he says so much about the concerns everyone has that he always gets a standing ovation."

"Take me to his next talk, I'd love to hear him speak," Rhosa poked the fire and watched as the flames took hold and spread. "Language is amazing, isn't it? How empty life would be if we couldn't talk like we are now. You wonder what the mechanism is that causes words to come into our minds without our seeming to think like chemical reactions. Put thoughts together and they produce words. But if I stopped to think how I do it, I'd be lost. I make sentences which have a subject, a verb and an object and follow rules of grammar. I am just grateful that not only do we think but we also have the throat, the tongue and the vocal chords to make words. Without them, the loneliness would be unbearable. And we need words to make change happen. What would the French Revolution have been without words?"

"You can understand why it started. But these revolutions, supposed to be for the good of people, always go too far; like this fire; it starts with a tiny flame and spreads to consume anything in its way." She threw another log into the flames and watched it become engulfed. "And if it gets out of this fireplace, it could spread out of control."

"I read an article in a magazine recently about the awful killing hundreds of years ago in the Vendee simply because the peasants tried to protect the priests who refused to take an oath of allegiance to the Revolutionary Government. General Turreau was ordered to kill everyone he saw. One hundred and seventy thousand men, women and children were massacred and Commander Carrier invented what he called systematic drowning," she shuddered, "I find it hard to think about it even after so many years have passed."

Jake nodded, "I read that article as well. Carrier tied women and their children together, floated them out on the Loire and sank the boats they were sitting in. He trampled children to death under the hooves of his horses."

"If you ask, is one individual more important than society, then there is no argument, but are one hundred and seventy thousand not more important than ideology? And what about the millions of blameless people slaughtered for the 'better' world of Communism?"

The log burst into flames and illuminated her face. "There's something about this house, Jay, whenever I'm here, I find myself thinking about man's inhumanity to man."

Jake decided that it was time to change the subject.

"I haven't seen you reading much lately, Rhosa."

She looked into the fire, leaned forward, picked up the poker, pushed the logs around and then said. "I sometimes think that I read too much."

"Too much, that's impossible, reading opens our minds."

"Sometimes it does the opposite." She shrugged. "I think I live too much with literature so I'm often disappointed by what happens in real life."

Jake debated with himself whether to reply but instead said. "I think right now, you need some music in your life. Haven't you got a break tomorrow before you go off on your tour?" When Rhosa nodded, he said. "Then I'll take you to the Festival Hall, I've been given tickets. There is a Czech pianist, can't remember his name, he's playing the sort of music you like, Chopin's Revolutionary and Rachmaninoff's Third. I'll book us a meal in the restaurant. I'll try to get a table looking over the Thames."

Rhosa got up and sat on his lap, putting her arm round his neck, laid her head on his chest. "Sounds divine," she said sleepily. In a few moments she was asleep, breathing heavily. Jake carefully carried her up to bed. He looked down on the turbulent mind so peacefully asleep. She always slept fitfully and he knew she would wake later and change into her nightclothes, so he left her to dream.

CHAPTER 17

Rhosa had only been back a few days from touring in America with a production of King Lear. To celebrate the success of the tour, she and Jake had gone out to a raucous party where the wine flowed very freely. The next morning was one of those days when he couldn't seem to wake up. He felt Rhosa shake him but when he sat up in the bed it was as though it was happening to someone else.

She jumped into bed beside him and passed him a pile of letters to open. Much of it was the usual junk advertising but the one which made him wake up was from the Alder Smit Institute.

He read it and passed it to Rhosa.

"Interesting," she said as she read it, "will you do it?"

"I think I will. I haven't spoken in public for some time but this will be different. I have to talk for a while and then be interviewed. It will be on that article I wrote for 'Current Management' about changing from what we have to a real democracy. So I've got all the facts - just need to put it into speech form - much of it is based on Haig's ideas so I'll send him a transcript. I could probably do the speech now without any rehearsal."

"Well, why don't you," she said, putting her cup on the table beside her and pushing herself down in the bed.

He looked to see if she were joking, saw she meant it; so he sat up in bed and talked. It came out so easily that, when he had finished, she said. "Marvellous, I'm convinced. We need all those changes, you never showed me the article, was it when I was away?"

"Haig Skarn inspired most of what I was writing about. I met him over a year ago. That was B.R."

"BR, whatever does that mean?"

"Bit like BC, before Christ. BR stands for 'before Rhosa'."

"Stupid man," Rhosa laughed. "Tell me more about this man Haig."

"Amazing guy with ideas which he hadn't ever publicised properly; he contacted me because he saw that I could give them an audience through journalism."

"You sure he didn't get his opinions from you? Many of the things you've just said you talked about even back in Stratford."

"In a way, you're right. What I wrote for 'Current Management' is a combination of his and my ideas. I haven't yet told you but he asked me to be his Press Officer."

"Will you, it sounds the sort of thing you'd be good at?"

"I don't think I'm ready for that yet - so many other things I want to do, like writing the book for a start."

"Perhaps you could work for him on an occasional basis."

No other woman had wanted to push out his boundaries before. He reached out and squeezed her hand in appreciation.

"Before I give this speech, I will have to talk it over with Haig; he might want to do it himself."

"No, Jay, the invitation is to you. This is your moment and you shouldn't let it pass."

He raised his eyebrows; this was a side of her he hadn't seen before.

"Where will it be?"

"I did a lot of reading in the Wren Library at Trinity College in Cambridge. It's an incredible room built hundreds of years ago. A bit small for a public meeting but it will do. I shall be talking revolution and it will provide just the antiquity to temper the message I'll leave them with." He smiled. "The place with its Greek pillars and busts of thinkers like Seneca around the bookcases is just incredible. When you walk in, you get the feeling that history is entering your mind."

"Go for it, Jay, it sounds marvellous, I can't wait. Great to hear you speak there."

CHAPTER 18

The publicity had been good. The hall was full and Jake picked up an air of expectancy in the audience as he sat down while the television interviewer, Reid McKenzie who was an old friend, introduced him.

"Tonight we are going to attempt something unusual, we might even say momentous. This evening is completely unrehearsed and none of us can be sure how it will work out. We are broadcasting what we shall call an interview but it will not follow the traditional rules, in fact there are no rules. If, while Jake is talking, you want to interrupt he's said he's happy for you to do that. Jake and I go back a long time and we both thrive on interaction, with readers in the case of Jake, and listeners in my case." The signal came that they were going on air. Reid straightened his tie, moved in his chair and spoke into the microphone.

"We are fortunate in having the well-known political columnist, Jake Dearsey to talk about an entirely new form of government. He and Haig Skarn, whom you will also have heard of, are convinced that this transformation will meet the needs of the 21st Century. Jake will talk first then I will ask a couple of questions, or if I think something he has said would benefit from being examined, I may interrupt him. I also have a series of questions which have been sent to me by a few who could not attend.

When we've both finished, we'll throw the meeting open with time for a few questions." The sound technician was gesticulating that he should speak up. He brought the microphone closer to his mouth and continued as the technician gave him the thumbs up sign. "Anyone who reads newspapers, listens to the radio or watches television will know that what we are all desperate for is change. Not just the nibbling around the edges sort which is all we get from our politicians. As Jake will explain, we need a revolution."

Jake made himself comfortable, filled his glass from the water jug in front of him and began.

"I imagine many of you are wondering why you are here in this magnificent hall." Jake smiled, taking time to glance around the room and make eye contact with some of the audience." And I have to admit that sometimes, I have wondered if I should be here myself when I could have been watching yet another production of Jane Austen's 'Pride and Prejudice' on television."

The murmur of laughter rippling through the audience pleased him - even if they didn't agree with what he was about to say, at least they were responsive.

"When I got the invitation to speak, one question kept going through my mind - why me? I have never considered standing for Parliament and have never claimed to be a typical political animal and, faced with the present Parties, I am, like Reid, probably 'apolitical'." He turned and smiled at Reid. "Haig Skarn is the founder of this movement – you will notice I say 'movement' and not Party because we believe that the Party system is obsolete. I see we are fortunate to have many representatives of the media here which is, of course, very important for the start of a revolution." He looked around at the faces to gauge their reaction before continuing.

"I notice some of you are perhaps a little uneasy at the use of the word 'revolution', which has unpleasant connotations. There is no need to be fearful though. This is not a revolution in which blood will be shed. Although it will be controversial it should ultimately be so convincing that there will not even be violent language. I am not so naïve that I am not prepared for dissent."

"As Reid said, there is a tide of dissatisfaction running through this nation and throughout the world which is growing in intensity as we see the results of the ineptitude of our politicians and their attitude to personal advantage." He cast his eyes from one side of the hall to the other and was pleased to see nodding of heads. "The tide, ladies and gentlemen, should not be diverted for much longer. What I want to talk to you about will be constructive and dramatic.

As Reid has implied, you will all leave this hall with your ideas changed. Some may claim not to be influenced in any way. I venture to say that such people will not have been honest with themselves."

The audience was quiet as Jake spent a few moments looking at their faces. Rhosa had told him to look at faces and change the pace or volume of his voice to mirror or direct their moods.

"We are fortunate tonight to be sitting in a hall which is many centuries old." He raised his hand to the medieval features of the old room with its statues and odour of mellowing books and dust. I deliberately made it a condition that I would only talk in this place. The reasons were twofold. I would like it to be used more often for this sort of event but, more importantly, this hall was here when another major revolution began in this country, I am referring of course to the origins of Parliament.

In the days when it was founded, this was a very different country. News travelled slowly and people living in outlying districts would learn of changes which might have profound effects on their lives days, months or years after. Sometimes they might never find out why they had lost their livelihoods or their lands and had been handed the profession of beggar."

"The King was omnipotent, able to act without any consideration for anyone but himself. The arbitrary imposition of taxes to permit the monarch to spend more money on himself and his household was little more than theft. The income of the King could also be reduced, as happened when Cardinal Wolsey raised taxes to such an extreme that businesses failed and men were thrown out of work. That experience should have provided a warning to our own politicians, but unfortunately they either do not know about it or choose to ignore it because the pattern is that taxes inexorably increase."

"The King needed enormous sums of money to fight his battles to settle a personal grudge. That could not be accomplished without loss of life of his subjects and of his opponents. To limit the power of the Monarch, Parliament was formed ostensibly to act for the people. I say ostensibly because its real aim was to act for the welfare of the barons."

"The Monarch and Royalty are now anachronisms, having no effective authority and being little more than part of the entertainment industry."

"The powerlessness of the monarchy is obvious to us all, but what is less well recognised is that Parliament is itself emasculated. I mentioned the poor communication of centuries ago. We can now broadcast news within seconds of events occurring and are able to receive the response of the people almost as quickly. This interview is being televised and audiences at home watching me will hear my voice even before you who are sitting at the back of the hall. For anyone who has the stomach for it, Parliament is also broadcast."

He took a drink so that the audience would have time to consider what he had said. He saw with gratification that there were some frowns on their faces.

Reid took the opportunity of the pause to ask. "You're not saying, are you, that there is no need for a debating forum where educated, informed people can analyse events, draw conclusions and make decisions?" he said with a grin.

"I notice that some of you are smiling at what Reid asked," Jake said, "amused because you know that Parliament is not like that. Any intelligent person listening to the debates in the House of Commons needs only a few minutes to realise that MPs are restricted by Party policy and must bend their own views accordingly."

"The rules, although never written down, are well understood by the participants. The weapons are the sneer, the snigger, the shout and the occasional raised fist. A loud and headmasterly voice is valuable as is the ability to feign righteous indignation on behalf of the oppressed and 'hard working' members of the public. To enter into impartial discussion would be considered a weakness. As a game aimed at selecting the most aggressive or even amusing speaker, it would have some point but as a method of government it is ineffective."

"Debate in the House of Lords is less Party-centric and we are spared the 'yah-boo-sucks' that is the inevitable accompaniment of speeches in the Commons. But many of us are concerned about unelected peers being appointed to Ministerial positions without any consultation with the electorate."

"The odd thing is that we accept the political structure we have inherited without seriously considering that there is an alternative." Jake had a pile of papers on the lectern in front of him and, although he was speaking without notes he deliberately looked them over to create a diversion.

Reid held up a card which said 'fifteen minutes left'. With a slight smile, Jake nodded at Reid and continued.

"Not only is Parliament unnecessary, it is also wasteful and positively destructive. Its function should be to consider the good of the community, but we all know that primary motivation is the livelihood of politicians."

"I recognise that there are many entirely sincere politicians but the system does not admire sincerity. Ruthlessness, aggression and verbal dexterity are much more highly regarded. This is why we have so many MPs from the legal profession whose skills are with words. Few have any experience of manufacturing, mining or making a tangible advance in the nation's capital; many have gained wealth by moving finance around or are from the legal and accounting profession."

"It is a truism that a lawyer can be paid hundreds of times more than a farm labourer and yet whereas most of us survive without the lawyer, we would quickly starve without the produce of the farm labourer. Society could not function without a legal framework and correct interpretation of the law by lawyers who can save much more than their fees, but the imbalance in society concerns many of us who see only unfairness."

"Many of us are able to understand the tides in society better than those we elect to represent our views. Yet we tolerate a situation in which we are allowed only to put a cross on a piece of paper to set in motion a machine which will run for five years, during which time it is not considered that Parliament needs any guidance from us. We are repeatedly told that the system is democratic. What does democracy mean when there is only a choice between three prospective candidates? Most of us would not choose the policies the parties have devised if there were real democracy. If the candidates were truthful, many of them would admit that the policies they follow so obediently are not their own." He paused to take a drink of the water in front of him and gauge the reactions in the audience.

To change the tempo, he looked at Reid to indicate that he would like to be asked a question.

"If I may summarise Jake," Reid said, "We are governed by people we would not choose if we were given a free voice, and these people carry out policies which do not represent our opinions and which we are powerless to influence, once an election has been held." Reid said.

Jake nodded. "I know that the committed will argue that we have access to our MPs and that it is their duty to make our views known in Parliament. But how many of us can remember when our representatives made a speech in the Commons. We rarely speak to our M.P.s unless we have a personal grievance. Many of you, I am sure will have written directly to ministers suggesting alternative policies, and have received a standard reply. 'The Minister thanks you for your suggestion but, as you will understand, he is very busy and will reply later.' Later means about a month when, if you are lucky, a letter comes from his secretary which effectively says 'thanks but no thanks'."

"It would be even less effective to ask your M.P. to change the policy of the Prime Minister or the Cabinet, because MPs know their opinions could influence their own careers. If Ministers rock the boat so much that it is in danger of sinking, they will be thrown out in what appears to be a civilised way. Sometimes they resign on the pretext of a sudden attack of ill health. In rare cases they are sacked, but the party machine, fearing a debilitating scandal, ensures that the P.M. writes them a letter praising their contribution. Intriguingly it gets published in the newspapers sometimes even before the recipient has read it."

"We also accept the ridiculous situations in which ministers who are expected to be experts in Education, Industry, Environment, etc., after often only a short period in office are expected overnight to become experts in Transport, Health, or Finance."

"How many of you with important positions in industry or commerce could leave your job in one day to someone who has no knowledge of what you have been doing while you take up his responsibilities. If the minister has personal reservations about the way the Ministry was run before taking it over, it is considered unethical for him to express such opinions."

It is argued that the Minister is only a figurehead and that civil servants actually determine and carry out policy. In which case it leaves one wondering why we need figureheads. Perhaps it allows the Opposition the pleasure of seeing Government ministers 'lambasted' in Parliament. If the minister's party loses the election, every opportunity to denigrate the newly elected minister must be taken."

Jake saw that Reid was signalling he would like to say something, so he picked up his papers and sat back.

"Thank you Jake," Reid said after the applause had subsided. "Let me just go over what I understand from your talk and I will include points from your articles which you have not had time to raise this evening." He looked down at his notes.

"You point out that we have members in Parliament to represent us who are there to further their own interests. Often they seek to be elected because they have no other platform on which to exercise their power hunger. Some appear to have the emotional maturity of children as judged by their behaviour during debate. Listening to a parliamentary broadcast is sufficient to make thinking people despair. We have inherited a structure which cannot work because MPs and ministers are inhibited from taking unpopular but critically important decisions because they might lose the support of vested interests and they want to be re-elected. Have I understood you correctly?"

"Thank you, Reid, I couldn't have said it better myself."

"There is time for you to continue, Jake."

Jake paused for a long moment while he looked up at the decorated ceiling, as if for inspiration, before saying "There is no room for subtlety in the speeches of MPs. They are haunted by bogeymen and fairy princesses. The bogeymen work for the opposition and the fairy princesses for their own side. We might query how it can be that one party is always right in its own judgement whereas, to the opposition, it is always wrong? Could it be that they are playing a game, or would you think me too cynical to suggest that? Now there is nothing wrong with playing a game but we pay them to govern, not to amuse us."

"Go to the visitors' gallery and see the small number of members who actually sit through the tedious charade they call debating but should more accurately be called 'posturing'."

Reid interceded again. "In one article you said we are suffering from Collective Delusion?"

Jake nodded. "We are so beguiled by the parliamentary system and the arguments put forward in its support under the oft repeated word 'democracy' that we never question why we continue to give our taxes to support a structure which demonstrably works to our detriment. Generally we are so disinterested in Parliament that a large number of us do not vote in elections. The victorious party is often elected by a minority of the population and we are so disillusioned that as few as one in four of us may have voted for the party in power."

"The only recourse of an aggrieved population is to march or riot in protest. Since for most of us this is abhorrent and, in any case, rarely effective, we can only attempt the equally futile exercise of collecting signatures for a petition."

"Do you not think that the democracy you criticise so effectively has not been a force for good?" Reid interrupted.

"Undoubtedly, in the past it has been of enormous benefit but, like so many institutions, it has become self-congratulatory, outmoded and tired. Whatever its past virtues, it is now an anachronism. Prime Ministers claim success in transforming the economy when they are impotent in the face of world market forces. Economic activity, inflation, employment and all other measures of the health of a nation, undergo global pressures. Take the example of Gordon Brown, who claimed that he had abolished boom and bust and had ushered in a 'Golden Age' of affluence. He was unable to see, or chose to ignore, the obvious fact that this 'affluence' was based entirely on borrowed time and finance. Within one year of his claim, the credit crisis was on us and he was blaming US sub-prime lending. Measured in terms of Gross National Product, some nations are more affluent than others but apart from China at the present time, they all follow the same sinusoidal curve, sometimes lagging, sometimes leading the rest."

"You have something to say about taxation I think." Reid said.

"Taxation is an effective tool of Parliament but the means by which it is collected is highly inefficient. The efficiency of taxation can be measured by a 'Cost of Collection over Value Ratio' we may simplify this to COVR. In an ideal world, tax should cost nothing to collect. If people were honest (and I'm not sufficiently naive to think they are) and they sent in their income tax through the post at their own cost, that would be the ideal. With human nature as it is, no one will pay a tax which can be avoided. We therefore need an army of tax inspectors who have powers which, in a democracy, we all find astonishing. VAT inspectors can practice the methods of a totalitarian regime and invade our premises at four in the morning in the name of tax collection. The cost of all these inspectors, assessors, clerical officers, buildings and reams of paper - the time employed by each one of us and particularly of companies in filling in returns, is enormous and if costed realistically, could even result in some taxes needing more to collect than the revenue they contribute. Any one of us here has paid taxes many times over, if I deal only with the well-known taxes which come easily to mind, they are, P.A.Y.E., V.A.T. Car Tax, Petrol Tax, Road Fund Licence, Business Rates, Corporation tax, National Health, Capital Gains Tax, Inheritance Tax, Stamp Duty. Eleven so far and I'm sure you can all think of many others. Taxation takes too much of the nation's resources and, in doing so it suppresses enterprise. It must be simplified and there are ways of doing this"

Reid signalled that he wanted to comment. "My job generally is to find errors but in the case of your tax ideas, I must admit that is difficult to criticise, if I understand you correctly." He turned his eyes up to the ceiling as though waiting for inspiration and then cast a glance at the clock before continuing. "So what is the alternative?"

Jake cleared his throat and took another drink of water. "As you will all know, many of the ideas I have talked about originated with Haig Skarn and he is the better man to talk about the mechanism by which taxation can be simplified. If he had been in this country, he would have given this talk but he won't return from his lecture tour in America for a month. You'll all have to come back here when he returns," he grinned at the audience. "I can tell you though that it is amazingly simple and, like all the best inventions, remarkable that no one has thought of it before. All taxes originate from wealth producers such as, for example, those who make motor cars, write software, buy and sell property, raise pigs, or any number of things which make society function. Haig's thesis is that only wealth producers should be taxed because they are the source of finance which provides the money to pay taxes of people they employ. The public and employees are able to pay their taxes because their income from the wealth producers is raised to provide an increment to cover these taxes."

Reid interrupted. "We did promise to have a few questions. He looked at the clock. "We probably have time for only two. He pointed to a well-dressed, middle aged man in the front who had raised his hand. "Can you explain why we and virtually all nations are happy to leave the direction of our lives in the hands of people in whom we have no confidence?" he asked. "We also accept that they act in their own self-interest, even manipulating economies to benefit their own parties. Is there a word which explains why have we not demanded a different system?"

"There is a word which describes our predicament." Jake said. "It is 'apathy'. We all know there must be a better way but we can't be bothered to do anything about it. Tonight you have all taken a step towards doing something about it. Mr. Skarn as you will probably have read hasn't yet given it a name. Perhaps you can concertedly come up with a name and email your suggestions to us." He raised his hands to include all the audience.

Reid looked round the sea of hands held up to ask questions and pointed to a striking looking older woman near the back.

When the microphone reached her, she said, "Our representatives argue that we, the general public are unable to make informed decisions."

"That would have been true in the thirteenth century when Simon de Montfort invited representatives from the various shires to 'parley' and thereby set up Parliament. Few people then had any education. As Dan Ilett has said we are using an organization as a global tool when it was only meant for a feudal society. Nowadays, we would dearly like to parley before our leaders make decisions on our behalf. I was an MP in the House in April 1999 when Deputy Prime Minister John Prescott stood in for Tony Blair. He was asked about the withholding tax which was aimed at preventing wealthy people avoiding taxation after putting their money offshore. Mr. Prescott obviously had not heard of the tax and thought it referred to people who were withholding their poll tax."

"He said, 'As Secretary of State for the Environment, that disastrous poll tax is one that I constantly have to deal with. You should bear in mind, that what we have now settled with the local authorities is the most generous settlement they have ever received!'"

The audience laughed and applauded. "As you said, Mr. Dearsey, we object to paying for the unqualified to amuse themselves at our expense."

Reid spoke when the applause subsided. "Thank you, Countess, as chairman, I should have cut you short but there didn't seem to be a pause when I could intercede." He smiled at her so that she would see that he was joking.

Reid pointed to a man in the front row with his hand raised. "We put our trust in the judgement of the people you describe. How many of us wanted to invade Iraq, Afghanistan or Libya? Do we still have no other resource than sending in gunboats and armies to kill innocent people and in the process suffer death and maiming of our own people? Our representatives convince themselves that we are unable to make judgements of that sort. They claim to have been given a mandate from us but no one ever asked me or anyone I know if we wanted to invade. Would Germany have attempted to defeat the world without the Kaiser or taken on the World powers with a certainty of defeat if the megalomaniac Hitler had not ordered it?"

"Politicians lead us into wars and after causing the deaths of vast numbers of people often come out of them personally unscathed."

Jake nodded. "I am, of course, in agreement with both of those questions. If," he smiled as he added as an aside, "they were meant to be questions. What I am saying may seem like old fashioned anarchy but I would be the last to suggest that we can exist without a government. We don't need politicians to waste their time debating subjects they don't fully understand and to bring in laws which are ill thought out. What Haig Skarn and I propose is not a lack of government, but a professional one. The nation demands that all other non-elected administrators such as judges, civil servants, teachers, doctors and so on should be trained and yet those who set policies for these critically important sections of the community need have no qualifications. To produce maximum gain for the nation we need efficient management by trained managers. So we would have an educationalist as the Minister for Education, a trained physician as Minister of Health, a transport specialist as Minister of Transport and so on."

He looked around as a few voices murmured. "I sense what you are thinking, would not these people also make mistakes. I don't deny that they would, they can be no more than fallible human beings but they would have a better understanding of the complexities of the decisions they have to make. We would never allow ourselves to have a surgical operation performed by a lawyer. Why then do we allow lawyers to decide on the resources that surgeons need? Why have we seen such a lack of decisiveness amongst European leaders over the Euro. One reason is the fear of losing an election, another is inexperience. The problems they have to deal with are highly complex. One Minister is reported to have said that the biggest thing he had looked after before was his constituency office but as a Minister he had to control a budget amounting to many billions. As MP Zac Goldsmith states, Parliament is dysfunctional, as he said in the Daily Telegraph of August 16th 2014, 'Politics is childish, superficial and rotten. I've seen people deliver powerful speeches and then vote with the government. You could replace many people in government with a laptop programmed to vote when needed'".

"We all have mobile phones, email and the internet so we can be consulted and can make our views known at any time. We do not need MPs to debate our interests, nor do we need elections or referenda."

"What we are proposing is indeed revolutionary and should be the subject of debate in the future so we would be pleased to see you at the next public meeting which will be held in two months."

Reid looked up at the clock, "I see that I have a choice, either I continue and lose the attention of some of you or we accept that there is a dictator which governs our lives - the stomach and it does need regular refreshment." There was a general laugh. "We allowed only a short time for questions deliberately because, as Jake has said, we want you to go away and debate amongst yourselves. Jake would be the first to confess that he does not know all the answers and concertedly we want your ideas for change. You will find the email address on your invitations. Thank you ladies and gentlemen, refreshments are in the reception."

Jake was pleased when the audience applauded loudly and quite a few stood while they were clapping. When he walked in to the side room, he was immediately surrounded by a large group, with most of them saying how pleased they were with what he had said. The nice looking older lady in an elegant red suit, whom Reid had called 'Countess', was asking him a question when he felt a hand squeeze his. Rhosa smiling her satisfaction stood on tiptoe and whispered in his ear.

"Marvellous, they were eating out of your hand," and turning to the questioner, she said, "my apologies, I was just congratulating Mr Dearsey on his speech."

"Deservedly, my dear; he has said things which should have been aired years ago. I'm Renda Margold, I was an MP for several years so I had plenty of time to despair of the system we have allowed ourselves to be saddled with. How can we possibly have informed debate when MPs have to accept only those policies adopted by their parties? Aristotle said you should choose your politicians from those with the most talent. We seem to have forgotten this and we choose those with the loudest voices."

Jake took the hand she proffered, a soft, delicate hand which held his with warmth "I resigned from the House – couldn't take the corruption any more. I don't mean bribery or, as they prefer to call it' sleaze'. It was the corruption of moral turpitude. My colleagues would subjugate their own principles and agree with what the Party wanted them to say even against their own judgement. This nation has no future unless we start to address issues honestly. We've lost our direction in a miasma of complacency. This once great country is now, as they say, a basket case and so bankrupt that we cannot afford to build the infrastructure we desperately need, and instead have to invite the Chinese and other nations to invest. Our people still have inventiveness, but our inventions go abroad." She stopped. "Sorry,

I'm dominating you. When you get to know me, you will find that I tend to do that. And I haven't allowed you to introduce yourself, Miss Cowen" she said, turning to Rhosa. "I sat behind you in the audience tonight and I just wanted to say that I saw you in that wonderful performance as Nerissa."

"Thank you, Countess," Rhosa said, instinctively bowing her head.

"Please, not Countess; the accident of my birth should not command respect. And certainly don't bow - call me Renda, please." She looked at her watch. "Time to snatch a drink." She gave Jake her card and took his. "Will you call me? I'd like to talk some more with you. Better still, I'll call you."

He took the card and as he walked beside her, back into the hall said "I should like that."

As he walked through the door, the Countess stood spontaneously and applauded. Hearing her, the others in the room stood and joined her. Reid called Jake to return to the platform.

Rhosa was behind him, gave his hand another squeeze and whispered, "Love you."

Guided by Reid, he again mounted the stairs to the stage. But even as he did, his thoughts were on Rhosa and the years not spent with her. In no other relationship had he felt so cared for. He stood in front of the audience put his hands up and nodded appreciation at the applause.

He turned to leave but had to turn back while the audience continued applauding.

Gradually the applause subsided and, with a smile and a slight bow, he left.

CHAPTER 19

A loud knock on the door of his study roused Jacob from a period of meditation, in which he had been unaware of where or who he was. It took him a few moments to waken to the sound of footsteps going away from his door. Pulling himself out of the chair with difficulty, he opened the door to see the back of Mistress Darkall.

"Mistress," he called but he heard her door being closed and was left wondering why she chose not to hear him.

Going to the closed door, he knocked and, after a few seconds, she tearfully appeared.

"Mistress, I am sorry, I was in another world. Did you want me?"

She looked flustered. "Sir, it is the time you asked me to call you."

Still not fully conscious, Jacob asked. "I... did?"

"It makes no matter, sir."

"Of course," his face cleared, "I am sorry it is time for learning. Do come downstairs and we will start. And bring us both some of that mead you made from the honey Mrs. Callenda gave us."

When she came downstairs, he took her arm. As his hand touched her bare skin he felt excited and wondered if she felt the same when, momentarily, she looked into his eyes and then as rapidly looked away.

In his office he sat her down and went to get the mead from the kitchen. When he returned, she was sitting uneasily with her hands in her lap. He passed her a horn cup which he had filled with the mead. She waited for him to drink before she raised the cup to her lips.

He had not planned the lesson, which he hoped would be more of a conversation, and pondered with his hand on his chin before he spoke. "Mistress," he said. "Let me repeat something we've talked about before; do you look around you and wonder why man is so far advanced?"

She stared at him, waiting for him to continue.

"Look at any animal - that dog out there," he pointed out of the window, "or that performing bear you can see at the corner of the road with his master."

She got up and looked through the window before answering. "Your meanin' I suppose, sir, is that they are not like we."

"Exactly; would it not be a surprise if that bear walked off and cooked himself a meal, or if that dog had made this mead? Or the horse that has just gone by, stopped to talk to that other horse you can see coming this way now with a rider on its back?"

"It would, sir," she said with a smile playing round her lips.

"I'm glad to see you smile, Mistress. It would indeed be strange if any of those things happened." He took a drink of the mead from the cup in his hand and she again followed him. "I know I've asked before but it is good to look at things in different ways. What makes us different from those animals?"

She looked down at her clothes.

"You are right, one of the things that marks us as different is the way we look and dress. But much more important is the fact that we have speech. I suspect that animals may communicate with each other but in a simpler manner. When you were going to make this mead, you had never made it before. I did not know how to do it, so we asked Mrs. Callenda. She told you how and next time you make it, you will not need her."

She frowned, "Sir?"

"When I first went to Italy, I could understand nothing but I found a teacher and now I too can speak to the Italians, not well but enough for business.

It is our ability to talk which enables us to pass on to others what we need to know - the easiest way to light this fire and how to cook meat in a way I like. I can tell you about places I have been to, like Florence. No animal has words like us and so they do not cook, make clothes, make mead or..." he picked up the cup and held it for her to look at, "make things like this. Do you see, Mistress?"

"I do see what you are saying, sir."

"It is the knowledge of how to do things which takes us past animals. No other creature comes anywhere near us."

"We aren't animals, sir."

"I have watched them closely and I find that they have feelings like us. They bear young, suckle them and teach them how to find food and to live in a difficult world. They fight and kill as we do but I have seen that they also love and suffer sadness when one of them dies. The one thing that marks animals as different is that they may in their grunts and squeaks and chirps be talking but it is very simple whereas we – as I am doing now – can talk about such varied subjects as pain, love, emotion or practical things like how to make the chair you are sitting on, and philosophical ideas like those of Aristotle."

She leaned forward enquiringly.

"Aristotle I have mentioned before, he was one of the Greek thinkers; he died many hundreds of years ago and seems to have considered almost every, including how to treat illnesses."

"And to cure you, Sir?"

"Thank you for thinking of me but, no, there is no cure for my strangeness that I know. Why do you ask, have I been afflicted again?"

"When I came to you this day, sir, you needed care."

"Did I, I thought I was just sleeping."

"Sir, no, I found you on the floor."

"Contorted?"

She nodded although she was not sure that she knew what he meant. "Bent up." He asked,

"I feel well now. When I woke, I was in the chair. I must thank you for putting me there."

She bowed her head in acknowledgement.

"Mistress, there is something I want to ask you."

"Sir?" she said, momentarily looking worried.

Seeing her concern, he said. "No, nothing serious it's just that I think it is time we changed the way we speak to each other," he paused, casting his eyes round the room as he searched for words. "I have called you 'Mistress' and you have called me 'sir or Mr. D'Arcy' for long enough, don't you think?" He raised his eyebrows enquiringly.

"What are you saying, sir?"

It was Jacob's turn to be tongue tied. "I think we need a name for you. Would you mind if I called you a short version of Mistress? Mistry, for instance."

"That sounds nice, sir. Silda was the only name I had and it was made up by Benjy who did not want anyone else to use it."

"Did your parents not want you to have a name?"

"Never had a mother that I knew since I was about three summers and they out there said my father took up with another woman 'fore I was born."

"My dear," Jacob put his hand on hers noticing with pleasure that she did not withdraw it. "We must make up for that and a name will be a start. From now on, I think you should be called Mistry. Mistry Darkall." He smiled at her. And she smiled back with pleasure. "I'm glad you like it. The name is you."

"Sir?"

"Now you have a full name that you like, it will shape your personality. It will identify you. You will cease to be that young woman who lived on the streets. We should begin your life from the day you came to this house."

The newly named Mistry hesitated. "Glad I am to have a name and start again but… you said the name will shape me but I don't want to forget my man and the life we had."

"I am sorry; I was forgetting your man who meant so much to you. Of course you must not forget him. Would you prefer to be called by his name for you?"

"You are kind to me, Mr. D'Arcy. My man is gone. I don't use the name he gave me any more. I will be Mistry." She leaned forward and, without thinking, kissed Jacob's hand. Realising what she had done, she coloured slightly.

"Mistress…" He corrected himself and self-consciously said. "Mistry," and noticed that she responded to her name with a slight smile. "In business, there are ways we must use names."

"How, Sir?"

"You will remain Mistress Darkall and I Mr. D'Arcy. I will show you how I write in my letters to my customers and we may get you to meet customers."

"But I will not know what to say."

"Gradually you will learn. Outside of business I will call you by your first name, Mistry, and you should do the same for me. My first name is Jacob."

"Sir, don't think I could do that. What'd your friends think?"

"When my friends and others are here, then you should call me 'sir'. But when we are in each other's company, I will be Jacob. Can you say that now?"

At first, she put her hand to her mouth but then drew it away and said in a low and uncertain voice. "Jacob."

The way she said his name sent a thrill through his body and he asked. "Can you say it again?"

This time she was more confident. She looked straight at him and said. "Jacob" and again he felt a pleasure which he had never known with Isabel. They looked directly at each other for an instant – brief enough for a message to pass between them before her eyes were cast down and her hands were folded in her lap. There was a momentary awkwardness before he spoke.

"We were talking about humans; for convenience, we use the term 'man' but that also includes women."

"But women is different, ain't they?"

Jacob nodded. "Physical differences but apart from that, my view is that men and women are otherwise equal."

Mistry frowned.

"I see you frowning which means you don't agree?"

"I was frowning because what you said is so different from what most people think." She looked into the distance before

212

continuing. "Is what you are saying like a Rinascita? Michael Dalgett told me it brought about a complete change in attitude."

Jacob was so amazed that he could think of nothing to say. He rested his chin on his hand and thought for a long time. "You are right, Mistry. Because men are physically stronger they have used this strength to push women down so that they even think themselves to be lower than men."

"Is't not so... Jacob?" she asked.

"Most men would disagree with me, as would many women, I think. But, no, it is not so."

Mistry looked surprised.

Seeing this, Jacob said. "I am talking about qualities which you have; I can see that there is a talent in you which has not been developed, but when it is it will surprise you."

"How, sir?"

"Jacob." He corrected.

"...Jacob," she said with hesitation.

"In business I have to be a good judge and I judged that you were different from the other women who wanted to work here. I saw, from the first day you came into the house with what I can only describe as the smell of the streets on you, looking unclean and unwashed. I saw in your eyes a look of... I can only describe it as intelligence." He turned in his chair to look at her, "I see it when I teach you about things which interest me."

"What be they... Jacob?"

"They be..." He said in mimicry of her. "You mean, what are they."

"I do," she hung her head slightly at what she saw as a rebuke.

"Don't be upset, Mistry. There will be many times when I correct you but it is all part of learning." He put his hand on hers to make contact, "but you asked what interests me."

He stood up and, walking to the front door, opened it and beckoned for her to come with him." he pointed at the crowd of people. "That life out there, those people hurrying by; they interest me more than anything else."

She looked out and waited for him to explain. "There, you see that man with the load on his back. What does it mean?"

"I've carried things like that and I feel a pain here." She pointed at her back.

"I've never had to carry such loads. But I can sense the sort of person that man is. I see that he has a look of intelligence. Yet he has been born to toil and I have been born to use only my brain and to watch from my window," Jacob grinned, "but I don't just watch, I try to think what he might be thinking. I want to know what makes him who he is. Did he choose to be what he is? I think he did not. What I would like you to think about is that we all have an ability to choose."

"Is't so, sir... Jacob?" she corrected herself.

"You look surprised, as though you think we have no choice. Looking at that man as he turns the corner and goes out of sight it would seem that his life is controlled. But he has choice."

"But I been there aside that man; he do what he does cause he casn't do no other."

"I'll explain. He has first the choice to live or to die, does he not?"

"Kill hisself?" she asked.

"That is so. But that is only one thing. Does he have children?"

"Eight little 'uns he have had, three died. Five are left"

"And they keep him poor, do they not?"

"That they do."

"You know how they come. You know that he could have decided to have them or not. Did you want to have children?"

"I did not; I'd never have enough to feed 'em."

"And that was your choice. If you had had a few children, you would not have been able to come to me as housekeeper. You may not have planned to do that but you did. That is what I am saying, even though we don't realise it, we all have choices which control our

214

lives." He walked to the shelves in his reading room and took a book down as Mistry closed the door and followed him.

"This is a book by a philosopher. I turn to him when I am full of doubt."

"You?" she raised her eyebrows again. "...doubt?"

"It is a curse I have to bear."

"How so?"

"My wife died from what the physician had first told me was a passing fever. I blame myself for her dying. Was there not something in all these books?" he waved his hand at the shelves. "Or could my friends know of a potion. One of our Scientificals was working on a medicine but he died in the last fever. What he was working on... it might have saved her?"

"You loved her... Jacob."

"I...," he hesitated wanting to say. 'I didn't know what love meant until I met you' but could not bring himself to say what he felt. "Isabel seemed right for me and I seemed right for her. We married without love but when she died I realised how much we had grown together."

"Sorry I am to hear that, Jacob," she said quietly, "I... my man died and left me empty. I wanted to die every day that I lived until... I... I came here."

"Your pain would have been even more than mine because you saw him being destroyed by a mob aroused by a lout in the garb of a priest."

He picked up the book and handed it to her. "You will find many answers in this book, so we must carry on with your reading lessons."

Mistry took the book and opened the pages slowly. "I can see that there is writing on these pages and I can read some of the words."

Jacob took the book back and from it took out a piece of paper which marked a page. "You will know that I am the fortunate possessor of a little money. I could have spent it on Hedonism - seeking wild pleasures – women, drink or gluttony - but I chose to follow the teachings of the philosopher Epicurus whose book this is.

I have an affliction which could have driven me to despair but I followed his Aponia principle which comes from limiting the desires within us. The highest pleasures come from knowledge, friendship and a virtuous and temperate life. Epicurus argued that one should not eat too richly, for it could lead to dissatisfaction if at some stage in your life you could not afford the same things. He also said that love making could lead to increased lust."

"It do sir, I've seen it. The man of the house where I did work had a passion for women, there were always several in the house and he would take one to bed every night and sometimes during the day. I know the women hated him and what he did but they could not say so for fear of being throwed out."

"Well, I think you are misguided as was Epicurus. God gave us the gift so that we can procreate."

Mistry nodded in understanding and then asked. "Why did you never have no childer?"

He picked up the book and idly turned a few pages. "My illness, you see…" He turned a few more pages trying to make it appear that he was reading. Then he looked up and said. "Isabel was afraid…"

"Afraid?" Mistry asked, "of bedding?"

"She was afraid that our children would have my illness."

"Jacob, poor man, how…?" she stopped herself thinking she was being too inquisitive.

"Did we prevent children?" He looked out of the window behind him. "I had a preventive made – from the intestine of a sheep. But it was little used…Isabel had no interest."

Mistry nodded. "Sad, you would've bin good with childer."

Jacob wanted to say, "Still might," but refrained – instead he said. "Isabel also read Epicurus."

"And?"

"Yes, she believed what he said about abstinence."

Again she said. "Poor man," and without thinking, put her hand on his for a moment but took it away when she realised what she had done.

216

He stood up and reached for another book. "This is not mine, I am looking after it for a friend...he has been imprisoned."

"Stealin'?"

"He committed no crime you would recognise." he sat down beside her, "he was foolish enough to complain in church that the priest was fatter than any of his parishioners at a time when some had died from starvation."

"But that be so, I seen that priest. He wobbles when he do walk."

"The Church considered that what my friend said was blasphemous."

CHAPTER 20

'The Merchant' did not run for long, but it and the television advertising which Rhosa did as a result of it, brought in a useful amount of money.

During the run, her aunt, the sister of her stepfather, of whom she had been particularly fond, died, leaving her a large sum of money. Jake was in the audience the evening that she heard of her aunt's death. Before she went on, he opened the door to her dressing room to find her distraught and weeping. "She was the sweetest of women. Always put herself second to others and particularly to me. It was she who paid for all my acting lessons. Without her I would have been a P.A. and no more than an echo of someone else. She never married; I think I was the daughter she always wanted. If ever I suffered a setback, she would fold her arms round me and kiss my head. Whenever I went on stage I felt as though her arms supported me. I owe her so much. If I tried to thank her, she said 'pay me back when you make some money or pay me back with your success - it never happened to me, Rhosa, but it gives me great happiness to see you growing'."

Rhosa turned her tear streaked face to Jake. "She has gone Jake. I never knew how much of her was me until now. Put your arms round me, I feel so empty without her."

Jake was sure she would not be able to do the performance but when she had put her makeup on, she assumed the personality of Nerissa. When she walked onto the stage, she gave the performance of her life. It happened to be the night when without his knowing, Anthony Garden, an ex-colleague of Jake's had been invited to the show.

Jake had known this television producer for many years but had lost touch as their paths had gone in different directions. Jake bumped into him in the bar looking excited. "Who is that girl; I'm sure I've seen her before in a restaurant with you?" he asked.

"Nerissa, you mean?" Jake asked.

"Of course, who else? She dazzles, doesn't she."

"Her name is Rhosa Cowen," Jake said.

Anthony sensed a reticence in Jake and said. "Come on, Jake, I can see her name in the programme as well as you. Why have I never heard of her before now. She's Nerissa personified. The rest of the cast are good but not outstanding. The play only works when she is on stage. Tell me how you know her, for God's sake?"

"I knew her ten years ago and recently met her again."

"I want to talk to her."

Jake nodded but his reluctance was obvious to Anthony.

"Come on Jake, you can't keep her to yourself, she's enchanting. Fix it for me to meet her. I may have a part for her."

Jake got a message to Rhosa's dressing room. He and Anthony walked to Jake's club, a short distance from the theatre where he frequently waited for Rhosa after shows. As long as Jake had known him, Anthony had always been unable to relax, it was all Jake could do to get him to sit and drink his Martini while they waited. Even while drinking he constantly looked at his watch, making Jake think he would get up and go before Rhosa arrived.

When she walked in, she was still Nerissa; it always took her a long time after a play for the chameleon to change colour and become Rhosa again. Anthony was as overcome with the way she looked as Jake was. He flung his arms round her and then, taking them both by surprise, looking straight into her eyes, he began Bassanio's speech from the Merchant.

"Madam, you have bereft me of all words… my blood speaks to you in my veins; and there is such confusion in my powers; as after some oration fairly spoke…' "

When he had finished Rhosa replied as Nerissa, "that have stood by and seen our wishes prosper, to cry, good joy…'."

When she stopped, he put his arms around her again. There was such empathy between them that Jake began to feel a tinge of jealousy, particularly when they went into a quiet corner to talk, leaving him rolling his glass between his fingers. He overheard that Anthony wanted Rhosa to be in a production he was doing of a new play, the first script from an unknown writer. "Very unusual

Existentialist theme." he told Rhosa, "deals with the ability the brain has to select its own destiny." Rhosa nodded and her eyes lit up.

Jake noticed that over the next few days, she talked a lot about Anthony and each time she did, another barb entered his skin. By that time he was not just in love - love happens a lot of times – this was far more. He was enchanted, besotted, obsessed but even those words were not adequate to describe the constant torment he was in. He kept thinking about the poetry of Sappho, describing love as an illness. For Jake it was worse - most illnesses have a palliative but the pain he felt was with him every waking moment. If he got up at night and she was not beside him, he was filled with fear that she was with someone else.

Rhosa always slept badly and, not wanting to disturb him, would often go downstairs to read. If he went down to see her, she would look up as he pushed open the door and for an instant it was as though he could see into her troubled soul, filled with so many fears. During the day she could rationalise them but not at night. Many times he would sit beside her and put his arms round her. She would look up and smile but it would be her actress's smile. He always knew that there was something disturbing her. At three o'clock one morning, he had found her sitting, staring at herself in the mirror. He asked her what the problem was.

"It's happening to me again, Jay."

"What is happening?"

"The terrors."

"When you are on stage? I thought you'd got over it."

"I had, but over the last few weeks it has come back and it's worse than ever. Last week when I was doing that last one woman recital, you must have noticed I was shaking with fear. You were in the audience; didn't you see? I froze, I just couldn't move. I wanted to do a Daniel Day-Lewis and run off stage and never come back."

"I didn't notice and I'm sure the audience didn't. Do you mean when you screamed out? That was in the script wasn't it."

"No it wasn't; I screamed because I couldn't stop myself."

"Well it was very effective. You should keep it in the act the next time you do it."

"If there is a next time. I haven't heard from my agent since."

Sometimes his presence was enough to release the barriers and she would sit back, close her eyes and remain silent. One night he tried to get her to talk but it was pointless, she was unable to speak and shook her head as though she was afraid that even articulating what was causing her distress would precipitate a crisis for her. The following day she told him, "I had nightmares about my ex-husband."

Another night when he went to her, he found her looking into a mirror, he had crept quietly down the stairs and she had not heard him open the door on her. She looked up surprised when he asked her if she was ok.

"What can I do about my nose," she said, "I am an actress and I must be attractive, but this nose would qualify me to play Shylock. I've waited long enough and now I've definitely decided I am going to have plastic surgery."

He was completely at a loss for a reply, she always looked lovely and he had never analysed why. He'd never even noticed her nose and now that he did, it certainly didn't seem to need any work done on it.

He had become used to her intermittent lack of confidence. Sometimes it became personified and she would complain about the size of her legs, her backside or her breasts.

He sat down on the floor beside her, took the mirror from her, held her face in his hands and looked into her eyes.

"How do I start," he said, giving himself time to think. "Well - you are the most attractive woman I know. When I sit opposite you I am looking at a work of art. I wonder at my luck in finding you again. I experience a peace just being in your presence and, when you smile at me, those things which used to worry me disappear.

When you talk about having your nose remodelled it is almost like suggesting that someone should scratch away the surface of a great work of art, disfiguring it and taking away its flawless appearance. God, Rhosa, what more do you want. Not only are you lovely to look at you have a personality to match. Do not change anything."

She smiled weekly. "'My Funny Valentine' you mean?"

He saw that she was listening and to break her mood, continued saying anything that came into his head. "You told me that we are a composite of so many things - school, childhood memories, sometimes little things which friends or acquaintances have said or we have overheard. The most important part of that composite personality is the face we show to the world. The face and the personality are inseparable and if you alter the face, you may alter the personality, I don't want you to take that risk, I like you just the way you are."

Rhosa nodded tentatively so Jake carried on. "Sometimes remodelling goes wrong and the work of art may never be the same again. That would be tragic. Your looks are as near perfect as anyone could hope for. Don't do it, dear girl, you don't need it. Just look at the effect you had on Anthony. Whenever we go anywhere together, I see so many other men drooling. I waited ten years outside in the cold, looking in through a window into a room from which you were absent, going through many relationships hoping I would be able to replace what I lost that day you turned up with Jed on your arm."

It worked; for once he was able to convince her and dispel her self-criticism. He picked up the mirror, held it in front of her. She looked at herself then back at him and smiled.

"Ok, perhaps I'll forget about it for now," she took his hand and kissed it, "why did I have to spend all those empty years without you, Jake, God must have known I needed you more than anything else," she looked up in the air and said, "thank you God for getting it right at last."

There were many other times when he could not change her mood and he would try talking about anything, it didn't matter what - his visit to Bhutan in search of solace during the marriage difficulties with Sabel - the journey up the Nile to marvel at the Egyptian ruins and to be amazed at the agriculture on the banks of the river, unchanged for thousands of years. She would transfer her distress at her own problems to concerns about the people he told her about, like the poverty of coffee pickers in Ethiopia paid so little that they could not save enough to afford even one cup of Starbucks coffee.

"How terrible to fall into a crude bed with aching limbs after a long day of physical effort. Too tired to laugh, sing, dance or think about anything except work…"

He would then have to dispel the guilt she felt for impoverished agricultural workers but this was easier than resolving the sorrows that hid in his own mind

After the meeting with Anthony and her obvious pleasure at conversation with the cultured man who held some of the keys to her future, his concerns grew. When he was suffering severe pangs of self-doubt he tormented himself wondering if she was with him because he happened to come into her life at a time when she needed someone. He had never before needed to look for signs - was that a smile of love or a smile of politeness – did the caress mean anything or was it nothing more than convention. He wondered many times about what she called her impotence and whether it was only with him. He wanted to ask Rhosa if she loved him but he knew that would be the worst thing to do – the last cry of a passé lover.

Some nights when she could not sleep she would say "I'd like a drink."

"Chocolate?"

"Whisky would be nice, it might make me relax."

His mood would sink - so often he would find she had alcohol on her breath. He knew enough to be concerned about the insidious way alcohol takes over a life. He had witnessed his first wife's decline into deceitfulness, the strong smell of peppermint around her which never did conceal what she had drunk. He had seen a woman; considerate and intelligent disappear to be replaced by a screaming harridan and dreaded it happening to Rhosa.

"I think you would be better with a milky drink, the calcium will make you sleep."

He was often able to convince her and would go off to the kitchen, returning with the hot drink.

"Could I have just a spoonful of whisky in it?" she would ask and he would go into the kitchen and put in only half a spoonful, take it up to bed for her to drink and wait till her heavy breathing told him she was asleep.

She let him down twice more in the following month. Once to celebrate an article on her in a Sunday colour supplement, he had prepared one of her favourite meals and got it all ready for eight when she had told him she would be back. At ten she turned up. She had obviously had a good evening and had forgotten that he was doing something special for her. She burst into the house and noticed the cooking smells. When she did, she put her hand over her mouth and poured out apologies.

Having sat for two hours not knowing what to do, Jake was angry but could not show it because of his fear that he was moving from conductor to first violin in her orchestra and he was being replaced by Anthony.

"Where have you been?" he merely asked casually.

"Anthony kept taking me over that difficult bit in the third act. You know the one where her husband had just walked out."

He nodded coolly. "I cooked you stroganoff, the sort you like."

"I'm not too late am I?" She looked tearful as she realised what she had done and how it must hurt him. "When we get stuck into something like that act three, time disappears; it's hellishly hard. I am terribly sorry, Jay, honestly, everything slipped my mind."

Strangely, he was not surprised that she was late and without thinking, had chosen to cook stroganoff, a meal that can be kept warm without drying out.

"Not too late. Sit down; I've got a nice wine I've already opened to let it breathe. I'll pour you a glass to have with the meal."

They ate in silence and, when Rhosa consumed very little, Jake assumed she had eaten with Anthony. When they had finished eating, she moved her chair so that she could sit beside him. She took his hand and said. "There is something I have to tell you."

Her words had an ominous tone, for him and without thinking he took his hand away which caused her to look surprised.

"About Anthony?" he asked.

"Yes, how did you know?"

"You are two hours late, you've been with him, it doesn't require a great deal of imagination. I've noticed how much time you are spending with him; it can't all be because he is helping you learn your part."

Carefully he put down his cutlery on his plate. "I expect he asked you to live with him somewhere," he was drained of emotion and prepared for her to tell him the worst, "and you have accepted."

Rhosa winced, screwing up her eyes in pain at what he had said. "Do you have so little faith in me, Jake?"

"Why, isn't that what happened?"

"The first bit is right. He has asked - you know he is married with two young kids don't you? The second bit is not right. I could never even think of living with him."

Jake had a job to control his reaction to what she was saying, he wanted to leap on the table and dance but he contented himself with throwing his arms round her.

She pushed him away. "Why are you surprised, did you really think I would prefer him to you? There are times when you are stupid, Jay. He is part of business."

"You've talked so much about him."

Suddenly she felt sad at the realisation that Jay had suffered because of a misunderstanding. She put her head on his shoulder.

"Just professional, there has never been anything more."

"But for an actress, he has a lot going for him," he said, "he's attractive, intelligent, well off and he could give you opportunities not many other men could."

"You want to know what I think of him?" she said, sitting up straight. "The man is creepy; so unctuous, so full of false compliments, he almost makes my flesh crawl. It was obvious what he wanted from the first time I spoke to him. He has cultivated heavily lidded eyes which he thinks are sexy. I just find him blatant." She put her elbows on the table and looked at the painting on the wall. "When you pay me a compliment, Jay, I know it's real, when he does, it is so obviously insincere. He has no give in his life, it is all take. I've met some selfish men in my stage career but never anyone quite like him. You see him preening all the time; catching sight of himself in a mirror, or anything that reflects."

She saw Jake smiling. "Yes, I mean it; he took me to a flashy bar for a drink after rehearsal one afternoon. Everything in the room was either a mirror or polished like a mirror. I had a job not to laugh it was so obvious that he loved the place because there were so many reflections of him wherever he turned. While we drank, he literally picked up the beer mat and looked at his hair to make sure it was perfect." She turned to put her hand in Jake's, "I'm flattered that you worried about me but… you <u>are</u> an old silly," she leaned over and kissed him behind the ear. How just a few words can change us, he thought, in that moment he felt as though he could fly.

Instead he took her upstairs to bed and left the dishes on the table till the morning.

He had been so concerned that he had lain awake many nights thinking about her, becoming so tired that he couldn't stop imagining her with her ex-husband or other men she had told him about.

He doubted if she always knew what happened to her in her alcohol confused states. Jake pictured her as he had known her when she was nineteen in Stratford when there was an easily aroused sexuality in her. At what stage did she lose her desire? Was it as she said that she had been so badly treated by her ex husband or was it simply that he was too old and she just found him physically unattractive.

One week end between rehearsals he had taken her to the faded but romantic Brighton.

When they got back to Firenze House she said as they got into bed. "I've had a lovely day, sorry I slept most of the journey back, I'm always like that on trains. Did I see you writing notes?"

"Remember that Art Deco café in Brighton."

"Yes, such a charming place."

"You said to me I should write down what I thought about the place because I might be able to use it."

"You'll use it somewhere, I'm sure."

"I jotted down a few notes after you met that old lady who kept you talking about how her Brighton had gone from the genteel place she had known as a girl to being drug ridden. The Trenchard magazine wants me to write something on social change and it will give me a theme."

Jake had settled his head on the pillow. "So many times I thank whatever it was that decided you to go to the pub that night," he said sleepily.

"It wasn't just chance, Jay."

"What does that mean?"

"A friend had told me she had seen you drinking there; I had to go three evenings before you finally walked in."

She pulled herself down beside him and in a whisper said, "I know that you must suffer, Jay. Give me time and I'll get over it, I know I will."

He pulled her close.

He was just drifting off when she said. "I was just thinking, Jay," she raised herself on her elbow so that he looked up at her. "Who is that other painting of - the one you moved downstairs, that woman wearing a hat? Young and, in a way quite beautiful - I've been sub-consciously aware of her many times but I only really thought about Jacob D'Arcy. I was looking at her tonight while we were talking; she's got those penetrating eyes which make me think she must have been something in her time."

"She came with the house, like the painting of the man. I never found out who she was, I just know about the covenant that the house can only be sold with the paintings of the man and the woman."

"Never heard of that with any other house before; quite romantic isn't it? Maybe through their shadows these people still inhabit the house."

"Mm." Jake responded, "I asked the previous owner about the paintings and the covenant. He was in the fruit business and struck me as the least enquiring of men. When I asked him, he just shrugged and said. 'That's the way it's always been, squire. There when I bought the place and there always I suppose.' He copied pages from a book for me but there was nothing about the paintings in it. That's about all I got out of him. As I said, I tried to find out about

Jacob but didn't get anywhere. Almost seems that there is a silence about the place."

"Silence, d' you really think that?" she said getting out of bed and putting her dressing gown on. "You know what I think, Jake? I'm sure there is a story about that woman. She must have been related in some way to Jacob D'Arcy. Now we've found they're not permanently stuck to the wall, I'm going to have a look at the back of the one of her; I won't sleep till I do."

Barefoot, she padded off down the stairs in spite of his calling after her, "I've looked, there's nothing there." With Rhosa gone, he couldn't sleep either so after five minutes he followed her down the stairs.

"Rhosa, can't it wait till the morning?"

She was already standing on a chair and trying to take the portrait down. It was very heavy so he took it from her and helped her get down from the chair. He laid the portrait on the table and looked at it and, as his eyes went over the image it gave him a strange feeling. It would have been difficult for him to put in words but it was as though the woman was trying to communicate. Rhosa turned the painting over and examined it under the light.

"Brown paper on the back," she said.

"Well that's what I told you. I've looked too - wanted to find out more about her."

"But isn't there something that puzzles you?"

He looked at the back again and said. "No, why should it? it just looks like ordinary brown paper to me."

"Haven't you noticed that it has been stuck on with sticky tape?"

"Yes," he said, wondering what she meant. "What about it?"

"Come on Jay, I know it's late but you did do a PhD about this period. Did you ever hear of the Tudors using sticky tape. Wouldn't have been around when this was painted or are you going to correct me on that," she grinned. "Do you mind if I take it off." He nodded and she got a pair of scissors from a drawer and carefully cut the brown paper away. Underneath there was an accumulation of dust and beneath it, some very indistinct writing in an ink which had been there for so long it had turned brown and almost illegible with age. She peered at it under the light.

"I'm not sure because the light is not good but it seems to be saying 'Mistry Darkall who changeth me.'

What does it mean?" Rhosa frowned. "I don't know if mystery has ever been written like that, it may be a spelling error but, if it was it would read Mistry that changeth me'. You know what the dictionary definition of mystery is? 'A doctrine of faith known only by divine revelation'. If it is meant to be 'mystery' one of us needs to go into a meditative state for divine revelation before we can understand," she said with a laugh.

"Maybe it's a phrase from poetry or from a book. If it is I've never heard of it; but literature is more in your line than mine. Is that something written below it or is it just creasing?" Jake asked.

She went to get the glasses she needed for scripts, put them on and pulled the table lamp closer.

"There is something. Not much more than a scrawl below this writing but I think it says 'Find me here'." Rhosa frowned. "That's even more puzzling. If we were in a cheap novel we'd find a map on the back of the paper I took off." She picked up the paper which she had removed and which had fallen to the floor. Holding it under the light, she said. "Absolutely nothing; what a shame."

"You've got a creative mind, Jay, what do you think?"

He shook his head. "Could mean a lot of things but there aren't enough clues here. Now you've satisfied your curiosity, let's go back to bed, it's nearly midnight if I stay up much longer, my brain will revert to party mode and I won't be able to sleep."

He was just settling off for the second time when Rhosa leapt up in bed. "Jay, listen to me. I've been puzzling over that name 'Mistry'"

"Can it wait till the morning?"

"Sorry, Jay, were you asleep? It's just come back to me, I've seen it before," she dragged him up. "You know how I take scripts to read in churchyards because I like the atmosphere. Well that's where I've seen it. On a gravestone, I mean. I can't remember where but I recall thinking it was unusual."

"What?" Jake said distantly.

"Mistry and I'm sure the second name was Darkall, I've seen it and recently. I thought it was a strange name for a sixteenth century woman. It sounds so modern doesn't it? Almost like a pop star. Let's go on Sunday and see if we can find it in some of the places I've been recently."

"Ok, but can I go to sleep now?"

CHAPTER 21

Jake always opened his emails before breakfast. As he heard Rhosa coming down the stairs he called over his shoulder.

"Interesting, I've had another invitation to give a talk. Sounds impressive, it's at the Athenaeum."

"You can't do the same speech again, can you, Jay?"

"No, they seem to have left the choice of topic to me so I'll talk on the future of Capitalism, no less."

"Exactly what you'd like to talk about isn't it."

"First time I've spoken on it though. I'll have to do a bit of thinking between now and the 23rd of next month."

The Athanaeum was impressive but the room where the meeting of 'Advance Society' was held was in the much more ordinary basement. The audience was different too. This time there was less of a cross section than at his last public meeting and, as he looked round he saw that there were more, older academics than young people.

After the introductions by the chairman, Martin Strangeby, Jake started by looking around for several moments before he said.

"You may wonder why I am not talking. I am doing what is called 'sensing the mood' and I think I now have it." Several people in the audience laughed with him.

"I've been given a short time to talk and you will see from the programme that I am to speak again in a couple of months so this evening I will only lay foundations."

"I don't need to tell you that we've been going through troubling times. It is obvious that a re-assessment of our future is critically important. We have got it all wrong and we should be debating whether the future we are rushing towards has anything to offer us. If we extrapolate the life we have with our obscene consumption, we could well be driven back to cave living where comfortable temperatures are maintained by the rocky surroundings." Several dissenting murmurs were heard from the audience. With a theatrical movement, Jake turned away to look at the clock on the wall behind him to allow people to settle. Gradually the murmurs subsided and he continued.

"There is a lot of critical media comment about the amount of money that business leaders take home. It is my view that we need the wealth stimulation that comes down from success seekers. But their success should not be measured only in dollars."

"Perhaps I may demonstrate by an imaginary event. Some years ago, you took your holidays on a tiny tropical island where the scenery was beautiful and the inhabitants managed to make a living from the land. You enjoyed the holiday but not the primitive accommodation you were given. While wandering around the island, you had an uneasy sense of guilt when you noticed that the locals had to work excessively hard to survive."

"On the flight home you meet an executive of a tour operating company. You tell him about your doubts. He replies that he can see how he can turn the situation into profit to the benefit of all. He persuades his company to build a holiday complex on the island. Encouraged by a willing government, land is compulsorily purchased cheaply. The tour operator and the island's politicians tell the media that jobs have been created; the island's population does not have sufficient skills so the company brings in immigrant labour. By charging Western tourist prices, the holiday company is assured of a healthy return on capital."

"Attracted by a glossy photograph in a brochure, showing luxurious facilities in idyllic surroundings, you return to the island. A lot of its farm land has been turned into an airport but, as the brochure claims, the development has been sympathetically carried out."

"Accommodation is in simulated native huts, air conditioned so that, provided you stay in the huts, you will always be comfortable. The huts blend with the landscape of the island and detract the eye from the ramshackle huts outside the complex. While sitting surrounded by a security fence to keep out undesirable people and looking at the immaculately cleaned beach, you have a tinge of regret that the island has lost the character that originally attracted you. But, at least now the native population has work and to survive no longer has to undertake backbreaking toil."

"At some stage you get bored with eating and drinking cocktails in the bar, eating in the 'Chief's' hut restaurant. Swimming in the temperature controlled pool also begins to pall. You want to see the real island, so you buy tickets and go for a tour in the air conditioned minibus provided by the tour operators."

"For the hour which the tour takes, you are surprised to see that there are many beggars in the nearby villagers. You can't remember seeing any when you previously visited the island. When you are back in the complex trying to enjoy the native dance cabaret, you ask the waiter where he comes from. In good English he tells you he is from Bangkok and came through the same agency on the mainland that had supplied the 'native' cabaret dancers, who also speak good English. He tells you that they learned the native dances in London, the city they grew up in."

"The waiter tells you that the natives of the island are not sufficiently educated for responsible jobs but are ok for gardening, cleaning and bed making."

"The island's community leaders have benefitted from the influx of capital and now have nice houses on the mainland. The tour operator makes a lot of money out of a modest investment which was subsidised by favourable finance from the World Bank and the mainland government. The shares in the operating company rise and the directors get large bonuses."

"Measured in purely financial terms the system is highly successful; land which was bought for just a few dollars an acre, is now worth millions and the holiday complex would be a target for takeover from a Disney type company who may want to put Mickey Mouse statues at strategic points throughout the island, to make the tourist smile and give them something to photograph for the folks back home."

"Everyone seems to have benefited, the mainland government which now gets more tax revenue, the cabaret dancers and hotel staff who have employment and tips and the tour operators' shareholders have increased their asset value."

"Yet you can't help being puzzled that the island population seems to have lost its livelihood when its farmland was bought and now can only advance by becoming coca-colanised and learning English so that the more employable of them are able to become hotel staff. They also have another option of learning how to do a version of native dances but many who are left are too old or infirm for these."

"You will be horrified as I am by the dissolution of island communities and by repeats of this scenario in many undeveloped part of the world."

"Looking around the audience, I can see many of you whom I expect will be retired and living on pensions. Your pension income is provided by companies whom you chose because they gave you a good rate of return on your capital and might even have shares in companies such as the tour operator for the island."

"We live in a world increasingly concerned by the damage being wreaked on the environment. The reasons for this can be seen by anyone who travels by car through the swathes cut through beautiful countryside by motorways and the proliferation on what was previously agricultural land of large sheds. These house 'distribution centres' which store goods imported from cheap labour countries."

"I expect that all of us here support the limitation of further destruction of land." Jake looked round and smiled as the audience responded with applause.

"Let me tell you the other side; a Chief Executive may decide to avoid exploitation and adopt environmental policies but these will almost inevitably reduce the profitability of his company. There will be one of two outcomes. One may be that the pension fund investment managers who hold large amounts of stock in the company will seek to get the CEO replaced with a man who is more cost-to-profit-efficient. Alternatively a predator would see that the company was not producing sufficient profits from its investment. By taking it over, getting rid of the CEO and his supporters, reversing the environmental policy and sacking the research people, it will increase profits. The new CEO who increases the profitability of the company could well be knighted for his services to industry and with an enhanced reputation will move on to wreak his destruction on other companies.

The chairman interrupted. "Can you tell us how this relates to your well known stance that leaders of nations must have more power, when it is commonly thought that they have too much already?"

"The reason I say this," Jake replied, "is that throughout the West, multi-nationals dictate to governments and establish subsidiaries only in countries where they are given the biggest subsidy. If governments are not co-operative, multi-nationals will close down plants in the inflexible country and move to more amenable and profitable regions of the world. They do it all so that ostensibly they can reduce the price of their products to you, the consumer and increase shareholder returns. We all know the real reason is that they want to maximise profits and thereby their own bonuses."

"Nothing wrong with profits, they are critical to the survival of companies and nations but we might contemplate Matthew in the Bible, 'what shall it profit a man if he gains the whole world but loses his soul'. Capitalism unrestricted puts profit far ahead of human happiness."

Jake looked around the nodding heads of many of those in the audience. "Yet isn't human happiness what we all want? It is a frequently stated truism that to paraphrase Matthew, 'Wealth doesn't bring happiness'. The wealthiest in the community can be miserable and misunderstood. A primary reason is that they are driven by their wealth and suffer dejection if they are not constantly expanding it."

"What are we talking about? Big corporations are only seen to be successful and admired if they constantly grow their profits. We have a world motivated entirely by finance, where the biggest returns come from moving money rather than making the products which employ people and create real wealth. For the sake of increased profits, people are being made redundant even though they have worked loyally for their employers. We wonder if the CEO of a major bank is justified in taking home nineteen million pounds in one year when the bank's shares actually declined in value. Or the CEO of a major supermarket who has presided over many years of declining profitability, is rewarded with ten million. The response of the bank is, if you want to retain the best people then you have to pay international rates. What this means is that the best brains always go to companies and not to the regulators who are supposed to control the banks."

"We are constantly told that we live in a global village. If this were the case, regulators could control obscene bonuses globally to people who are exploiting the community which would mean that the regulator could also attract the best brains."

"We live in a world in which there is finite wealth measured in terms of farm land, minerals, sea etc, yet the amount of money in circulation is growing exponentially. No matter how big it grows, the real wealth changes very little."

"Who controls the Capitalist system? Do any of you in the audience?" Jake waved his hand to encompass all corners of the hall. "No one here? Is there really not a President of Capitalism? Is no one in charge?" he said, feigning surprise but knowing that he would not get an answer.

"And yet, as I've said, I can see several senior executives in the audience. So let me ask if there is anyone here who feels they have enough power to change the capitalist system either individually or concertedly?" He looked around knowing that he had posed a barbed question and confident that no one would accept such a challenge. "No one," he said, "and yet, I repeat, we have many very influential people here. Amongst the senior executives, I see Members of Parliament and some MEPs."

"Globalism applies only to large businesses, we the public have no global consensus. Until we have, nations will continue to be manipulated by multi-nationals. This means that every one of us," he waved his had around the audience, "will indirectly be dictated to by the unknown entity. We have a Wild West economic system where only the heavily armed will survive. Are you happy with that or will you join me in my efforts to encourage a sane global structure?"

He leaned forward, conspiratorially and stretched out his arms, seeming to draw the audience into his confidence.

"I am just about to finish but I'd like to ask one last question. Is anyone here confident that what we have is sustainable?"

He sat down to applause. Several people rose to clap but a middle aged man also stood up. He did not applaud and did not look pleased. Beside him was a girl with a microphone which he snatched from her.

"I wonder if you are aware that what you would call the 'excesses of capitalism' are what feeds and clothes all of us in this room. It is very easy to criticise but I will bet that you do not have any viable alternative to offer." He continued to stand while the girl tried to take the microphone back. When she failed to do so, the chairman interrupted.

"To begin with, you have not been selected to ask a question. You have also failed to give your name and occupation and in taking the microphone without it being offered to you, you have acted with indiscretion which in my experience is without precedent. I am tempted to ask you to quietly leave the hall but I will take advice from our speaker."

He turned to Jake who said. "I am happy to reply." He leaned towards the microphone in front of him.

"Before you do," the chairman put a restraining hand on Jake's arm, "perhaps the questioner would be good enough to follow our tradition and announce himself."

"As I think you all know, I am Harold Deppard, Financial Advisor to some of the wealthier people in the community. I hope now you will now allow the speaker to answer my question."

Jake picked up his microphone. "Perhaps you think that capitalism is without fault. If you do, I suspect that you would be one of a small minority in the audience. I earn my living by selling my abilities at a profit. Like you I am fed and clothed by free enterprise. I support your view that there is no better system but I would be naive," he paused to let the import of the word become obvious to the questioner, "if I were unable to recognise the many and glaring faults in Capitalism. Not least of which is the strange fact that those who move wealth make much more than those who produce wealth. If food from farmers stopped coming to this city, we would last less than a week. But if the money inflators ceased to work, most of us would not notice or suffer for years or even lifetimes. Businesses are becoming aware that they have responsibilities not just to shareholders but also to society. The difference is between short term

237

and long term gain. In short term gain, companies declare redundancies, throw people onto welfare, take over competitors, make sure they maximise profit by moving to countries with health and safety standards which would not be tolerated in the West. There is a US company which currently returns a profit of thirty five per cent. Its products come from China where workers are so exploited that many have committed suicide. Its profit comes mainly from selling in the West. As a result it contributes indirectly to the decline of the West. This company is held up as an example of successful capitalism but, carried to its limit, it will result in the West descending into poverty."

Harold Deppard tried to respond but by this time the microphone had been taken from him and his voice was lost while another questioner spoke.

Most of the other questions were supportive. One or two expressed the views that only by returning to religious values could capitalism be made more human. Many hands were raised by people wanting to contribute but the chairman, looking at the clock said. "We have had a most illuminating discussion this evening but I am afraid we have overstayed our welcome and I will have to call the meeting to a close."

CHAPTER 22

"Jacob." Mistry had a look of anguish on her face as she spoke.

"Yes?" he asked anxiously. "You look worried,"

"The man who came here in a black cloak with his hood over his face," she looked to see if Jacob understood. When he nodded, she continued. "I seen him today in a carriage."

Mistry's speech had improved rapidly but occasionally, especially when she was disturbed, she slipped back to street grammar. "Did you see his face?"

"No, 'twas turned away."

"How could you be sure it was him?"

"I seen his ring, with that five point star in gold, the same ring I saw when he came to see you. His hand was by the window of the carriage."

"That must have been a shock for you."

"Made me afeard - desperate scared."

"I know he seems frightening, it bothered me a little when he first came here but I think he is a good man." Jacob said, watching her reaction before he continued.

" I think we should get on with your lessons. It will take a time and we'll get thirsty; would you like to get us both some of that ale again?"

When she returned he said, "What I am going to tell you is complicated but it will help you understand what I and my friends talk about when we meet. We are an unusual group, you know and that's one of the things I like about it. You've met Michael Dalgett, most of us are serious people but there are others who are amusing like Michael, but," he smiled, "we have no one as outrageous."

He poured ale into decorated glasses which he had bought when he had been to Venice on business and took a drink, savouring the flavour and nodding his appreciation. "He is coming next week to give you another lesson. What do you think of him?"

"He makes me laugh and I saw you laughing," she hesitated, "which I liked to see."

"We need more like him, people of learning who also love to play-act. You are right in saying I need to laugh more. My wife was serious you know, there was not much laughter in this house."

Mistry, not sure what to say, sat beside him and waited attentively.

"We are going through a time of change such as we have never seen before, Mistry. This could be the beginning of a new world for all of us, new in almost everything we do. In the days of my father, Columbus sailed to discover a new passage to India; instead he found a new land which has only been explored in parts."

"There are many ideas spreading from Italy to other countries and they are now beginning to affect all of us in England. We are learning from new ideas and from the different people who have come here with skills which we need. Business has increased because of international finance, trading ships and a growing group of wealthy people who invest their money. By wealthy, I mean people who have big houses with land and servants and also much gold or coin. All of these things bring benefits to everyone and that includes you and me."

He finished the ale and poured himself another. Mistry had not yet touched hers but, for a while, held it in her hand to warm it while she was thinking and then said, "I was cleaning the room which was your Isabel's - there is a big box with a lot of carving on it."

"Isabel's virginal. She loved playing it. Many winter evenings she would sit and please me with her music, it sounded throughout the house." He mused. "Open it and try it if you like, it makes a beautiful sound."

"I'd like that. The grandfather at the last house I worked was nice, they had a virginal when all the others were away he taught me some playing."

"Then you must think of the instrument as yours. Music is one of my great pleasures and I often hear it when I am invited to big houses."

"There is so much happening, Mistry; I find clever people who have new ideas whenever I go." Turning in his chair to see if Mistry was listening he found her eyes glowing with interest.

"One of the most important inventions is, as I have said, the printing press. This has been a revolution as powerful as the cannon and," he laughed, "much quieter. Now, a book which could have taken many years to produce by hand, can be done in a matter of hours and can be read by anyone who can read."

Mistry stopped him by putting her hand on his arm. "Because of your teaching I can read more but I want to read better."

"It will take time, but soon you will read easily," he said, putting his hand on hers, "the important thing about the printing press is that books can now be printed in large numbers. Many are in English and not the Latin used in monasteries where books were copied by hand before printing was invented," he stopped as a thought struck him, "I have told you my wonder at the beauty of language. Can you imagine if we could only grunt like beasts, how poor our lives would be? There is a man I know who lives in Italy. He is very clever and also very wealthy so he can afford to buy beautiful things. He has many clay tablets which it is said the Egyptians used. There is writing on them which cannot be understood. But can you imagine how amazing it is to hold these tablets which could be read if only we knew how. The Incas in the land which Columbus discovered do not have writing like that but use strings which are knotted in patterns to act as records."

"Jacob, I love to hear you talk. I am trying to read your books but there are some very difficult words in them."

"I am amazed that you are reading and writing so quickly. Later I will teach you Latin, which many of my books are written in. The Church still uses it just to make the word of God mysterious. It was this as much as anything which provokes the desire for a Reformation. There are changes which will have an effect on us both, Mistry. Our Group which meets in this house has begun to question the way we are governed."

"Governed?" Mistry asked.

"I mean those people who think they are our masters – the King, the lord of the manor, the Priests, Bishops, Parliament, the Pope and his Cardinals. We want to know what right they have to control us. It's not just me and my friends; there are many other groups we have met and talked with." He pointed through the window to the stalls selling their wares outside.

"Those people out there have been hurt by a drop in wages. It all changes so slowly that most people don't notice it but talk to an older person and they will tell you how they lived much better when they were young. They used to be able to afford meat but because the population has grown, wages have dropped from the level they were after the Plague."

"I've talked about the balance between money and goods that is changing constantly. There is an example in Spain; much gold and silver was coming in from the world which Columbus discovered, the result was that the same amount bought less goods so the effect is that money becomes less valuable."

"But don't things have a fixed price and it's only the men who sell things on the stalls who charge what they like?" Mistry looked enquiringly.

"No, there's more to it than that" Jacob continued. "I have talked to you about business and the balance between money and goods. When we have a good summer, more food is grown, the price drops so money becomes more valuable. If the summer is bad, less food is grown, the price inflates so that money is able to buy less food."

"A hungry man is an angry man, Mistry, so we have seen fighting between different people because their wages dropped as landlords became greedier and demanded more rent from tenants who were unable to pay. Those who can no longer find work have been so hungry that they have rioted against those who had grabbed more and more land. The result is that people became homeless. We see them all around us, begging on street corners, some of them so hungry and weak that they starve."

"I've been near death with wanting food," Mistry said, grimacing, "especially since my man did die. The worst about it is that you just want to sleep and many don't wake up."

"What a terror that must have been, Mistry," he wanted to get up to comfort her but felt that would be a wrong thing to do in a lesson. "The working men in London and many of the other port cities where trade is carried on with other nations are not as badly off as in smaller towns which rely on food grown nearby. Unfortunately in London and many other ports that I have seen, there is a lot of drunkenness and rowdiness. You hear them coming from the taverns, shouting, singing and fighting."

"It does not please me. Sometimes I've been hit."

"Have you? I hope not while you have been here. If it happens again, tell me. There are some stout fellows whom I have used to keep the peace and I know they would be glad to help."

"I've seen 'em start riots in the streets so that people leave their houses to get away then those doing the rioting can break into houses without any fear of being seen."

"I've seen that in Italy where there are a lot of wealthy people."

"Can you tell me more about Italy?"

"I don't think Michael Dalgett has yet told you but one of the advances in knowledge was brought about by François, the king of France; he introduced the new thinking of the Italian Rinascita to his country and encouraged new learning which found its way to England via King Henry."

"When I buy from the stalls, they tell me the King is not well," she said.

"He would do well to follow the teachings of Epicurus I told you about. The King is greedy and gluttonous, womanising, and profligate. In my view it will be a good thing when he goes, he has been evil and selfish."

"Our King?" she said raising her eyebrows, "people do seem to like him."

"They would not if they knew the truth about him. He married many wives and found reasons for putting them to death."

"People I do hear complain about monasteries. The King got rid of 'em."

"Yes, with that I agree. There was too much power in the monasteries. The king was without mercy; he destroyed small monasteries then moved to larger ones. In four years, he and his minister Thomas Cromwell closed almost all of them, took their precious jewellry and ornaments and melted them down to feed the King's appetites. Many who stood in his way were hung, drawn and quartered."

Mistry grimaced. "But I did hear the King did much good."

"Oh he certainly did; we had always been afraid to write anything or get it printed because of Pope Leo's decree that all books on any subject had to be reviewed by the Church and by an inquisitor."

"There was a clever man called Copernicus, who was convinced that the earth went round the sun when the Church had accepted the teaching of Aristotle who claimed the earth was at the centre of the universe. He waited until he was close to dying before the book was published."

"When our King was ex-communicated, the Pope lost his power in this country. Thanks to King Henry, we are not now punished by Rome for writing about scientifical things."

"But breaking away from Rome was only so that he could take another wife and also steal from the monasteries. There was so much he could have done with the wealth of the monasteries."

"What could he do?"

"Look outside; what do you notice most when you walk out there on very hot days."

Mistry pondered and then said. "The stink, it near makes me spew."

"Exactly, King Henry could have spent the money on improving the drains in our streets. There is a town called Lavenham where I get my cloth dyed blue. They had the same smells only worse. They now have their dirty water carried away in pipes beneath the ground where it flows into a river and is washed away. If King Henry cared enough about his people, he would have used the money from the monasteries to lay the same drains for everyone in London and he could have paid people to take away rubbish which is thrown into the streets because there is nothing else to do with it. You would then be able to walk the streets without feeling sick and I am sure that the putrid matter breeds disease. You know, Mistry, I think that may be one reason my wife fell ill."

He grimaced for a moment and then, with a forced smile, picked up a letter and held it in his hand. "Today we must think of happy things. Tonight we will have something to celebrate. A messenger arrived with an order that I am to supply many yards of my finest cloth to Lord de Sangen. He sent the money with the order. What shall we have for dinner to celebrate?"

"You liked the rabbit I cooked when you last had a big order. The same warrener who sold us the rabbit then is back in the tavern. I could get another one of his rabbits and cook a pie with it."

Jacob smiled his pleasure. Mistry went to get the rabbit, but returned quickly, looking ashen faced and panting for breath.

"What is it, Mistress?" Jacob asked.

"The man… in the cloak. I seen his carriage coming toward me. I ran back," she said between panting from exertion.

The smile left Jacob's lips.

"If he is coming here, we must have something to offer him," he said trying to appear unconcerned.

Shortly after, a hammering was heard on the door. Mistry went and returned, followed by the cloaked figure.

"I must speak with you, sir, but again I must insist on our being alone," the muffled voice said from behind his hood.

"Can you fetch some mead for me when you get the food for dinner?" Jacob asked Mistry. For some moments, she stood transfixed, staring at the back of the gaunt figure. Then she seemed to come to life and turning quickly, rushed from the house.

Jacob had stood as the figure entered the room. "Sir, I had no knowledge that you were coming and I have no drink or provisions in the house."

A hand was raised from the long sleeves. "My thanks, I have eaten and drunk in sufficiency."

Jacob pulled a chair close to the fire and directed his guest to warm himself. It was cold and in the manner of companions, both men held their hands in the heat from the fire.

"You will be wondering why I have returned, Mr. D'Arcy," he paused and eased his hood back slightly to allow the warmth to reach his face. "I have heard reports about you from some of your compatriots."

Jacob leaned forward apprehensively, wondering what could have happened. He felt sure he could trust Mistry but wondered if she may have been careless in talking to people outside.

The visitor's hands moved away from the fire and fumbled in the cloak. From one of the pockets, a small Bible, chased with gold was produced.

"I want you to swear that you will keep all I am going to tell you to yourself and reveal it to no other person unless I tell you that you can."

Jacob put his hand on the Bible and said. "I swear by God Almighty that whatever I hear tonight shall be kept secret unless your honour permits me otherwise." He took his hand from the bible and said. "Before I speak, I need you also to swear on the bible that what I say will not be passed to anyone else, Reverend Sir"

At the words the hooded figure started in surprise. "Why do you say, Reverend Sir? You do not know me."

"I know you sir as a man of the Church."

"But you cannot know me. I have not revealed my face."

"It is not necessary to see your face." Jacob said. "It is sufficient to say that I know you." He turned to the fire and added another log. "We are playing the same game as last time we met because you do not know if you can trust me and I don't yet know if I can trust you. We must both swear on the Bible that we shall tell no one of what is said between us."

"I agree," the figure said, pulling the hood back slightly, revealing an aquiline nose.

Jacob stood up, went to the book case and took out a Bible. He passed the Bible to the figure who repeated the oath and then said, "I want you to tell me what you think of the Pope."

"I am still a Catholic, although I do not make it obvious in this country. I only go to church a long way from here where I am not known. I can tell you that I dislike what the Church has become. My views are not just my own, they are shared by many others. This Pope and others before him have followed their own pleasures. I have heard in the past of orgies in the Vatican in which a prize is given for the holy man who deflowers the most women of easy virtue. The prize can also go to the Pope himself. There are many other examples of corruption in the Vatican."

"We have talked of Martin Luther, who expressed his concern but received no satisfaction. The Pope supposedly rules 'for the good of the people' but he practices tyranny to support what he would call the will of God. This is just the same as all Kings who are supposedly there to maintain law and peace but achieve it by suppressing the people. The King and his nobles have different laws which allow them freedoms which ordinary people do not have."

"But Luther says that all Christians have a role as priests and leaders. If Luther is correct, then the State is the rightful governor of the people and the Pope should be a servant to the State. We have a Parliament supposed to represent the people but the King is so powerful that he surrounds himself with his supporters. I look forward to the time when we, the people are able to choose our own Parliament."

"Sir, you have ideas above what I had expected." the hooded figure said.

At his words, Jacob froze, fearing that he had said too much. He waited for the other man to speak but when he did not Jacob broke the silence, saying. "I have told you my views. We have both sworn on the bible. I am not prepared to say any more until you reveal your identity."

"I have two reasons for being cloaked." The man said as he slowly pulled back the hood.

Jacob stifled a gasp as he saw the man's pock marked face. "But we've met, sir. We shared a meal at the home of Marco Bideri in Florence. But you were there dressed in ordinary clothes I did not know you were a man of God then."

247

"You will see the two reasons for remaining covered. I try to conceal my pock marked face to save embarrassment to my congregation. And also I did not want you to see me until we had talked. I was sure when we met in the Bideri house that you and I shared the same sorrow at what we have become. Of course, we could not talk and I wanted to be sure of you before you knew who I was."

"The Church has sharp ears, I know, sir, and listens at many corners. You can rely on my silence." With an effort, Jacob looked at the man's face, studying the lines between the pocks. "When we met, you were not introduced by name."

"My name is Valenti, Lucca Valenti."

At the name, Jacob's mouth fell open. "Cardinal Valenti?"

The other nodded slowly. "You know my name?"

"I have heard you spoken of as a good man. I see why you did not show your face. I am afraid that you have tricked me into telling you of my feelings about the governance by the Vatican."

"No, my son, I did not come here to trick you."

"Then why?"

Cardinal Valenti got up, pulled aside the curtain to the window and looked out, then went to the door and quickly opened and closed it before returning to his seat and warming his hands again. "You are a man who can help us," he said quietly.

"Help you? But you have so many people around you in the Vatican, what help can I give that you do not already have?"

"It is a different sort of help that we need from that given by the sycophantic servants who surround me."

"But why me, your grace?"

"When we met at Signor Bideri's house, I recognised that you were a man of integrity, and when you had gone I spoke to Marco about you."

Jacob looked anxious. "What did he tell you about me?"

"No, have no fear, he did not tell me anything which you need worry about. But he said that you have some unusual abilities.

248

That you are able to see things so clearly that people of all ranks come to you with their problems."

Jacob nodded, "but why does that interest you, a man of such great power?"

"I have something to tell you and something to ask you but before I do I must consult with others. Can I take it that you are willing to help?"

"I cannot answer until you tell me what you want."

"I can only repeat what I have told you before that we want to make changes. There have already been some attempts."

"You are referring again to Martin Luther?"

The Cardinal nodded "We do not agree with him entirely or with the way he chose to publish his complaints but I am sure he would understand what I want to talk to you about," he looked intently at Jacob. "Are you ready?"

"I am ready to listen." Jacob replied, carefully weighing his words.

"That is all I can ask of you." He said and rose to his feet. "I will consult with my friends and will meet with you again."

Both men got up, when Jacob opened the door, the Cardinal stopped and listened, saying, "what is the music?"

"My servant - she plays on the virginal which belonged to my late wife. She has made amazing progress."

When his visitor had gone, Jacob climbed the stairs and stood on the landing listening. Mistry made many mistakes but even after a few weeks, listening to her playing brought him much pleasure.

CHAPTER 23

During the time that rehearsals for the play were suspended so that the author could rewrite a scene, Rhosa would go to the library to read.

"I've missed you Rhosa. What have you been doing in the library?" Jake asked when she came in at six one evening, "Why don't you borrow the book and bring it home."

"It's not just one book, there are several," she said, putting down her briefcase. "Anyway I know you prefer to be alone when you write. And I'm not reading, I'm writing."

"Not planning to be a competitor to me are you?" Jake said with a smile. "Or are you at last writing your Pinter play."

"Neither," she replied. "I've nearly finished what I'm doing. I'll let you read it when I'm happy with it."

"What's it about?"

"Patience, I'll tell you when it's finished. I don't want to tell you now because I may change it."

"Fiction then?"

"You'll find out in a few days."

On the following Friday afternoon, Rhosa came in from the library and put a notebook on the desk in front of him while she went to fix something for them both.

She returned with a tray to find Jake with his feet on the desk, reading from the notebook.

"Sorry about the errors, Jay, I've re-written it three times and it's still not finished."

Jake, with his usual total concentration hardly looked up even when she put a sandwich in front of him. She saw the frown on his face. "I know it's depressing, Jay, but that's how I've felt ever since you told me about the KGB... I just had to write it out. You know

250

how you said writing is a therapy…you were right, I do feel better for it."

Jake finished reading, put the notebook on the table and said, "God, Rhosa, this is powerful. I know it will have helped but I thought you'd write…" he shrugged, "well a romance, not future fiction. Have you ever done anything like this before?"

"First time I've written."

"Not counting poetry, of course," he smiled. "Will you read it to me?"

"Are you sure you want me to, you've just read it."

"I'm sure; I've only skimmed it," he nodded, "I'm just intrigued at your ideas. I want to hear it read, and by a famous actress of course," he said with a smile.

"I'm not sure I can, Jay, I wrote it to try to forget what you said about Russia which really distressed me; I tried to write out my distress." Rhosa sat down and picked up the notebook. When she had finished, she said. "Reading it makes me worried about the future we are shaping. What you said about the people watching me at the grave of Gregory started me thinking. Will we end up as I've said in this story, closetted in one room, allowed out only when the authorities permit, to meet only those selected by the regulators and then only in approved places."

She looked up from the notebook to see Jay with his eyes closed. When he said nothing, she asked, "Did you not like it, Jay?"

He opened his eyes. "Like is not the right word. I'm sure you didn't write it to be liked. No I didn't like it because it is too close to what the future might become. You warn what I've suspected for many years that we are headed for a disaster scenario."

"Me too and up until now I've been successful. As I wrote it, I became more and more depressed," she stood up and looked out of the window at the domesticity of the scene outside. Mothers were pushing their babies in prams, fathers flying airplanes with their sons and toddlers throwing bread to the ducks. "Look out there, Jake, isn't that all we want, just peace and stability. Why is it that we constantly need to progress?" she asked. "When will we accept that advances are not always improvements but are sometimes retrograde? Scientists are hell bent on understanding human thinking and trying to perfect the process with software. Why do we want neural networks? Why are we trying to make computers cleverer than we are? I read in the Library that as far back as the late Fifties, there was a 'Perceptron' which tried to copy human thought, fortunately it wasn't very good. But who knows what the future holds?" She turned her back to the window. "I delight in the imperfectability of human beings. I don't like arguments but I do like disagreements; they bring us excitement."

She picked up her notebook and leafed through it. "There is so much more I could have written. I read that biologists are studying ant communities. Individual ants have no value and they die to ensure that the community survives. I'm sure some scientists want us to be like that."

"Come on, Rhosa, let's change the subject." Jake said forcing a laugh to bring humour into the situation. "You're getting into one of your morbid moods."

"I would love a whisky." Rhosa looked pleadingly at him, knowing Jake didn't like her to drink spirits.

He knew what she was thinking. "Sorry we don't have any whisky; Arthur Deckin drank the lot last night and left without even giving me a commission for another article."

"What a waste, it was a malt whisky too."

"If you need a drink, I have a sherry."

As Jake passed her the sherry he saw on the opened page of her notebook. 'Write to Marina'

"Who is Marina?" Jay asked.

"I met her some years ago when I was last in Moscow, she was a bar girl in the hotel I told you about," she opened her album of photographs, took out a letter and passed it to Jay.

"That was the letter she wrote me before I went to Moscow a couple of years ago. She has just emailed telling me she has moved to London and would like to meet me. From what she says, she will be missing Moscow. She took me round the city and many of the sights she talks about in that letter when I was last there."

Jake sat back and read. When he had finished, he re-read it.

"She makes Moscow come to life doesn't she?" Rhosa said.

Jake nodded, "even though she obviously has difficulty with English she writes a very intelligent letter for a bar girl."

"Bar girl only while she was between jobs. She had been a manager of a design company but left because she had an affair with the boss and could not face his wife." Rhosa said. "I've got another letter; I'll let you read it, it's as interesting as the one you've just read, she included some of her poems, just short but beautiful. She has a very creative mind."

"I'd like to read them. Or, better still, I'd like you to read them to me."

Rhosa stood up, "I'll get the letter she sent with some of her poetry." Her slippers clattered on the wooden stairs as she went up and again as she came down. She was reading as she sat down. Jake waited expectantly while she read.

"Sorry, this poem is particularly beautiful," she said as she turned a page and passed it to him.

"Mm,"Jake said appreciatively. "Reads like part of a longer poem."

"They are all like that, they leave you thinking you'd like another verse or I wonder what she meant?' She says here that she wrote that, after finishing an affair with a married man. Leaving him was devastating for her. All her poems are like impressionist paintings. You see unexpressed emotions."

She looked over at Jake and, seeing that his eyes were closed said. "Jay, are you listening to me or are you asleep."

"I'm listening, it's just that your voice reading those poems is hypnotic. Please go on."

She read several more to him. When she had finished they both remained quiet with their thoughts. Jake broke the silence. "I see what you mean; so much is there between the lines. We might get them published, I wonder if she has many more."

"She has, I have a lot and I doubt that she has sent me all of them."

"Is she going to live in London?"

"Apart from a phone call a couple of days ago, her email is the first I have heard of her since I was last in Moscow, so I don't know."

"What's she doing?"

"Modelling, amongst other things, she has a stunning figure and real poise; holds herself very elegantly."

"Like you, good dress sense then?"

"Not that sort of modelling. She poses for artists."

Jay raised his eyebrows in mock appreciation.

Rhosa got up and playfully punched him in the stomach. "You beast," she said, jumped on his lap and put her arms round his shoulders, laughing. "Haven't there been enough women in your life?"

"Probably," he grinned, "Marina can't be as lovely as you though, can she?"

"She was very attractive but I haven't seen her for a few years. Anyway, she has asked me to meet her over lunch next week so I'll find out what she's like now, she was hardly twenty when I met her so she's probably changed. "

"For the better, I expect," he teased.

"Go and make me a cup of tea, I need to get the taste of that sherry out of my mouth. Where did you get it?"

When he came back carrying a tray, the cups rattling with his movement, Rhosa was re-reading the poems. "You know, I think you are right, we should see if we can get these published along with any others she has written. There is that publisher friend of yours, Mark Rindell; these are the sort he ought to have in his catalogue aren't they."

"If she is in London, why don't you get her to come to my office here one day in the next couple of weeks?"

"You *are* interested in her Jay, aren't you, like you were with Lilyana, whom you haven't yet met?" Rhosa said, raising her eyebrows. "I hope it's not because I said she had a stunning figure and that she does nude modelling." she said, teasing him.

Jake thought he noticed an undertone to her voice.

"I've never even seen a photograph of her so I could hardly be interested," he laughed.

"No," she laughed back, "but I sense there are fires that burn within you, Mr. Dearsey; fires that I don't put out." Jake looked surprised at her remark, but said nothing.

CHAPTER 24

The years since they had last seen each other fell away when Rhosa met Marina at the newly re-opened Savoy Hotel. They wrapped their arms around each other.

"Rhosa, delight to see you. It has been long and my life in Moscow has too difficult."

Rhosa looked at Marina and said, "Do I see sadness in your eyes, Marina, why is that?"

"Always I trouble with men."

"You had ended your affair with that married man when we first met."

"Nearly ended me; I cried days and did not live anything. But I could not with him carry on. His wife come into office where Hugo and I work and she look at me and say nothing, just nothing but her look tell me. I am honest girl and her look make me full of guilt they had nice children that I loved and it was them I could not hurt."

"That was many years ago. What has happened since then?"

The question brought a smile to Marina's lips. "So many," her eyes wandered admiringly round the room, "they come they go. Some few nights, some stay long time.

I come to England to live with nice English boy, but when I come he is different, not nice any more. Just want me for my body, not my mind. Tell me I stupid with no ideas. So glad we departed."

"Will you stay here?"

"I stay. London is nice, living here is easier."

"Easier?"

"No one to pay; in Moscow everything has price, driving test-pay, passport - pay, driving licence- pay."

"Bribery?"

Marina nodded. "I like London, no one to pay, I don't feel like immigrant, so many Russian, French, Indian, all people. I feel more at home than in Russia. You like London?"

"I live here because I am happy in England. If someone is nice to me here, I know they are not doing it because of the size of my wallet." Rhosa smiled, "I was born in Egypt. When I came here I hated it. I couldn't speak proper English and I was made to feel stupid by the girls at school. I worked hard and studied Shakespeare and grew to love English literature. When I moved to another school, they thought I was English. By then I knew more about Shakespeare than they did." She became pensive. "It's just occurred to me that probably as much as anything, Shakespeare keeps me here – I want to be in the city where his plays were heard."

A couple of weeks later, the phone rang in Jake's office. The voice at the other end was unfamiliar and he had to ask her to repeat what she had said. "Rhosa and I met last week, talked you a lot and told to me to ring, I am Marina," she said in her heavily accented voice.

"Oh, Marina, sorry I wasn't expecting you. I was miles away thinking about some research I am doing," he replied. "Yes, Rhosa read me your poems. Do you want to drop round and we can talk about them? That is if the idea interests you."

"Are you unoccupied now, I have just finish photograph session in Richmond park so only bus ride away."

"Yes, come round, I've got to a stage in my writing where I need a break. Has Rhosa told you where the house is?"

"I know it, I like to walking Common and round Barnes so your house I have passed it."

He was taken aback at how young Marina looked when he opened the door to her and for a brief moment, he stared at her in surprise. She obviously sensed his feelings and said. "You expected someone other did you?"

"No," he replied standing back to let her in and trying to regain his composure, "I have seen your photograph, Rhosa showed it to me; I recognised you from that, but photographs only show one dimension. Do come in."

When she was seated, he said. "Can I get you something to drink?"

"I'd love a ground coffee but not if it's too difficult."

"My mornings are punctuated by breaks and I'm just about to have one so you're in luck. I've even got some biscuits which Rhosa told me you liked."

Marina stood up. "I help you," she said, following Jake, "what large kitchen, it must be nice to work."

"You like cooking?"

"For me therapy."

"You need therapy?"

"Is there anyone who not at times?"

Jake was tempted to correct her English but thought it added to her enigmatic charm. He frequently found himself wondering why language was so often illogical. Why must we say 'I came home' instead of the more logical versions a child uses 'I comed home'

He was washing his hands when he noticed that Marina had found the cafetiere and the ground coffee, had boiled the water, made coffee and was walking into the lounge with it on a tray.

"You learn quickly."

"Comes being bar girl and waitress," she smiled, filling the cups, "yours you like black."

"How do you know that," Jake asked

"You think telepathy?" she smiled, "or one thing Rhosa tell to me about you?"

"Odd thing to talk about my taste in coffee."

"I tell to you, we ate in a restaurant, had coffee at finish. When I say to her 'mine black', she say, 'same as Jay'."

"And you remembered."

"Having waitress mind I have to remember that sort of thing. Steak well done with chips or vegetables, apple pie with cream and black coffee; sometimes for ten eating people but each different."

Looking at him she said, "Rhosa say you like my poetries and thought them to publish."

"Don't want to raise your hopes. I would not be able to publish them myself but I could show them to a publisher I know. He might be interested."

"I would like. I know he might not want publishing them but I write them for myself and for someone read them would please me."

"I've only heard a few, perhaps a dozen, do you have more?"

"Fifty maybe."

"That would be enough. Send them to me; are they typed nicely?"

"Some but the others I type for you and will make them pretty."

"Those that I have heard are very good English."

"You have notice my English is not good?" Marina smiled, "My boyfriend was English. He corrected for me. He was reason I came to England. I thought I loved him but..." she shrugged, "sometimes..."

"We are driven aren't we?"

"What means that?"

Jake wondered if he should embark on one of his interests. Marina was looking at him expectantly so he continued. "Lots of pressures act on us; friends, relatives, the world of pop music and Hollywood. All shape our behaviour and expectations of relationships. Into our lives comes what seems to be that mate. So we choose - deciding to spend the rest of our lives in union. But then disillusionment begins and that happy state breaks up."

Marina looked worried, "You and Rhosa?"

Jake shook his head. "No, Rhosa and I have something which I think, or perhaps I should say I hope, will last, but who can tell, things change all the time." he shrugged, thinking back to his doubts about Rhosa and Anthony Garden.

Marina just nodded in a way which filled Jake with doubt again, wondering if Rhosa had confided something to her?

Marina stood up and said. "Thank you for lovely talk, Rhosa tell to me we would get on well. I must go, have an appointment."

As she stood before him, Jake noticed again her beautiful figure and wondered about the 'appointment'. "Modelling?"

"Yes, Rhosa tell you? Something I've done for a while. You'd surprised how hard work. Sitting still for long time. You have an itch or you want to sneeze and you terrify because the pose has always be the same. If it isn't, the artists lose dimension. Sit or stand for two hours and ache in all body." She saw his eyes looking at her and felt a certain pleasure at his admiration.

"Is it something you need to do?" he hesitated, not wanting to appear to pry into her private thoughts.

"Young life is short. In ten, twenty year I will be not slim and..." she put her hands under her breasts as though weighing them, "they will drop. I can make a living, not good but survive with other work. You say 'need to do' – it is also freedom. Many people stupid about body. Should celebrate it. Why must always be clothed, exciting to have liberty, feel wind blowing on my skin."

"You model in the open air?"

"Best time to run - my hair flow behind me."

"While you are being filmed?"

"Yes, for art film," she smiled, "they say will be shown in Tate Gallery."

"Perhaps I will be invited," Jay grinned.

Marina looked at him from under her brows directing a smile at him. "Perhaps but now I go," she said, blowing him a kiss as she looked over her shoulder.

Jake followed her as she walked away, watched the bounce in her step and was pleased when she turned to wave goodbye to him.

He went back into his office and tried to start writing again. After half an hour, he looked at the page in front of him, read what he had written and deleted it all.

As he did, he picked up the cold cup of coffee, went to the window and looked out over the pond, drank and thought about Marina.

CHAPTER 25

A few days later Jacob heard Mistry go to the door and shortly return with a letter in her hands. He took it, broke open the seal and grimaced as he saw that it was written in Latin.

"Mistry," he sat down as he read and indicated for her to sit as well, "it is a letter from the man in the cloak," he said.

She nodded. "The messenger did not say who he was but he also was wearing a cloak and as soon as I took the letter he ran off."

"The same man who came here?"

"No he was much smaller and with a crooked back."

"Mm, in the letter, the man who came to see me wants me to meet some other people."

"Do there not be dangers in that, sir," she said, reverting to addressing him formally.

"It may be a trap to catch me in heresy, but I shall go."

"Sir, I want you not to…" she stopped herself in mid-sentence as she realised that it would not be correct for her to restrict his freedom.

"Thank you for caring. The danger is worth risking." Seeing the concern on her face, he said, "I shall not be alone. I will take three strong men with me; they have been my shield before. They will not be seen because they will mix with people outside the house where I shall meet the hooded man and his companions. I have a sign which the young men understand. If I go to the window and make the mark of a cross on my forehead, they will force their way in. They will have weapons beneath their cloaks and I would pitch them against twice their number."

"But can you then come back here?"

"If I can, I will but, even if there is too much danger. I have other safe houses where I can stay."

Mistry's face showed her concern.

"You are wondering about yourself, Mistry, are you not?"

"I am more worried about you but a little bit about what I could do. I think I would die if I went back to the streets."

"You need not fear. I have made some arrangements and you can be sure you will be taken care of."

She smiled and bowed her head in thanks.

"Sit down beside me, Mistry. I want to talk about lessons."

"You have taught me a lot and I want to learn more."

"We never stop learning." For some moments, their eyes met until she turned her gaze to the floor.

"We live in changing times, Mistry. There has never before been such a time. So many things that we are told is God's truth cannot be proven. Some years ago, a man called Magellan sailed with a crew from Spain and went round the world. The journey proved that the world is round. Do you see what that means, Mistress?"

"I'd like to hear more."

"I told you about Copernicus, who contradicted the Church, but it refused to accept his evidence."

"Does that matter, Jacob?"

"If by that you mean, does it make any difference to the world, then no, it does not matter. Mankind will survive but the Church which is the most powerful body we have punishes all who have ideas which conflict with their teachings. It is more powerful than kings, more powerful than armies, more powerful than countries."

"Is that because what God has decided cannot be altered?" she asked with a smile.

"You remembered what I said." Jacob smiled with her. "The minds of the people have been enslaved and they fear that if they do not obey, they will suffer eternal damnation in Hell."

She turned her head away and he saw that she was distressed.

"Are you thinking of your man?"

"Sir, they did say those words to him. Even when they pulled his drowned self from the water, the priest shouted 'To Hell' at his dear face all blown up with the water. I wanted so much to go to Hell with him."

"And all this, his death and your wanting to die is all because the Church has foundations so weak that it cannot accept any challenge for fear it might collapse."

"But what of the King?"

"What I am saying must never be repeated, you understand?"

"Sir, my life is here, with you. I do say nought to anyone outside."

"The King we have is as deceitful as the Pope. He wrote a book praising the Church but only so he could ask for favours. In gratitude for his praise, the Pope made King Henry, Defender of the Faith. The King is a very rich man at a time when many people die from want. It is no wonder that there are riots. Land is stolen from the people and enclosed by fencing so that they can't enter it. People tear down the hedges and fences that are meant to keep them out but wealthy landowners execute them".

"Execute?" she asked.

"They are hanged with a rope tied around their necks until they are dead."

Jacob could see she was overcome by the memory of her man.

"I think it's time for some ale, Mistry. Can we have some of that which Jack brewed for us?"

"I will get some," she said, going into the kitchen.

Together, they sat and drank the ale. When Jacob could see that she was more settled, he continued. "I share your sadness about the death of your man."

CHAPTER 26

It was a cold, grey and drizzling morning, where to be in front of a fire, with a hot drink, reading a good novel was tempting. Jake was all for staying in and waiting for a fine day but Rhosa had a break in her rehearsal schedule and insisted that this had to be the day they would do their exploration. Clad in raincoats they ventured out to look for the grave of Mistry Darkall. The wind became so strong that it almost tore open the umbrella they shared. As they walked, Jake tried again to convince her to come back on a better day, but Rhosa insisted that they carry on. They had been into four churchyards without finding what they were looking for.

After fruitlessly looking round many churchyards he was becoming irritated and said he was going home to the fire. But by this time, Rhosa was too excited to stop. She dragged him to St. Andrew's churchyard, where the service here was later than in the other churches. The bells were ringing with a noise so loud it made Jake feel uneasy, he thanked the Lord when the congregation stopped rushing past them.

Rhosa squeezed his arm as she looked around the gravestones. "This is it, Jake. I'm sure it's somewhere in this churchyard."

And she was right. There behind the church, probably unnoticed for hundreds of years. By this time Jake was beginning to get as enthusiastic as Rhosa and, shielded by the church, the weather ceased to bother him. When she saw it, Rhosa almost cried.

The inscription on a small gravestone read:

Mistry Darkall
Who Changeth Me
Keep Me Here
With You

Rhosa leaned forward and rubbed her gloved hand over the stone to remove the moss which partially obscured the writing. Suddenly she leapt up, grabbed his arm and pointed. "Look Jay. See what it says at the bottom."

They were in the shadow of the church and the light was bad but there it was, worn down by four hundred years of hostile weather but still distinguishable –

'By Jacob D'Arcy, With Gratitude for a Life'

"Don't you feel – I don't know - overawed, Jay?" Rhosa said. "It must be the same woman as in the painting; too much of a coincidence otherwise."

"Presumably she lived in the same house as Jacob D'Arcy but she has a different name so they were obviously not married." Jay said.

"Could she have been his mistress, I wonder?" Rhosa asked.

"I was wondering that too."

They stared in silence at the gravestone and felt a strange bond with the woman who was buried beneath.

Rhosa shivered. "I want to go into the church."

"To get warm?"

"No, it's not that; I sense there is something in this church."

"There's a service on."

"We'll go in quietly and sit in the back."

Jake was often awkward in unfamiliar situations. Going into the church where people were worshipping was one of them. Against his better judgement he allowed himself to follow Rhosa through the entrance. The door creaked noisily as they opened it and many eyes turned to see who the intruders were. They couldn't have chosen a more intrusive time to go in, because the priest was in the middle of his sermon. Worse still, he stopped and said loudly to them. "Welcome to you."

His greeting prompted those who had kept their gaze forward to turn in enquiry and watch while the newcomers self-consciously found a place to sit. The pew they sat on was cold and creaked beneath them. Whenever they moved the priest paused in his sermon as though emphasising that although he had used the phrase 'welcome', it applied only if they merged into the background and remained silent. In trying to avoid moving, Jake and Rhosa found they were so uncomfortable that they couldn't avoid shifting. Jake issued a silent sigh when the sermon ended and they all stood to sing. He tugged at Rhosa's arm and indicated that they should leave while the congregation was singing and they would not be heard. She shook her head determinedly and whispered that she wanted to stay. When the service was over, he again tried to leave but Rhosa held his coat, preventing him from rising. The congregation filed out with many of them staring at the new couple and a few nodded their heads with a smile to make them feel 'at home'. The priest came to give them his greetings, apologising that he had to leave and hoped that they would come again, as he walked to the entrance to say goodbye to his parishioners.

Jake and Rhosa remained seated until everyone had left.

"Why can't we go?" he asked.

Silently, she pointed at the stalls. "Can't you see?" she whispered

"No, what am I supposed to be looking at?"

"The worn brass plate on that stall"

He had always been rather short sighted and had been advised to wear glasses all the time but was convinced they didn't suit him. He told himself it was not just vanity that stopped him. He earned his living by impressing people and he seemed to do better if he didn't wear his prescription lenses. "What does it say?" he asked.

"It says 'D'Arcy Family'."

"God, Rhosa. Like you said before 'this is getting creepy.'"

"Not to me it isn't; I think we are beginning to get somewhere. I have to know more about your man in the portrait." Rhosa pulled his arm. "Jake, I want to go and sit in that stall."

He wasn't sure he wanted to but followed her obediently, musing to himself that this was the first relationship he had been in where he was happy to be led. With his two previous wives and the intervening girlfriends he had always been the one to make decisions.

Sitting on the hard wooden bench in the pew that Jacob D'Arcy would have sat on was a very moving experience for both of them. Rhosa took Jake's hand and squeezed it hard.

Momentarily, the clouds outside cleared and a ray of sun shone through the window. "Jay, look," Rhosa said.

He frowned, "look at what?"

"Your shadow!"

He glanced at his shadow and with some tingling in the nerves on the back of his neck saw that his shadow made him look like a different man. The same sensation overtook him as when he had found the bible in the hole in the wall of Firenze House.

They sat, absorbing the atmosphere, for several minutes before Rhosa spoke.

"That's it, Jay, it all fits," she said with a distant smile, "the shadows on the wall there, must be saying something."

"Yes," he said, confused.

"Jacob D'Arcy would have sat here and his shadow would have been cast on the pew wall as yours is, and the sound of his voice would have echoed in this church as it would have done at Firenze House."

"Sorry, you've lost me."

"Jacob D'Arcy left his thoughts for you."

Neither of them could think of anything to say. Eventually, she slid her hand under his leg as it rested on the pew and he felt the warmth which he had built up around him beginning to drain away into her cold hand.

"You will be sitting next to a block of ice if we don't move, Jay, I think I must walk around," she said.

They got up and walked past the few stragglers standing in the porch talking to the priest.

They passed the gravestone and were about to get into the car when they saw the outer door to the church hall was open and refreshments were being served. Without saying anything, they both changed direction and went into the warmth. The scene which greeted them was familiar, smelling of steam from the urns standing beside rock cakes falling from overfilled plates. The lady behind the counter was typical – seen better days, slightly overweight, with a pinafore over her large bosom. Jake and Rhosa walked to a table with their tea and cakes, still so overcome by their experience in the church that they did not want to speak.

After they had drunk the hot sweet tea they felt warmer. Jake broke the silence and joked that perhaps Mistry had even pushed her hand under Jacob's leg on cold days.

Rhosa laughed at the thought and she said. "You know, it's funny, I didn't mean to do that, it sort of just happened. Afterwards, I almost felt like apologising because it seemed that I was invading your warmth."

He smiled. "Do that anytime your hand is cold."

Rhosa smiled back, squeezed his knee and ran her hand along his thigh. He looked over at the pinafored woman, who quickly looked away, but not before Jake saw that she was looking at what Rhosa's hand was doing with more than just interest. When later they found that she was the Vicar's wife, Rhosa mused on the way she had looked at them in what seemed an envious manner. At the time, they joked that probably nothing like that had ever happened in her life.

They finished the aptly-named rock cakes as best they could and dashed to the car in a vain attempt to avoid the rain, which had started again.

"We've got to come back here when the weather is better, Jay," Rhosa said as they drove off.

The following Saturday was sunny and this time they walked to the church through a winding path in a wood, lush with undergrowth. They were sitting on the same stall in the church when the vicar came in. He remembered who they were and was pleased to see them.

"Reverend Joshua Williams, I am very pleased to see you both again." he said shaking hands with them.

Rhosa looked stunning and Jake thought it would be more correct to say that the priest was pleased to see her. He noticed while they talked that the vicar almost always directed his questions at Rhosa.

He was obviously intrigued that unlike most casual visitors, they had attended one service and were now in his church for the second time.

Rhosa sensed his bemusement. "You may be wondering why we are here, Vicar," she said.

"It's very nice to see new faces, especially young ones." It was one of those rhetorical comments designed to invite an explanation, so Rhosa continued.

"It's just a co-incidence that Jake has a house nearby in Barnes."

Jake saw that the priest was looking down at her wedding ring finger, trying to sort out their relationship.

"And the man whose name is on this pew was the original owner of Firenze House. What's more, you have Mistry Darkall buried in the churchyard and she also lived in the same house, we think."

"Jacob D'Arcy," he said, looking at the name on the stall, "was one of the benefactors of this church. I don't know about Mistry Darkall. Jacob was a Catholic I understand, but converted to the Church of England before he died. He left an annuity in perpetuity. It was quite a large one and has grown into a fair size. It enables us to endow an alms house and leaves enough for some maintenance on the church. He is buried up there near the altar, did you know?"

He took them up to the altar so that they could see the elaborately carved plaque which seemed to read Jacopus D'Arcius. It was quite beautiful and Rhosa gasped both at its intricacy and at the discovery of another connection with D'Arcy.

"Do you know anything about him?" she asked the priest.

"I don't I'm afraid, nor do I know why he was given that Latin sounding name, I suspect it was done by an ill-educated stone mason," he smiled wanly at what they assumed must have been meant as a joke. "There is a man whom I have met who is an historian. He's writing a book on the village of Barnes as it was in the sixteenth century. I know that Jacob D'Arcy was quite important in his day and perhaps there will be something about him in his book."

"Do you know his name?" Jake asked.

"Yes, I have his details in my address book. If you want to come in to the rectory, I'll look it up."

They followed him out of the church and across the graveyard to the rectory, which still retained traces of its medieval origins.

As they walked in, they passed the kitchen door and a woman came out, whom initially they did not recognise without her pinafore on.

"Hello again," she said. The vicar looked up, surprised until she explained. "This is the young couple I was telling you about, Joshua, they came to the hall after the service last Sunday."

Jake wondered if she had told him about Rhosa's hand on his thigh.

"I remember them because they seemed to enjoy my cakes." Something about the way she spoke made Rhosa think there was a note of triumph in her voice. Her vivid imagination sensed layers in the relationship of the vicar and his wife; she being the cook and provider and he the complainer. Her husband appeared not to notice the implication in her voice.

Rhosa introduced herself and Jake by first name only as though determined not to explain their relationship.

"Jennifer Williams," the Vicar's wife said smiling and holding out her hand. Jake saw that in her own surroundings and without the pinafore, she was an attractive woman.

The Vicar asked her, "You remember the man in your reading circle who has written a book about the village in the sixteenth century, do you have his address?"

"Daniel Freidan, yes, why do you want to know?"

"These young people have a house in Barnes and want to find out about the original owner. They think it is the man who is buried near the altar behind that beautiful plaque."

"Jacopus D'Arcius, isn't it?" Jake asked.

"The Latinised name someone chose for him when he was buried here." Reverend Williams said directing his words at his wife, "and this couple think that his friend, Mistry Darkall who is buried in the graveyard, may also have lived in the same house."

"Daniel will be interested," she said as she wrote down his name and address, which they noted she obviously carried in her head. As she said the name, Jake saw a glance passing between her and her husband. "For the next couple of weeks, he is away in Italy with the reading group – the one I was invited to go on," she said, looking at her husband with lidded eyes. "When he comes back, I'm sure he would like to talk to you. I'll speak to him if you like."

"Thank you." Rhosa said. "That would be nice. I'm intrigued to know more about the man who built Firenze House."

Two weeks passed, during which time they tried to find more about D'Arcy. And then the 'phone rang one evening when Rhosa was out rehearsing.

"Mr. Dearsey, Daniel is back, I've spoken to him and he's willing to meet you."

"I appreciate that, thank you. When would be convenient?"

"As it happens, I am meeting him to talk about the tour he organised. The group has been visiting the sites of Etruscan settlements, which were the subject of the book we have just read. He is a fascinating and very busy man; he could fit you in at his house next Thursday afternoon at 2pm."

When Jake heard that she found him fascinating, he hesitated for a moment. "I'd be delighted to come but Rhosa will not be available." He knew that she was rehearsing but he also knew that she could finish early if she wanted to. Knowing Rhosa's interest in intellectual men, he decided to assess him before he introduced her.

Thursday morning came and Jake told another white lie to Rhosa. "Oh, I had a call from Jennifer Williams, the wife of the vicar. She suggests I drop in this afternoon. She is meeting with that Daniel fellow who is the historian. I'll go and ask him about D'Arcy, see if he knows anything."

"She invited you? That's surprising."

"Why surprising?"

"Didn't you get the vibrations when we met her with her husband?"

"How do you mean?"

"It was all there in the look her husband gave her and in the guarded way they spoke."

Jake stared at her vacantly.

"You aren't normally unobservant. Are you deliberately being obtuse?" she teased him. "I'll spell it out – listen - Jennifer Williams is a frustrated wife – she is bored with her husband, the vicar. The vicar knows it - didn't want her going away with that Daniel character because he was afraid she would jump into the tent with him."

Jake had subconsciously sensed this but had not been particularly aware because neither Jennifer Williams nor the vicar had impinged much on his consciousness.

"So that's why I'm surprised that she invited you." Rhosa said.

He looked quizzically at her.

"Because I would have thought you would get in her way." she said as a thought struck her. "Unless… unless it's a three in a bed situation." She laughed.

Jake was pleased to see the beginnings of jealousy, if only feigned, in her humour, but defused the situation by saying. "If you are right about her and the historian, she probably wants me there so that she can tell the vicar that the reason for her seeing him is to introduce me."

"You are beginning to wake up, Jay. If that's the reason, you will be shunted off early, having served your purpose."

CHAPTER 27

Daniel Freidan's house was an elegant Victorian place on Castelnau Road, leading to Hammersmith Bridge, white painted with well-proportioned windows. It spoke of money. The door was opened not by Daniel but, he was surprised to see, by Jennifer.

"Come in, Mr. Dearsey, Daniel is in the garden doing research." Jake followed her down a long corridor and out into bright sun, contrasting with the rain which had soaked the earth for the past week. His eyes blinked as he walked into the long garden which sloped down to the reservoir behind the house. Sitting beneath the shade of a tree sat a dark haired man, dressed in clothes which marked him as an artist. Daniel Freidan appeared so absorbed in his reading that he did not look up as they approached him. He looked insignificant, bent over papers lifting at their edges in the light breeze blowing through the garden. Jake judged him to be about the same age as himself and saw that he had an austere, academic-looking face. When Jake stood in front of him, he glanced up in a distracted manner, his hands tapping on his lips and his eyes focussed on the distance. After a measured pause, he stood up and with only a slight smile held his hand out. "Mr. Dearsey, I assume." he said without warmth, "I'm told you've come to learn more about the man whose stone in Jennifer's church is marked Jacopus Darcius." he indicate a chair and without turning said, "Jennifer, I'm sure Mr. Dearsey would welcome some of the fresh lemonade you made."

Jake could have felt irritated that Freidan should assume what he thought he should like, and also that Jennifer would get it for him, but after the hot walk in the sun, the thought of cool lemonade was welcome.

From the moment he met him, it was apparent to Jake that this man was a poser and would be a pretentious bore so he said nothing and waited for the lemonade to be poured by Jennifer.

"Now, Mr. Dearsey, fate has brought you here and you've come to the right place, no one knows more about Barnes or Jacopus than I. What is it you want to know?"

Jake took a drink from the glass in front of him partly to give himself time to think and partly to play Freidan at his own game so that he would see him as being at his own level of intellect, not, as it appeared from Freidan's attitude, an inferior.

"I have the enquiring mind of a journalist and would like to know all you can tell me about him."

"A journalist! Are you planning to write an article on Jacopus? If so, is our conversation on a commercial basis?"

Jake, taken aback, was momentarily lost for words.

"No, I am not planning an article; I meant only that I am interested in facts, particularly historical ones."

"Mm." Freidan said, nodding and again tapping his lips with the fingers of one hand. "Very well but, perhaps you will be cognisant of the fact that, if at a later date you do write an article, my efforts will be recognised, I have worked exhaustively on the history of the sixteenth century and the man reputed to have extended your house."

"Of course," Jake smiled ingratiatingly, "I do understand that knowledge such as yours is only acquired by considerable effort."

Freidan inclined his head in mute acknowledgement and Jake saw that he glanced at Jennifer to ensure that she had noted the compliment.

"By multifarious and circuitous routes, I have been able to gather a body of data about him and of course many other people but there are considerable gaps, you understand. If you were planning to write about him, a lot more research would be needed, which I should be glad to undertake at my usual fees of course. Jennifer acts as my secretary and can inform you of my fee structure."

"What I have found is that Jacob D'Arcy was a remarkable man. A Renaissance man before that body of thought which started in Italy became widely disseminated in these islands." He stopped, stroked his chin with his hand and said. "One is looking for a suitable point to begin."

"What did he do for a living?"

"Ah yes, the first question of the man in the street." he said in what seemed calculated to be disparaging; he glanced at Jennifer as though expecting an approving glance from her. "He was a merchant and from my research, seemingly a very successful one. There are records of gifts and endowments he made which, even to this day benefit the unfortunates."

"What was his business?"

"Wool, of course or more precisely, fine English cloth; many merchants in this country were in the cloth trade. It formed the basis of the wealth of England. Raw wool, treated wool, weaving, dyeing or making into garments, areas like the Cotswolds were built on the woollen trade. If you have been to Halifax, where some of my studies took me and where Jacopus would buy some of his raw wool and get it woven and dyed, you will have seen the residue of what must have been an extremely wealthy town, now sadly in considerable decline. Quite a lot of his business was with Italy and often with Florence."

"The Medici bank financed his family business, that was until the bank fell on hard times and called in loans. Along with many other businesses the D'Arcy family was almost destroyed, but that was long before Jacopus became involved. It was largely through hard work and the talents of Jacopus that the family trade became re-established. The house you live in was originally built for the D'Arcy family dowagers but Jacopus; we call him that name only because that is what is on his memorial in Jennifer's church - had the house extended as his home and a base for the business."

Jake noticed that he referred to the church as being Jennifer's and not the Vicar's.

Freidan stopped talking and indulged in one of his meditations. They were so contrived that Jake interrupted Freidan.

"And what sort of man was he?"

"You go too fast, Mr. Dearsey. I wanted to explain more about the acumen of our Jacopus, for he was, as I say, a Renaissance man, not just an intellectual but also a man of commerce. He took over an ailing business and in the modern parlance, 'turned it round'."

"In doing that, he cut out a lot of waste - people who had been taking large amounts from the company while contributing nothing. Stocks that had lain unused for many years, he sold off -

sometimes at below cost, just to get capital back into the business. Having done that, he managed the business so successfully that, when he died, he left a fortune - a small sum by today's standards but, as I say, a fortune then."

He became meditative again and to fill the silence, Jake took a drink and turned to Jennifer with a smile of thanks for the lemonade. As they made contact he saw in her eyes what seemed to him to be a shadow of fear, but it quickly passed and was replaced by the same polite smile he had given her.

He wondered about that look for a moment but then began to suspect that he had been mistaken. He was so pre-occupied that he missed what Freidan was saying as he stroked his chin, trying, Jake felt sure, to look enigmatic. He obviously did not notice Jake's lack of attention and was still droning on when Jake interrupted.

"What is known of Mistry Darkall?"

"Oh, Darkall, just his servant, she would have had no involvement in his life."

"Other than providing for his needs?"

"Yes," he said distractedly, "of no consequence at all."

"And yet…" Jake was about to explain about the painting and the message on the back of it but Freidan was away, talking about Henry the Eighth and Tyndale's bible and how in the 1520s the Catholic authorities ordered all copies of the English translation of the Bible to be destroyed, to stop what they considered the dangerous thirst for freedom, flowing from Luther's Germany.

He took a drink of his lemonade as Jake tried to tell him that the period was the subject of his own Ph.D. and that he had seen a copy of the Tyndale bible in Firenze House but Freidan, intoxicated by his own voice, was not listening to him.

"This was the Protestant Reformation which came in reaction to Roman Catholicism." He did a histrionic frown as though struggling to bring deep knowledge from his 'learned mind'. Jake began to wish he could find an excuse to leave but Freidan was away again. "You know Mr. Dearsey, the Reformation was predicated in England by John Wycliffe in the fourteenth century. But he and his group, the Lollards, were suppressed, and it is commonly thought that

England in the early sixteenth century had only the Catholic religion. It wasn't till 1517, that Martin Luther, a monk and professor at the University of Wittenberg, opposed the Pope and the Catholic Church, claiming that it had become corrupted by its political influence."

"You see, Catholicism was able to enrich its priests and to dominate the leaders of other countries. Luther deplored the sale of indulgences by the Church. You've heard of these I hope." Freidan waited for Jake to nod. "They allowed people to expiate their sins and avoid punishment and, you may be surprised to learn that the sales formed a large part of the wealth of the Vatican." He looked up at the few clouds drifting across the sky and said, "I am a man of reason, not of religion and you will understand why I say that it is my opinion that the Vatican is the world's biggest confidence trick."

"Can you imagine anything cleverer than to be able to exploit mankind's need for an omnipotent being whom they called God? This God loves everyone and is all forgiving but demands extreme loyalty. He so abhors what he calls sin that he has invented places called Hell and Purgatory to which the people he purportedly loves will be sent if they misbehave. There they suffer the fires of eternal damnation unless they or their families pay large sums to the Church for masses to be sung and for the purchase of indulgences."

"One can't help feeling that the Mafia followed the same principles in the protection rackets." Jake said, for a moment feeling an affinity with Freidan's views.

"Substantial difference being that it is easy to show that the Mafia exists and the Hellfire that comes from the barrels of their guns requires no proof. The Church is not expected to prove the existence of God, the devil or of Heaven and Hell. Anyone asking for proof would have been condemned as a heretic."

Jake nodded his agreement, and would have spoken, but Freidan was off again.

"Only if we follow the dictates of the Church will this perfect God let us go to Heaven. They will there suffer a life where everyone is good and there is no sin and which anyone with a mind as enquiring as mine would find tedious and boring."

"The Church claimed to be empowered by God to decide what is to be called 'sin' and thereby to deny us any of the pleasures nature has given us to enjoy. I have looked far and wide at paintings, sculptures and images of religious men and women. Nowhere have I seen anyone smiling and enjoying themselves except in lewd Bacchanalian rites intended to show simple believers how not to behave. Saints have to have a long suffering look, their eyes cast up to heaven showing that they have denied themselves enjoyment. Nature has given us the desire to have many partners for the purpose of so spreading our seed that humankind is made stronger. You may have read the work of Dr. Jack Dominian opposing the Declaration of the Catholic Church on Sexual Ethics. Dominian wrote that sex is one of the gifts of God, worthy of exaltation and the springs of joy, pleasure and loving communication. We see it in the animal kingdom where those fortunate creatures have not been cursed with a morality which denies them excitement. In the animal world one of the greatest pleasures is freely available. Let me tell you an interesting story. It has been found that the dawn chorus comes earlier in those birds that nest near street lighting. Female birds nested in woodland away from the lights, fly to the lit areas to copulate with other male birds. They then fly back in time for the dawn chorus in their own mates' territory." He cast a glance at Jennifer and Jake was convinced that he saw a faint smile of acquiescence in her eyes.

Jake wanted to say that he would be discussing the denial of pleasure in the book he was writing, but said nothing for fear that Freidan would demand payment for the idea. Instead, he waited while Freidan cast his eyes around the garden as though needing inspiration. With an exhalation of breath he started on an unrelated topic. "You may have heard the name Calvin. He had a profound effect and perhaps even inspired King Henry in his sacking of the monasteries." He eased himself into a more comfortable position and checked that not only was his guest listening but also that Jennifer was impressed with his erudition.

"Initially, at least, the Reformation was resisted in England, and King Henry denounced Luther and the grateful Pope awarded him the title of 'Defender of the Faith', which is, of course, why we still have Fid Def. on our coins.

"Translations of the Scriptures into English were burned. Protestants were persecuted, or arrested, tried and executed. So that he could marry Anne Boleyn Henry wanted a divorce from Catherine of Aragon who had failed to produce an heir."

"The Pope refused to grant a divorce so in 1531 Henry charged the Church in England with having usurped royal authority. Realising that the best course of action was cooperation, the Convocation of the Clergy made a donation to the royal coffers of over £100,000, and accepted the King as 'Supreme head of the English Church and clergy'."

"In 1533 Henry divorced Catherine and married Anne Boleyn who became queen but, as you may know, he tired of her after a few years and an excuse was found to behead her on the grounds of infidelity. Henry was excommunicated by Pope Clement VII. Monks and clergy who objected that the king, a layman could not be Head of the Church of England were hung, drawn, and quartered. Of such character was our Merry Henry. It is even suspected that he had the Earl of Surrey executed because Henry was envious of his looks." Before continuing Freidan repeated the tapping of his lips with his fingers while he watched to see if Jake was impressed.

"Fisher and Thomas More were accused of treason and beheaded. And from then till 1539, the monasteries were suppressed and their vast wealth passed to the King. This did not mean that the freedom to be a Protestant was established in England. On one day alone, twenty five Protestant Anabaptists were burned for heresy. In spite of the King's depredations, the Reformation slowly grew in England, probably covertly, and we must recognise the heroism of men and women who preferred martyrdom to changing their faith. I am telling you all this because you will thereby be aware of the dangers which Jacopus faced and of his courage in opposing the Church."

"Just as in our present day, technology came to their aid, in the form of the printing press to which you owe your livelihood, Mr. Dearsey." He smiled prissily at his attempt at humour. "Protestants found they could send their messages around the country and defy the Church."

"'How many printing presses there be in the world,' John Foxe, the Protestant asked, 'so many blockhouses there be against the high castle so that either the Pope must abolish knowledge and printing or printing at length will root him out.' As we know, Mr. Dearsey, that prediction is yet to eventuate."

Freidan stood up and without apology or comment, walked to the bottom of the garden amongst the shrubs and appeared to be looking out over the reservoir. Jake had heard enough and was about to get up to leave when he saw his host returning.

While he was walking back, Jennifer and Jake exchanged pleasantries. Jake wondered if Freiden could have moved away because he had run out of ideas and needed to read notes from his pocket.

"You will be interested, Mr. Dearsey," he continued as he sat down in the chair he had vacated, "to hear about the rebellion during the life of Jacopus. We can only ponder on what his involvement might have been. By assiduous effort, I have been able to find other documents relating to him and his contemporaries. They reveal many other acts of dissension. I am still researching if he was involved with lawyer Robert Aske who, with a priest, led a rebellion involving a large number of people. They seized several cities and castles in England and demanded of the King that monasteries be reinstated. The King appeared ready to acquiesce but this was obviously a strategy to defuse the situation and in 1537, he executed one hundred and thirty people, including the leaders." Freidan nodded his head sagely and tapped his lips with his index finger. He fixed his visitor with what Jake was sure was intended to be a penetrating gaze. "You might wonder why I am telling you all this, Mr. Dearsey?"

Jake hadn't wondered at all and was convinced that the purpose was twofold, the first to impress him but more importantly, to impress Jennifer. When Jake didn't reply, Freidan continued.

"The reason is that I want you to be aware firstly of the effort I have expended and secondly of the qualities of our Jacopus. You see, he was part of that renaissance of ideas. Somehow his name escaped the history books but in my extensive research I have been able to uncover letters." He looked up at Jake. "I see you look surprised, Mr. Dearsey but don't be, I am tireless when I feel there are documents I should obtain. The letters are of course in code and would have remained un-deciphered were it not for the fact that I happen to be an expert in code breaking." He looked over his glasses at his guest and at Jennifer. Jake didn't see the need to respond but Jennifer's voice broke the silence as she said.

"We all admire your abilities, Daniel, and are fortunate to have you leading our circle of learners," Jennifer said.

He beamed at her and expecting similar approbation, turned to Jake who could think of nothing to say other than. "Interesting."

There was hardly anything Freidan had said with which Jake was not already familiar, and the mechanical delivery made him think Freidan had been rehearsing what he had told Jake.

Since he had not fallen at Freidan's feet in worship Jake suspected he was a disappointment and stood to leave.

Without getting up from his chair, Freidan shook the proffered hand and said. "I trust you found this afternoon useful, Mr Dearsey. If you need any more information, I am sure I can help, particularly if you start to write your article or," with a quizzical smile on his face, "is it a book you are writing?"

"Thank you Mr. Freidan, I have only an interest in learning a bit about the man who built Firenze House and have no intention of writing about him."

When saying goodbye, Freidan placed one hand on top of Jake's so that the large pentacle ring he had on his finger would be visible.

Freidan remained seated while Jennifer showed Jake out of the house. Before she closed the door, she put her hand on his arm, seeming to gain comfort from the contact. "Do come again," she said, and the way she spoke made it sound almost like a plea.

CHAPTER 28

Shortly after he got in, Jake heard Rhosa's key in the front door. She came into the study looking stunning, wearing an outfit which could have come straight from Vogue, a lime green woollen top coat with a pale green turtle necked sweater and matching flared trousers over the top of lime green suede boots. She gave him an affectionate kiss while she explained that she had been trapped on the train and was desperate for a drink; 'anything would do'. While Rhosa took off her coat, he passed her the newspaper she always liked to read and went into the kitchen. When he returned, he put the mugs and the biscuit barrel on the table in front of her. "Well." Rhosa said, looking up from her reading as he came into the room. "How did it go with the vicar's wife and her lover?"

"You're being cynical about Jennifer. I've no reason to believe they are anything more than members of a history group."

"I have though. Acting makes one very aware of atmosphere. The look holding simmering anger in a brief glance when the vicar was talking to his wife was enough for me. I couldn't know whether she and your Mr. Freidan are actually lovers in the true sense but there is certainly something more than 'members of a history group' between them."

"I hadn't thought that far," he responded. "It could be even more than you suspect. The atmosphere in the Freidan house was almost eerie."

"What do you mean, eerie?"

"You remember the Gerald Du Maurier novel Svengali?"

"Should do, I took the part of Trilby. One of the first plays I did."

"I didn't know that," he said with some surprise, "but I wouldn't have known you then. Our Daniel Freidan doesn't look like a Svengali but I'm sure he has a hold on Jennifer somehow."

"How interesting, the play lasted only two weeks but it's such a demanding role that I was Trilby long after the run ended." She shuddered. "Did you learn anything about Jacob D'Arcy?"

He related to her the few things Freidan had told him about Jacob.

"Nothing we couldn't have guessed, I suppose." Rhosa said. "But did you ask about Mistry?"

"Oh, yes. He was very disparaging about her – just a servant – he said in a way which made me think he was trying to dissuade me from showing any more interest in her."

"That makes me even more intrigued by her. He couldn't have seen what D'Arcy wrote on the back of the painting or on her gravestone could he? Otherwise he wouldn't have said that. I wish I'd come with you, rehearsals finished early so I could have," she paused. "Nice house?"

"Couldn't really say, I only saw the hall and a corridor, nice on the outside though, and in a lovely area. We've driven up Castelnau Road to Hammersmith Bridge many times so you know the sort of place it is. Jennifer let me in, by the way."

"Jennifer did! But she was supposed to be a guest like you."

"Yes, I thought it was peculiar when she came to the door. She also showed me out and he got her to give me lemonade which she had made. Her Daniel Freidan did not even come to the door to say goodbye."

"Not a cripple, is he?"

"Possibly an emotional one but definitely not a physical one; at one stage, he got up, left me with Jennifer and walked to the shrubs at the end of the garden."

"An old trick of the stage," Rhosa laughed. "Forget your lines, walk away to where you've written them down or the prompt will tell you. Done well it can create quite an atmosphere of suspense."

He smiled. "I wondered about that too. He was pouring history at me and then stopped, walked off and returned with more history which he delivered at full tilt. I did wonder."

"Think he may have had a history book hidden?"

"Or notes in his pocket which he didn't want me to see."

"The old fraud. I wonder if he has been an actor." she frowned. "Daniel Freidan. It's quite a good name so he may have used it on stage. I'll look him up."

"You can do that?"

"Oh certainly, every actor or actress is recorded and sometimes actors have to change their names because another actor already has it."

"So I might have to change my name from Jacob Dearsey if I had wanted to take the part your director virtually offered me."

"Yes, you might need to be Jacob D'Arcy." she smiled quizzically. "Funny, isn't it how similar your name is to his?"

"I did wonder about that too - just a coincidence of course."

"P'raps," she said, shrugging her shoulders, "but I think there is more to it than that."

CHAPTER 29

Jacob looked up from the book he was reading. "Mistry," he said as she raised herself from tending the fire, "there is something I have wanted to talk to you about."

She could see that he felt awkward so wiped her hands on her apron and waited for him to speak.

"My friends have collected some money for my birthday. They want me to get my portrait painted."

"That would be very nice."

"It will but I wondered something..."

"Yes?"

"I wanted to thank you, Mistry; you've become part of this house, so much so that I can't imagine it without you. Well...," he stumbled, "would you like to have your portrait done also. In our group, we have an artist who has seen you when you were in the streets and he thought you had a face he would like to paint. At the time, you were with some people whom he said looked unpleasant. He was surprised when he came here and saw you again. He told me he found you even more attractive than when he first saw you."

"Me? But I am only a servant; why should he want to paint me?"

"You should not think of yourself as a servant; that is only what people outside see. Francis, the artist says that you have a serenity which he has never experienced before."

"Serenity?"

"A peace about you," he said, "He wants to paint that peace."

A smile settled around her lips as she said "'t'would be nice."

"You have brought such contentment into this house that I want your portrait fixed to the walls so that it will always remain here. We are not on this earth for long and the house will be sold many times after we've gone so I will write to my lawyer that the portrait must always stay on the walls of this house."

"I would be happy with that if your portrait was also to be the same," she said quietly.

"It will be so, then," cautiously he took her hand, "you and I will remain forever in this house through our portraits and the shadows we cast." He noticed that she did not take her hand away from his and was so overcome that he felt compelled to get up and go to the window to steady his whirling emotions.

"The artist will be here in an hour, I have asked him to eat with us - just bread and cheese and ale. Do you have enough?"

"Unless he do eat masses, there be enough in the larder for four meals," she looked up at Jacob with a slight smile as he turned away from the window. "Sorry Jacob, I forgot myself for a moment, I should speak properly; I should have said 'unless he eats masses there is enough in the larder."

Jacob allowed himself a smile of satisfaction as she left the room to busy herself laying out the food.

Mistry had expected the artist to be a handsome young man but when he arrived at the door he was small and insignificant, dressed in untidy clothes which were stained with paint.

He smiled at her and introduced himself. "Francis Pomroy, Mistress Darkall. I am here to paint Jacob's likeness and if you agree, I would like to paint yours as well."

Mistry curtsied as Jacob had taught her. "I am pleased, sir."

"I prefer to be called Francis. I don't like these formalities," he said as he walked through the door she held open for him. Taking off his hat and coat, he said. "I have seen you many times buying produce from the stall holders and Jacob has told me about you."

Mistry showed him into Jacob's study and stood with her hands together while he and Jacob exchanged greetings. When they had sat, Jacob indicated that she should sit beside them.

"Shall I bring in the food for you gentlemen?" she asked.

"Some ale would also be welcome I feel, Francis."

When Mistry had brought the ale and poured it, Jacob stood as she took the seat which he held for her.

"I'm very glad that you, Mistress would also like me to paint you. I've asked Jacob several times before but I fear it's taken him very long to suggest it to you. I can't think why." Francis said with a smile.

"I am honoured, sir...Francis," she said.

"I see from your hesitation that you are unsure about me." Francis said to her. "Let me put your mind at rest. Jacob has told me how you came to him and the sort of life you led beforehand. To begin with, I share his views on people. We are all different and all have qualities of our own".

"Jacob has told me that you have a great interest in learning and he is amazed at how quickly you pick things up. You are fortunate to live in the home of a man of immense knowledge who can understand complex subjects which most of us find incomprehensible. "

"It is your fate and mine to be born in different situations. I, like Jacob, had parents who were financially comfortable so I have never had to live as you did. I'm sure I could not and I would have died long ago. Probably killed by a mob because I am also an ugly man with a stoop and they don't like anyone who is different." He put down his emptied enamelled glass goblet. "Jacob told me about your man and I am very sorry to hear about the way he was treated." Mistry refilled his goblet from the pitcher on the table. As he downed the drink, he said, "Jacob tells me that he suspects that if you had been born into a well-off family as we were, you would have been an important person because of your intelligence."

"I am happy here, sir...Francis." Mistry coloured slightly and seeing her consternation, Francis continued. "Why am I saying this? Because I want you to know that I am like Jacob and do not hold with the stupidity which gives people titles and respect simply because of the family they come from. You have my respect and indeed my admiration for having lifted yourself out of the awful conditions out there." He pointed through the window, "We are here as equals; I will call you Mistry, the name Jacob gave you and you should call me Francis. I am sure we will become friends. That is the only way a painting can be done. I see many very poor paintings and the reason is that the painter and the sitter did not get to know each other. You see, I do not want just to paint a likeness, I want to bring out the person behind the face."

"I should have explained, Mistry, that Francis is not like any other painter I have met," Jacob said.

"I want to reveal their happiness, their loves, doubts and their fears if they have any." Francis put down his glass and with a twinkle in his eye, said "did you not say you had some fine Barnes cheese and bread, Jacob. I confess to not having eaten today, overcome with the thought of meeting your lovely maid."

Mistry felt so relaxed in the company of this man that she beamed at his compliments. Moments later, she brought the food to the table; Francis took it from her and cut the bread into slices, put a piece on the three plates, poured more ale and sat back to eat.

"What could be more enchanting than to eat in the company of such an attractive young woman," he raised his goblet, "and her equally intelligent but somewhat less attractive companion," he grinned at Jacob who laughed along with his guest.

"Now, tell me," Francis said between mouthfuls, "do you share Jacob's opinion on the Church?"

Before answering, she looked at Jacob. When he nodded, she said, "I have love of God but none for the Church. My man was drowned…" she stopped, unable to speak.

"I can understand how you feel," he put his hand on hers momentarily, "I had a cousin, a dearly loved friend who expressed opinions which opposed those held by the Church. Jacob may have told you about him. He was imprisoned for heresy. Can you imagine it, they are so afraid of anyone criticising them that they take away the liberty and often the life of a critic. How can they even think that the all-loving God commands them to do such a thing?" He sensed that Mistry was saddened by her memories. "I am going to paint Jacob in the clothes of a wool merchant."

He looked at Mistry so intently that she began to self-consciously smooth down her clothes. "And my painting as a servant?" she asked.

"Indeed no, Jacob told me about how elegant you looked when he took you to Hampton Court so I want to paint you as a lady. He told me of the dress you wore and I wonder if you would agree to let me see you wearing it and perhaps let me look at some others. I will need to do a few sketches of you both first."

Mistry looked at Jacob who nodded his agreement. She tried on three dresses before Francis was satisfied. When he left he had several sketches which he said he would work on before choosing the best.

After he left, Mistry said, "Jacob," she used his first name but it was still an effort for her. "I like that man, he... he makes me feel that I really could be a... lady." She coloured with embarrassment at her presumption.

Jacob looked into her face and said hesitantly, "To me you are a lady."

They both felt awkward and Mistry busied herself by clearing the table and wiping the crumbs which Francis had left. She took the things into the kitchen. When she returned she stood for a while before speaking.

"Last time you talked about history you did use the word crusade. What does that mean?"

Jacob was pleased to hear her question. A year had passed since she had first come into the house; her transformation filled him with pleasure. She now sat with him most evenings while he read and wrote with his quill pen while she either sewed or read the books he had selected for her, frequently asking him to explain difficult words.

"The Crusades are a name given to disguise what were vicious wars against the countries of Islam. The Pope, the Protector of the Roman Empire, wanted them to win back lands which had once belonged to Christianity; the Crusades caused great loss of life and destruction."

"Why did they want them then?"

"We have to go back a long way to explain," his brow wrinkled as he dredged facts from his memory. "We and much of Europe were governed by the Romans. They brought laws and civilisation to us for several hundred years. But nothing lasts forever and the Romans were defeated by invaders. Some of them were Muslims from Turkey. I've told you about Muslims, just as we follow Christ, they follow their saviour Mohammed. The Muslims captured Jerusalem which was the birthplace of Christ and to us a holy city. They also captured many other cities in the Holy Land."

"Christ said we should love each other, but war brings hate."

"You are right, Mistry." Jacob smiled with pleasure at her understanding. "And that is one of the puzzling things about the Church. It sees itself as God's offspring that can do no wrong and whom God will bless above all others. I have met many Muslims during a visit to the countries where they live; they are a loving people much like ourselves." He was pleased to see her nodding in understanding.

"It may seem stupid and you might wonder why we don't talk out our differences which are in reality unimportant. But that is the way of the world," he said, "we are told to hate what we don't understand. This attitude controls the way we work, the way we behave, the policies of our rulers, the wars they fight and even worse, the education of our children, trained from the beginning to see the Church as the earthly presence of God and therefore not to be questioned. We are governed by what is called Canon Law but which is obviously unfair. If I commit murder I would be punished with death but if a priest kills, the worst that could happen would be that he would be made a layman. There are many other examples of unfair treatment - you know that if a woman is discovered doing her washing on a Sunday, she could be whipped with knotted cord on her bare back."

Mistry nodded and looked to him to continue. Jacob put his elbows on the table and rested his chin on his hands as he thought about what he should say to her. "Sometimes, Mistry, I wonder if God is just an invention and nothing more than a cruel subterfuge of to keep us suppressed."

"Do you mean, for you there is no God?"

"That's not a question I could answer. We have no proof that he exists so it is just a matter of faith. I admit I am not convinced that an all-loving God would not understand that we are weak beings who often stray."

Mistry took a long time replying but, hesitating, said. "And have you strayed, Jacob?"

He put his hand on his forehead and looked away while he meditated.

"There was a time…" he paused. "My wife you see…she was very unemotional and…well, I was not. There was a woman who gave me comfort; she was about the same age as my wife. She lived nearby. She was not a lady like my wife but she understood a man's need for love."

"And now?"

"She too has died, her name was Ruth. She and Isabel were friends, they shared everything and when Isabel was stricken with the fever and I was away, she nursed her and must have caught the fever as well."

Mistry put her hand on his and said. "Poor man to lose two women from your life."

He nodded his head and said. "Yes, although Isabel and I did not have the sort of love which many men have, we were close, but fever took them both."

They both sat silent for a while. Then Jacob realised that she was waiting for him to continue. "Mistry, do you ever think about what influences us."

She looked puzzled and then asked, "God, do you mean?"

"No, I don't mean God, I mean the way our minds work and why we all behave in different ways."

"I wouldn't be knowing, Jacob, what is it?"

"Most thinkers still believe Hippocrates, an ancient Greek who wrote about medicine about two thousand years ago. He said that we behave as we do because of four humours, blood, yellow bile, black bile and phlegm. If one of these dominates we behave in particular ways, we are either sanguine which is courageous, optimistic and amorous, or choleric, the sort of person you meet who is bad tempered and easily angered, or melancholic which I tend to be. I am pessimistic and often unable to sleep and sometimes I can be irritable; the last is phlegmatic which I think you are – calm and not easily roused to anger. If these humours become unbalanced we suffer illness."

"Another man, Galen believed that certain foods were able to change us because they affected the humours. Warm foods could produce yellow bile and cold foods produced phlegm. If we eat food which is suitable for us, we experience eucrasia or good health."

"You told me that those words are the sort Epicurus would have used."

"Mistry, I am so glad you remembered about Epicurus, I told you about him a long while ago."

Mistry smiled broadly. "Can we change ourselves by our food?"

"They thought we could by eating suitable food by being in the right surroundings and the right season of the year. You will see that I sometimes cure my irritability and find sleep when I am agitated by lying on the earth - that is my element. I know how often you wash so perhaps water is your element."

"But water took my man."

"I have wondered about that many times." Jacob lapsed into thought before saying. "You might not like what I will say but it is my feeling that that was symbolic."

"Symbolic? What do you mean by that?"

"That you were the water and as he went under, he entered you," he looked up to see how Mistry was responding before continuing, "you know what I mean by that, by what I am saying?"

He saw that she was looking confused.

"He I hope would have died happy to be held in the arms of the water and therefore also of you," apprehensive that he might have distressed her, he reached out and took her hand. She stared into his eyes and he saw that she was smiling with her thoughts.

"That pleases me, Jacob. It has fretted me always; I feared he had died with terror."

"Did you see his face?"

"No, the mob did hold me back, I saw only his back."

Jacob nodded his head. "When I got to him I saw his face and I am sure he was at peace. It seems to me, looking back that he must have been thinking of you." He saw that Mistry was on the verge of weeping, so stood up and went to the window. He heard the door open and close and then the sound of water being poured. It was a long time before she opened the door again. As he sat down, he saw with some amusement that she had brought a jug of water which was steaming. She poured some out for them both and he smiled as he noticed it was hot.

"Why do you smile, Jacob?"

"The water," he saw the look of puzzlement on her face, "Hippocrates said that cold water is not good for women, it causes bad and painful bleeding. The Chinese also preferred water which had been boiled."

CHAPTER 30

Rhosa had a break in rehearsals and decided to read more philosophy. Together she and Jake started on Schopenhauer. Jake had notes he had made at university and Rhosa got a book from the library. Jake found it interesting that their responses were very different.

One evening they were both reading. She put her book down and laid her head back so that she looked up at the ceiling.

"This is interesting, Jay." She said after thinking. "I'm just reading about his '*wille zum leben*' you know he always had difficulty with his will to live. I've just got on to where he says that we select a mate based on opposites so that our own deficiencies will be corrected in our children by the other's strengths. But relationships become unstable because opposite characteristics are not a good basis for a long life together." She got up and came and sat beside him. "Do you feel that, Jake?"

"It's something I've often thought about."

"Oh," she said. "Then how does that leave us? Do you mean, we are different or the same and do we have the basis for a long term relationship?"

He laughed. "There's something in what he says, but we should not let it influence us too much, don't forget that he was a very disillusioned man. It's easy to fall into the trap of accepting that these philosophers knew what they were talking about. Most of them were struggling to solve their own problems and assumed that they were common to all other people. Ludwig Wittgenstein was haunted by self-doubt. Wealthy family but the wealth did not bring solace to Ludwig. Three of his brothers killed themselves; one of them, Hans, composed music at the age of four so he might have been another Mozart. Wittgenstein who, incidentally went to school with Hitler, was also Austrian but very unsociable, elegantly dressed, highly formal. He wanted to be called Herr Ludwig by his associates. He constantly changed his career, sometimes being a professor, giving it up and becoming a gardener or, at other times a very unsuccessful elementary school teacher. For some odd reason he gave the fortune inherited from his father to his siblings who were already very wealthy. That is a man considered perhaps the most influential philosopher of the 20th century even though he was obviously flawed.

Philosophers should not be mentors for your life." Jake mused. "Schopenhauer was so anti-social I wonder how he could have coined the phrase 'post coitum homo tristes es' when he seems to have had no success with women. I don't know if you read this but he fell for a young woman. They were on a boat and he gave her a bunch of grapes as a gift. She took them but allowed them to fall into the river. She said in her diary, 'I didn't want them because old Schopenhauer had touched them.' He was then about forty!"

"How sad - to be so despised," she said. "As you say, interesting that with little experience of living a normal life, he's had such an influence." She turned back to her reading and then, as another thought struck her said. "I remember you found his idea of the 'blissful repose of nothingness' attractive. Not sure I understand why; perhaps you were thinking of relaxing in Firenze House but what he meant was the repose before birth and after death."

"Perhaps one reason he's had so much influence is that he provides solace for the anxious?" Jake said

"How do you mean?"

"He, like many others I know find their lives filled with pressure, anxiety or guilt. It would be a comfort to be told by a Schopenhauer that living is to be endured, not enjoyed." He grinned and after a moment said, "I just thought that could be applied to me."

"Now you are getting maudlin. Perhaps you should write your book on philosophy. I'll do it with you."

"My philosophy or yours?"

"Both, of course, they are synonymous aren't they?" She asked.

He nodded very slightly but, when he thought about it, he wasn't convinced that her philosophy and his were the same or even that he would have wanted them to be. Jake delighted in her differences and had even grown to accept that her occasional unreliability made her more human. Knowing the way Rhosa was about sex he found it ironic that she should be the only woman he had ever wanted to have a family with and often found himself wondering what their children would be like. When they began reading again he found he could not concentrate. He put the book down.

"Did you ever think of having children, Rhosa?"

"With Martin, you mean? God no! I got to the stage where I couldn't even be in the same room with him. Martin would have been paranoid about contact with kids and their germ-ridden nappies. He would have been a dreadful father; like Wittgenstein he was just confused about everything. I wouldn't have wanted my children to suffer what he made me go through."

He was about to ask her if this had been why she had turned to alcohol but thought better of it. So he asked if she also meant her first husband, Jed.

"I must have been stupid to have married him." She put the book down. "It's funny what we do, isn't it? Looking back I can see that I always knew what he would be like even before I married him. He had those dark brooding eyes which gave him an 'air of mystery' as a Mills and Boon novels would say. I suppose what made me fall for him was that I had always been interested with the way we cope with stress; his erratic behaviour intrigued me. I looked on him as an object for study. I thought I would be able to change him, sort out some of his mental tics." She shrugged. "Probably the reason was that after you left my life, I was lost. While I thrashed around, Jed seemed to fill the gap you left. I was completely aimless - wanted something which would give me a purpose. I suppose also, there was a hope that he might give my career a new direction, you know, some of the glory which surrounded him would envelope me."

"Did it?"

"A bit - he talked to a director and got me an audition. I did a film with him called 'Flame Inside' moderately successful too but it wasn't my style. The script was banal but Jed loved it - a chance to explore his own problems. In the early days it was that which made him successful as an actor. You know those dramas where men would sulk and have tantrums. He fitted them perfectly. But he had one style and he couldn't change. The fashion passed but that was something he never accepted. He was convinced that if he 'honed his style' he would keep getting parts."

"Back to drama school, you mean?"

"In a way except that I was the drama school. He did all those Jimmy Porter spoilt brat things but directed them at me. I was the reason he had lost his way. Marriage had taken him out of the single and desirable league. Women no longer fawned over him and he was convinced that my acting in 'Flame Inside" was the reason it had not been shown internationally. He had been stupid to get me into it - he and the director had wanted Liz Bryton - she would have been able to bring out the nuances in the script which I had missed - he had only got me the part to please me. He constantly reminded me of what he had done for me and it was always accompanied by screaming, shouting and sometimes even weeping." She picked up her book to continue reading then put it down and said. "Such a relief when we parted. New life for us both; he went straight out and resumed his womanising. But he never got another film part. The last I heard of him was that he was in rep. travelling around the North of England."

"And for you," he asked, "what did the end of Jed do for you?"

"I was only slightly less stupid than I had been with Jed," she said. "Martin was a rebound. Until we married, I thought he was fascinating, probably that was because he was so unlike Jed. For the first few weeks of the marriage with Martin I was alone in the flat every night while he went out celebrating. He'd come home in the early hours of the morning, sleep a couple of hours, swallow some stimulants and then be off to the trading floor. When I complained, I saw that the aggression he had in his job was not confined to business."

"How did you cope?"

With some reluctance she nodded. "Make up helped but sometimes it was so bad, I didn't feel I could leave the house."

Jake wanted to say something to her. Something that would take the memories away but words didn't seem right – I'm sorry – can I do anything – the oft used phrases but which generally have no meaning. He tried to find other words but they didn't come. What he felt most was anger, intense anger against the two men who had hurt her. If he had been able to he would have taken Martin to a cliff and pushed him off and would have punched Jed so hard that he would never be a pretty boy able to attract women into his web.

Eventually he said. "I want to take all that away, Rhosa." he knew it wasn't a very good line but it must have been right because she said.

"You have, Jake." She came and put her arms round him. "Jed was nothing more than an actor in a play in which I had a bad part and in which the script was all wrong. The play is over now and the misery is over too."

"And Martin?" Jake asked.

"For a long time, I used to wake up from a dream – no, not a dream, a nightmare in which Martin was hitting me again. That's all gone. When I wake up now, I look across the bed and with relief I see that he is not there." She sighed with pleasure. "When I am in Firenze House surrounding you is not anger but peace. Thank you, Jake, for giving my my life back. So sad you did not see that Jed was transitory, I just wanted you to marry me and give me babies. Look," she pointed at two empty chairs, "over there would be a Portia and a Marcus. Marcus would be around ten years old and Portia nine."

"Was that your plan, then?"

"Within a couple of weeks of meeting you, I had chosen their names. When you just asked me if I had ever thought of having children, I should have answered only with you'."

"That's nice," Jake said, "and now?"

"Oh, Jake, we often share the same bed - you know how Martin left me. On the outside I am still the same woman but the soul which was there when I first loved you is lost, blown away like a dead leaf in the wind."

"But," Jake said quietly, "it'll be back."

She gave him a kiss on the cheek which was about as far as she ever went with him. Many men would have felt repressed but somehow it didn't matter, he understood the way she was and only occasionally felt rejected. Before meeting her again, he had an active sex life but now, he was experiencing for the first time that selflessness which comes with real love. That feeling that the object of one's love is more important than oneself.

She picked up her book again, read a little and then said. "You know what drove Martin to make so much money."

"Let me guess. Was he proving he was the working class hero?"

"Right first time - brought up on a council estate, father left home when Martin was five, and mother earned her living as a cleaner. Had his first bike when he was ten so he could do a paper round, went to school in torn clothes, always claimed to have been brought up in total poverty."

"Mm."

"What does 'Mm mean?" Rhosa quizzed.

"Just that nasty word, poverty," he replied, "so imprecise that it doesn't mean much. The reality is that we left the old definition of poverty behind in this country decades ago."

She raised her eyebrows. "Aren't you being a bit fascist, Jake? Don't know what the actual figures are but it may be that thirteen million people in this country live below the poverty line, I think,"

"The poverty line varies with each era. Compare them with previous generations. In 1926, in Jarrow, sixty per cent were unemployed, malnutrition was common, kids had no shoes, and infant mortality was one in ten. Many houses had no baths, toilets or running water and were rat infested. Even in London, four undernourished families would live in one room and were often starving. I'm in the middle of reading Frederick Engels on the condition of the working classes in 1844." He picked up a book from the table and opened it at a marked page and read. *'we found a complete layer of human beings stretched upon the floor, often fifteen to twenty, some clad, others naked, men and women indiscriminately. Their bed was a litter of mouldy straw, mixed with rags…Theft and prostitution form the chief means of subsistence of this population.'*

I am not stupid enough to say that there is no poverty today but the sort of conditions Engels found have gone."

"There is still relative poverty though."

"Oh, I agree. We measure ourselves against others. If we are far down the income scale then we consider ourselves to have failed. That failure can be as degrading as the conditions Engels described."

"It may be even more so because when all around you are in the same situation that becomes the norm. Those in poverty nowadays often live alone and do not feel a community spirit and depression may be more common. Over eating and obesity are now the more serious problems."

"Just shows how we are conditioned," she said, looking pensive. "Makes you wonder how free our thinking is. As Keynes said, more damage is done by ignorance than by evil. D'you think our illusions are implanted by what we read?"

"You mean by journalists? Getting back to my dislike of my work aren't we?" Jake grinned. "What we read does colour our lives. Because we are encouraged to think disaster is imminent, we tend to think that the concerns we have now are unique but go back to 1829, Thomas Carlyle wrote about the advance of machines which were taking the skill out of work and, he even claimed, education. We deplore what we see as threats to our stability but read George Eliot's 'A Midland Journey' where she talks of riots and trades union meetings. Then look at the letters from Captain Swing where a farmer is told to destroy his 'thrashing machine' or else, and General Ludd's followers who spread riots and smashed machines."

CHAPTER 31

Jacob walked to the house where the meeting with Cardinal Valenti was to be held, followed at a distance by the three men he used as guards. The evening was windless and warm and the stench of rotting vegetation and night soil was everywhere. Night watchmen with torches in their hands regarded the four suspiciously as they carefully picked their way along the streets. Jacob had put wooden platforms on his shoes because he did not want to arrive stinking. In spite of his care, as he turned a corner to pass by a butcher's, his foot skidded on decaying offal and he shouted an uncharacteristic oath as his clogs sank deep into the decaying rubbish.

When he arrived at the house, he took off the platforms and tried as best he could to clean his shoes on the grass. The house which stood in front of him was large, dark and overgrown with creeper, giving it a desolate appearance. The three men he had brought with him set themselves down quietly in different spots in a tavern and casually looked around them at fellow drinkers.

Jacob knocked and the door of the gaunt house opened almost immediately. He followed a beckoning monk in a cloak which was similar to that which had been worn by Cardinal Valenti.

He was shown into a room in which he saw with disappointment that the shutters were closed and he would not be able to signal to the men outside.

In the room were three men, each seated with their backs against different walls and each cloaked and hooded. Beside each man was a candle, flickering in draughts blowing in through windows and doors.

As Jacob walked in, one of the figures rose and spoke in English. "We would like to extend our gratitude to you, Mr. D'Arcy for being kind enough to answer our summons. We will speak in Latin during this meeting for the sake of one of our friends here who is from Poland and does not speak English or Italian."

Jacob recognised the voice as that of Cardinal Valenti. In the centre of the room was a solitary table and beside it a chair which he was directed to sit on. There was a bible in front of him and in front of each of the figures.

"We will all swear on the bible never to discuss anything we talk about today to anyone except those who become allied to us."

Jacob recalled the passage from the bible which warned against swearing oaths, 'let your 'yes' be your yes and 'no' be your no. Everything else is from the evil one". But against his better judgement he followed the other three who picked up the bibles and swore to keep silence.

Cardinal Valenti said. "When we last met, we spoke about Robert Aske. Symbolically his followers used the five wounds of Christ as their sign." He waited to see the effect of this on Jacob.

When Jacob showed no emotion, a man only dimly visible in the darkened room said. "What we want to ask you firstly Mr. D'Arcy is, like Robert Aske and Martin Luther, do you agree that the Church needs reform, and secondly, if we can rely on your support?"

Jacob turned to the speaker and could just make out a small bent man, cloaked and hooded so that he could not be recognised. Although slightly at an angle, Jacob could still make out a familiar distorted body.

"Sir, we have met. You were at the same meal at Marco Bideri's house at which I met Cardinal Valenti, were you not."

The figure bowed slightly and continued, "Indeed I was and you will recall that we talked about the fact that you felt that the Church was in danger of losing some of its followers."

"I did and you appeared to disagree with me."

"The word is 'appeared'; none of us is free, Mr. D'Arcy. The more senior one becomes, the more restricted one is. In Marco Bideri's house were people whom I felt would see it as their duty to discredit me. You may know that our Church has many ways of dealing with those who have dissenting views." His voice stopped as he waited for Jacob to reply. "Do you understand?"

"I do. I saw that a glance passed between two of them when I expressed my feelings and they leaned forward to more clearly hear your reply. In my business, I have sometimes met similar people. They have small minds and envy success. There are always ways of distorting facts. I know for example that two of my businesses ventures were destroyed by such men."

"I am sorry to hear that, Mr. D'Arcy. I hope that you overcame that set back."

"God always has a reason for sending us tribulation. By them, we become stronger and they force us to strive harder. Yes, thank you, I put more effort into compensating for the loss they caused and by God's grace, the effort was rewarded many fold." Jacob replied.

"I hear from others that you are financially secure now?" Cardinal Valenti said.

"I fail to see the reason for your question, Cardinal, but that is the case."

"Forgive me, my question was not meant to cause you concern. I merely want to build an image of you... to get to know you better."

Jacob bowed slightly in acknowledgement.

"Mr. D'Arcy, I know you will understand that my companions here will want to remain nameless."

The look on Jacob's face changed to one of disappointment and he began to rise from his chair. "Then, gentlemen, I must leave you. We are dealing with a situation which is accompanied by considerable risk. If we do not have complete trust in each other," he stood behind his chair leaning against it with his hands resting on the back, "then I cannot be involved." He walked to the door, turned the handle but found that it was locked.

"A precaution, Mr. D'Arcy, we want no one to enter or leave while we are talking. The door, you will see, is solid and, unless we raise our voices, no sound of what we say will pass through it."

"I am a prisoner here?" Jacob said and began to walk to the window wondering how he could signal to the three men who had accompanied him and who would have positioned themselves in view of every window.

"You most definitely are not. You are free to leave and, since we have discussed nothing, there will be no let or hindrance on you."

One of the others stood up and pulling back his hood, walked to Jacob with his hand outstretched. "I am Cardinal Vincenzo. I can understand your need to know all of us and indeed I admire your principles. My companion here is a Cardinal also, he is Cardinal Bardonski."

Jacob shook the hands proffered and returned their smiles of greeting.

"I must apologise for the air of mystery, Mr. D'Arcy. You will appreciate that it is necessary. Now that we all know each other, we will sit at the larger table." The other two pulled the oak table into the centre of the room and arranged their chairs around it.

The three Cardinals lowered their heads in prayer before Valenti began to speak in a subdued voice and with his head bowed.

"We are here in the service of God. We acknowledge that there are deficiencies for which God has no responsibility. We all know that the next life when we meet our maker is more important than this life. We have, therefore come together to seek out ways of bringing the Church back to its rightful place in the world," he said and then raised his eyes to look at Jacob. "Mr. D'Arcy, before we start, we all want to again express our gratitude to you for coming here today."

"My opinions I think accord with yours. There can be no better basis for my being here." Jacob said. "I am only puzzled that you should want me to help. What can a merchant like me do?"

"It is not as a merchant that we want your help." The rotund figure of Cardinal Bardonski said. "We know that you have many other talents. We are told that you have a reputation for performing wonders."

"I have never performed wonders."

"How do you explain all that is said about you? Perhaps I should rephrase my statement, you have a reputation for making things happen."

"If I have a talent, it is for understanding people."

The three Cardinals looked at each other for inspiration, each hoping that the other would explain what Jacob meant. No one spoke so Cardinal Bardonski asked.

"Can you explain your meaning?"

"It is in the nature of man that he wants heroes and he wants miracles. When I explain simple truths to them they see this as performing wonders."

"You are seen by them as a superior person?" Cardinal asked.

"In the world we live in, if I thought that it could be seen as blasphemous. I prefer to be thought as a manifestation of a parent."

"Yes, I see." Cardinal Bardonski said but in a tone which suggested that he did not understand. "But tell me, what you know about poisons."

"Poisons!" Jacob replied with surprise. "I have studied potions and many of them can be poisons if too much is consumed. Why do you ask?"

"And do you know of any delayed action poisons."

"Delayed action?" Jacob hesitated, wondering what was behind the question before replying. "I cannot be sure about a delayed action. Most of the potions have been for curing illnesses. The right amount is necessary for a medicine to work, too much of certain potions can turn it into a poison. Is your question about a poison acting on people, is that what you mean?"

Cardinal Valenti took a long time to speak and when he did his voice was halting. "Not people no, we mean on a person."

"A person?" Jacob's eyes opened in surprise. "I have tested potions on animals that their owner believed was possessed of a devil. I have never tried them on a person, nor do I intend to, I can only say that I have no reason to doubt my potions are able to poison a person when administered in excess." He looked into Cardinal Valenti's eyes. "What is the purpose of your enquiry?"

Valenti looked at his two companions who inclined their heads towards him.

"This is the most critical part of our meeting Mr. D'Arcy and the main reason we asked you to come here." He fell silent.

Jacob waited for him to continue but when he saw that Valenti was obviously waiting for a response, said. "I am here, sir, I have sworn my secrecy, I can do no more than wait for you to speak."

With obvious difficulty Valenti continued. "There is someone we feel the world would be better without."

"And you want to administer poison?" Jacob raised his eyebrows in astonishment. "But why a delayed action poison?"

"He has a taster who tries all his food before he eats."

"Then he is an important man. Is he an aristocrat?"

"In a way you are right." Valenti said and lowering his voice, continued. "The man we want to poison is…" he looked at the others who both nodded cursorily, "the Pope."

Jacob's mouth fell open; he turned white with horror and gasped aloud. "The Pope! Do you mean… the Pope in Rome?"

The three men remained silent, looking at him. Then Cardinal Vincenzo spoke for the first time, his voice guttural and strained. "You, Mr. D'Arcy have expressed opinions about the Vatican enclave. We are here to tell you that we share the same concerns. There are many with our views and a large number of those in the Vatican are equally appalled at what they know has happened and what even now is happening. None of us here can condone the sale of indulgences. The common man accepts what he is told and believes that the Pope is holy and God's representative but let me tell you a few truths. The lewdness and depravity which the Borgia Pope Alexander VI encouraged and indulged in was particularly disgusting. It is commonly held that not only did he have many mistresses and bastard children by them, he even coupled and lived with Rosa Vannozza, the child of one of his mistresses. He arranged for her marriage because he found it titillating to couple with a married woman."

"Lucrezia's brother Cesare whom Pope Alexander made a cardinal, was a multiple murderer but was protected from punishment when he was appointed. The Pope's daughter, Lucrezia Borgia was even more depraved. The Pope declared her husband impotent which, as you will understand, is an insult. It is suspected that the Pope had fabricated this story so that he himself could sleep with Lucrezia. Lucrezia was married and the Pope wanted the marriage annulled because he had arranged a politically advantageous marriage for his daughter Lucrezia. To do this he decided to declare that her marriage had not been consummated. But she was six months pregnant by a man who was not her husband. The Pope arranged for Canonical judges to declare that she was a virgin."

"Pope Paul fathered children by several women; one of his children, Ranuccio Farnese he made a cardinal at the age of fifteen and another he made a Duke. Can that be right – of course it is not. He created one of his illegitimate children to be Duke of Parma and his daughter became his lover. When he was made Pope, he made his grandsons cardinals when one of them, Alessandro was only fourteen. The present Pope we are told has murdered relatives, including his mother and niece, for personal gain. By actions like this he became Pope. It is rumoured that he was irritated by arguments between two cardinals and a Polish bishop. To settle the dispute, he had all three men hacked to death. He would sell any position and he is said to take a proportion of the earnings of a large number of prostitutes in Rome."

"I had no idea there was that sort of corruption." Jacob said, shaking his head.

"We are told by the Vatican about an evil man, Martin Luther, but I know I speak for my colleagues when I say that we have a great deal of sympathy with what he is preaching. We know that you travel a lot, Mr. D'Arcy, and will have seen that in all countries of Christendom, there is heart breaking poverty but from such people alms are demanded. Yet their alms go to supporting the Pope and his entourage in luxury, and what is worse, depraved luxury." He looked around at the others to see that they agreed with what he was saying and waited for their nods before continuing.

"All that I have said we have been told by others but the sources are reliable and we want to be no part of this corruption of which I speak. Crimes are committed for which there is no punishment. We all think that the position of Pope is one of such power that it cannot fail to corrupt. "

"I see that you are honourable men," Jacob said, "how can you live with this knowledge. Are you not constantly preyed on by your consciences?"

"You see, Mr. D'Arcy, we three were only recently made cardinals but we are only now aware about the extent of corruption in the Vatican. When we have to tell our flocks that they should love

God and their neighbours, obey the commandments and do good works, we cannot any longer be part of that deception without taking action. That is why we are sitting here before you." Cardinal Vincenzo said.

"There is no easy way to explain how we have got into this situation." Cardinal Valenti stood up as he spoke and walked behind his chair, placing his hand on the back as Jacob had and leaned slightly forward. "There are probably things which you do in business which you never question because everyone else is doing them. There is also a gradual attrition; we see things we do not like but they are small and of little significance until one day, there is change or we are told of things which we had not suspected and suddenly one begins to question the whole system." He looked at the others as though waiting for their agreement.

Cardinal Bardonski broke the silence. "We have reached that plateau, Mr. D'Arcy and we find that we are unable to continue with easy consciences. You may ask how we came together when even to express our concerns publicly could result in our deaths or at least excommunication."

"It must have been a torment for you." Jacob said.

"In the Vatican there are many eyes. We three only meet when we are away and are sure that no one suspects that we share the same doubts." Bardonski said.

"But the more we met the more our concerns grew," said Valenti.

"And now - what of now?" Jacob asked.

"We feel shame," said Bardonski. "Shame that by ignorance we are party to those obscenities and disgust at what the Church has become. It is no longer God's Church but a creation of powerful men, set to beguile ordinary people with promises of heaven in the afterlife. It is just surprising to us all that the stink does not reach high heaven and cause God to be sickened and to destroy the wrong doers."

"We are not permanently in the Vatican," Cardinal Valenti said, frowning. "We have administrative duties and are not personally involved in the excesses. Part of my work is to visit monasteries and what I see shocks me but, even more am I shocked when I visit some nunneries which have forgotten what they were set up for and have degenerated into little more than," his voice dropped, " brothels, granting favours to visiting priests and monks in return for donations."

"You are confirming rumours which I have heard but never believed,"said Jacob.

"I too had heard rumours and took them to be stories spread by enemies," said Bardonski, "it was not until I met Cardinal Valenti for the first time since we had studied together more than twenty years ago that I learned the truth about nunneries."

"What is worse, Mr. D'Arcy," said Cardinal Vincenzo, "I know from my own work that these monasteries and nunneries are expiating their sins by buying indulgences from the Vatican."

"It appears we all share the same dismay at the state God's office has fallen into," Jacob said.

"Let us pray that God watches over our endeavours, for each one of us is a dead man if any word of what we have talked about gets out," Valenti said.

With the bibles on the table in front of them, the four men linked hands and bowed their heads, each seeking solace while they communed in prayer. As they sat in silence, the wind outside grew in ferocity. The candles in the corners of the room nearest the door and the window guttered wildly and blew out. The three Cardinals sat upright, their gazes turned quickly to see if a door had been opened suddenly and Jacob felt their hands tense in his. When they saw the door and windows were still closed their grips softened and their bodies relaxed. But it was several minutes before Bardonski said in a hoarse whisper.

"You are right, Mr. D'Arcy, all of us here share disgust at the behaviour of the the head of what is still called 'The Holy Roman Empire'. In reality it is just 'The Empire' it has not been 'Holy' for many decades, if not centuries."

"I can understand your abhorrence at what you see in the Vatican but I must tell you that I am deeply shocked at what you are suggesting. I have always tried to protect life and here you are asking me to be part of administering death." Jacob spoke with difficulty.

"If you saw a man intent on killing hundreds of innocent people, would you not feel justified in taking his life to save theirs?" Cardinal Vincenzo said. "That is all we are asking of you." Instinctively he placed his hands together as in prayer, "We would abolish the position. When the Pope is gone, his place would be taken by at least five Cardinals devoted to God. We know the Cardinal who would be the senior member. He is a very devout man, born of a very rich family but he has given his wealth to the poor and he has endowed an orphanage, a school for disabled children and a hospital. He is well known to the three of us."

"I need time to think about what you have said."

"It grieves me deeply to say this Mr. D'Arcy because I know you to be a good man but if you are not now able to join us then we must detain you until you are."

There followed a long silence disturbed only by creaking of floorboards on the other side of the door as someone walked up and down the corridor.

Jacob looked at what in the dim light, he could see of the faces of each of the Cardinals.

He nodded slowly to himself and then said in a voice broken with emotion, "I am with you, gentlemen." As he spoke, a sigh came from the Cardinals.

"I must tell you though that I need to think carefully. It may not be possible to do what you are asking of me with poison. It is easy to get a poison which acts quickly but one with delayed action is much more difficult."

The three Cardinals stood and each in turn embraced Jacob.

Jacob remained immobile; hardly noticing their affection while he thought. "It is possible gentlemen to take poison in very small amounts and to increase the dosage as the stomach becomes used to it. It may take six months before large amounts can be taken with little effect. I know of people who have trained their bodies to be little affected by some common poisons. The taster could do this and..."

"That is interesting but would not suit our purpose. The Pope chooses his own taster from a man in whom he has complete trust. If we took the taster into our confidence, he would inform the Pope because he would lose his position if the Pope dies. No Mr. D'Arcy, we need a man with your knowledge of poisons and also one who lives away from suspicious eyes, as you would in England, where you have a King who has no favour with the Pope." Cardinal Bardonski said.

Cardinal Valenti cleared his throat. "Shall we meet here this day in the month? If in that time you find you have an answer, place a red book in your window and I will arrange for us all to meet here again."

Jacob nodded his agreement and, as he turned to leave, Valenti said, "And Mr. D'Arcy, there will be no need to bring your three companions with you. You are among friends here."

"A precaution only," he said as he bowed his goodbye.

"Wise," said Valenti, "but unnecessary, God will watch over us." He closed his hands together in prayer as Jacob left.

When the door closed, he turned to the other two and said. "We have our man, gentlemen." All three Cardinals knelt together in front of the table and prayed.

Jacob felt a mixture of emotions as he walked home after dismissing the three strong men he had thought would have been necessary for protection. With each step, his mood changed as he assessed and reassessed the bizarre meeting he had just had. Sometimes he felt he had walked into a trap and the three men were even now plotting to expose his words to their masters. Perhaps they were not even Cardinals but had dressed just to deceive him and gain his confidence. At other times he felt elation that they had chosen him. It was in this mood that he arrived home, quietly closing the door behind him so as not to waken Mistry. He was saddened to hear Mistry crying to herself as he tiptoed past her room. He stopped to listen and then, knocking lightly, he pushed on the door and went in to speak to her.

"What is ailing you, Mistress?" He asked, reverting to her old title because of his concern.

"Sir, 'tis nothing."

"It cannot be nothing if it makes you like this. You must tell me. I insist; I shall be cross with you if you do not tell me. Has someone said something to hurt you?"

She composed herself, wiping her eyes with her apron before speaking. "There were a lady came here when you were out."

"Lady, what sort of lady."

"Older than me and taller and dressed in fine raiment."

"What did she say that upset you?"

"Asked who I was?"

"And?"

"I said I was your servant. She said she knew what I was after."

"Yes?"

"Your money, sir; she said I was using my guiles to get your money."

"That is all nonsense. Who was this woman, did she give her name?"

"When she left, she said her name was Bedella and I was to tell you that she would be away for two weeks."

Jacob almost shouted the name, "Katarina Bedella."

"She is a friend, Jacob?"

"The story is long, Mistry. We first met in Florence when I was there on business. Her husband, Lorenzo, was my agent in Italy. When they married he was a strong and a successful man but gradually he declined both in health and in his business. When I met him first, he was very active but in later years he was always unwell. Katarina was not able to accept that the man who had kept her in wealth could change so much that he would have to lean on her both mentally and physically." Jacob stopped while he thought for a moment. "You see, Mistry…," he hesitated, "she transferred her affections from Lorenzo to me."

"Was that to your liking?"

"To begin with, I have to admit I found it flattering. She is not without certain charm and I, as you will know, am not a man that the ladies find much to their liking." Mistry opened her mouth to contradict him but Jacob held up his hand to quell her. "But soon I found it an embarrassment, especially since Katarina made no secret of her affections even in front of her sick husband."

"But if you met her in Italy and her husband is there, how is she here?"

"Lorenzo is dead. Katarina is now living here."

"Because of you, sir?"

Jacob nodded. "She is living with her mother and father — they have a house near here." As he spoke, he could see tears welling up in his maid's eyes and was both distressed and perversely pleased because of the depth of her own affection for him.

Momentarily she touched his hand with hers, looked up at him and smiled fleetingly expressing her regard for him.

He went into the next room and brought a chair so that he could sit beside her and was delighted when she repeated the momentary touch and held his hand in hers.

"I was also afraid that you would not come back from the meeting with that be-cloaked man."

"He was there with two other Cardinals and the meeting went well. They want me to help them."

"Oh, sir," she said, slipping back into her old way of speaking. "Is that safe for you?"

"Sometimes we have to trust our instincts and weigh things in the balance. With them I am able to help. I am ashamed of what I see around me. I would like you to help me if you would. " He stopped and thought for a moment. "I am sure you could."

"How can I help? I am just one, I can make no difference."

"If we all said that, nothing would change. Do you know of Joan of Arc?"

"You have not told me about her."

"Her part of France was occupied by the English. She heard voices which told her to destroy the enemy. She was about the same age as you and had little learning. Just on her own, she led the French army into battle"

"You would not want me to lead an army with my little broomstick, would you?" she joked but, seeing that he was pre-occupied, said. "What is it they want you to do, Jacob?"

He leaned his elbows on the table, put his hands in front of his face as though in prayer while he considered what to say. When he finally spoke, he even surprised himself with his candour. "Kill the Pope."

Mistry's voice failed her, she opened her mouth to speak but no sound came out.

"You are shocked, are you not, Mistry?" Jacob said, "I do not mean me alone, there will be others."

Finally finding her voice, she said, "Others?" and when Jacob continued to watch her, waiting for her reaction, asked. "The man in the cloak, with his face covered?"

Jacob nodded his head. "He has many important friends who, like you and me, also hate corruption."

"But kill the Pope!"

"The Pope as head of the Church makes us into puppets, destined to follow a leader without question, be he malicious, self-seeking or bestial. They all bear scars of guilt, from the Pope down to the very priest who destroyed your man." Jacob waited while Mistry thought about what he was saying.

"But not you, Jacob, you bear not their scars."

"Even as a young man I saw evil, not in God but in the clergy who called themselves the messengers of God." He moved in his chair to be closer to her and continued. "I'd like to talk to you about what I mean. It will be difficult to understand so it would be best if we move closer to the fire. I could do with another drink if you would get me one, please."

While they drank, they looked into the fire.

"Man is a peculiar creature, Mistry," Jacob said meditatively, "he wants to be free but needs a leader to govern him and to whom he gives complete authority. So this is the first schism – schism means a division - freedom always fights against authority. Since authority can only survive if it grows and remains stronger than the governed, it adopts ever harsher methods to maintain its domination over people.

This is the reality we are in now. Spain devised an Inquisition to seek out and destroy anyone who could be considered a threat. Any criticism of the Church would be considered heresy even if it was no more than a minor comment. The decision on what was heresy was entirely arbitrary. By employing torture, innocent believers confessed and were put to death."

"It is a paradox that mankind has never yet been able to invent a system which limits the powers of our rulers. There is something in the human mind which, when given power, wants more and then more. To survive our rulers surround themselves with similar minded people who benefit from the continuance of power." He took another drink and meditated.

"That is what is happening now, Mistry. Men have been pushed too far. They are prepared to risk their lives for change." He held his hands in front of the fire to warm them. "As I am also, Mistry."

"I understand all you have just said, Jacob and I know that I want to be with you. I wanted to die when they killed my man. If you are to risk your life, I will be with you." She spoke with an eloquence which pleased him.

The following morning while Jacob was working on his accounts, there was a knock on the front door. Mistress Darkall opened the door to Cardinal Valenti who bowed to her as she let him in.

Jacob stood as she opened the door to his office and showed the Cardinal in.

"You may be surprised to see me. Mr. D'Arcy but I bring good news." He said as the two men sat. "We are all pleased that you have joined us in our mission. Together we prayed that the blessing of God will descend on you. I am come to say that there is no time to waste. In six months' time, the Pope will give a banquet where he will be entertaining a great number of important people who want to impress him and whom he wants to impress. His appetites are so great that he is in need of money and his guests are there because they want advancement for their families. At the last meal he had sixty five courses with delicacies such as peacock's tongues and nightingales which flew out of pies. The wine flowed so freely that most of the guests fell asleep before the meal was over. We think it would be propitious to show our displeasure at this next meal." He looked into Jacob's eyes. "Can you do this?"

Jacob stared over the shoulder of the Cardinal. "For most of last night I read through my books on poisons. There are some which I can work on but I can make no promises. We must be prepared if there are none which are suitable for your needs, your grace."

"For 'our' needs, Mr. D'Arcy; do not forget that you are one of us."

"I confess, your grace, that I have apprehension." Jacob stood up and walked around the room slowly. "It was for that reason that I did not sleep last night."

"Apprehension! What do you mean?" The cardinal said raising his voice. "May I remind you of your oath? We cannot have doubt at this time."

"Sir, I have given my word and I will never go back on that."

"Then, pray tell me your apprehension."

"I do hear stories about the Papacy which I find shocking but I also hear of the good works which has been done by the Vatican." Seeing that the Cardinal was ready to listen, Jacob indicated that he should sit and pulled a chair close to him, sat down and leaned forward. "I have been told by a customer from Florence of the good works of Pope Leo."

"And what were they, pray?"

"He spent much money on Rome, they say. He built the Via Ripetta, restored the church of Santa Maria and he had a clever man, Leonardo Da Vinci draw up a plan to drain the Pontine Marshes. To increase the reputation of Rome, he invited scholars to the city. I have seen his works and the citizens still benefit from them and they are grateful."

"Those works he accomplished, certainly. But do you know where the money came from to carry them out?"

"No, your Grace, I do not."

"I don't know the exact number but I suspect he sold the office of Cardinal many hundreds of times. Many of the recipients were completely unsuitable and wanted the position for personal gain.

They could immediately gain power and could themselves sell positions of power to others."

"He would also have sold indulgences to those who had committed crimes even the crime of murder. The criminal, if he paid enough to Pope Leo, would be granted absolution. Pope Leo was hated by many and underwent unsuccessful attempts to assassinate him. The Pope ordered the murder of those involved. Some had flesh torn from their bodies with red hot tools and then were dragged through the streets by horses so that more flesh was torn from them before they were hung on a bridge for all to see. Another source of money for the Pope was brothels but even with around seven thousand prostitutes there was not enough income to support his profligate lifestyle." As though ashamed of what he was relating, his eyes were cast to the ground while he spoke. "There is much more I could tell you about Leo and Pope Clement who followed Leo, and now we have Pope Paul. There are stories of his misdeeds which say that he murdered his own mother and niece so that he would inherit from them. He committed incest on both his male and female children. He has had priests and bishops murdered because they disagreed with him. I can think of many Popes who have become corrupted by their power, one of those was Gregory who was accused of murdering four other Popes and of sleeping with the richest landowner in Italy, Matilda. He had a hatred of your King Henry IV and hired an assassin to kill him by dropping a stone on him when he was praying." He raised his eyes. "Are you convinced, Mr. D'Arcy?"

Jacob said in a restrained voice. "I am with you."

CHAPTER 32

One evening when Jake came back late from a meeting, he walked in to the house quietly so as not to disturb Rhosa, who had worked all the previous day doing a children's play in the morning, a matinee in the afternoon followed by the play in the evening and then had gone to a final curtain party with the rest of the cast. As he went past the study, he saw her with her head on the table.

He went to her, took her hand as he sat down and said. "What is it?" he suspected she might just be drained of mental energy. "Are you very tired?"

"Yes, that is probably what it is." She wiped her eyes on the back of her hand and her cheeks with her fingers, smearing her mascara.

"Sorry," she said, "I didn't hear you come in."

She looked up plaintively and tried to smile. "How did your meeting go?"

"Well; I'll tell you about it when you tell me why you're upset."

He could see that she wanted to speak but was unable to. Suspecting that she needed to be in different surroundings, he took her to the settee.

He saw that she was still distressed, so talked to relax her. "My meeting went well. One of the things we talked about is the way the mind works under stress. I shall have to do some research because they want me to do an article on it." Rhosa raised her head so that she could listen to what he was saying.

"When I was younger I read Freud, Jung and R.D. Laing. Don't agree with any of them but I was intrigued. In 'The Divided Self', Laing claims that we exist only as defined by others who know us. They carry a model of us in their heads and we also carry models of them in our heads." He deliberately spoke quietly so as not to break her peace. "These models have an influence on us. Laing, who

317

of course had his own mental problems, never convinced me, except for his models where I was with him. Cities and conurbations of people are often hostile to us but we choose to live in them because we are surrounded by models with which to compare ourselves. That way we remain sane. We become irrational if we are denied interaction with other humans. When we sit on a crowded train we are constantly observing and being observed."

"Put us in a pod away from any interaction with others and when we come out, we are jibbering idiots. Psychiatrists disagree with each other so it is evident that none of them has a true understanding of the way the psyche works. That's what I will write about."

He saw with pleasure that she had drifted off and wondered about the compulsion that drove her so hard that she almost reached breaking point. He stroked her hair gently and marvelled at the fineness of her features and his fortune at being with her. So as not to disturb her, he covered her with a blanket and crept out of the room.

The next morning, she brought a drink, gave him a kiss to waken him and said. "I was being silly last night. I had acted so many different characters yesterday that I didn't know who I was. Thank you for understanding." She smiled at him. "I have woken up a different Rhosa."

Later she absent mindedly began to lay the table for dinner.

Jake grinned at what she was doing and said. "Have you got something on your mind?"

She sat down at the table and said. "I woke from a vivid dream about this house. I think I know how it affects us."

Jake raised his eyebrows and said. "Go on."

"It's pretty deep but here goes." She talked while Jake took up the dinner places and re-laid the table with breakfast things. "You know how we're born knowing some things – how to suck for instance."

"Thank God, the human race would die out without it." Jake said as he toasted bread.

"As well as being born with information, we draw from the bank of human knowledge recorded over centuries."

"Mm," Jake nodded, waiting for her to continue.

"D'you see what I mean, Jake?"

He frowned. "You're still puzzling me, tell me a bit more."

"This house is part of that bank of knowledge. By osmosis we are influenced by it and if we are sensitive enough, we may even get the same emotions as previous occupants of this house. That's why we are being so affected by this building. D'you see?"

"I do and the same idea occurred to me as well."

"Why didn't you stop me then?" Rhosa said feigning annoyance.

"I just like to hear you talking." He said, jokingly and taking her hand to bring her to the table for breakfast which he had finished laying while she had been talking. "Come on, forget the meta-physical and satisfy the physical. I've got some of that rye bread you said you liked."

Rhosa got up and kissed him on his cheek. "Jay, dear, you must be the only man who has ever wooed a woman with rye bread. But there's always a first time for everything."

CHAPTER 33

A few months later, the clatter of horse hooves on the cobbles outside the house roused Jacob from his book-keeping. He wiped the misted window and looked out to see a messenger on horseback, dismounting, coming to the front door and knocking loudly. Mistry went to the door, took an envelope with a large red seal on it, thanked the messenger and carried the envelope to Jacob.

"What is it?" he said, taking the envelope. He examined the seal, broke it open and as he read, his face broke into a smile. "Good news. I am summoned to Florence to visit a new customer who wants to talk about a contract to buy our best quality cloth. I have met him before but he doesn't yet know what he wants so I will need to take some new samples with me. Let me see," he said, turning the pages of a diary. "I could go in about a month's time if the wagons I use are running. I would normally get samples transported but this could be a big contract so I will need to do some negotiating."

"I am pleased for you, sir," Mistry said lapsing back into calling him 'sir'. Jacob thought he saw a cloud pass across her face as she spoke. "Will we be long without you?"

"I suspect it will be at least two months."

"I will keep the house ready for you." She turned and walked from the room.

Jacob sat in silence, re-reading the letter and thinking about Mistry. On impulse, he got up and went to the kitchen where she was working. He turned her towards him and saw her distress. When he asked her what was troubling her, she said. "I shall be sorrow that you will be away for so long,"

"I should be glad if you would come with me. The journey can be lonely and tedious. I would enjoy your company."

"As you wish, sir," she said noncommittally but he could see her shoulders lift.

"No, Mistry, I am not commanding you, you must decide if you want to come."

She turned towards him and he could see that she could hardly contain her pleasure. "It'd be my pleasure, Jacob but never before have I travelled. I wouldn't know what to do."

"I will tell you everything you need to know; you learn quickly, already you sound like an educated lady, so you will have no difficulties."

Jacob spent time preparing and organising travel arrangements while Mistry sorted out clothes for them both. Her pleasure in everything she did and saw was obvious to Jacob. He had given her several outfits which his wife had owned, many of which had come from Italy when he had travelled there.

On the wagon which had been made reasonably comfortable with cushions and a cover to keep out the weather, he noticed the admiring eyes of the male passengers and quizzical glances between them as they wondered about the relationship between the young woman and the older man. Before they had started the journey, Jacob had said that they should revert to formal titles and if he were asked he would introduce her as Mistress Darkall his servant. For this reason, in hostels she always had the smallest of rooms and the most uncomfortable of beds. She never even commented to Jacob about any discomfort.

The journey was, as he had told her, tedious and there were several occasions when the carriage broke down or the horses went lame and they had to wait endless hours while changes were made. There were arguments and fights amongst their fellow passengers who accused the groom of deliberately going slow, suspecting that he had been bribed to deliver them to inns where the beds would be flea ridden and the food intolerable.

Jacob had a great interest in the way people naturally developed a structure, forming what he told Mistry were loosely knit 'tribes'. After a couple of days, those passengers who were going all the way to Florence developed an affinity with each other. Those who were only staying for short distances they instinctively excluded. Jacob, by travelling all the way to Florence was considered a superior person.

321

Mistress Darkall, although covertly admired was, as a servant, never spoken to directly. This pleased her because she would have been too terrified to reply. For the first few days, only by holding her hands tightly beneath a muff could she stop them from shaking with fright. She used the muff even when, as they journeyed south, the weather became hot. She despaired of ever feeling at ease and many times she was tempted to jump from the vehicle and walk back to Firenze House.

One of the younger men who had joined the wagon at the last stop often looked at her and when he did, she would quickly turn her head to look at the constantly changing scenery. She was particularly interested in the small towns they passed through where people were working; carpenters sawing, farriers shodding horses, houses being built, farmers gathering in crops and women washing and sewing at the doors of their houses. She always knew when they were approaching a town by the smell which wafted into her nose long before they arrived. Each town was different but when she had been in the place for a short time, she ceased to notice and wondered if, when she returned to Barnes, it would have an odour which she would recognise.

Whenever she turned her eyes back from looking outside, she became aware of the gaze of the young man. He had a face that pleased her and when their eyes met, a smile flickered on his lips. At the next stop, night was falling and only a guttering taper lit the area so he stepped down first and turning, took her hand to guide her safely to the ground.

She waited to collect their bags and began struggling with them to the inn.

"Allow me," the young man said in a friendly voice.

"Sir…" she stammered awkwardly, "I am Mr. D'Arcy's servant. My job is to carry bags."

"I insist," he said, taking the bag from her and depositing it in the entrance to the inn. Jacob had taught her how to curtsy but not well, as she did so, she almost fell and he caught her arm to steady her. "You must be tired after your journey."

She found she could not speak but managed to nod. At that moment, Jacob, carrying his own case, caught up with her.

"I fear your maid is fatigued, sir," the young man said. "Allow me to introduce myself. I am Captain George S'Aderson, I am travelling to Milan to join my regiment." He rummaged in his bag, "here, I have a little brandy in a pocket flask. I think it might help revive your maid, sir."

Mistry had sat down on a wall, her face pale. She looked at Jacob, who nodded his encouragement and passed her the flask. Mistry drank a mouthful and grimaced. Captain S'Aderson leapt forward and caught her as she fainted. Together, he and Jacob carried her into the hostelry where a woman directed them to a white painted room which being on the shade side of the inn was cooler than other parts of the building.

The two men laid Mistry on the bed. Jacob thanked the Captain, saying that he would take care of her. The captain nodded his understanding and closed the door quietly as he left. On the table was a jug of water which Jacob, sitting on the bed beside her, poured onto a cloth and wiped her forehead, sprinkling some of the water on her lips. In a few moments she had revived and swung her legs off the bed and sat up shakily.

"What happened," she asked, still confused. "The man gave me a drink and then…"

"It is the journey, you need to sleep. I will leave you to undress yourself and get into bed."

Mistry held the dark green velvet drape of his sleeve. "Don't 'e leave me, Jacob, I am afeard here." Her anxiety caused her speech to revert to that of the streets she had grown up in.

"I will not leave you," he pointed to the other door in the room, "I am in the room there. I will leave the door open so that you can reach me whenever you want."

Mistry, stood up but almost immediately fell back on the bed.

Jacob knelt down by the bed, held her hand and said, "My dear, you are unwell, you must sleep."

Mistry, her face drained of colour, sat up slowly. "I am sick, Jacob, I fear I will spew."

Jacob reached for the bowl on the wash stand and held it while Mistry emptied her stomach contents into the bowl. When she had stopped, he took the bowl to the girl in the hostel who grimaced but gave him another bowl. When he went back to Mistry, he wiped her mouth with his handkerchief and when she had lain back, stroked her damp forehead. She tried to undo her buttons but her hands were shaking so much that she could not control them.

"Allow me, Mistry," Jacob said. She lay back and smiled her thanks. "I will take off your outer garments.

As he started to take her clothes off, he saw how hot and feverish she had become with beads of perspiration standing on her brow and her upper lip.

"I am so hot, Jacob,"

"You have so many clothes on; you are not in England now. You are probably suffering with the heat. I think you need to remove all your clothes, Do that and I'll leave you now that I've taken off the bulky outer clothes?"

"Sir…, Jacob, I have no strength, can you do it for me?"

He started to do as she asked with hands that were shaking with arousal as he took off her outer clothes and saw her pale, beautiful skin. He covered her with a sheet and sat down on the hard wooden chair beside the bed while she closed her eyes.

In a few moments, her body began to shake. Jacob put out his hand to restrain her and she opened her eyes and smiled weakly.

"Mayn't I die, Jacob?"

For answer, he squeezed her hand to pass on some of his strength.

"I would like to be with you Jacob." She took his hand and pulled him towards her. He hesitated before taking of his shoes and his outer clothes and getting clumsily onto the small bed. He put his arms round her as she laid her head on his shoulder and he noticed that the body she pressed against him had stopped shaking.

"Jacob, if I am to die, I need to tell you of my love for you," she whispered to him.

"And I for you, Mistry but do not talk of dying. I have seen the sort of illness you have and it will pass."

"If I had not come to be your housekeeper, I would have died on the streets I was so near to starving. So I am not afraid of death. Living only began when I came to you." She was near to sleeping and her voice was so quiet, he could hardly hear her. "You are the kindest man. I want to tell you that my love for you came from the first day and it has been with me every day. When I wake, I think of you, when I sleep I dream of you. To care for you gives me more pleasure than a woman like me deserves. You see, I have sinned many times and given harm to my God. I could do nothing else; there was no way to live without sin."

"It matters not, Mistry, God will understand as do I." He said. "I too bless the day you came into my house. I knew such loneliness that I wondered if I wanted to live but you have taken that all away and you are always in my thoughts and... in my heart."

For a moment their eyes met and he allowed himself to think that she was asking him to come to her. Even so he was unsure of what to do...this was a moment like nothing he had experienced before. He went to her carefully, afraid that she like a bird might ascend into the sky if he approached too quickly. She was struggling with her buttons with her hands shaking so much that she could not control them. Unable to remove her underclothes she let her hands fall back. Jacob's hands began to perspire as he knelt down beside the bed and stroked her hair. Intense pleasure coursed through his body with the excitement of touching her.

Unable to contain himself, he said. "I've thought about this since almost the first day you came into Firenze House, Mistry."

She looked with longing at him and said slowly. "Those thoughts filled my mind as well."

"I lived with my wife for many years and have never felt as I do now. There was a time when I came on you washing yourself; you didn't know I was there. You stood unclothed before me and such a desire for you went through me that I could hardly stop myself. You weren't aware I was seeing you."

"No, I knew you were there," Mistry said, "and knowing that you saw me made me tremble inside. When you left and went upstairs I was disappointed."

"You were," he cried, "I had no idea; I thought that being so much older and in ill-health I would never interest you."

"Oh, dear man, you are the gentlest person I have met. I never thought I could meet a man so kind. My dreams are always of what we could do together."

He had undone all her buttons and pulled her naked body towards him. She was still cold so he put his arms round her to warm her. As he did, there was a stirring in his body. Mistry sensed the change in him and reached down to caress him. He had tried to conceal his ardour by moving away but the bed was too small and he would have fallen out. She kissed his head, his lips, his neck and his hands. In a bliss which he had never experienced, he cupped her breasts, allowed his hands to slide over her lissom body until he found the area of desire. "I have so little knowledge, Mistry, touching you is new to me," he whispered in her ear.

Their roles had changed - Mistry, the experienced teacher and Jacob the neophyte. She guided his hand, showing him what she liked a man to do. As he entered the warmth of her body, he exploded and was concerned for her but when he saw the pleasure he was giving her he continued with even more force. The little wooden bed creaked beneath them as they moved in ecstasy. In her passion, she bit into his shoulder. The exquisite pain made him more violent. And then the peace when she held him tightly her legs and arms entwining his

After the passion, she looked up at him as he lay above her and said. "Now I can die happily."

"You will not die now that we have found each other."

He saw tears in her eyes. "What is making you unhappy, dear girl?"

She pressed her eyes on his shoulder."I love you so much, Jacob that I cannot stop my tears but they are of happiness that I am with you."

They lay together for almost an hour; Mistry became still and silent and he constantly put his hand on her breast to make sure she was still breathing. Gradually she drifted into sleep and soon after he slept.

The next morning he woke as she was getting out of bed. He saw with pleasure the lines of her young body and marvelled at her beauty. Feigning sleep, through half lidded eyes, he watched her move around the room, pour the spring water in the bowl and sponge herself down and collect the clothes which Jacob had scattered on the floor. When she had put on her day clothes, she went to open the shutters, sat on the chair in front of the window and looked out over green hills and valleys. Quietly he got out of bed and went to stand behind her. He thought she had not heard but without saying anything, she raised her hand to catch his and pressed her head backwards to look up into his eyes. She did it so naturally that he wondered if she had known that he had been awake and admiring her. The thought of the closeness that had grown between them, elated him.

"You were right, Jacob, I am better."

"The countryside around here would make anyone feel better but I am so glad you are well now," he smiled down at her upturned face. "Are you ready to eat, I imagine you are starving - you haven't eaten for almost a day." As Mistry nodded, he said, "I will go and get some bread and cheese which is all they serve here in the morning. I've stayed here many times before on my journey to Florence. The wagon goes today but I have enquired and there is another going tomorrow, I will go to the drivers and ask if we can get on the wagon tomorrow or another day. I think you need a rest. So, when we've eaten and if you feel well enough, we may walk along the river you see there, he pointed through the open window. We can take food from this inn and have what the French call a picnique. The water here is sweet and cool it comes straight from the spring which wells up in the nearby hill. I think it will be less hot today because the sky is cloudy but we can anyhow sit beneath the shade of trees.

When he returned with a tray, he laid it on the small table. Mistry sat and ate while Jacob picked only at a few morsels.

"You may have eaten something which was not good," he said, "I suspect it was the rabbit you had for dinner the night before last. I didn't like the inn keeper, quite an evil looking man and he looked at you in a most objectionable way."

Mistry smiled to herself. "I thought him to look handsome," she teased.

Jacob looked at her anxiously: he had seen several men pass admiring glances at her including Captain S'Aderson. Whenever she was the subject of admiration a momentary sensation of pride tempered with slight jealousy filled his mind. He had caught her many times looking at herself in a mirror. Now that she could read, write and speak well, when they were in hostels with other guests whom they had not met before, she was frequently taken for a lady from a good family.

He wore only old clothes when he was travelling and had on one occasion been mistaken for her servant, admittedly by a man with bad sight. This so shocked him that he gave his travelling clothes away to a beggar and replaced them with garments more suitable to his station.

As she sat before him now in a thin silk gown which he had given her before they left, he looked with satisfaction at her slim figure and the elegant way she held herself as she sat in the chair in front of him.

He was about to express his admiration when there was a knock on the door.

Jacob stood up and opened the door a few inches only, "Thank you, Captain, she is still weak but recovering. She may be well enough to take the air later."

He stepped outside, closing the door behind him.

A murmured voice reached Mistry's ears and she was about to rise when Jacob quietly came back and closed the door.

"Who was that, Jacob?"

"The Captain from yesterday was enquiring about your health."

"Did you not invite him to share the meal with us?"

"He told me last evening that he has hired a horse and is going to visit a friend," he lied

"Oh," she said, "I hope we shall see more of him on the journey."

"We may but he suspects he may not be able to take the same vehicle that we travel on because the friend he is visiting is a long way away and he will probably not get back here for many days." He had in fact told S'Aderson they would travel by the same vehicle which would be leaving three hours later that same day.

"That will be sad; he seemed a nice man and good company for the long journey."

"For myself, I preferred the conversation of the two older men sitting beside me. They are also in business."

"Yes, but they did not address one word to me," she pouted, "and the older lady sitting beside me seemed to sleep and snore most of the time."

"I'm sure she is a charming lady but I suspect she is not well. You will notice she keeps breathing from her nosegay. I spoke a little with her. She is returning to her family in Milan where she has a good doctor. No one, she says, can understand her ailment in London. I do fear for her well-being, I am suspicious that sometimes when we think she is sleeping, she may have fainted off."

"But she snores so loudly I'm surprised she does not waken herself. Even above the noise of the horses and the wheels, I can still hear her," she smiled. "You have taught me so much about your business, I would have liked to speak to the two old men about their work one of them with diamonds and the other with ladies clothes but I know they would not speak with a woman."

"If we go on by another wagon, we will not see the same travellers again. On the next journey, shall I introduce you as my business partner which is anyhow what you are slowly becoming?"

"I should like that but I am not sure I can. I heard what they were saying and I would want to talk about many things, new things."

"Do you indeed!" Jacob raised his eyebrows, "what things do you mean?" He was pleased to see Mistry was better and eating well.

"When I was on the streets I used to watch people working. It seemed to me that there would be better ways they could do it."

"Tell me, I'd be interested to know." Jacob said.

"One of the things was using mare's urine on cloth. I saw it once when my man Benjy took me to an old crone's house in Putney, she had horses running around and she had put a blanket over one which was ill, when it pissed, some of it splashed on the blanket and the dye changed its colour."

"The smell must have been very unpleasant."

"I can still remember it. Before your lessons I would have said 'it did fair make I puke'," she laughed, "but of course now I know better."

"What did it do once you had stopped 'puking'?" Jacob found himself laughing with her and realised that he had not laughed much since before he had married Isabel. She had been of a serious disposition and he had adopted her behaviour which had stayed with him even after her death.

"Where it had been splashed, red colours looked pink and had a shiny surface, I expect that with a brush you could do interesting designs."

Jacob looked surprised and then said, "I don't think you should tell our fellow travellers any of your ideas, we should keep that to ourselves, we will try the mares' urine when we get back to Firenze House. If it works, it could give us a new trade. It is your idea, I won't forget that."

CHAPTER 34

Throughout his life Jake had been what most people would call a day dreamer. There were many times when he would sit in a chair and meditate sometimes so intensely that he would seem to an outside observer to be inanimate. Rhosa was understanding and happy to see him relaxed and peaceful. It was at these times when he would often have what he could only describe as visions. These were frequent and intense since he had moved into Firenze House.

For much of one March afternoon, when the weather had been too foul to venture out, he had felt the sensation of somnolence come over him. Sitting in an armchair in the lounge, he stared out of the window at the driving rain. Slowly his eyes became heavy and he had drifted away, not into sleep but into a meditative state. When he next looked at the casement clock in the hallway adjoining the lounge, more than an hour had passed and the air was filled with the aroma of cooking.

Rhosa heard his footstep as she closed the oven door and turned to smile at him. "You've had a long session, Jay," she gave him a kiss on the cheek, "I left you to sleep. Did you have a dream?"

"I did but it is vague. Jacob D'Arcy was involved."

"Try to remember about it while we eat, I'm just about to serve."

Throughout the meal, he found his mind struggling to remember what he had been dreaming about. Rhosa kept glancing at him while she ate and, eventually asked. "What is it, Jay, you are very quiet, have I said something to upset you?"

"No, not at all; it's just that the dream I had is still with me and I'm beginning to sort out what it was."

"Tell me what you remember."

"I was listening to a talk by D'Arcy. It must have been triggered by what you were saying about Russia and totalitarian regimes. He said that man is a peculiar creature; he needs to be free but at the same time he needs a leader to dominate him but always fights against authority." She saw he was eating a little and served him more.

"Rhosa, are you sure you want me to talk about this while we are eating?" he asked.

"It's obviously bothering you. I didn't say but last night I also had an odd dream about the cruelty that the Church adopted to protect itself." Rhosa said.

"You're almost reading my mind," Jake responded in surprise. "I've no idea why but I can remember now that I was thinking about the Cathars who reacted against the spiritual corruption of the Church. Pope Sylvester suppressed them with appalling acts of violence."

Putting down her fork, Rhosa frowned and said. "Not just the Church is it? It is the same with dictators. Their sons succeed them and nations inherit weak and impotent rulers." She started to clear the plates. "You've not eaten much, Jay, normally you have a huge appetite."

"Sorry, Rhosa, I'm still with the Cathars. It really took me over. Then I got to thinking about the way we treat our prophets – you know the appalling treatment of Tom Paine – condemned to death in Britain because he wanted democracy – just escaped being guillotined in France and despised in America because he criticised corruption." He stood up to help her clear away but Rhosa saw that his mind was still distant so she sat him down.

When she returned with the dessert, she said "Paradox, isn't it, that we allow rulers obscene powers and they surround themselves by similar minded people."

"It sometimes shoots them in the foot though, or more literally, in the head," Jake said, beginning to regain his sense of humour. He stopped, suddenly unable to think of anything more to say.

Rhosa waited to see if he was going to continue and, when she sensed that he had finished, said. "It's funny, but I was sure that you had been thinking something like that."

"How could you?"

"I was cooking while you were drifting into your mind," she reached for her wine and drank pensively looking into the distance. "And I was convinced I was getting the same ideas that you were. I thought that in my case it was because I was stuck thinking about Russia."

"I don't recall anything special before I drifted off."

Jake had always believed in telepathy and with Rhosa, there were many times when they were alone together she would thinking about the same things. He was once meditating on the Hawthorne effect which demonstrates how simple changes can build morale. Within minutes, Rhosa was saying that she was intrigued by the way we all work together and how we are more productive when in company.

She could be excited by intelligent conversation; as though her mind and not her body was the centre of her erogenous zone.

She often told him of her worry that people had become too interdependent which made them vulnerable.

"Don't worry, man is an amazing survivor." Jake told her.

"Until the Apocalypse. That terrifies me as well," she said.

"We can only hope that it is quick, like Pompeii must have been."

"Mm," Jake murmured, "I'm planning a chapter in the book devoted to the environment and our profligacy. Everyone says 'Why don't 'they' do something about it?' when the reality is that it is the responsibility of every one of us."

"My fear is that the end may be a whimper and not a bang."

"How do you mean?"

"That we are already in the whimper stage and are gradually making the world so inhospitable that we shall die out but only slowly."

Professor Shorning's influence on the way her mind worked meant that being with her was both interesting and challenging. To keep up Jay took to reading whenever he had a few moments. Many of the subjects were foreign to him. When they were in bed, she was always at her most talkative.

On the many occasions when, because of the excitement of acting, she could not sleep, she would curl up beside him and say, "Talk to me, Jay."

He'd pick a subject which he had just read about and would just talk. As he did, her body would tighten her grip on him like other women would during the sex act.

He would talk until he heard her heavy breathing on his shoulder. When he knew she was asleep, a sense of peace would come over him. When she was not working, she was unable to relax either waiting for her agent to ring suffering the constant doubt that she would ever get another acting role or that her performance on stage would be a disaster.

He had known many successful, always-smiling actors trying to convince the public that they were leading marvellous lives. Now, he realised that it was all gloss and they were shrouded by the same fears that Rhosa suffered.

In the will of her aunt she had been left enough to keep her comfortable but because she had never wanted to have an easy road to travel it had the opposite effect of adding to her self doubt. Taking money from her account made her fear that she was draining her reserves faster than she was replenishing them.

She often received invitations to parties where 'Hello darling, you look gorgeous,' would be repeated ad nauseam along with myriad other empty phrases of congratulation.

Jake would usually plead prior appointment but for Rhosa, it was necessary for her to be seen at the parties. When there was an invitation from Anthony Garden, she pleaded with Jake to go with her. She dreaded going alone because she wasn't sure what Anthony's motives were. His parties were held at his London home and his wife would never be invited. 'Looking after the kids in the country,' he would say to anyone who enquired about her."

Rhosa passed the invitation to Jake and said, "Please come with me, Jake, I need you to be there." She seemed nervous about going but laughed and said, "If I see him on my own, I might vomit all over him."

Jake was amused but also wondered if she was trying to reinforce what she had said about Anthony when he had suspected her of having an affair with him.

"You know how much I dislike these events" he said but when she did her 'little girl tearful' act, he grinned and said, "Ok. if it means so much to you, I'll come."

"Can you reply for me? I don't want to do it."

"It says Rhosa and partner on the invitation so I'll reply but I don't think it is me Anthony will want to see."

"I'll bet he does, probably wants you to write a piece on the plans he has for a play."

A note came back from Anthony's secretary saying that because he was having modifications to his house, the venue would be changed. Jake knew the new address, a nice part of Kensington and jotted the address on his mobile 'phone.

On the evening of the party, he called a taxi. Rhosa had not been well; she had been working too hard and had exhausted herself. In the taxi, she fell asleep on his shoulder. She was only half awake when they walked to the front door but, when it was opened by a maid, Rhosa suddenly started to shake, the colour drained from her face and she seemed about to faint. Jake managed to guide her to a chair in a small room and explained to the maid that Rhosa needed to sit for a while but would be better soon and he would take her in to the reception when she had recovered.

"Rhosa, tell me what's wrong, are you unwell?" he asked when the maid had left them.

She could not speak so he waited, holding her hand which had become cold.

"Get me away from here," she said in an almost inaudible voice. When he looked into her eyes he saw that she was terrified.

At that moment, the maid came back to see if she could do anything.

"I'm afraid Miss Cowen is unwell, I wonder if you can apologise to Mr. Garden for us."

"Mr. Garden?" she looked puzzled, "which one is he?"

"He's the man who is holding this party. Dark haired, greying at the temples – handsome, I'm told by women who admire him." he grinned.

"Oh, him" she said with a slight curling of her lips.

"How is it you don't know him, you work for him, don't you."

"No, thank God, I'll be leaving in four hours, I'm a temp. I'll tell him – Cowen did you say?"

He nodded as he helped Rhosa to her feet and walked along the hall and out of the front door with her leaning on his arm.

The air outside seemed to revive her and he was pleased to see that she stepped unaided into the taxi which had just decanted more guests for the party. She remained quiet throughout the taxi journey and even when they got into Firenze House still did not speak.

"What was it that made you so unwell?" he said 'unwell' but had had wanted to say disturbed but didn't want to distress her more than she already had been.

She took his hand in hers and, without looking up, said. "Don't ever leave me Jay, I couldn't survive without you." She was unable to say anything more as he sat her down, knelt before her and waited.

"That was the house," she said inaudibly.

"The house; you mean, you know it?"

"It all happened there, my last husband – he and I lived there for less than two years but for me it seemed like eternity."

"D'you want to tell me about it?"

"I can't, Jake. I'm sorry but what he did…" she broke off. "That's why I'm like I am." He felt her squeezing his hand in what seemed like desperation. "I know it's hard for you and… cruel of me to share your bed when I'm like I am," she squeezed his hand again. "Jake, if you think it best if you can't take it any more I would understand and you could lead a normal life with someone," she hesitated, "who is… more responsive."

He saw that what she was saying was not what she wanted to happen and pulled her head onto his shoulder.

"Rhosa, for once in my life I am fulfilled and happy. You just asked me not to leave you; this is for life, you and me. "

She looked up tearfully and just said. "Thank you."

"I think you should go to bed early and get some sleep. You feel so cold, you should have a soak in the bath to relax you and I'll put a hot water bottle in bed."

She pouted. "I'd sooner have you than a hot water bottle."

He laughed, "Spoilt brat. Ok, I'll take a book up and bring the bed to body heat while you have your bath."

Bed was always a luxury but it was usually tinged with guilt - he should be up and stirring the world with activity instead of lazing. But this was one of the times when he could experience the full womb-like exhilaration. He had 'snuggled' in the enveloping calm of clean sheets and tried to read the book he had taken from the shelves. His mind was distracted by wandering forward to the moment when Rhosa would join. When she came in, she picked up the book from the floor where it had thudded as he had drifted into sleep. He awoke with a start as she put the book on the cabinet beside the bed.

"Oh," his fuddled voice said, "I just slipped away."

"Poor thing, you were sound. You must have been tired."

She climbed in beside him and began to wrap her legs around him. Although drowsy, he found it hard to suppress his desire for her when her legs gripped him tighter. When he looked into her eyes, he saw that she was still scared. He went through a reversal and suppressed his feelings.

He'd never thought himself a particularly kind sort of man. People in the circles he moved in considered that thrusting aggression was the ultimate quality and that anything as feminine as caring was weakness. But Rhosa brought out the hitherto suppressed protective side of his character.

The next morning, they had been due to work on his book but, somehow it didn't seem right and they both decided to have a day together.

"Jay, I need to forget what happened last night at that house," Rhosa said as she filled his cup. "I don't have any rehearsal and I want to do something completely blah. Let's go back to that church. I just know there is something we haven't noticed."

"Woman's instinct I suppose. If it were up to me, a mere male, I'd say we've seen everything."

So they went and when they got to the church, he suddenly felt she was right. The last time they had been there, the weather was foul but on this Saturday the sun shone and the church looked inspiring. Rhosa wanted to walk round the graveyard but he just wanted to sit and look at the church, thinking about all that it had lived through - the Plague, Martin Luther, Cardinal Wolsey, Henry the Eighth, Elizabeth the First, Oliver Cromwell, the Industrial Revolution and the twentieth century in which Britain lost the drive which had made it a world leader. She left him to sit and went off to the shops. Hearing a noise, he looked up to see her carrying a large paper bag.

"With all the fuss last night, I wound up not eating, I'd skipped lunch yesterday as well so that I could eat at the party we never went to," she smiled, "It's just caught up with me, while I was looking around the gravestones, I felt light-headed. There's a nice deli over there so I bought us some things to make sandwiches. I even managed to get the sort of cheese you like." She started to un-wrap the food on the grass. "Come on, Jay, sit down here, I bought a newspaper for you to sit on. It's got one of your articles in so I've taken that page out."

"God, Rhosa, you've got enough food for ten people."

"It won't be wasted, I'll take what's left back and we'll have it for supper tonight."

"And tomorrow and tomorrow and tomorrow," he said, quoting Macbeth and knowing that it would get her going.

Her eyes rose to look at the top of the steeple as she said,

"To-morrow, and to-morrow, and to-morrow,
Creeps in this petty pace from day to day,
To the last syllable of recorded time;

And all our yesterdays have lighted fools
The way to dusty death. Out, out, brief candle!
Life's but a walking shadow, a poor player,
That struts and frets his hour upon the stage,
And then is heard no more. It is a tale
Told by an idiot, full of sound and fury,
Signifying nothing."

It always stirred him both for the meaning in the words but also because when he had first seen her on stage in Stratford, giving a one woman recital, she had captivated the audience and ensnared him by those same words.

"I saw that you were thinking about something, Jake, what was it?"

"You, of course."

"No, seriously."

"I always get melancholic when I come to a place like this. I see around me the mementoes to people who have died many of them in despair. I was also thinking about our Jacob D'Arcy and this woman Mistry."

While he talked, Rhosa, began making the sandwiches and passing them to him.

"What about them?"

"Do you really want to hear? It's such a nice day, we ought to spend it light-heartedly."

"I do want to hear. I often see you thinking and when I enquire, you make some flippant remark. We've got hours to spare. Tell me what was going through the mind you keep locked." She poured juice into a paper cup for him, taking a mouthful herself first and then with a bendy plastic knife, started to cut up the sandwiches on a cardboard plate.

"This church was built in the 12th Century. It has lived through times of glory and of terror." He looked up at the cross on the top of the steeple. "We think of these places as our stability, 'Rock

339

of Ages,… let me hide myself in thee'. If we want fair treatment, if we want honesty, if we want love and understanding, we've been conditioned to turn to the Church. Daniel Freidan said 'It's probably the biggest confidence trick in the history of mankind'." He grinned. "I suspect he says that to anyone who will listen to him."

She passed him the sandwich she had made.

"Don't stop, Jay, I don't often get you talking, it's like music."

He finished the sandwich and watched her while her eyes wandered over the church. "Go on, please, fill me with new information about the vagaries of religion."

He thought for a moment. "Ok, while you were away I was thinking about the violence of religion. Let's go back to the Cathars, doing no harm to anyone except that they wanted to behave in a manner the Pope did not like. In 1208, the Pope sent an army to destroy them. Beziers was surrounded. When the Abbot of Citreaux was asked how to decide who was a Cathar, the Pope said 'You can't. Kill them all, God will know who is a Catholic and who is a Cathar.' Ironically the name of the Pope was 'Innocent'. When it was over, the army leader sent a message to Pope Innocent saying, 'Your Holiness, today, twenty thousand people, men, women and children were put to the sword'." Jake found it hard to talk about such cruelty. Rhosa saw that he was concerned and waited while he recovered his composure." Can you imagine a situation where worshippers could be murdered simply becaue they wanted change? The murderers were convinced by His Holiness that the killings were for the greater glory of God."

Rhosa was pensive. "It occurred to me when you were telling me about Chapter 9 in your book that mankind has a remarkable ability to screen out unpalatable truths. You are talking about religion but we are also conveniently blind to the excesses of our politicians. We all know how they manipulate to ensure that they become re-elected but we ignore it. They don't commit murder directly but, by their actions, they cause war deaths."

"We also are hypocrites, you mean?" he said with a slight grin.

"By our apathy, yes," she grimaced, "but carry on with what you were saying."

He took another drink from the cardboard cup and rolled the oversweet liquid around his tongue. "In the time of our Jacob D'Arcy, they were trying to exert ever more restrictive discipline. In 1545 till 1563, the Council of Trent met and laid down a series of rules which are still mandatory. Can you imagine any other human endeavour which would make a decision and never change it over hundreds of years? In those years society has undergone revolutions."

As he spoke, he realised that damp from the grass was penetrating his clothes. "I'm going to have to move, otherwise I shall have a numb bum and rheumatism in later life." he joked.

"Glad you said that, my jeans are beginning to stick to me but I didn't want to stop you talking. Let's move over to the bench in the shade. I'm cold in the bottom but hot in the head here in the sun." Rhosa said as she got up and moved to a bench.

Later he wondered why they had chosen that particular bench, there were at least two others which were nearer and had equally as much shade.

"Carry on talking." Rhosa said as she passed him another sandwich.

"Hope the bum soon dries out." he said and then without warning laughed aloud.

"Why are you laughing?" She said.

"It suddenly struck me, if you'd been a member of the Council of Trent and had had the sort of damp bum you have now, it would have been decreed the will of God and you and all females would have been condemned to forever have cold bums." They both laughed as Rhosa stood up and showed him the wet patch on her jeans.

He finished the sandwich and then carried on. "When we look around this sun-blessed churchyard it seems so peaceful. But during its time people have suffered oppression, even for proving that the earth went round the sun when the Church had convinced itself that the earth was the centre of the universe."

"Galileo was a house prisoner because his telescope showed that Copernicus was right. What was that you told me about a fellow called Bruno? "

Jake nodded, "Galileo at least was allowed to live. His reputation saved him, Bruno's books were banned but they couldn't touch him because he had moved to England. He was invited to Venice to act as tutor to well-known man. What he didn't know was that the Venetian was a member of the Inquisition. Bruno was imprisoned for seven years and then burned at the stake. Later, his body was exhumed and his bones ground to powder."

Rhosa put her hand over her mouth. "Ugh, that's revolting, to hate a man so much that you have to destroy even his bones."

"Not so much hatred as fear - afraid that he could have become a martyr if his bones had been dug up and used emblematically."

"I suppose so, but it is still revolting. Bruno wasn't the only one."

"There were thousands of people they called 'heretics'."

Rhosa noticed his distress and said. "I know the power of the Church; I had a difficult experience with my second husband. He was Catholic but not very devout. The priest was always coming round to visit us and talk about our duty. Before he left, he would stand so close to me that I could smell his sour breath. He would constantly ask what my plans for children were. Through his thick pebble glasses, he would look me in the eye and say, 'It is your duty, Mrs. Raysent, to serve your Lord by having a large family to spread God's fellowship.' I hated the false piety and the narrowness. It was pointless to get into a discussion with him; he was like a politician with only one message and he would reiterate it endlessly."

"Wouldn't it have been interesting to have asked your priest about his views on Pope Paul V's attitude to Piccinardi whom I've just been reading about? He happened to mention to a friend that he had an unpublished book in which he compared Pope Paul to the previous Pope and his interest in young boys. The Pope imprisoned him and had him hung from a bridge until his body decayed."

Rhosa grimaced and said. "He would just have denied that it ever happened and said something meaningless like 'Popes have always watched over the interests of their flocks'."

"The position changes the person."

"Tell me more."

"Cardinal Barberini was a friend and supporter of Galileo but when he was elevated to be Pope Urban he rapidly changed, became paranoid, suspected everyone, got rid of his assistants and changed his food tasters. He requested that the bodies of heretics be taken from their graves and burned. He was convinced that Galileo in his 'Dialogues' had defamed him."

At that moment, a sudden gust of wind took the paper napkin from Jake's hand and blew it against a gravestone. Rhosa, accepting the food arrangements as her responsibility, leapt up and ran after it as a gust took it away and onto another gravestone, much larger and of carved obsidian. She picked up the napkin and was beginning to return when she turned back.

"Jake," she called, "come here quickly."

He could not see the need for urgency so walked slowly to her.

"What is it?" he asked, "a beautiful memorial?"

"It is beautiful but it's the inscription. Have a look."

He had walked in through bright sunshine into shade and, while his eyes became accustomed to the light, he could not see what she was talking about. When he was finally able to read, his mouth opened in surprise. It read:

'Beneath this stone is buried Cardinal Valenti.

Dear Friend of Jacob D'Arcy, for Whom He Gave Life

To Protect the Interests of All People

From the Ravages of \\\\\\\\\\\\\\\\\\\\\\\\\\\'

The rest of the inscription had been obliterated by chisel marks.

"Jacob D'Arcy! He must have been close to this Cardinal Valenti, whoever he was and it looks like someone has removed the last few words. What could they have said that was so important that they have been obliterated?" Rhosa asked and turning to Jake asked, "Why are you frowning?"

He had heard the name, 'Cardinal Valenti' but could not remember where until suddenly, a memory struck him.

"Jay, what's wrong, you've got an odd look on your face?"

He took her arm and walked her back to the seat. They had sat down before he was able to sort his words out. "In Rome there is a gallery. More than ten years ago, I visited it with my ex-wife who was very interested in the Renaissance - one of the few things we had in common - she took me to the gallery to see a Piero Della Francesca painting. But, when we got there, we were both overcome by another painting. Can you guess what the subject was?"

Rhosa shook her head but said, "Portrait by Leonardo or Michelangelo?"

"Good guess but no, it was neither of them" He waited with a stage-like pause which he had seen Rhosa use, "The painting was of the man whose body is in that grave - Cardinal Valenti, he looked a bit like Savanarola; his face was partly shrouded by a hood but the eyes commanded attention and he was holding his left hand in a manner which showed off his ring." He saw Rhosa looking enquiringly. "Sorry, I haven't explained have I, the ring was a pentacle of gold in a precious stone." he waited to see her reaction, when she said nothing, he continued, "I've seen that ring recently."

"Seen it! Where?"

"When I went to his house, Daniel Freidan was wearing the same ring."

Rhosa looked stunned. "Wearing the ring Cardinal Valenti was wearing in the portrait, you mean?"

"It looked exactly the same, I remember being so impressed with the portrait and the ring Valenti was wearing that I took a photograph. I could probably find it filed away somewhere" he said, "what's more, Freidan kept playing with it. I'm sure he wanted me to see it on his finger because he kept turning it round and looking at it."

"And Valenti is buried in the same church as your Mr. D'Arcy and Mistry. Gets even more mysterious, doesn't it?"

"More than a bit," he said, "I'm beginning to wonder."

"Wonder?" she said over her shoulder as she walked back to the Valenti grave and looked at the rear of the gravestone. "Come and look at this, Jake."

She was pointing at the centre of the stone. "Is that the design on the ring?"

With the sole of his shoe, he scraped away lichen which was obscuring some of the carving and was able to see clearly the same pentacle which had been on the ring worn by Valenti in his portrait and on the ring on Friedan's finger.

They were both unable to take their eyes of the carving as they tried to reason out the coincidences.

"It seems to me that we're being told something, Jay. I'm just wondering if it has something to do with Firenze House. You said before that it has a personality which is unlike any other house you've lived in"

A cold wind blew through the churchyard. They went back to the seat, put their things in the bag Rhosa had brought the food in and began to walk out past the porch of the church.

As they did so, a voice called, "Hello."

They turned and saw the ample figure of Jennifer Williams, smiling broadly, walking up the path and carrying an armful of flowers for the church.

"Glad to see you've come back, I thought we'd lost you. I've just collected these from Gladys Waller. She has a most beautiful garden, lives alone and has no one to admire her flowers so she gives them to us. She has a hothouse too, so we get them from her practically all year round."

She had so many blooms in her arms that she was finding it difficult to walk so Jake opened the church door for her.

"Thank you, Mr. Dearsey," she said as she struggled through the door and put her flowers onto a table, where there were several large vases. She turned and said, "Do come in, these flowers are for a wedding, the church looks a picture."

Rhosa and Jake looked at each other and eye signals passed between them.

"I'm passionate about flowers," Rhosa said to Jennifer and gasped in astonishment as they walked in. "So beautiful, makes me wish I'd been married here."

Jennifer looked quickly at Rhosa's ring finger and said, hesitantly. "Where were you are married, Mrs. Dearsey?"

"Not Mrs. Dearsey and not married," Rhosa said, "we live together – well sort of, we both have our own houses."

"What a happy arrangement," Jennifer said and, her voice had undertones of envy, "to be companions or lovers and yet to have the freedom to choose."

"That's the theory," Rhosa said, "but the reality is that most of the time I stay with Jake; my house is tastelessly modern and his is much more interesting."

"Firenze House, yes, I know what you mean, I've been inside, it has a unique atmosphere of history doesn't it." Jennifer said as she indicated chairs for them to sit on.

"Does it?" Rhosa raised her eyebrows. "It certainly has an atmosphere but a friendly one. What do you mean by 'history'?"

"Surprised you didn't know." Jennifer Williams said as she arranged the floral display in vases. "Quite fascinating; before the last owner lived there, we used to have our history meetings there with Mrs. D'Aldernay who owned the place then. She had done a great deal of research on the house going back to the early part of the fifteenth century. It had been attached to a warehouse for the woollen trade then owned by a wealthy merchant's family."

"The D'Arcy family?" Jake asked.

"Yes, Daniel told you about Jacob. His portrait is still in the house. It's part of the covenant, I understand."

"Yes, quite a fine painting," Jake said, "and there is also a painting of Mistry which is also beautifully done."

"Mistry!" She looked puzzled. "Is there? I've never noticed that and I once looked round all the rooms with Mrs. D'Aldernay," Her frown cleared. "Now I recall, there was a silk hanging next to the painting of Jacob D'Arcy, perhaps it concealed the portrait of Mistry. I wonder for what reason it could have been obscured. Mrs. D'Aldernay was very strait laced, perhaps she thought Mistry was Jacob's mistress and she preferred not to have it known. She was always discovering new things in the house, you know, things like hidden cupboards behind the panelling – one of them had documents in Latin. Daniel Freidan translated them - he is very clever you know. The documents were obviously put there during the time of Jacob

D'Arcy, that's what I mean by 'history'." She turned to Rhosa and said, "my back has been playing up, I wonder if you'd be very kind and carry this vase up to the altar, it goes on the left hand side."

When Rhosa was out of earshot, Jennifer asked. "Before I say what was in the documents, are you happy for your lady friend to listen, some of it can be quite revealing, even in our enlightened age? Is she a Catholic?"

Her question took him by surprise and he hesitated before replying. "Of course I am happy for her to hear, Rhosa and I share everything and, no, she isn't a Catholic and neither am I. Why do you ask?"

"What is in the documents reflects badly on the Catholic Church as it was in the sixteenth century, you see."

"I studied that period so I am unlikely to be shocked or even surprised."

Rhosa had returned so Jake asked her, "I've never asked - but you're not Catholic are you?"

Rhosa looked quizzically at him. "With a name like Cowen it would be unlikely. My step father is Jewish and my mother converted herself and me, but I'm not practising. Why do you ask?"

"Jennifer says there were documents found in Firenze House which are critical of the Vatican and the Catholic Church in the 16th Century."

"What's new? For as long as history, man has criticised authority."

Jake sensed she was deliberately being cynical to appear to be disinterested. He went along with her and said, "I suppose you're right."

"It's rather more than that." Jennifer said in a manner which made it seem that she was surprised at Rhosa's attitude. "I've finished the flowers. Come to the vicarage, I've made some cakes, my husband is away and I can show you a photocopy of one of the documents. I found it very distressing when Hannah D'Aldernay first showed it to me."

347

Jake was intrigued that she had said 'my husband is away' and wondered if she would not have been able to show it if he had been at home.

"Sorry, I was forgetting myself, you wouldn't prefer something stronger, port, sherry or we do have a nice malt whisky?"

Rhosa cast a glance at Jake for his agreement but, before she could reply, he said, "No, it's too early in the day but thank you," and saw Rhosa pout at him.

When Jennifer left, Rhosa said, "Pig, I would have liked to try her malt whisky."

"Tea is much better for you. Full of anti-oxidants - keep you young and healthy. Career enhancing for you," he grinned.

Jennifer returned with an ornate Victorian pot and poured the tea into matching cups. She offered them biscuits from an elaborately chased silver biscuit barrel.

She saw her guests admiring glances and said. "Lovely aren't they? Not ours though, they go with the house like your paintings, Mr. Dearsey."

"It's Jake."

"Short for Jacob?" Jennifer asked

Jake nodded, "Why do you ask?"

Jennifer shrugged, "Just coincidence," she poured the tea and passed it to them. "Jacob Dearsey could easily be a derivative of Jacob D'Arcy, the man in your portrait"

"It doesn't stop there," Rhosa said, "I think Jake even looks a bit like him, don't you?"

"I'm not familiar enough with the painting to be able to say but it's an interesting thought," Jennifer said, turning away. "I'll get the copy of the document I told you about."

She was away for more than five minutes while Jake and Rhosa, exchanging glances, drank in silence. When she returned, Rhosa was looking at the books in the bookcases.

"Pretty boring, I'm afraid, mostly on theological subjects. My husband uses them for his sermons." She said. "But I've got a disappointment and a puzzle. The document I was going to show you is not where it should be. I'm sure it was there when we had the history meeting here last week."

"With Mr. Freidan?" Rhosa asked.

"Yes, he chairs all our meetings, an amazing man. Why do you ask?"

"No reason, just that Jake told me about him but I've never had the pleasure of meeting him."

"You'd be very welcome to come to our meetings – both of you, if you wish."

CHAPTER 35

"Jay," Rhosa said, as she leaned on his shoulders while he sat at his desk, "I've waited nearly a week while you've done your research and typed away on your computer. I think it's time I was allowed to read your chapter on 'Is There a Future for the Human Brain?' Isn't it ready yet?"

"I've got all the ideas down, I'm just working on a few more details," he said, standing up and stretching, "have a look."

She sat down, put her glasses on and was quiet. Like him, she had the ability to concentrate on what she was doing to the exclusion of everything around her. He knew there would be no point in speaking to her until she had finished so went out into the garden to sit in the sun for a few moments. A few minutes of activity were all he allowed himself. He picked up the newspaper and tried to read but all the time his mind was wondering what Rhosa's reaction would be. He tried to concentrate on an article about the economy in Japan but was just not taking it in. With pleasure he heard her footsteps as she came and sat beside him. She said nothing and he began to wonder if she had found what he had written objectionable.

"What do you think?" he asked.

"Amazing, you say so much that I would like to say but I know I couldn't. There is such a lot in this chapter that I want to read it again – no, even better, I'll read it aloud to you."

"As though Shakespeare had written it?" he laughed obviously pleased at what she was saying.

"I'll try," she laughed with him. "While I speak, you can jot down any changes. Come on into the study, I don't feel like reading out here, the sun's too damned hot."

She laid out the pages of type and read.

"Man has always had an odd relationship with progress. Saint Bernard of Clairvaux, the most influential Christian thinker of the 12th century, declared that the pursuit of knowledge was pagan and

350

vile. He stated that to kill a Pagan was to bring Christ closer." She stopped reading. "That doesn't read well. You need something to join that last sentence to the next paragraph." She pencilled in a note. "I think you want to add something about the Church. Like, 'In 1302, Pope Boniface said 'Everyone answers to me and I answer only to God.'

"Even during what we call the Industrial Revolution mankind resisted progress. James Watt, who is credited with inventing the steam engine, scoffed at steam locomotives manufactured by Symington and Murdoch and his attitude delayed the development of the Railways. In the early part of the nineteenth Century, the Luddites destroyed weaving machinery because they were terrified of losing their work, even though the new developments had the ability to relieve them of drudgery and improve their living standards."

"This is good, Jay but if I'm going to read all of it I'll have to have a drink. Could you do me a G & T?"

For once, Jay was happy to get her a drink. When she had the glass in her hand, she continued reading aloud.

"The disjoint was also characterised by William Morris and the Arts and Crafts Movement which deplored the growth of factory-made goods and the loss of the character of what they called honest toil."

Rhosa stopped. "I think you ought to put in something like 'It is ironic that the movement was sustained by Morris's family wealth which came from men going down into copper and arsenic mines in often appalling conditions'. You could also put in that the machine-made goods he deplored improved the standards of millions. *The machines largely invented in the 19th century and improved in the 20th century have dispensed with much of what those who do not have to indulge in it were wont to call 'honest toil'. They conveniently ignored the rheumatism, silicosis, pneumonia and many other diseases which resulted in the early deaths of miners."* She scribbled another note on the page and said. *"Every invention throughout the intervening decades has provided a better standard of living which we appreciate when switching on our central heating, taking tablets to cope with our ailments and walking from hospital beds with new hip joints."*

Jake nodded as he wrote down what she had said. "Yes, I'll put that in."

Rhosa carried on. "We cannot fail to be grateful for the inventions of ingenious men who lived before us. We now live longer, healthier and wealthier lives than ever before. Every invention which removed physical hardship can be blessed but, in recent times we are seeing the growth of more insidious developments which are making man's brain redundant. There are groups all over the industrialised world who are straining to be the first to perfect neural networks so computers will function better, faster and more productively than the human brain.

They are not there yet, but if you are planning to be a novelist, go to many universities' Creative Writing courses. You will be introduced to software which creates passably good stories. You have taught yourself to compose music – play a simple theme into a computer's memory and within a few hours it will play back to you its own compositions which to most people will be as good as those professional musicians.

You are a sculptor. No need to work physically. Place a sitter in front of a laser scanner and very quickly, a computer will instruct a machine to make a copy of the sitter's face. You have spent ten years becoming a medical doctor. Shame, the computer will beat you to analysing a patient's many symptoms and could also prescribe a drug as a cure. Even better, the patient will feel that the computer listened more patiently and analytically. Perhaps you decided to become a psychiatrist - pity you wasted all those years of study; the computer will listen to problems with endless patience and draw on an infinite resource of cases so your meagre knowledge will be left behind I'm sorry to say. Is your mind legally trained? There is much more information on case law available on CDs or on the internet than you can ever have learned of during your university training or your lengthy career. You work as a stockbroker? Programmed machines buy and sell stock without any human interference. You may argue that computers are not as good at solving problems as the human brain. Wait a few years, they are already communicating with each other and not just with those around them, they are part of a network linking individual machines, stretching around the world. By logging on to the machine on your desk, you will be able to discover details of a problem solved in New Zealand, Brazil, Egypt, anywhere.

The 'progress' we have every day is often driven simply by the need to have progress. Ostensibly the purpose is to make our lives easier. We must ask ourselves if that is what we want. Our minds need challenge, just as our bodies need exercise. Remove the challenge and the zest goes out of our lives.

We speak to computers who reply with a series of standard answers. We are, of course, not standard people but that is just our misfortune and we should learn to conform to systems. Capitalism is concerned only with making profit and treats people as units of wealth. The recent mis-selling by banks and investment companies of products which are virtually worthless and have only one purpose, to make the sellers large profits, is convincing evidence. Capitalism has forgotten that its purpose should be to foster human well-being. This is an illness which will grow into a wasting disease. It may never die but it can become an amorphous leech, sucking out the blood of the people it purportedly serves."

When she had finished, he was as pleased as she was. The way she had read it gave it an extra dimension. He had found her reading of it so helpful that together they decided that the rest of the book should have the same treatment, he writing followed by her reading aloud.

He sat back and said. "Rhosa, I've just thought about that story you wrote about life as it might be in fifty years time. We could use that as an example of what will happen if we continue with what Capitalists call 'progress'."

"It terrified me when I wrote it. I've never looked at it again. I suppose you're right. Yes, why not?"

CHAPTER 36

When she was not appearing or rehearsing, Rhosa settled happily into housewife mode and would find pleasure in tasks she would normally have found tedious. Each morning, she would rise first, pad down the stairs, make the breakfast, collect the mail and take it back to bed. Jake would be awake and sitting up as she passed him the tray.

"Nice lot of post today," she said as she got in beside him." Most of them bills though. Nothing for me; I keep hoping that I'll get a letter with a contract saying I've got that part."

"Thought you said it wasn't your sort of thing,"

"It's not really but I need something to get my mind into gear. I do love being at home here with you but only if I have something in the future. Don't think I could just be a hausfrau for good." She drank her juice as Jake picked up a letter with a green envelope. "Yes, I wondered what that one was, never had a green envelope letter before." Rhosa said.

Jake opened the envelope and read. "It's from Renda, apologising for not replying to my email but she's not computer literate, got in a mess and lost my email address. She's invited us both to dinner at her place." He put the letter face down. "Where do you think she lives?"

"I'm hardly awake. My blood sugar level is low - I've not yet eaten my toast and jam. You'll have to tell me."

"Mayfair, she has a top floor flat in Albemarle St, close to that gallery where you saw the Prince of Wales watercolours. This Friday if we can make it; I'm ok; are you free."

"Wouldn't miss it."

"It's just the two of us apparently. Pretty long letter too, you read it, it'll help you wake up."

He passed the letter to Rhosa who gulped down her orange juice as she read. "'I've taken up with a new young man who loves cooking.'" Rhosa laughed as she read. "Good for her. 'Fortunate for me because I can't make toast without burning it. We shall be able to talk while he indulges his passion on a new dish - his own invention he tells me. We are still like newly-weds; when I said 'passion' I meant it literally, I don't know how it works but cooking 'enlivens' him if you understand me. So if we end the evening around 10ish, you'll understand won't you. Here I am at sixty and he has made me feel like the women I always wanted to be when I was in my twenties. Don't entirely know why he has chosen me. Partly because I'm well off I should think and he at forty has gone through a disastrous marriage and divorce which has left him virtually penniless, paying alimony to keep two youngsters at a special school.

You may be wondering why I have asked you; I want to meet you both, talk about your political theories Jake and your acting, Rhosa, your life together and - you know - everything. I've got lots of stuffy friends who repeat the obvious and frankly I'm bored, bored, bored with their conversations. I need young people like you and I want to show you off to him and show him off to you. Hope that doesn't sound too contrived. It obviously is but that's what I'm like. This life we have been given is too short for the conventions. That's partly why I left politics. Like lawyers, politicians get paid by the word. I wanted to say to them all 'for God's sake get on with it. Decisions shouldn't be so agonising. Why does it often take years for a Bill to be passed and even when it does, it turns out to be full of holes and has to be amended? Do be sure to come even if you have to cancel other things'." Rhosa smiled as she passed the letter back. "Goes on a bit but it's all interesting. I'll phone her today and accept."

On the Friday evening, they stepped from the lift at the conventionally correct ten minutes late.

As soon as they rang the bell, the door was flung open and Renda was standing there beaming.

"Thought you were never going to get here," she laughed, "come in." She took them into the lounge and sat them down.

They were both surprised to see that the flat was minimalist with Cubist and Vorticist paintings on the wall and furniture in the same style.

Renda noticed their reaction. "I guess you weren't expecting furniture like this." She looked down at her ample figure. "Not what you'd expect of a matron like me. Have to admit it took me by surprise at first."

"I love it," Rhosa said, "just wish I had the nerve to do it."

"So do I."

"You got an interior designer in?" Jake asked.

"Gerhardt," Renda said smiling, "that's what he does and he's damned good at it." She asked them what they wanted to drink and poured out drinks from the polished aluminium cabinet. "Do either of you speak German?"

"Rhosa has a few words but I can only ask for 'zwei bier bitte' and then I've run out of conversation," Jake said. "Why do you ask?"

"Gerhardt again, he is German and unusually he does not have any English conversation." She grimaced as though sharing a confidence. "Met him a couple of years ago in Bonn when I was on a fact finding mission and he was working on fitting out the hotel where we were staying. My family were Jewish, left Germany to escape Nazism but they insisted I speak German in the home they made in London." She shrugged. "I married a couple of times; first one lasted three weeks, next one ten years. I was close to forty when the last one walked out on me, same age as Gerhardt is now. Vowed I'd never look at another man and didn't until Gerhardt smiled at me. It's love you know," her face glowed as she spoke. "Can you imagine my delight? You think the fire has gone out for good and the only way to keep warm is to turn on central heating, suddenly along comes someone special and the embers burst into flame more fiercely than ever before."

"I was beginning to wonder about language and its effect on national character too. The men I married were English and just couldn't take what they called my bossiness. You'll find me quite an opinionated woman. Gerhardt doesn't even notice it when I order him around in German." She laughed suddenly. "Don't like to admit it even to myself but I've got to say that the way he speaks to me does get my goat. I guess I like the way the English treat a woman even if it can be difficult to tell if they are telling you the truth or only what you want to hear." She got up to refill their glasses and said, "sorry, my dears, I'm doing what I always do – talking too much." She sat down. "Your turn now and if I interrupt, just tell me to shut up."

"Mm," Jake said awkwardly, "how will we speak to Gerhardt?"

"Oh, don't worry about him. He will be in his chef and servant mood so you won't see much of him. He probably won't even eat till after you've left this evening or maybe even tomorrow. A smile goes a long way with him."

As she spoke, the door opened and a tall slim man carrying canapes came in, smiling at them. "Good evening, mein friends," he said in guttural and halting English then after a silence, bowed slightly and left.

"Must say I can see why you found him attractive." Rhosa said. "He is very handsome. Bit like George Sanders the actor."

Renda looked surprised at the mention of a name from the 1940s.

Rhosa saw her surprise and continued. "I loved all those old films. When I came to England from Egypt at the age of ten, I watched every film I could, I watched George Sanders in 'All About Eve' at least a dozen times, I went to every play I could and read Shakespeare till I knew every word."

"Explains why you're so good now."

Rhosa smiled her thanks at the compliment.

"We will eat in thirty minutes," Renda said. "Gerhardt ticks along like clockwork. While we wait, tell me more about your political ideas."

"The originator is Haig Skarn, I've just added to his ideas." Jake said modestly. "I'm sure he would have liked to have been here but he's lecturing. It's a long flight across the Atlantic so I will be second best."

"No matter, I will meet him later," Renda said, selecting a canapé and passing the plate to her guests. "Let me say that what you are doing is, in my view, critical for this country. Politics as we know it has outlived its usefulness and has become as Prince Charles might have said, 'like a monstrous carbuncle on the face of an old friend.' It not only disfigures, it drains strength and mental vigour from the nation. In an election year, our politicians are so intent on retaining power that they push the economy into growth mode when we all know they should have applied the brakes. Why do we let them get away with it?" She stopped as a thought struck her. "Rhosa, I'm sorry, I did not think to ask you if you minded if we talk about politics."

"Of course not, I am here so that I can join in. I suspect I am as much a political animal as you are. And Jake definitely is."

"I am usually right in my judgement of people; except of course with my husbands, I've made a dreadful mess there." She grinned as she popped another canapé into her mouth. "I was just asking why we let MPs get away with indulging their complete self-interest. Just a few people are objecting. One of the most remarkable fighters is a journalist, Heather Brooke. She's British but has lived most of her life in USA and when she came back to this country she was appalled at the secrecy with which our leaders surround themselves. In the US she was always able to find out what she wanted to know but here everything is suppressed."

"But we now have the Freedom of Information Act." Rhosa said.

Renda smiled. "Don't ever try to get information in a hurry, Rhosa. Two years is common and even after that, the data is sanitised. Read Heather Brooke's book, 'The Silent State'. Under a cloak which they call democracy we are slowly moving towards a secret police state; a fair chunk of the taxes you pay are used to keep track on all your activities but also to prevent you finding out what your records contain. You could have a bad credit rating and never know about it until you go for a loan. Every call you make on your mobile, every email you write, every time you visit your doctor or apply for a licence is in a database."

"The lives of every one of us are observed." Jake said. "Walk the streets of London and you may be filmed hundreds of times a day and be recorded. But if you take photographs of those that spy on you, you will be investigated. The inquisitiveness of the state is justified on the premise of protecting your security."

Renda nodded in agreement. "We now have a situation where prevention is worse than the disease." She got up and refilled their glasses again. "Enjoy the freedom to drink what you want. The State would love to restrict your intake - they haven't yet been able to find a way to do it - but they will. What they would love is for us to live in cupboards so that we don't interfere with them."

Jake smiled, "Coincidentally Rhosa has written a short story which almost paraphrases what you've just said."

"I must read it." Renda said.

As she spoke, the door opened and a smiling Gerhardt came in again. He said something in German to Renda which Rhosa and Jake did not understand.

Renda looked at her watch and grinned. "What did I say? Exactly on time, Gerhardt is ready to serve."

When they were seated and Gerhardt had served the starter, Renda said between mouthfuls, "I'm haunted, you know."

Jake frowned. "This flat, you mean?"

"No, this country - my spectre is that this land which I have made my home and which I love, is in decline; the flame is flickering and we have lost the vital spark to re-ignite it."

"Like you I have chosen to make my home in this country," Rhosa said. "And I see it declining too but it has been doing so since at least 1880 when the US and Germany started to dominate."

"In spite of this, we are still able to afford to eat Gerhardt's smoked salmon pate over a century later," Jake grinned as he spread Melba toast with the starter. "I understand what you mean about his cooking. Just a shame he's not enjoying it with us."

"You'll see why when he brings in the main course. I've watched him cooking. Everything is measured precisely, cooked for a calculated time at a carefully set temperature. Think of the best restaurant you've eaten in and double it. That's my Gerhardt."

"Going to be very difficult if you come back to us for a meal; I haven't progressed much past learning how eggs are boiled."

"Suits me well, I love what he cooks but the palette becomes jaded and needs to be refreshed with the classic baked bean supper now and then."

Jake and Rhosa smiled as they put down the cutlery on their plates, the door opened and a smiling Gerhardt cleared away the plates.

"Sehr gut, Gerhard, danke schön." Rhosa said in halting German.

"Sie sind sehr freundlich." Gerhardt beamed at her as he carried the plates into his kitchen.

Renda pushed her chair back, went to a bookshelf and came back with a book.

"This is the book I was telling you about, 'The Silent State'. If you haven't read it, borrow it. In any sane society, this book ought to start a revolution. As you say the only reason we accept a system which works against our interests is simply because most of us are apathetic."

She opened the book to page 233. "Heather Brooke had applied under the Freedom of Information Act for details of the expenses claimed by MPs. After she was told that it would cost too much to disclose how MPs were spending our money, she applied again and was told she could only ask for ten MPs' expenses. Before she received the information, a private members' bill was introduced quietly around Christmas time to amend the Freedom of Information Act to exempt MPs from their own law. Can you believe that, the 'do as I say and not as I do' system of government still exists."

Jake and Rhosa shook their heads.

"Hold on, it gets worse, fill your glasses, you'll need alcohol to dull the senses," Renda continued. "Listen to this from page 234 for the sort of doublespeak which Orwell would have been proud to have invented to justify MP exemption from the Freedom of Information Act. This is what he says. '*When we write on behalf of constituents... we must be able to look them in the eye and say that in all circumstances what they tell us will not get out... It is like the relationship with a priest.*' Does that sound to you like a justification for MPs being exempted from the Act they introduced? Can you imagine why we pay these people to work in our interests? It would be a pious hope that they should show themselves more intelligent than we are so that at least they could understand their own convoluted legislation," she shook her head in mock disbelief. "We could not be expected to understand the complexities which would obviously go over our heads. Yet here is one of those 'intelligent' representatives using arguments that even we with our simple minds can see are blatantly fatuous."

"Glad you suggested we fortify ourselves with a drink before you read that," Jake said, "about as convincing as saying 'we will not let the public have fuel in their cars because if we did they would think that the Government was allowing them to drive and they could have accidents and kill themselves and this would be a cost to the nation'."

Renda stood up and walked to open the door to the kitchen.

"Sorry, Gerhardt, doing my usual, talking too much," she said in English and then, corrected herself, repeating what she had said in German.

She sat down again while Gerhardt was serving, Rhosa noticed with pleasure that when he passed Renda, he kissed the top of her head affectionately.

When the meal was served, Renda said, "I'm sure I've distressed you enough and you now want to enjoy what Gerhardt has prepared, so we'll leave politics till we've finished, shall we?"

As they ate a stroganoff the like of which neither Rhosa nor Jake had had before, Renda made polite conversation asking about the theatre and impressing Rhosa with her knowledge of Shakespeare's Troilus and Cressida.

"I'm surprised that you know the play so well, Renda," Rhosa said, "it's not often performed."

Renda laughed impishly. "Looking at overweight me sitting here indulging my appetite when I really ought to be toying with the classic lettuce leaf you would be surprised to hear that I played Cressida when I was in my early twenties."

"Renda Margold!" Rhosa said. "Of course, I thought your name sounded familiar. You appeared in one of the televised versions, I never saw it but the critics said your performance was a triumph and now I think about it, I remember seeing a photograph of you in the part."

Renda opened her eyes in surprise. "D'you know, you're the only person under forty who has ever heard of the career I left far too early. Should never have married - jealous you see, insisted I be a wife and not an actress; I'm sure I would have made something. I miss the excitement that comes only when you walk on stage to an expectant audience. There's nothing like it is there, Rhosa?" She looked at her watch. "Just coming up to ten." She said with a twinkle in her eye.

Rhosa and Jake left smiling at Renda's eagerness to go to bed.

CHAPTER 37

Jake was sleeping in the chair one dreary Sunday afternoon when Rhosa came in from the library. "Jay, something funny's going on; the books have moved."

He woke up bemused but still managed to joke, "what, all of them?"

"No, half a dozen. They seem to have just fallen over."

"Probably the ex-cleaning lady. She's got a key to the place and I'd told her she could borrow books for a new Open University course she is doing."

"She still has a key? Bit risky, Jay, what's to stop her coming in at night when we're not here?"

"Bit stupid I suppose. I never asked her for the key back. Guess I should, shouldn't I. But she usually leaves me a note if she has been in for a book."

"Would be an idea to limit the number of keys around, Jay. But it couldn't have been her, I saw the books a couple of hours ago and they were all tidy. Your lady doesn't come in the afternoon like a silent wraith without knocking, does she?" she asked as she sat down on the floor beside him.

"No, but I've always told her to come and go when she wants," he frowned as he began to wake up. "Now I remember it couldn't have been her she told me she was going to see her son and his wife in Glastonbury."

"Glastonbury?" Rhosa smiled, "into mysticism is she?"

"Bit strange, I know but after his father died her son went off the rails, he's a Druid or something like that."

"I know the sort," Rhosa affected a shudder, "I had a revolting experience with a man like that. I'd just separated from my husband and was introduced on a blind date by someone I thought was a friend. She 'phoned and said 'Why don't you spend the evening with us? I'll introduce you to this man I know. You like people who are different and he certainly is.' At the time it seemed like a good idea so I got ready and jumped in the car. The arrangement was that I would pick him up because he didn't have a car. First of all I couldn't find where he lived, when I did, it was little more than a hut. I knocked on the door and he came out, dressed in black with a sweat band on his forehead and a big feather sticking out of it. He seemed pleased to see me, flung his arms round me and tried to kiss me on the lips. Revolting…"

"Body odour?" Jake asked.

"How did you guess?"

"It comes with the story doesn't it?"

"Ugh, acrid, I pulled away and said we had to rush because we were late. I then had to drive two miles with him sitting beside me. Fairly cold night but I had to have the windows open; I guessed he never washed and didn't even have water in the hut."

"Is there a happy ending?"

"Not till I left. The most self-indulgent man I ever met – that is apart perhaps from Anthony Garden who at least redeems himself by being clean. You know the sort who can talk only about themselves and never even think that other people have opinions. He was convinced that by attuning himself to the energy of the earth, he had discovered solutions to the world's problems." She shuddered. "Funny, all that evening I thought about you and how easy it was to talk to you."

"We'll talk about something else then." Jake stopped to think, "One thing that intrigues me is that you never tell me about your origins. Not about your mother or the grandmother who provided for you. About the only thing you've told me is that she travels a lot but still has a home in Egypt, I think. Fascinating country but you never seem to want to go back."

"For a tourist it is fascinating. But one thing you are forgetting is that I am of a different faith and even worse, Jewish."

"So?"

"In Egypt I could be despised, denied any privileges, unable to work, threatened with violence."

"This is the twenty first century. Is it really that bad?"

"It is that bad. My grandmother still has a house there, yes, but she would never live in it. I've only met her fleetingly when she arrived with a young man on her arm as she was passing through London. I was captivated, couldn't keep my eyes off her, which of course was what she wanted."

"What, the sort, aging glamour on the lines of Gloria Swanson in 'Sunset Boulevard' do you mean?" Jake asked.

"You've got it." Rhosa smiled. "Not the least bit interested in me or my mother, her only daughter, though." She sat down in the chair in front of her.

"That's why I never talk about my grandmother. I've told you all I know in one sentence. My mother is quite like her, very self-interested. No time for me after her marriage. I rarely meet her these days. Just occasionally we talk on the 'phone. I did see her when you went to York for that journalist's conference. She was more interested in you; wanted to know about what you were doing. She reads your articles."

"I'm impressed," Jake grinned. "She sound like an intelligent woman."

"She's still with my stepfather, I'm certain she would have left him if it hadn't been for the prestige which spins off from his position in the university. I'm sure that, like me, she can see that he is a self-centred, selfish prig who treats her and always treated me with condescension. She's happy to be his wife because for her, love is not important, she is only interested in status."

"I'm not like her, don't have her need to be involved in that sort of society. Got to admit though that I would have liked some appreciation from him of what I've done."

"You, a successful actress, don't you know he is impressed with you?"

"Didn't go to university - no degree, you see."

"Is he as facile as that?"

"He's as facile as that and even more. Even if, like you, I had a PhD, he would still remember me as that ill-educated wretch with a dreadful Egyptian accent."

"Does that still live with you?"

"Even when I am taking curtain calls and surrounded by applause, I am thinking, why does he still have no respect for me?"

"He does, you know - perhaps wouldn't admit it to you but I met one of his colleagues over dinner one evening who told me your stepfather was boasting about his lovely actress daughter and her success in Shakespeare."

"Doesn't sound like him." Quickly, she broke into a smile. "Ok, you're joking aren't you?"

"I'm not joking, Rhosa, your stepfather talks about you endlessly, so this fellow said. And he meant endlessly."

Rhosa stared at him obviously confused, then said "Well that's a surprise?" She looked slightly bemused.

A couple of minutes passed before she said "That's shaken me as much as those books that seemed to have moved without anybody being near."

Jake got up and went into the library with Rhosa following him. When he saw that a few of the books certainly were out of position he looked mystified. "Mm," he said, surprised, "I don't think they were like that when I was here a little while ago."

"I was with you and they were all straight as far as I remember."

"Wait a minute," Jake said, "that's where I found the Tyndale bible - behind those books."

"Tyndale bible what's that?"

"The first bible in English, printed in 1525, bibles were always in Latin which few people understood; one of the ways the Church kept control. If no one understood, no one could complain."

"Oh, yes, I have heard of it, wasn't Tyndale unpopular with the Church?"

"Tragic story. All he wanted was for English people to be able to read the bible in their own language."

"A Tyndale bible behind these books – a real one?"

"Yes, there's a hollowed-out bit in the wall with a loose panel over it."

"You never told me," she said, "Why didn't you?"

"I don't know, always so tongue tied in your presence, I suppose," he joked.

"Thanks for the compliment," Rhosa grinned with him, "but I'd actually have liked to have seen the bible. Is it still behind these books?"

"Yes, I put it back, didn't want to move it, it's been there many hundreds of years I suppose. I somehow felt it should be left in its home."

"What a nice romantic idea," and then added with feigned sarcasm. "Is it asking too much for me to see it?"

He thought back to when he had found the bible and the eerie feeling it gave him until he'd put it back. Since it had been returned to its hiding place he had felt more at ease in the house.

"Um – it's not that I don't want you to see it."

"Yes – then why don't we look at it?"

"It has an…" he searched for a word which would explain but not alarm her, "an aura."

"Aura! D'you mean it's haunted or something?"

"I don't know; it's just…well I get to imagining things when I hold it."

"Ghosts, d'you mean?" Rhosa put her hand over her mouth, holding back a laugh, "Jake, you are just not like that, I know you are imaginative but you are definitely not the type who would believe in the supernatural."

"I'm not but," he hesitated, "it's hard to explain - I had this image of a man and a woman in medieval clothing."

"Are you serious? A man and a woman, what did they look like?"

He thought for a while before replying. "I couldn't be sure because the images were very indistinct."

"Well … how about trying to explain."

He took a breath, exhaled slowly and said, "I thought it might have been Tyndale but now I've looked more at the paintings here, they looked like Jacob D'Arcy and his mistress, - no, not 'mistress' I don't know what she was."

"Jay, you hadn't been taking LSD or something?"

"No, I was very tired though."

"That's probably it," she said, "you can reach a stage of exhaustion; it's happened to me, where reality and vision become blurred. You were probably very tired and had the memory of the paintings so vividly that they appeared in your conscious mind."

"That sounds right." he said without conviction, wondering if she was agreeing because she just didn't want to worry him. But he knew that what he had 'seen' was more real than she was implying. "I'll go and look at the Jacob D'Arcy painting again."

Rhosa folded her arms across her chest and looked quizzically at him. "Jay," she said, "you are prevaricating. Tell me how to get at the bible."

The room was well lit, it was warm and modern jazz was playing on the radio in the next room. Everything should have made him feel relaxed but still he was apprehensive. Rhosa saw his hesitation and said with just slight irritation in her voice. "Come on Jay, you are behaving as though you've got something to hide."

"No, I'm not," he said without conviction, "it's just that I feel the bible should be left where it was meant to be."

"By whom?"

"I...don't know – perhaps it was put there by D'Arcy himself."

"Perhaps," she said. "Jay, can't you see I'm dying to know more about it, what it's doing there, who hid it and why. Tell me where it is."

He pointed to the middle of the book case at the books leaning on their sides. Rhosa pulled them out, reached to the back of the case, felt the loose panel and pulled at it with her fingertips. As it moved, she pulled her hand abruptly away. Jake could see that she had also become uneasy. "It's dark there; I need a torch, Jay."

There was one in his desk drawer which he had put there, meaning to re-explore the cavity where the Tyndale bible was kept, but had never summoned up the determination to do it. He took it from the drawer and passed it to Rhosa, by which time she had pulled aside the panel and had taken out the bible which she placed on the table in almost the same position as he had laid it in when he had discovered it. Carefully and almost reverentially, she turned over the pages with a hand which Jake could see was shaking with excitement.

"Jay, what an incredible feeling to look at a book which has probably been hidden for several hundred years," she said in a hushed tone. "Tell me about Tyndale, I know almost nothing about him."

"Remarkable man, studied at Cambridge and could speak French, Greek, German, Italian, Spanish, his own tongue English and, of course, Latin. It is thought that he may have studied under Erasmus."

"He thought that the way to God was through the bible and decided that Englishmen should be able to read the bible in their own language. A priest said to him 'We had better be without God's laws than the Pope's.' and Tyndale replied, 'I defy the Pope, and all his laws; and if God spares my life, I will cause the boy that drives the plough in England to know more of the Scriptures than the Pope himself.' He left England for Cologne. His bible was first printed in Worms, a city that had converted to Luther's doctrines.

The bible was smuggled into England, where many people read it before the church condemned it, after which, all known copies were burned. Tyndale went into hiding but was betrayed and captured."

"Then what happened?"

"He was burned at the stake."

"Just for translating the bible?" Rhosa said, open-mouthed.

"You have to put it into context. Those were days of violence, when life was cheap."

Rhosa nodded absently, absorbed in reading the bible. "This is just so moving, Jay. I can read it even though it uses language hundreds of years old.

It's like modern English written by someone who had bad dyslexia but it is still understandable. But you go back to the 'Craft of Deyng' 'this vrechit warlde, the quhilk is callit dede, femys harde'. It's so different."

"Remarkable that you know 14th Century poetry?"

"The life of an actress is punctuated by long periods of 'resting', usually at a time when you want to be immersed in work. On the basis that one day it might be useful, I kept up my spirit by reading and learning."

He was about to say jokingly 'and drinking?' but stopped himself. Instead he said, "I doubt if there are many careers where a knowledge of Louthiane Inglis, which incidentally, was not English but Scots, would have been useful."

She smiled, "the point was not for it to be useful but simply to immerse my mind in something - anything. It's funny how memory works, when I said 'this vrechit warlde' I was back in my own wretched world and wondering why I wasted all those years when you were not around," as she looked at the bible, her hand wandered across the table until it found his fingers. He moved his towards hers leaving an imprint in the polished surface. He looked at the mark and was back with Sabel when they were newly married and had sat at this same table when they ate in their dining room. It occurred to him that if he had accurate enough instruments, he would be able to detect the residues of Sabel's handprints. He was very sensitive to atmosphere and for a brief moment, in the darkened room, he saw Sabel in the place where Rhosa was sitting. The thought disturbed him and, to pass it off he got up and poured them both a glass of sherry.

Rhosa, carefully turning over the pages of the bible, took the glass and drank. Suddenly, with a bang, she put the glass down, spilling drops of sherry on the table, which Jake wiped with his handkerchief, thinking how angry his ex-wife would have been that he had stained the handkerchief and that she would have to wash it. Rhosa was different and did not even notice his action – reasonably clean and tidy herself but for her, mess was synonymous with creation. He was constantly falling over her discarded clothes, books and scripts but it was part of her and he even liked to see a bit of mess, a reaction, he supposed to Sabel's 'next to Godliness'.

"What is it, Rhosa, what have you seen?" he asked.

She could not speak for several moments and then said. "D'you ever get that cold feeling up the back?"

Jake nodded, "that happens whenever I hear 'One Fine Day'. When Madam Butterfly sings the words 'I know'. Why do you ask?"

For reply, she passed him a small piece of paper which she had taken from the bible. On it was written 'Knowest thou that whatever happens, I am here and think of me and happiness, Jacob'

"Jay," Rhosa said, "what is this we've uncovered?" she caught her breath and he saw the intensity of her emotion when she wiped her eyes with the back of her hand. "Is Jacob D'Arcy reaching out over the centuries to us through this bible?"

A sensation of unreality gripped him and he remained silent while his mind tried to rationalise his turmoil. "You're saying that there is a supernatural." He pursed his lips. "No this 'supernatural' could be answered by physics. The energy of the human voice causes atoms to vibrate in such a way that they become permanently changed and record events and voices."

"The way houses are haunted, you mean; the walls act like recorders?" Rhosa asked.

"D'Arcy's words are still here?" he asked. "I was so cold when we were in St. Andrew's church that I didn't follow what you said when we saw my shadow but now I see what you meant."

He picked up the Tyndale. "If there is any sense in what we're saying, he's probably left his shadow in this bible as well and that's why I had a vision when I held it." He walked around the room again, looking at the walls, the ceiling and the floors. "But why should he choose us, there must have been scores of people who have lived here, why not them?"

"I don't know," she shrugged, "you're a journalist, perhaps he wants you to write what he was unable to do in his time."

"Pretty imprecise way of telling me."

"At the time he was around, there would have been nothing better." Rhosa continued looking at the paper she had found in the bible and then said. "Have you ever looked in the cavity where the bible was?"

"No," he said hesitantly. "Somehow I hadn't wanted to disturb it."

She moved some books aside, picked up the torch and directed it into the cavity. "Ugh," she cried out, "there's a spider on the bookshelf there. Deal with it, can you, Jay?"

Squeamish about spiders himself, he grabbed it in rolled-up tissue and threw the corpse into the fireplace while Rhosa grimaced in horror.

"You look in there first, Jay, there might be another spider." She shone the torch into the recess and turned away.

"Spider free now," he said, "but, you know, there is something there."

Rhosa looking over his shoulder said, "my God, Jay it looks like a roll of papers pushed right to the back."

He reached in and pulled the papers out. Something had nibbled the edges, perhaps, he wondered, centuries of the ancestors of the spider he had just disposed of, but otherwise they seemed intact.

He watched Rhosa's hands as she took the papers from him and carefully untied the ribbon holding them together.

Apart from some fraying at the edges, the documents were in good condition considering their age. They were dry and the outer sheet had cracked but he managed to carefully separate most of them. Jake took them immediately to the photocopier so that he had copies which would not be damaged. While she waited for the copier to warm up, Rhosa was almost jumping up and down with frustration at not being able to read them straight away.

When he had peeled the outer two sheets away, he opened the third and they saw writing on it. Involuntarily, Rhosa called out, "Jay!" and, when he looked at her he could see her amazement.

The writing was indistinct but Jay was able to read a few words written in Italian.

"Italian! Surprising it's not in Latin," she said. I've got a reasonable understanding of Italian; did a couple of seasons in Milan in 'The Cherry Orchard'. But this isn't the modern Italian that I can read."

On the shelves was his Italian English dictionary which he passed her, she sat down and began to make some sense of the writing.

Her mouth fell open as she looked down to the bottom of the page. "Jay, you'll never guess who this is from."

"Go on, don't keep me waiting."

"Would you believe," she stood open mouthed, "Valenti?"

For a moment the name meant nothing to him and then he remembered. "You mean the gravestone in the churchyard in Jennifer Williams'church."

"I bet neither the Vicar nor Jennifer know who Valenti was." Rhosa said.

"But what about your Mr. Freidan?"

"I keep wondering about that missing copy of the document that Jennifer wanted to show us." he saw her frowning. "Is there a pattern building? You were drawn to this house without knowing why. It has portraits of D'Arcy and Mistry which supposedly can't be moved. You find this bible and now these papers. You visited a gallery in Vienna where you saw the painting of Valenti wearing that unusual ring on his finger."

He nodded. "What's more, the ring was worn by Freidan when I went to visit him. The pentacle sign has been used in witchcraft, as a source of energy," he was beginning to get a cold feeling up his spine. "What is he saying in the letter?"

"Don't know yet. Although it's old Italian, I can only pick out some of the words. The seal on the back of this letter is in the form of a pentacle. You'll have to give me time to try to read this, my Italian is not very good and this is handwritten. I'll need your dictionary and a bit of quiet. You go and get on with your book."

It was several hours later when she came over to him, looking tired but triumphant.

"I haven't done much of it; many of the words are meaningless to me. There's only a couple of letters which are in Italian but in the others, there is a name that comes up a lot. Does Cardinal Bardonski mean anything?" she asked.

Jake shook his head. "Don't know why but it has a familiar ring about it."

"We might need to find an academic who could translate and get more sense than I can but I think I can understand the gist of this first letter." She laid the paper out on the desk and took a chair to sit beside him.

"It is a letter from Valenti to D'Arcy, it sounds serious from what I can make out."

"Why was he writing in Italian to D'Arcy who must have been able to read it? Even stranger, why is a Catholic Cardinal buried in St. Andrew's in what would have been a small village a long way from London."

"Apparently they were both part of a group who were…"

"Go on, Rhosa, who were…"

"I can't be sure because my knowledge of old Italian doesn't exist but I'm sure there's something about death."

"Our gentle-looking Jacob D'Arcy involved in killing!"

"There's something about poison in this letter but I think we'll have to read the other papers to find out."

"Is that something you can do?" he asked.

Rhosa shook her head. "No, I've looked through them. I can't do anything with Latin."

"Latin! I suppose that makes sense - he was a Catholic Cardinal. But why send only one letter in Italian?"

"Think about it," she smiled tauntingly.

"Sorry I'm lost."

"Bardonski, does that sound an Italian name? Could he possibly be a Polish man who could not read Italian and this letter was meant to be unreadable by Bardonski." She shrugged. "I know that sounds way out – it's just a theory."

"I don't have your brilliant mind do I? I wonder how you put up with me," he joked.

"You make up for it in other ways," She put her arm round his shoulder and winked her eye provocatively.

"Thanks." He stopped as a thought struck him. "I've just remembered where I know the name from. In that gallery in Rome where I saw the painting of Valenti, there was one of a Cardinal and I'm sure it was Bardonski, that's why I though it sounded familiar. I must see if I can remember where I would have put the photograph, I'm sure it had the Valenti portrait and I think also one of Bardonski"

"Nice?" Rhosa asked.

"No, 'nice' is not the epithet I would have used. Shrewish and evil looking would be closer."

She carefully turned over the other letters. "What can we do about the Latin?"

"I'll bet our Daniel Freidan reads Latin." Jake said.

"What - you're saying take them to him?"

"No, I'm uneasy about that man; I'm sure he's a fraud and as I said, wearing what to me looked like the same ring that Valenti had in the painting must have some purpose," he meditated. "I was just remembering that funny thing with Jennifer when she couldn't find those papers for us."

"You wonder if he stole them because they said something he didn't want known. An old fraud?" Suddenly she laughed. "Wouldn't it be interesting if he was running a white slave racket with Jennifer as the madam? Would make great headlines in the Sunday newspapers?"

Jake laughed with her.

"In your business you must know someone who speaks Latin, Jay."

"Hold on, yes, there is someone I know. At university I had a friend who was reading Theology, Armand Mistrand, odd name and an odd guy, too," Jake said. "We'd be in the pub, drinking with the other students talking about football or their latest conquests and Armand would startle us with a disquisition on Thucydides, whom he found him fascinating - would read him in the original Greek. One evening when a group of us were in a pub, Armand was obviously not listening because he interrupted in the middle of a hilarious joke one of the students was telling us. 'Thucydides knew that wars were not caused by the Gods but by men', he said. Quite ruined the playful atmosphere and we all fell silent after that. Having a drink with Armand was like having a drink with the parson that we all thought he was destined to be.

That was until he met a girl, a real stunner, Joli Bryant, who was his intellectual equal. He even started confiding in me about his sexual prowess."

"Very amusing, Jay, but how does that help us."

"Sorry, I didn't explain, did I. He's both a Latin and a Greek scholar and I'm pretty sure he also has Italian because he told me he had read Dante in the original language."

"Have you kept in touch with him? Or I should say do you know where we could talk to him?"

"Actually, I saw him in the British Library a couple of weeks ago when I was doing some research. He's writing a book on Greek thinkers, I'll bet he's there at this moment, he almost lives there," he looked at his watch and saw that it was very late. "Perhaps not now but he'll be there virtually any day."

"And the stunning woman?" Rhosa raised one eyebrow.

"No, she doesn't live at the British Library.," he grinned. "She tired of him, told him he bored her with his monoculture mind. She went on to become a professor of psychology, lives in a little flat in Notting Hill."

"You know her that well then?"

"Um, quite well, we had a brief fling about the time you and I lost contact with each other."

"I hate professors of psychology," Rhosa joked, "is she still a stunner?"

"No, she isn't, she was always very busty. That should have been a sign; she has now turned to fat and is what is termed 'obese'. Those stunning looks disappeared under several layers of over-indulgence."

"I'll change my views on lady professors of psychology then. Is she still interesting?"

"Interesting," he pondered, "yes, in a way but when an attractive woman talks about Jung, she commands attention but, if the same things are said by a woman who waddles…" he shrugged.

"Don't be sexist, Jake. Are you saying that she is interesting or not?"

"Sounds very superficial of me but – no," he hesitated and then said. "That is the way things are, I often wonder why we place so much credence on appearance but we do. Nature throughout the generations has driven us to select good looking people. It is a matter of surprise that after aeons of selective breeding one would have thought that mediocre looks would have been bred out and we would all be beautiful."

"It is very surprising." Rhosa said. "From photographs I've seen, my ex-husband, Martin's parents were both attractive but he certainly was not."

"What drew you to him then?"

"His mind; he had the most amazingly quick brain, he could solve any mathematical problem even before others had started. Whenever I met his colleagues, they always said he was streets ahead of them in analysing risk and his ability to invest in stocks which they would not touch but which produced good returns. I adored that side of him. When I met him he was even likeable but gradually his arrogant nature took over. He demanded one hundred per cent from everyone."

"And from you?"

"From me?" she said, "after the first few months there was nothing I could do to please him. But let's not talk about that. What were you saying about your friend?"

"Armand? I'm pretty sure he'd be able to translate these papers."

"Would he want to be paid – can we 'phone and ask him?"

"We can't 'phone, he won't spend money on that sort of thing. I don't think he'll want paying much. I was able to get him the research project which now keeps him occupied and brings in an income - so he owes me a favour. He's so bright; Latin for him will be like me reading nursery rhymes."

The next day Jake went to the library with photocopies of the papers in his briefcase. As he expected, Armand was there. He looked up fleetingly as he heard Jake's muffled footsteps and lowered his head slightly in acknowledgement.

Jake shook his outstretched hand and took the seat beside him. "How is Thucydides today?" he asked in a whisper. He had taken to addressing Armand by the name of his Greek hero.

"Trying to discover as much as I can about his early life. I want to make a start soon on the writing."

"Are the publishers happy to wait? It's been nearly two years since you started."

"They'll have to wait, won't they, there's no magic wand. I can't produce facts from nowhere." He said with an irritation directed as much at himself as at the publishers. Jake knew they had advanced just enough to keep him in his bedsit and off the streets. Initially he had been grateful to Jake for finding him the commission and could not conceal his excitement at being able to research his favourite topic and be paid for it. But after the initial euphoria, it was obvious that commercial reality was staring him in the face.

Jake was shocked to see how thin Armand had become since he had last seen him. "I feel a bit peckish, fancy popping across the road and picking up something?" He asked to get him away from the library, which he suspected was probably beginning to feel like a prison to Armand.

In the warm, slightly steamy atmosphere of the café, he could see Armand relax as he sipped his sugary drink and ate a sticky bun. The haunted look around his eyes softened as he leaned back in his chair and stretched out his legs.

"Marvellous place that library, it certainly saves me a lot in heating and lighting but it can become depressing, especially in the winter." Armand said as he bit hungrily into the bun.

It struck Jake that the haunted look was because Armand was ravenously hungry. "They do a nice breakfast here," Jake said, "I could do with something, do you want to join me." The last thing he wanted was a fried breakfast, having eaten with Rhosa already. But he knew Armand well enough to know that if he thought Jake was buying a meal because he suspected he was hungry, he would have refused.

"I've eaten already but if you are having one, I'll keep you company," Armand said, his face visibly brightening.

Jake caught the eye of the Polish waitress. She took their order with a genuine smile and, as she walked away, to make conversation with the normally monosyllabic Armand, Jake said. "Wonder where all the English girls have gone, they never seem to work as waitresses nowadays."

"I don't eat out much so I've never noticed."

Jake had been a few times to the dingy bedsit for the 'quick bite' Armand sometimes invited him to. It was a tiny room, pervaded by a smell of stale cooking drifting from the un-cleaned cooker. In one corner was a crumpled bed on which Armand would sit while his guest shifted uncomfortably in the armchair so that its protruding spring would reach a position where it ceased to be painful. On one wall of the room was a damp patch where an outside drain pipe must have leaked. It had been leaking for so long that the wall was beginning to effloresce.

Jake would drink tea with the occasional custard cream which were usually soft because Armand would only buy when he could get two packets for the price of one. Whenever he went there, Jake would leave feeling depressed that Armand with the great promise he'd had as a younger man could end up in such a hovel. It made Jake wonder if his own work, so precariously reliant on his ability to turn out interesting articles, could go out of fashion and leave him without an income.

Jake noticed that, whereas he had chosen just scrambled egg, Armand had asked for everything on the menu.

"Funny isn't it, I was not hungry until I saw the menu and those photographs of the food they serve, then my appetite opened up," he said

"I'm usually like that but I've noticed my weight creeping up and I have to cut down." Jake lied as he patted his stomach.

He had intended to speak about the D'Arcy documents while he was eating but Armand was so preoccupied with the breakfast that he left him to it and ate his scrambled eggs quietly. When Armand had finished, he had two cups of coffee to wash down the toast and marmalade which he had also ordered.

He looked a much happier man after he had eaten and said "Now Jake, you wouldn't have come to the library on the off chance of seeing me, what was it you wanted?"

"I wanted to use that erudite brain of yours."

Armand looked interested. Jake guessed that, in the bed-sit life he led compliments were rare and it struck him that he could have done a disservice to Armand by diverting him away from what might have been more lucrative opportunities. He recalled that, when he had suggested that he contact the publishers, Armand had said that a university was also considering offering him a teaching post. Jake noticed frayed sleeves, grubby fingernails and a general air of grime about his old friend but resisted saying, 'things will get better, Armand' to him.

"I begin to wonder about the erudite brain you refer to after the time I am taking on this book," Arman said, "but, yes, go on, what did you want to ask?"

Jake took out the photocopies and placed them on the table. Armand looked at them and then at Jake.

"Latin! And looks old; 16th century I'd guess from the style of writing." He ran his eyes down the page. "Nice hand but difficult to decipher. What do I have to do, not translate I hope."

"That's what I was hoping."

"What, all of these?" he asked, picking up the pile and flicking them over with his thumb "there must be ten letters here and closely written too. If you want me to do them all, I'll need to do a bit of research."

"Will you?" Jake raised his eyebrows, "I thought that, because Latin is not a spoken language, it would not have changed and for you it would be like reading English."

"Latin hasn't changed but our own words have. I speak modern English, very different from the English spoken at the time this was written. I'll have to transmute the English as well."

Jake looked puzzled so Armand continued. "Take a word like 'antic' which in the 16th century meant a grotesque shape and which Byron used as 'half naked, loving, natural and Greek' but we use just to mean old and collectable. If I translate, I have to know the changes in English words as well." He looked at Jake to see if he had understood.

Jake nodded but had failed to understand. "What will it come to?"

"I'll tell you what I'll do. I'll do this first page for nothing. I'll get an idea of how long it will take and then give you a price for the rest."

"Sounds good to me," Jake said. "Oh, one other thing, can you keep it entirely to yourself."

He raised his eyebrows. "This is all legal, I hope."

"Completely legal, I found these in my house. I just don't know what it's all about, that's all. They were hidden in a wall so there's a bit of a mystery about them. They may be nothing," he shrugged, "I'd just like to be able to read them."

After getting him some more toast and marmalade, Jake left Armand with his head down frowning over the first piece of paper, so engrossed that he didn't even notice Jake leaving.

CHAPTER 38

Rhosa looked up from her reading when Jake walked into the room that she used as a study.

She stood up excitedly. "What did Armand say the papers were about?"

"Steady," he joked, "it's not as simple as that. Firstly, translation from Latin to modern English requires some research and secondly he is going to charge me a fee."

"Miserable creature, after all that you've done for him. You should have taken me along," she smiled, "female charm would have reduced the cost."

"Not sure that would have been a good thing to do. I don't think he has had any relationships with women since the stunning Joli. I suspect that seeing you could easily have unhinged him."

"You're joking, aren't you?"

"A bit, but only a bit; I don't think he's completely stable and a very attractive woman like you might tip the balance."

"Unlikely," she smiled. "You sure you're not keeping him away because I might find him very interesting?"

"If I tell 'fastidious you' that there is a distinct grubbiness about him, you'll see what I mean."

Rhosa pulled a face. "Ugh! Like I said about Jed, that's one thing I can't stand in a man."

Jake grinned. "Then there's Armand's conversation; get him on the ancient Greeks and he'd keep you entertained all night and I mean all night if Joli was telling the truth - she confessed to me that the sexual prowess he used to tell us about, consisted of lying in bed naked and talking about mythology." He grinned, "So I have no fear that you might find him attractive."

"Ok, you've convinced me," she said with a smile, "what's he charging you for the translation though?"

"He's going to do the first page without charge and then he'll know what to charge for the rest. I suspect it'll be a hundred quid or something like that."

"But when, when, when? I can hardly sleep wondering what's in those letters."

"When I tell you he has been over two years on Thucydides and other Greek thinkers and the publishers have received nothing, I wouldn't hold your breath."

Suddenly she frowned. "Jay, I know this sounds melodramatic but we don't know what is in those papers, there could be something about hidden money. Can you rely on your Armand?"

"You may be surprised that I had thought of that."

"Yes, what did you do?"

"I looked up the Latin for all things to do with money, coins, jewels, riches, treasure and I went over each page looking for those words." He shook his head slowly, "I'm afraid that those papers will not help us to find treasure or anything like that."

"That's a relief. I don't particularly want to get rich quick but it would be a shame if we had passed instructions to Armand and he got there first."

"If you'd been to his bedsit, you'd think it a kind gesture." He looked away pensively.

"What is it Jay, you look upset."

"No, I'm not upset," he sat down beside her.

"Well what is the meaning of that frown then?"

"I was just thinking about Armand. He was the most intelligent one amongst us, got a first without even trying. Many of the lecturers were in awe of his ability to absorb and analyse knowledge – they even used to get him to vet papers they were writing for publication."

"Impressive but it isn't that which is making you frown is it?"

"With promise like that, how does it all go wrong? Could it happen to me, could I find myself out of joint with what readers need and could I slide down into a smelly bedsit?"

"There are times when I think you are more neurotic than I am, and that's saying something." Rhosa said, laughing. She leaned over and said in a conspiratorial manner. "I don't know why I am telling you this because you could tell me as easily but here goes anyway. Success is not just the result of intelligence; you need that extra something indefinable but immediately recognisable. You have it, I saw it the first time I met you and I see it every day I am with you. People want to spend time in your company. You enthuse them like you do me. Even if you'd had no education, that extra something would carry you through. There is no way you will slide downwards so don't worry about it," she squeezed his hand tightly, "and anyway, you've got me. Armand is like he is because he hasn't got that something extra and you told me that apart from Joli he never had a woman."

He grinned, "Thanks Miss Mentor. All we need do then is to clone you and all Armand's problems disappear. Does that apply to all men?"

Rhosa playfully punched him on the chest.

A week later, a letter arrived. Jake opened it at the breakfast table while Rhosa was putting finishing touches to her make-up and reviewing the effects in her compact mirror as she came into the room. In between reading, Jake followed her with his eyes and marvelled at how amazing she looked in a yellow sweater and a tan skirt. He caught sight of himself in the mirror on the wall and suddenly felt depressed at his ordinary looks,

"From Armand?" she asked.

"Yes." Jake nodded, "he apologises that it has taken him longer than he thought but it's not simple Latin but the sort priests would use and there are a lot of code words. He enjoyed doing it so much that he's done several other letters. The first one is just enquiring about business and the health of Jacob D'Arcy and which to you and me would not be of any interest. I told you Armand was highly intelligent didn't I? Well, from what he's done, he's shown himself a star. He has used word substitution - I don't pretend to understand what he means by that - may be like using fish in French for the word poison - but he says that when he does his substitution, the letter becomes very different. He has found that our Jacob was involved with Cardinals Valenti, Bardonski and one called Vincenzo.

They wanted him involved because he understood poisons. Apparently he had a book which had been written by Piero d'Albano. He was accused of heresy simply because of his adaptation of Averroes' idea of the soul. He died before the Church got to him so they were too late to try him for heresy so they did the usual, dug up his body and burned it."

"Following God's will, I suppose they would claim." She said in disgust. "After what Armand has said, I want to find out if there is anything else in the letters, don't you?"

"We should get the rest of the letters translated. Armand's given me a price for doing them which I think is very reasonable."

"Do it then, Jake, certainly what we've found out so far has got me aroused."

He looked at her quizzically but said nothing; even though she was almost completely anglicised, there were still times when she used words which could be misconstrued.

"In this letter Armand has translated, there is a lot about a Captain S'Aderson."

"Wonder who he is?" Rhosa called over her shoulder as she went out of the room to pick up a script she was going to read.

"I don't know but when I looked over the other letters his name often appeared. In this letter that Armand has done for us, S'Aderson was in league with Cardinal Bardonski if I read between the lines."

"What does that mean, I wonder and anyway, what happened to Jacob and Mistry?"

"We've only got a summary but when I meet up with Armand, he'll give me more details of a very sad letter to Jacob from Nathaniel Borrit who seems to have been one of a group that Jacob ran that he calls 'Scientificals'. As well as the letter from Borrit, Armand says there is another from Jacob, both of them are in Latin."

"What's sad about the letters?"

"The Church…" Jake found it hard to speak. "Sorry, I find it very disturbing." He carried on after a pause.

"Nathaniel knew Mistry when she lived in the streets. He used often to give her food."

"What a terrible life. She looks like a lady in the portrait." Rhosa said.

"In one of the letters to a Michael Dalgett, Jacob talks of how pleased he is with his housekeeper, Mistress Darkall, who amazes him with her intelligence."

Rhosa interrupted. "Of course, that's where the name Mistry came from, a short form of Mistress."

Jake nodded. "Apparently, for a couple of years, she had been the mistress of a clever man called Benjy who was accused by the Church of being a male witch. He was subjected to trial by water and was drowned."

"God, how appalling. Was Mistry accused as well?" Rhosa put her hand to her mouth.

"No, the crowd thought she was too simple and they weren't interested in her."

"So she lived and must have then become housekeeper to Jacob?" Rhosa asked.

"Must have been for a long time; Armand writes about another letter which is dated much later and is from Borritt. It's about a woman called Katarina Bedella who had also loved Jacob but he had preferred Mistry. When she found how happy Jacob was with Mistry, she went to the Church and made an accusation against Mistry. She said that Mistry only pretended to be simple but that she was a witch."

"But there would have been no evidence would there?"

"The Church did not need evidence, an accusation was sufficient."

"What happened to Mistry?"

Jake breathed heavily and pursed his lips. "Another trial by water."

"They didn't drown her as well?"

Jake, obviously moved said, "Jacob thought that Mistry had left him and he was in agony wondering why she should have done it.

He obviously loved her deeply. He had been married before but it seems that Mistry was the love of his life."

"Poor man, and he thought that she had left him because she didn't care for him?"

"Even worse, when he got Nathaniel's letter telling him what had happened to Mistry and where she was, he rushed to the place to find her decaying body still floating in the water. His anguish was so great that he tried to attack the priest who had come back with a crowd and was issuing incantations. Jacob wanted to kill the priest but his friends held him back, he was so violent that they hit him over the head with a heavy stick so that they could carry him off to safety."

"We've seen the grave of Mistry, though."

"Yes, his friends collected the body later; Jacob bribed a priest to allow her to be buried in consecrated ground."

"Risky thing for him to do."

"The amount the priest was bribed probably salved his conscience and sealed his lips." Jake feigned a wry smile. "Equal to £10,000 in today's money I think."

"I see why you were sad." Rhosa said. "What sort of a woman was she - do we know."

"This letter," he turned and picked up one of Armand's translations, "written after her death when Jacob was obviously in despair but even if half of it is right, she must have been impressive. She came to him without education. She had an enquiring mind, was interested in science and learning and, in a way, quickly became Jacob's adviser, almost to the extent that she was advising him on what to do even on business matters. He says he would turn to her whenever there was a problem with the business or even with his alchemy. He even thought that, if she had lived she would have been a member of the Scientificals in her own right."

"What was her relationship to him – did they marry?"

"No mention of marriage or of anything like going to bed together, it may have been a Platonic relationship although from the tone of his letter, he must have been passionate about her. The few comments he makes about her response to him make me think that she felt the same."

"When I look at his portrait, that fits, he looks as though he was too much of a gentleman to try anything." Rhosa said.

"I sense that in him too and it comes over in his letter. So many times he refers to her intelligence but also to her beauty. You know what it's like when you watch a modern film with a scene of a man and a woman, you expect they are going to finish up in each other's arms and until they do, you feel unsatisfied. That's the way I feel when I read what Armand tells us Jacob has written, I want them to get together."

Rhosa said. "So tragic; I never cease to feel grateful that I live in the present time and in Europe."

"Be even more grateful you don't live in Israel. There was a forest fire recently which killed forty one people. It was reported in the Telegraph that Ovadia Yosef, the spiritual leader of a powerful religious party said there was little doubt that the fire was sent by God to punish people for not respecting the Sabbath."

Rhosa shook her head in surprise. "As I told you, if I lived in Egypt I would have been attacked just for being a non-believer."

Jake turned over Armand's notes and said, "Rhosa, there is something else."

"What is it Jake? There's a strange look in your eyes." She said frowning.

"Jacob talks about a diary that he got Mistry to keep after he had taught her to write. She had given it to him to read." He frowned. "It's lost. Could it be that the papers Jennifer wanted to show us but which had disappeared were the diary."

"She didn't make it sound like a diary."

"No, she didn't but I'm just wondering. They're not the sort of things that anyone would steal; they'd be valueless to anyone except a historian."

"What are you saying?" Rhosa asked.

"I had that weird meeting with Freidan when as I told you, he seemed to be going off into the wings for inspiration."

"What about it?"

"Very dismissive about her, said something like 'just a servant, nothing else.' At the time I felt there was a lot more about Mistry he could have told me."

"Tangled web we're weaving, Jake."

CHAPTER 39

At ten o'clock one night Jake was in bed reading and taking notes when he heard Rhosa's key in the lock. The door closed with a slam and in moments he heard her running up the stairs. She burst in full of smiles and happiness.

"What is it? You look as though you've won the lottery"

"No better than that – much better," she said.

"Is there anything better than that?" he joked.

"Well just being here with you is better than that."

"Tell me then, if you don't I think you will explode and leave enough mess to ruin the carpet."

"I got the part. When the play I'm doing finishes, I'll be rehearsing Juliet in Romeo and Juliet." She came and sat down on the bed beside him and playfully bit his ear.

Jake gave her his congratulations and said, "I knew you'd get it, there was no one else who could do it as well as you."

"What are you reading?" she asked, leaning over to look at the cover of the book he had laid on the bed. "'Rosencrantz and Guildenstern are Dead'," she read. "Pretty impressive stuff; Stoppard's the modern equivalent of Shakespeare in my opinion."

"Humble opinion," he joked

"Of course, sorry – my humble opinion," she laughed with him.

"I'm serious, though, he has such beautiful language with the advantage that the 20th Century invented the Surrealism. Shakespeare didn't have that."

"Stoppard also had four centuries more of philosophy to play with, like the improbability of a coin falling the same side down ninety two times in Act 1."

"Let me take my make up off and get ready for bed and you can read Act 2 to me."

Jake's eyelids were beginning to drop by the time she had undressed and put on her dressing gown.

"Did I rouse you?" she asked, "Sorry, do you want to sleep?"

"No, you know what I'm like – if I read in bed, tiredness overcomes me. No, I'm awake now," he said, picking up the book which had fallen onto the bed cover. He was about to read when he sensed that something was wrong. "You look upset, Rhosa?" he said. "You were so happy when you came home, what is it that's upset you?"

"I found a letter for me in the rack."

"Yes, I know, I put it there."

"You wouldn't have recognised the handwriting."

"No, why should I, it meant nothing to me."

Rhosa pulled away from the bed. "It does to me."

"Do you want to tell me?" Jake asked.

"Did you not see the address on the back – Martin Investments? The letter is from him."

"Your husband?" He pursed his lips. "I noticed but it meant nothing I'd forgotten the name of his company, you hardly ever speak about him - thought it was someone wanting to invest your money."

"Not as simple as that…he wants me to go back to him. Probably seen my pictures in the papers and would like his trophy wife back."

"He can't, you're divorced now."

"He said he'd made a big mistake, wants me to go with him to Monaco, he has a house there."

"Sounds better than your place in Acton." Jake joked and then, as what she was saying hit him, said anxiously "Are you tempted?"

Hearing the words, Rhosa turned and pummelled his chest angrily. "How can you say that or even think it?" she screamed, hitting him so hard that he began to wince. "The man is a sadist, honed and polished on the outside; a beast inside."

Suddenly, she stopped, realising what she was doing. "Jay, that was stupid of me. I don't know why I did that; have I hurt you?"

"Broken rib and internal bleeding, that's all, I'll probably recover in a month," he joked.

"Don't laugh it off, I feel dreadful, it was a stupid thing to do, it's not your fault I'm upset," she said, breaking down in tears and laying her head on the bed.

Jake put his arms round her. Several minutes later she was calmer and said, "I want to tell you…" a sigh escaped from her mouth.

"Yes, what is it?" he asked beginning to feel worried.

"I know I have been unfair to you," she said, wiping her eyes on the sleeve of her dressing gown, "and I don't want that anymore."

"How do you mean 'unfair'?"

"I know how much you will have been hurt by my not seeming to want you and, all this time we've been with each other you accepted the way I am without complaining." She lifted her head from the bed and looked up at him. "You've never asked me to tell you why I'm like it…" she stopped to think. "It all came flooding back when I saw his letter. It made me tremble with fear. Can I…?"

"Yes, tell me. What is it?" he said reaching out for her hand.

She took a while to speak.

"I…" her body shook. "I can't while we are like this." She stood and sat in the armchair on the other side of the room. "Can you come and sit beside me?"

Jake got out of the bed, put a blanket round her shoulders and sat beside her on the arm of the chair

She laid her head against his chest and put her arms round him, her body still shaking.

"He used to get high on drink and drugs when he'd been to his club. He'd come in sometimes as late as three in the morning. He'd rip the bedclothes off me and indulge himself," she shuddered at the memory, "I hated it and I hated him…it was rape, nothing more than rape, for me it was bestial." Overcome, she was unable to speak for several minutes, while Jake stroked her hair to calm her.

"I became pregnant. He had always said he never wanted children so for a while I didn't tell him that I was missing my periods.

When I did tell him he went into a screaming fury, threatened to kill me if I didn't get rid of it. I refused; it seemed to me the only good thing that had come out of the marriage. Two days later, I was sitting on the bed reading a script. The door burst open and he came in with a woman, an older woman, someone I'd never seen before. Without saying anything, he picked me up, flung me on the bed. I tried to scream but he forced a towel in my mouth and held me down, tore my clothes off and the two of them…" she shuddered again, "even though I struggled to get away, he was very strong and I couldn't stop him. They killed my child. As soon as it was over, he paid the woman and left with her without saying anything to me." Jake held her shaking body tightly until she was calmer. "I just couldn't move. I was paralysed."

She turned her head away as though unable to look at him. "I've tried to forget," her voice wavered, "sometimes I know you have wondered why I was silent and appeared to be ignoring you." She turned her gaze to him. "It wasn't you, Jake, it was just the memory. It would come back whenever things didn't go as I wanted them to. I tried very hard to change my mood but I just couldn't. I know you think I am too fond of alcohol but it was the only thing I had, it helped me forget." She put her hand out to reach his.

"I know I am unreasonable at times and I do get to feel very low." She kissed his hand. "When I came to this country my mother went on her hunt to find a husband, the hunt ended up with her marrying my revolting stepfather. While she was out with him, I was left on my own a lot. I would sit in my room reading. It was then that I found some sort of satisfaction in denying myself food; it was the only power I had left. I had always loved eating but when I looked at myself I saw my body growing with puberty. You can't imagine the sensation of control I felt as I measured my waist and saw that I had lost several centimetres after only a week denying myself food. I was gratified when my mother noticed. After her marriage to a man who despised me she had completely lost interest in me. She said one evening when she came into the bathroom that I was getting thin. She tried to frighten me by saying I would die from lack of food. Somehow that made me more determined. I didn't worry about the harm it would do. All I could see was that I was now in command."

"Anorexia?" Jake said looking concerned.

"I didn't know the word then, I just knew the feeling of satisfaction. I felt at the time that I was a funny looking thing and when I see the few photographs of myself at the age of twelve, I can see why. I was beginning to be attracted to boys suffering the pangs of sexual desire which got worse as my breasts grew and were signalling my readiness to enter that experience which I had only read about. But at school, boys did not even look at me. They gazed over my shoulder at prettier girls. So I suppressed my desires, subjecting my body to abstinence from food. It made me feel stronger and I found myself walking more erectly where previously I had slouched to make myself look inconspicuous.

Walking more confidently and with a slimmer figure had an effect. Boys saw me for the first time and I had several flings."

"Did you recover from the anorexia?" Jake asked.

"Took a while but yes it did; I had got used to my mother's lack of interest and several of us would go around together and we ate as a group. My dislike of food never returned until that dreadful time when my child was taken away from me by my husband. Then it all came back. I suppose it was my way of punishing him. I got so thin that even he became worried. You see, I was his flag; he waved me whenever he was in company. Apart from sex that was about all he needed from me and insisted I should always be at home whenever he came in. He wanted me to be seen to be attractive and, when I began to waste away, he was embarrassed. He was so embarrassed that he paid for me to go to a clinic where there was a psychotherapist, a lovely man with whom I fell in love with a little because of my emotionally dependent state. He became like the father I had never had. He took such an interest in me and introduced me to theatre friends of his. Even though I stayed in the clinic, they offered me an audition for a role in a small amateur theatre company. Shaw's 'The Apple Cart'. I played Orinthia, the mistress to the King. The King was gorgeous; I fell in love with him as well. The play didn't run for long but it worked for me. I began to feel that I was worth something again."

She raised her head so that she could look at him and said quietly, "Can you understand why I haven't been able to think of sex since?"

"As I said before, it has been enough for me to be with you." He was so overcome that he was unable to say anything more. Instead, he put his arms round her, lifted her up and carried her to bed.

"Read to me, Jay, read anything just so I can hear your voice and think of something else. Read me some of Stoppard, it's there on the table," she said as he lowered her into the bed and got in with her.

Rhosa burrowed down beside him and put her arm around his body. As he read, he noticed that she became more affectionate and her hand began to caress him in a way which she had not done before.

When he had finished reading the second Act, he stopped and she said quietly, "that was wonderful, Jay."

"What, the way I read it, the words or the way your hand was moving?"

"All of those but more - it was just you; your kindness, your intelligence, just … you." Her hand wandered across his body. "Can I be so lucky as to have you in bed and reading Stoppard? You know, when we were in Stratford all those years ago how literature could get me into the right mood?"

Jake cast his mind back to the times when they had shared a bed.

"Jay, I think I've come over now that I've told you why I've been so disappointing. I've never been able to tell anyone else." She stroked her hand up and down his chest. "I'm going to try not to think about the depressing things that happened to me during the time you and I were apart. They happened to someone else, not to me, didn't they?" She looked up at him for re-assurance. "Here in your arms I am secure from all those terrors which my husband forced on me. Now I can choose for myself."

"What are you saying?"

She kissed his hands as they held the book he had been reading to her and said in a whisper. "I am saying … I am ready for you. The hurt from my ex-husband will be in the past." Her lips touched his chest and moved down his body, "I know I don't need to say this but will you be gentle with me, Jay, I am still apprehensive."

She raised her head to kiss his ear and whispered, "I have such a longing for you. I've been waiting for ten years. Since you walked out of my life in Stratford there has never been a day when I have not thought about you. You were that beacon of light I was always reaching out for. Take me, Jay take those empty years from me. Fill me with your desire. I have wept inside many times for returning your kindness with what you probably thought was disdain. Let me caress you, let me kiss all your body, let me put you between my lips. I want to show you how much I need you now that the fear has left me. My darling I have hurt you, confused you with the pain he left me with. Forgive me." Tears drifted down her face and onto Jay's shoulder. He raised himself up and kissed her salty cheeks and she pulled herself closer to him, clinging to him as support. Fervidly she tore at his clothes and threw them aside while he pulled her nightdress above her head and, in the dim light, marvelled at the beauty of the body she had concealed from him. As he kissed her longingly, she reached down and caressed him. Jake was delicate and gentle at first as she had asked him to be and then with more passion.

Afterwards, they behaved as if they were a honeymoon couple, Rhosa, now freed of her terrors took every opportunity for physical union with Jake. For them both it was their happiest time, a union of soul and body.

Like most honeymoons, there came a time when the real world intervened. Now that she had expiated her terrors, Rhosa seemed to want to establish her independence. Jake began to wonder if the bond between them had remained only while she needed the support he had given her. The play she was in was receiving bad reviews, not of her performances but of the cast and the production. Even so, she still took the disapproval as a personal affront and began to worry about her career.

She drifted back to being late for the dinners he cooked and, when he looked disappointed, responded by saying, "You just have to realise that Anthony and I are doing everything we can to bring this play together."

"Ok, ok, but all you've got to do is ring and tell me when you'll be home."

"You've seen how things are, when I'm rehearsing, everything goes out of my mind."

"Including me?" he put the plates on the table and began to serve while she remained silent, pre-occupied with her own thoughts.

Her mind was so often obsessed with the difficulties with the play that she spent less and less time working with Jake on his book. His disappointment began to build within him. He said nothing but Rhosa interpreted his moodiness as his wanting to push her away.

CHAPTER 40

A few weeks passed before Jake, sitting in his office writing, had a 'phone call from Armand. His call invited them to go round to his bedsit.

"Rhosa," he said as he walked through to the lounge where she was reading, "here is a test for you."

"Test! What do you mean?"

"I've told you about Armand."

"Armand, the man you are afraid to let me meet? Yes, what has he done?"

"He has finished the translations."

"Why is that a test for me?"

"He has asked us to go round to his bedsit."

"And you're worried I might throw up."

"Well it is a bit on the nose."

"Jay, you pig, are you implying I might be finicky?"

"You may need a nosegay and they went out of fashion when hygiene came in." Jake laughed. "Anyway, I pre-empted you and told him you would be coming."

"Why didn't he want to meet us at the café where you gave him the papers? You could have bought him another of those all-day breakfasts you told me he enjoyed."

"Dunno, seems a bit mysterious but that's what he asked."

On the following Saturday morning, Jake and Rhosa rang the doorbell to 39 Clayhewn Mansions. Armand came to the door with a just washed look and wearing a clean white shirt and crisply pressed navy slacks. He introduced himself to Rhosa with a formal "How do you do, Miss Cowen?"

As Jake walked in, he saw that the place had been tidied up. Books which had previously been scattered over the floor were now piled on each other and below the cooker and sink all the decaying food scraps which had been there when Jake had previously visited had been removed.

Armand noticed Jake's gaze wandering round the room and said. "The landlady has been in to clean up a bit. She comes in every week. I'm not much good at tidying."

Rhosa beneath lowered eyelids glanced momentarily at Jake.

"Does she also do the ironing?" Jake asked, nodding at Armand's crisp white shirt.

"Mothers me a bit; this used to be her son's room before he escaped to an American university to become a Professor of Anthropology. She is lost without him to dote on. I've sort of become her surrogate son. She's been ill in hospital for a long time. You may have noticed that the place had got pretty messy when you last came."

"Had it?" Jake said and suppressed a wince when Rhosa punched him in the back as Armand went to the sink to fill the kettle.

Armand had laid a clean white cloth over the table. He spent a long time preparing tea. He poured into Worcester china cups and handed round the sugar lumps in a silver bowl with silver tongs.

"Miss Cowen," he said offering her biscuits. Jake noticed that they were better quality than the custard creams he normally served.

"Rhosa," she corrected him.

Armand smiled ingratiatingly. "I've never been lucky enough to meet an actress of your stature before. I thought I'd have to be more formal."

"Rhosa is what I like to be called," she said, slightly taken aback by Armand's old world attitude. "Have you seen me on stage then?"

"The Taming of the Shrew; I thought your performance was magnificent and in The Merchant, I was entranced."

"Thank you." Rhosa smiled as she took one of his biscuits.

Jake had never seen Armand in a deferential mood before but understood why. He had to admit that Rhosa looked terrific. He wondered how he would have reacted if he had met her for the first time now that she was being recognised as a great actress.

Armand talked plays with her and it was obvious he was an ardent theatre goer and that he and Rhosa shared the same passion for Shakespeare. They seemed to have so much to talk about that Jake began to feel redundant, ate the shortbread biscuits and took over the role of refilling their cups.

They were talking about Sophocles play 'Oedipus' and Jake was on his third cup of tea when Armand stopped and said. "I'm sorry, Jake, you've come to hear about the letters you gave me, and here am I indulging myself in the theatre."

"I hadn't realised that it was such an interest of yours."

"Passionate about it. It's one of the seven pivotal principles of society. Psychology, Philosophy, Politics, Sociology, Music, Theatre, Literature - take any one away and civilisation would stagger, if not collapse."

Jake was tempted to add a few more such as Medicine and Language but decided that he should bring the conversation back to Armand's translations.

"I could go through each piece of paper in detail if you like." Armand said, "I've got them all typed out and copied but I've also done a summary which is probably all you need now for the moment. I can wade through the details later if it becomes important."

"That's just what we need," Rhosa said, "I've got to get to a reading in an hour or so."

Armand picked up the summary. "These documents are not just letters; there are some which are commendations to Jacob D'Arcy. I don't mind telling you, they are quite intriguing. I've taken longer than I thought I would because I became fascinated. I've done some background work and also been to check on the family tree of D'Arcy and there is a surprise there which I'll tell you about. From all of this I can tell you that D'Arcy was a remarkable man."

"He looks to be a gentleman if the portrait Jay has in his house is anything to go by." Rhosa said.

"That was his reputation apparently. He was active in trying to get a voice for the common man." Armand turned over the papers and looked down at the one in his hand. "I've got some details about D'Arcy, partly from the letters and partly from other research I've done. If he'd lived today, he would have been featured in the papers for his business success. Apparently his family business had been practically destroyed by the Medici bank but he'd done what we now call rationalisation, changed its direction, got rid of a lot of old stock. Partly he was able to do this because he married a young woman fourteen years old – that would also have got him into today's papers - she was from a wealthy family of merchants. He transformed his wife's family business as well. She died of a fever and he took in a maid; from the letters that she was completely uneducated. I don't know if she was his mistress but she is often referred to as Mistress Darkall. Later there is a woman called Mistry who may be the same woman."

Rhosa interrupted, clapping her hands in excitement. "We've been to her grave in Barnes."

"Have you indeed, you must take me there."

"I will," she said.

Jake started slightly, wondering if the invitation included him.

"Before I get stuck into this, can I get you anything else? I do have a very nice sherry."

"I have had enough tea. Thank you, I would like to try your sherry." Rhosa said.

"Jake, sherry for you?" Armand asked.

"Too early in the day for me, thanks." Jake said hoping his words would have an effect on Rhosa. She gave him a quick look and took the proffered drink from Armand who filled his own glass.

For a moment, Jake felt left out as Rhosa and Armand drank sherry, obviously enjoying communing together.

"What did you mean by a voice for the common man?" Jake's interruption was partially aimed at breaking the atmosphere.

"I know what you read at university Jake, so I don't need to tell you that the Church was dominant in his day and also corrupt." Armand said, putting down his glass on the tray in front of him, "and you'll know that corruption existed in many different guises."

"At the time Henry sacked the monasteries, the Church probably owned forty per cent of the land in this country and the pattern was roughly the same throughout Europe. The Church wears

401

a cloak which says it is working for the common good but some, like Jacob, saw through the holes in the clothes at the bloated man beneath." He refilled his and Rhosa's glasses and continued. "One of the skills D'Arcy had was a knowledge of poisons."

"To poison the Pope," Rhosa said, "Jake had worked that out from your translation of the first documents but I wondered if we were reading too much into the letters."

"Obviously they didn't succeed, though," Jake said, "otherwise we would have known about it from history books."

"This letter possibly explains why they didn't. Look here," Armand picked up one of his translations and pointed half way down the page, "Valenti is talking about coming to England to see D'Arcy, apparently Valenti suspected one of the other two Cardinals involved in the plot but doesn't know which one. He was setting a trap to find which one it was."

"Was one of the Cardinals called Bardonski?" Rhosa asked.

"Have you heard of Bardonski?"

"Only in the letter in Italian, I was able to read a bit of it and there was a name which seemed to be Bardonski. I brought the photocopy with me -" she opened her handbag "- yes, one is called Cardinal Vincenzo and the other is," she screwed up her eyes in an effort to read the writing, "difficult to be sure but it seems like Cardinal Bardonski."

"Well, it is Bardonski whom Valenti suspects." Armand said. "What he seems to be saying is that Bardonski is junior to him and Valenti thinks that he is looking for promotion and would expose anyone whose disappearance would help his advancement. Valenti thinks that Bardonski wants to be Pope himself and that was why he was stirring up feelings against the existing incumbent."

"Quite clever," Rhosa said. "Get to know all that he can, denounce the plan, and by his action, become ingratiated with the Pope and advance his own career."

"What's new," Jake smiled. "In many newspapers I've worked for plots against the editor are rife."

"The only difference is that they generally stop at murder."

"Murder, why do you say that?"

"If my translation is correct, that is what he is saying," Armand looked up at Jay to see if he understood, "that he suspects that Bardonski wants to kill him."

"What, poison him?"

"More subtle than that. If they are successful, after the Pope dies, Valenti suspects that Bardonski will denounce him. Valenti and Vincenzo will then suffer being put to death, probably by burning at the stake. So Bardonski disposes of two rivals while appearing blameless."

"Apparently there was another man involved, who called himself Captain S'Aderson, who had been employed by Cardinal Bardonski. He had followed D'Arcy and Mistry and met them on a journey to Florence, where D'Arcy had business. There were two reasons for the journey, one selling cloth and the other was to meet with the Cardinals. D'Arcy says S'Aderson tried to ingratiate himself with him and with Mistry, making what we would call a pass at Mistry, which seems to have got up D'Arcy's nose, but he managed to give S'Aderson the slip."

"D'Arcy visited the Cardinals in a secret house and was astonished to see S'Aderson there. He feigned surprise when he saw D'Arcy, who was initially suspicious of him until Bardonski vouched for him. D'Arcy revealed that he had perfected a poison which worked on animals and was based on work done by d'Abano. Amongst the documents are letters between D'Arcy and Valenti. Valenti had his own spies in Bardonski's household who reported to Valenti that the plot was rumbled and that the Pope had been informed."

"There must have been a great deal of subterfuge because Valenti was convinced about the treachery of Bardonski. Vincenzo had been murdered, which as far as I can tell Valenti suspected was a crime committed by S'Aderson."

"There is another woman, Katarina Bedella, who apparently was doing her best to implicate D'Arcy. There is a letter from her to Bardonski. I don't know how it could have got into the other documents; perhaps one of Valenti's spies had stolen it. A lot of what Bedella says is illogical and, to my mind, the result of an overdeveloped imagination. She is so vitriolic that I wonder if she was just 'a woman scorned' as they say. In one of the first letters I read, I told you how she had denounced Mistress Darkall. Valenti wrote by special messenger to D'Arcy asking for refuge. He must have fled the Vatican because the next letter is from England where I presume D'Arcy had managed to arrange for him to stay at a safe house in the countryside nearby. There are several letters without addresses from Valenti to D'Arcy. Valenti had managed to bring all his precious jewels and valuables with him because he talks of selling some to pay for his stay in England. There is a sad letter as well from Valenti in which he commiserates with Jacob about the death of his wife Mistry. He refers to her beauty and intelligence."

Armand put the papers down with an air of satisfaction and, seeing that Rhosa had emptied her glass, refilled it again.

As she drank, Rhosa said. "So Mistry really was his wife, not a woman of no consequence as Jennifer's lover tried to make out to you, Jay. I wonder what his motives were in belittling her." Suddenly she looked at Jake. "Could this have anything to do with the jewels and things that Valenti brought to England, I mean, what about the Valenti ring you told me about?"

"A story worthy of Shakespeare," Jake said.

"Indeed but here comes the interesting bit. In the D'Arcy family history there are records which reveal that D'Arcy and Mistry were married by – who do you think – by a priest called Valenti and, what's more, they had a son, his name is recorded as Walter Dearsey. That may have been a spelling error but in a letter, Jacob D'Arcy states that he does not object because he is afraid that his name had become a risk. In all subsequent letters, he calls himself Dearsey. I was astonished when I followed the records down that it leads to – you've guessed it – to you, Jake."

"Jay, this is amazing," Rhosa said, "it's true then, not only do you look a bit like him, you are related to Jacob D'Arcy."

"My God!" Jake said, open-mouthed. For several moments, he was unable to speak. "Firenze House…when I first saw it I had no choice but to buy it," he frowned. "I'm just wondering if Jacob D'Arcy's memory lives on in the house. He could not have known who would have found the letters but it seems to me that some power guided me to them."

"Guided me as well," Rhosa said, "Don't forget it was I who rummaged around in the hole and found them."

"It was you, wasn't it, you're right; perhaps he looked on you as a D'Arcy."

"Is that a backhanded proposal?" Rhosa laughed.

Jake was interrupted by Armand. "I'm intrigued; I want to do more research on your man and the plot against the Pope. To my knowledge it was not known before you found these papers."

"You might be in conflict with a man I met, Daniel Freidan who purports to be a scholar on the subject."

"Freidan! D'you know him?" Armand opened his eyes in surprise. "That man is a charlatan. I was once foolish enough to go to one of his lectures. I could have got as much out of the Encyclopaedia Britannica."

Jake burst out laughing on hearing this.

"Why do you laugh?" Armand asked joining in the frivolity.

"When he was lecturing me, I came to the conclusion that he was reading from an encyclopaedia - I was sort of inveigled to go to him because I was told he was a scholar, he treated me as semi-literate and told me nothing I didn't know already. I was at first baffled when he suddenly got up and walked down his garden. Only when he came back was he able to continue with his diatribe."

"And was it a woman who told you he was a scholar?" Armand asked.

"Yes, as a matter of fact it was, why do you ask?" Jake replied.

"I suspect there's something going on there." Armand grinned. "He seems to have set up a history group specifically to attract women - mostly disenchanted marrieds it seems. I'm sure he gives them advice based on what he says is an intimate knowledge of history, psychology and I suspect, extra-marital liaisons. His reputation is of being a guru, possessor of divine wisdom, that sort of nonsense. No situation is unique; he claims that by selecting a historical parallel, all problems can be resolved. I suspect that he has a sexual appetite – and part of his success would be enforcing a promise of complete secrecy from the women he's ensnared. It's one of life's unsolved quandaries – how one person can so dominate his followers that he can lead them even to Hell. Remember the Jones Cult where nine hundred people died as parents took poison and gave it to their own children because Jones told them that by doing so they would find salvation. I suspect Freidan has that power - on a smaller scale, of course."

"He wears a ring which was worn by Cardinal Valenti, how is that? We know Valenti is buried in Barnes. Could it be that Valenti brought his jewellery to England?"

"You mean the pentacle inlaid in gold. Did he make you very aware of it?"

"Oh yes, he kept twisting it and making the sun glint off it into my eyes."

"The ring is a fake, I know the jeweller who made it for him. I got to know him when my mother wanted me to get some repairs done on her jewellery collection."

"You never mentioned your mother or her jewellery collection?"

"Not something I talk about, she's dead now," he shrugged. "Left me everything, not because she was fond of me it's just that I'm the last of the Mistrands."

Jake looked around the cramped and cluttered room. Armand followed his gaze. "You're wondering why I still live here when I could live in her house in Chelsea?"

"I was a bit," Jake smiled.

"It suits me here, the landlady is nice and she looks after all my needs. I'm an untidy bastard. If I lived anywhere bigger, I'd soon have it filled with books and rubbish. Besides, I just can't spend money; apart from that, the house in Chelsea has too many ghosts for me." He picked up a photograph and passed it to Jake, "Remarkable woman, my mother, everyone liked her but as soon as I could get away from her I did. She had the curse of the Mistrands, a feeling of superiority and the conviction that I should follow in the traditions of the male members of the family. She wanted me to go into commerce, exploit every one and make the family fortune even bigger. I just can't be bothered. I don't even touch the money or her jewellery; it is in investments, some of it in bank vaults, growing larger all the time, I don't doubt."

Jake noticed the time and said he had to go to a meeting. Rhosa looked at her watch and said she must dash soon. Jake got up to leave expecting Rhosa to accompany him but was surprised that she accepted Armand's suggestion of another drink and sat down after offering her cheek for Jake to kiss goodbye.

CHAPTER 41

When Rhosa got back late the night after meeting Armand, she came into the room where Jake was reading, sat down on the floor beside him and said, "You old reprobate, Mr. D'Arcy. How do you feel about this house now that you know where you came from?"

"I now know why it's my home."

"And you were also trying to fool me about Armand - an intelligent man. Not a trace of the body odour about him that you warned me of. Why did you try to discourage me from meeting him?"

"Must admit I was surprised; he was quite different. When he heard you were coming, he must have made a big effort." he shrugged, "I've been treating him as though he was a pauper - no idea that he was from a wealthy family. He'd never even mentioned his relatives; we all assumed he'd been found floating on the Nile and had never had a mother."

"Doesn't surprise me, don't forget you've never told me much about your own mother."

"I suppose it never came up in conversation but, as I said before, you never talked of yours." Jake said.

"I am eternally grateful to her for my need to keep studying. She came to England to expand her education. As I learned recently that includes reading your articles."

"How does she know which name I use and which journals to read?"

"She wrote and asked me when she saw that photograph of the two of us in the papers." Rhosa looked into his eyes, "you don't realise what influence you have. She's an intelligent woman; I don't know how she puts up with the tedium of life with my stepfather. I always hoped she would strike out on her own."

"What d'you mean - leave your stepfather?"

Rhosa nodded. "She could make a career in anything she put her mind to she's full of business ideas. The professor wants her as an adjunct only and dismisses any ideas she has."

"How little we know our parents," Jake smiled. "Or our friend's parents if it comes to that."

"Armand, you mean?"

"Yes, I wonder if his mother was as difficult as he makes out. He must have got his talents from someone." Suddenly he said. "Of course, I read a paper by a Maria Mistrand, a researcher at Cambridge. There was a photograph of her I recall, quite a striking woman and a well-researched piece of writing. It's a sufficiently unusual name so I bet she was his mother." He grinned. "Armand Mistrand, you sly old devil."

Rhosa smiled as she recalled Armand in his clean pressed clothes. "Interesting that he loves the theatre. I'm going to get him a ticket for the play, he asked me to go to dinner with him to talk about it."

"Fast worker! Did he arrange that in the few minutes you were with him after I left for the meeting?"

"Not a fast worker, just very interested in the theatre." She thought for a second. "Now he's well off, he may be a potential as a Business Angel for the next play; Anthony needs to raise funds for it."

Jake looked at her quizzically. "You've never been interested in money before."

"Not for me, idiot, for Anthony's play. You can't believe how a production can eat money. It's a new writer, you see, he has never been produced before. It's much easier if you're established and with successes behind you. The public is very fickle; it asks for new writing but only goes to see well known playwrights. That's why we get so many Cherry Orchards and why television keeps churning out the same Jane Austen plays that you comment on."

"And Shakespeare?" he teased.

"Well, yes in a way but Shakespeare is different."

"Because you love him?"

Rhosa frowned. "Are you trying to wind me up, Jake? I've had a hard day and I'm not in the mood for it."

He noticed the irritation in her voice and turned back to his desk.

Seeing that he had opted out, she said, "I'm going to bed, I'm shattered."

While he listened to her going up the stairs and the floorboards creak as she moved around the bedroom, he thought about the way she had responded to Armand and her comment about financing Anthony Garden's play.

When eventually he went to bed, Rhosa was asleep. The next morning was Sunday and they usually had a lie in and had breakfast in bed. When he woke, she was downstairs. He padded down and found her in the laundry, washing her clothes. She waved cursorily at him. When he called to ask what she wanted for breakfast, she said. "I've had mine; you were sound when I got up so I left you to sleep."

The table was laid with his breakfast and she had left the cafetière on the heated pad.

He ate in silence; when he had finished he went into the laundry. She stopped ironing and waited for him to speak.

"You hadn't told me you were still involved with Anthony Garden raising finance." Jake said.

"Didn't seem worth mentioning; he hasn't been able to raise money for the play he wanted me in, so we've been pushing for an alternative and 'Strange Meeting' is the one we've chosen. It's still only an idea. "

"It must be more than that if you are out looking for finance."

"The script is written, the main parts are chosen but there have been only a few angels. There, that's as far as it's got." She turned to face him. "Are you happy now?" she said defiantly.

It was one of those moments of confrontation which happen between partners. It could develop into a full blown row, it could simmer beneath the surface or it could be defused by a gesture or a smile. Such things can become the pivot on which relationships are destroyed. Jake suspected that there was more to the Anthony Garden business than Rhosa was saying and she was being distant with him because she needed her freedom. He said nothing while they each sat

410

staring silently into the distance and inwardly debated what action he should take. With a mental shrug, he said, "Let's go to that place on the Thames at Richmond. The food's not marvellous but it's full of activity."

Rhosa took his hand, acknowledging that the tiff was softening and said. "That sounds nice. I'll finish the ironing while you're in the shower." She looked out of the window. "Looks like a nice day for a walk along the Thames path."

Walking is the best way to carry on a dialogue. There is so much activity that pauses in the flow of conversation is natural. Both Jake and Rhosa had difficulties to resolve with each other and in the hour's walk, interspersed with comments about the birds, trees and people, they came together again, at least for the time being.

They walked without speaking while they watched for the weak sun to break through the clouds. Eventually, Rhosa ended the silence which was becoming awkward for them both. "I know living with me is not easy, Jay, I'm moody, erratic and unreliable and I know you don't like it when I have a drink, but that's me." She climbed the style and took his hand as he steadied her and continued. "That first night, when you cooked for me and I was late; I could see that you wanted to fly off at me but you knew that would have been the end of us so you bottled up your annoyance. I've let you down several times since haven't I." They waited at the side of a road while the traffic cleared and then ran across.

"I know how you felt and I wanted to say something but I couldn't think of the right way. Acting is my life, it's as important as writing is to you."

"I've never doubted that and I've never stood in your way have I?" Jake asked.

"No, you haven't but you make it obvious that it takes it out of you."

An elderly couple had stopped in front of them, throwing bread to the ducks. Seeing Rhosa's smile, they passed some of it to Rhosa who thanked them and stopped to feed the ducks.

"Life in microcosm isn't it?" she said to the couple, "that greedy drake beats all the others. He would be the boss man if he were human." They laughed and Jake and Rhosa walked on.

"Nice couple," she said.

"I don't see why you say that I make it obvious, I haven't complained. Can you tell me any time when I've objected?"

"You don't have to put it into words, there's a tightness in the lips and a body language that says the same thing."

They stopped to watch a rowing team working in harmony, the Cox calling out instructions through a megaphone.

When they walked on, Jake said. "Rhosa, I think you are just being too sensitive."

"Maybe but can you honestly say that I don't irritate you when I lapse from what you expect of me? I have to concentrate and do everything I can to do what I set myself. It takes a lot out of me especially at a time like this when I have no work after the show finishes tonight."

They had arrived at the restaurant and waited to be seated. They ordered a sandwich each and jug of water. "Let's enjoy the food and sun and talk later." Jake said.

"I'd like that," she said, and rubbed her thigh against his.

The next day, Jake was working from home. Rhosa had left to meet her agent, who had phoned to ask if she could call in to discuss a proposition.

Later a letter was delivered through the door.

It was from a new magazine, 'Future Politic'. Jake opened it and found a letter from the owner, whom he had met at a function.

Dear Jake,

When we met for lunch at the RSA restaurant, I was very taken with your ideas on society and politics. I told you I was planning to expand our range of magazines into more serious subjects. No doubt you have read the publicity about 'Future Politic'. I raised your name with the board; they read your articles and coincidentally, one of the board members was at your lecture. Unanimously we have decided to ask you if you would do us the honour of becoming our first Editor.

No doubt this will come as something of a surprise to you but, if you are agreeable, it will only remain to discuss terms which I am sure will meet your requirements. I am out of the country for a while but if you could call my secretary, Lavinia, we'll meet at a time convenient to us both to finalise terms.

Yours.

Harry Grahame.

Jake read the letter through once more, picked up the 'phone to ring Lavinia, who had a voice to match her middle class name. When he said he was in principle very pleased to accept, she said that she would find it a pleasure to work with him and reminded him that they had met at the Royal Society of Arts briefly. He of course remembered her, blonde flouncy hair and bright bubbly personality.

He then rang Rhosa, who told him she was just going in to see her agent, so arranged to see her at a café in town at 3.30 after her meeting.

The café was one of the few Art Deco places left that had not been pushed out by the chains and converted to the ersatz style of never-read books on simulated library shelves. They arrived at the same time. Rhosa looked pre-occupied as they sat at a table in the window and ordered tea and cake. While it was coming, Jake, noticing her mood asked, "Well, what did he say?"

"What did he say?" Rhosa said as the waitress went to get their order. "Just what any actress would give her right arm for."

"Great, a six month run of 'The Merchant'?"

"Think bigger," she said, trying to hold back a smile. "They want me to go to L.A. They are offering a five film contract. They want me there next week." As she said it, Rhosa could contain herself no longer as tears welled in her eyes. "Sorry…I'm a bit emotional." she said as he passed her his handkerchief.

Like the trouper she was, she recovered but still had to wipe her eyes.

"And what did you say?" Jake asked his heart racing with apprehension.

"What could I say – it's the chance of a lifetime. I've worked all these years and looking back it seems that I've only fiddled around the edges. This is the big chance at last."

"Rhosa, I am so very pleased for you. " Jake said although his heart had sunk at the news that she would be leaving London. "More than anyone, you deserve this. Funny, I had a feeling this would happen. When I saw the audience at your last performance, they practically went wild when you took the curtain call, I was sorry for the other members of the cast. That performance was the culmination of what you've been doing. I understand that you must feel you've done all you can here."

Their order had been delivered by a waitress slightly overawed at serving the well-known actress Rhosa Cowen in tears.

Rhosa said to her. "Sorry, I've just had some very good news." She blew her nose and was back to herself.

"I couldn't help hearing Miss Cowen. I think it's wonderful news," she said, not wanting to leave them. "I wonder if... I've got the programme of the play you are in - would it be too much to ask if you could sign it for my father. He's not well and he is such a fan of yours. I'm sure it would cheer him up."

"I'd be delighted."

The waitress had the programme already under the tray.

"Thank you so much. His name is George Sawyer."

"George Sawyer, the critic, I didn't know he was unwell."

"He's had an operation and the surgeon says it's just a matter of convalescence now, so he'll be back at his desk in a month but he can't put up with being inactive and it's made him very low. He wants to see the play when he gets out of hospital and this programme from you will cheer him up."

"I'll do better than that. If you write the name of the hospital down on the bill, I'll take it to him myself; I'm free tomorrow afternoon if that will suit."

The waitress, an attractive young woman, gave Rhosa a kiss on the cheek and turned to wipe a tear from her own eye before she scribbled the hospital address on a bill and passed it to Rhosa.

"That was a nice thing to do, Rhosa," Jake said as the waitress left them. "I've got some news as well. I've been offered the editorship of that new magazine I told you about, 'Future Politic'". At the news, Rhosa cried with delight. Jake put down his cup and looking round the café, asked, "Do you think we ought to go, people are beginning to stare. Don't think either of us is hungry anymore."

They bolted down the tea which had cooled to drinking temperature and left. In the street outside they threaded their way between shoppers and then turned down the first street, which they were pleased to see led them into Grosvenor Square. The Millennium Hotel faced them and they could have gone in there to lose themselves in the anonymity of a clientele who, although they might notice Rhosa, would treat her as just another celebrity amongst the many who frequented the place.

"Do you want to sit in the Millennium, Rhosa."

"Sooner sit in the Square; we'll catch what sun there is on the bench over there. Let's get as far away from the American Embassy as we can, it destroys an elegant square."

When they were seated, Jake took out two plastic bottles of water from his briefcase, passed one to Rhosa and silently they drank, looking around at the houses. "I often look at houses like these and wonder what lives are going on behind the closed doors and windows." Rhosa said, trying to keep a conversation going. "When I was younger, I had to hold myself back from ringing a bell just to see what would happen. I pictured myself asking, is this where Robert Taylor or some name lives? In my mind, they would say 'No, but do come in and have a drink'. Then I would be able to satisfy my curiosity."

They both knew she was using words just to delay the moment in which they would need to talk about their future after leaving England.

When she stopped, Jake looked down at the grass beneath his feet and said quietly. "Is this the end?"

Rhosa, still in an emotional state and trying to hold back tears of joy mingled with sadness at what she knew was a precipitate moment in their relationship. Fearful of what Jake's reaction would be, she looked over at the Millennium and said, her voice drifting off into the Square. "Not the end, a new beginning."

"For you?"

415

"And for you; you have the editorship you always wanted of a journal which I am sure will be respected and which will drive political ideas."

"Don't prevaricate, Rhosa, you know that's not what I meant."

"What did you mean, then?" she asked, feeling herself being driven into a corner.

"We know each other too well to play games. Do we cease to be the lovers we have only recently become? That is what I mean by 'is this the end', not some pleasantries about our careers."

"If you are in London and I am in L.A., there is a certain physical and geographical problem with our being lovers."

"That's your decision then?"

"Not my 'decision', it's one that has made itself."

"Do we then stand up from this hard bench and walk in opposite directions."

This time Rhosa was unable to hold back tears, worsened by pain in her stomach and her emotional state from the first day of her period. She turned away to look at the Hotel and, when she could control her shaking body, said. "If that's what you think is best."

The solid bench did not creak as Jake stood up while she continued to look away, unable to say anything. When Rhosa had calmed, she turned back to speak to him and was going to say. "Can we talk tomorrow, you know what I'm like on the first day of my period and I've come out without any painkillers." But she just saw his receding figure as he turned into a side street. She got up to run after him but fell as her high heels stuck in the earth, softened by a heavy rain the night before. When she had brushed herself down, he had disappeared.

"Jake," she shouted, her voice disappearing on the wind.

That night, when she had taken the final curtain call on the last night of the show, cleaned her face of stage make-up, she asked the taxi to take her back to her own house.

All the next day, she kept trying to call Jake but his 'phone was on answer and she didn't want just to leave a message.

Late in the day she was distraught at what had happened and took her car round to Firenze House. As soon as she put her key in the lock, she knew that the house was empty. She walked in and was faced with the portrait of Jacob D'Arcy. Jake had moved it to a position where he would see it as soon as he entered the house. Rhosa stared at it and immediately felt again the strange emanation of the man. She walked into the lounge and saw a pile of cardboard boxes packed with her things. On top was a note from Jake:

'Sad, Rhosa but I suppose it was inevitable the great screen would eventually claim you. Sorry that it had to end like the song, 'Just one of Those Things'.

Goodbye to my love, enjoy your new life. Jake

It was the second day of her period but seeing his letter brought back all the emotion and the pain in her stomach of the day before. She fell into the chair where they had so often sat together and wept in desperation.

It was not until much later that she learned from a mutual friend in Los Angeles that Jake had been asked by Harry Grahame's secretary if he would go to Paris, where Mr. Grahame had been delayed but wanted to finalise their contract. While he was there Jake decided to extend his visit and get some background on the French political situation for the first edition. With Rhosa gone, he had no reason to rush back and bought a French SIM card for his phone so he could call his contacts in Paris and get their opinions. When he returned to Firenze House it was after Rhosa had flown to L.A.; the boxes he had packed had gone. On the table was a note from Rhosa which just said:

Dear Jake,

For me it was never 'just one of those things'. It was always a trip to the moon. Goodbye, thank you for giving me back my life, Rhosa.

Jake read the note several times each time putting a different interpretation on it but always coming back to disappointment. What depressed him most was the shortness of it and its finality. He screwed it up so that the cleaning lady would not read it and put it into the waste bin. He poured himself a drink, sat down and tried to calm his racing heart.

That night, he went to bed early, ostensibly to read himself to sleep, but he could neither read nor sleep. He even felt cold in bed without Rhosa, something that had not happened since she had started to spend nights with him. The next morning, he took out the letter from the waste paper basket, straightened it out and put it in an envelope in his desk drawer.

His thoughts would so often centre on Rhosa and to find out what she was doing, he took out a subscription to 'Heady', a magazine devoted to celebrity gossip. When it was delivered and Lavinia brought it in to his new office, he read it through telling himself that he was looking for social angles but in reality he wanted only to see if Rhosa was featured. Whenever he read about her in the papers or saw her on television being interviewed, he became sad again and his mind re-ran that last note. He thought several times of sending her a chatty letter but from her publicity, it was obvious she was a great success. He saw her often in the gossip columns on the arm of well-known actors, always smiling up at the man.

She wrote a few times but her letters became less meaningful and more automatic – 'went to a reception where I was feted. I am unable to believe that little Rhosa from Egypt could be so admired. All those years when I struggled and no one seemed interested." Jake read what she wrote but it was so patently a self-praising paean that he felt impelled to write her out of his life, and did not reply.

He took up with other women including Lavinia who, as well as being Harry Grahame's secretary, worked as P.A for Jake. She was quite amusing but there was no depth to her. She could talk constantly about fashion and celebrity gossip – she also read the magazine 'Heady' which she had recommended to him and talked endlessly about the stars and their lives.

He also got to know more of Kate the cleaning lady who had taken care of his house and, having tried other jobs, had now returned. She had just finished her Open University studies and being qualified, had been applying for jobs and been offered work as a librarian at Imperial College.

"Working with you made me see there is a great deal of satisfaction in manual work, particularly the sort that requires no mental effort so that the mind can wander and go into a sort of

418

trance. I'm a member of Mensa, they talk about the Pacific state of happiness where ideas come and go without reason. That's the way I've been here."

Jake turned from his reading to listen to her. "Interesting thought," he said, "people who go to underdeveloped countries often comment on how happy workers in the fields can be. Perhaps it's the Pacific feeling and they are just daydreaming."

"Maybe it's just me; I've always been a bit of a dreamer."

Jake looked at his watch. "Listen, we should do something to mark your new job. There's that new Italian restaurant down the road, they're open all day. Why don't I take you there for lunch?"

When they were sitting in the dimmed light in the restaurant after they had ordered, Jake looked at Kate with different eyes now that she was leaving her role as cleaning lady. He saw that, although she was probably a bit older than he was, she was still attractive. As they ate their pasta, he occasionally looked at her and pondered on how the human mind needs to typecast people and put them into categories on the basis that they will always remain in them - this is a teenager, therefore...a problem - this is a middle aged woman, therefore... - this is a pensioner, therefore... - this is a cleaning lady, therefore.... Now that she sat before him as a librarian, she opened up and talked about history which she knew, from reading the books on his shelves, interested him.

"My husband always wanted me to be a housewife, someone who would be there when he brought his business contacts home and who would cook a meal that they would remember and listen to their tales of business successes with wide-eyed wonder."

"Were you happy to do that?" Jake asked as he poured her a glass of wine from the carafe he had ordered.

"Don't know that I was happy," she said, taking a drink, smiling appreciatively at the rather nice white wine and looking at Jake, "at the back of my mind was amazement that I, a girl from Hackney, who grew up in a council flat, should be living in what is almost a small mansion in 'leafy' Putney." She put down her glass and looking around the restaurant, said, "and eating in a nice place with you, Mr. Dearsey" she turned back to look in his eyes, "thank you."

419

"I never liked 'Mr. Dearsey', it was something you seemed to want. Now you are leaving, it should be Jake."

"Then thank you," she reached out and touched the tips of his fingers, "Jake."

Without thinking why, he withdrew his fingers ostensibly to pick up his glass. He was still going through the transformation and could not completely accept that this woman who had always treated him deferentially was now making passes at him.

"Nice place," he said, "first time I've eaten here - I'd heard that the food was good."

"Yes it is," she said, sensing that she had gone too far in touching his hand.

She took up the librarian's job a week later and Jake started to see her more often, sometimes going to one of the many free lectures which are given in London, sometimes to concerts or the theatre where he was often given complimentary tickets.

Kate obviously wanted the friendship to become more intense but, for Jake, it never got past enjoying each other's company. Always interested in a woman's intelligence, he had initially thought that Kate's interests would mean she could replace the lost Rhosa. He soon found that she had academic knowledge but none of Rhosa's creativity. Also, she wanted to talk only about herself, and had no more than a passing interest in what he was doing or the book he was writing.

They had been seeing each other for three months when, in the same Italian restaurant she took his hand once again and said. "Jake, we have known each other long enough now. I think it's time to cement the relationship, don't you?"

Jake was completely taken aback and, for a moment was unable to reply. He wondered if she was suggesting that they should have a sexual union. It was a scenario which he had given little thought to; although she was attractive, he had no physical desire for her.

She saw his reaction, stood up, leaving her half eaten meal, "I'm sorry," she said, "I have embarrassed you," picked up her coat and left.

He occasionally bumped into her when he went to the library to do research. They exchanged politenesses but they never again went anywhere together.

He had not seen Marina for several weeks when she rang him out of the blue.

"It is I, Marina." She had continued with her English studies, and was often more correct in her grammar than most native speakers, but not always. "Would like to see you."

"Sounds a nice idea, what did you have in mind?"

"I am having a recital my poetry. You know like the ones your publisher printed. I have more now. There is a special evening of new poetry in the Putney Arts Theatre. I'd like if you come, next Tuesday if that's ok for you."

As it happened Jake had arranged to meet a colleague, Charlie Wendell, but without hesitation he said yes, knowing that he could see Charlie another evening.

He had been to the theatre many times and always found the productions very good, sometimes even better than professional West End shows. He arrived early, had a drink in the foyer and drifted into his seat, surprised at how full the auditorium was. He sat through recitals of many very amateur poems, read by a range of types including schoolgirls, some matrons bemoaning lost loves, and a scattering of Harris tweed-coated men, one with a leather strap leading to the fob watch in his top pocket which he consulted three times during his lengthy poem. The recital was to last only an hour and Marina was the last. As soon as she came barefoot on the stage, the audience responded to her. The lighting was dim so Jake could not be sure but it appeared that her dress, a simple black chiffon shift covering her from head to toe seemed to be the only clothes she was wearing. When she spoke with her Russian accent everyone was silent. She started with voice whispered like a soft wind. Gradually she built to a crescendo and her last verses were delivered in staccato which held the audience to the end.

"… A voice called me
Where can I find you now

421

Close were you so that your breath mingled
Close were you so that your body was mine
We were together alway with life precious to me
You had all my mind and I all yours.
Come back and open me again."

She stopped, looked at the audience who, in expectation that she was going to continue, waited as she turned and seemed to glide noiselessly off the stage. The lights went up and the other poets came back on to polite applause but, in spite of the anticipation of the males in the audience, hoping to see if Marina really was naked beneath the shift, she did not return, even at curtain call.

Jake had arranged to meet her in a nearby restaurant close to the theatre; when he got there she was waiting for him. She was wearing a smart suit but he saw that she was shaking.

"Are you cold?"

"Not cold, scared."

Jake sat down beside her, "You didn't seem scared when you were on stage."

"I was terrified, that was why I spoke only in whisper, I couldn't speak loud to start with."

"I and the audience thought you were doing it for effect. It was very dramatic."

"Towards the end I relaxed and began to feel my meaning," she said.

"You didn't come back at the end with the others? Every man wanted to see if you were unclothed beneath your shift."

"What you think?" she smiled, beginning to relax a little.

"Knowing you and the freedom you like I was sure you had nothing on beneath it."

Marina nodded, "nothing at all, such a sensation was the feeling, like being a wraith, no restraint, no inhibition, wind blowing on the moors through me. I felt exhilarated but that didn't stop me to terrify."

Being with Marina somehow made Rhosa seem closer to him. The two women were very different from each other but both vulnerable and struggling to find themselves.

From that evening he met Marina several times a week. The more he knew her, the more she seemed like Christopher Isherwood's Sally Bowles. He even thought there was a similarity to Lisa Minelli in the film 'Cabaret' in her. Like Sally Bowles, she had many men friends and seemed to move from one bed to another and yet she was devoutly religious.

Sometimes, if she was feeling miserable, she would drop into Firenze House unannounced and, because she found cooking therapeutic, she would be laden with provisions which she had picked up on the way.

She would often want to be silent with her own thoughts. Jake would sense her mood, know that she was having man problems and would work while she cooked or read. One evening when they were eating a meal she had cooked for him, she was obviously very happy and wanted to talk and he said. "It intrigues me that you are a devout church member but you have many men."

"In my church we have not the same repressive Augustinian inhibition that Western churches do," she stopped eating and looked around the room at ornaments on the shelves, "my religion is inside, my rules are made in here," she touched her head. "God has given me pleasure, why should I not?"

Jake nodded his understanding and smiled at her.

"My body it will not last. Has maybe ten, twenty years and will be gone. So," she shrugged, "I must use talents I have."

"Modelling?"

"That also; I am student and can't work so I must earn enough in other ways to keep myself in London. Is very expensive city so I must sell what I can."

Jake looked quizzically at her, wondering what she meant. She had such an innocent and honest face that he was sure that the obvious interpretation of her remark could not be correct.

"You are a photographer, have you sold any of your photographs?"

"Yes, I have sold a few to an art magazine run by friend."

Marina continued eating for a few moments and Jake sensed that she was thinking.

She talked into the night while he listened, feeling like an older priest in a confessional as she told him about her problems with men until they fell asleep still sitting on the settee, she with her bare feet in his lap.

During breakfast the next morning, she said. "I want to get away from London for a while. So many things make me unhappy."

"Where will you go?"

"Where will we go?"

"We?"

She nodded, "I'd like you come with me," she stopped for a moment. "Will you, Jake. Will you show me this green and pleasant land? Outside of London nothing do I know of it. I want to go to place of poetry. I need to be immersed in words, not in emotions."

"You know there is a land of mysticism, where you can imagine demons and fairies, a place where poets have been inspired and which is like no other place in this England."

"Take me there, where is it?"

"A place of hills and water which is almost like another country. It drew poets and artists. Robert Southey, Wordsworth, Tennyson, Coleridge and a woman you will not have heard of Emma Millward. She died more than ten years ago, hardly anyone has read her poetry but, for me, she is an unrecognised genius. She was a great aunt of my father's. She had no children and left her house to me, so if you want you could stay there. It overlooks Lake Windermere and is surrounded by hills. There is a jetty where Emma kept a boat. She would row out most mornings in the summer and write her poetry which was mostly about her lost life. She always seemed so content on her own. I never realised how lonely she must have been and how much living she had lost until after she died and I read her poetry and the diary she kept where every thought was recorded. It was all there, the torments, the depressions, the longing to find a man, the desperate desire for children. You see, she was what is called 'plain' and in this superficial life, looks open doors."

"Jake, how sad; will you come me to the house, so that I am not lonely like your Emma?" He saw loneliness in her eyes.

"Why, will you be lonely on your own?"

She rested her head in her hands and closed her eyes before she spoke. "Jake," she said quietly, "I have ghosts."

"Ghosts? Who are your ghosts?"

"You know I cannot say no to men. So many I not remember names."

"Men, are they your ghosts?"

"No, not men... children unborn. Three abortions...they do not leave me." Tears coursed down her face and fell onto the table.

Jake put his arms round her and pulled her close. She held him tightly in a caress of despair.

"What would they be if they had lived?" she said, looking up and wiping her eyes with the handkerchief Jake gave her.

"Now you've suggested it, I think I do need some solitude myself," he said.

"Then please take me to your Emma house. But, Jake, it will only be as friends... nothing more."

"I will come with you. I should warn you, the house is little more than a cabin, if you want a bath, you have to light the stove - not only did she leave me the house, she left a huge pile of logs, enough for more than her lifetime."

When they got to the Lake District, the journey along winding roads was tedious for Jake. The house had the barest of furniture but Marina was enchanted, transfixed by the views over the lake. A storm was building up and was rolling over the hills in the distance. They had picked up food at the village nearby and Marina took charge of it, filling the 'fridge and the cupboards with much more than they would need.

Jake followed her round, aimlessly trying to help until she took him by the hand, sat him down in the conservatory, picked a book from the shelves and said. "You read, I cook one of my special dinners."

Between looking at the view and attempting to read, he savoured the perfume of cooking.

When the meal was ready, she served it at a small table in the conservatory.

After the meal, Marina put her arms around herself and said. "This all I need, Jake, I had to get away from people."

"London?"

"Not London. All cities I visit. But London is home. No, just so many hectics: I could take no more. So for couple weeks, I want look out at a view," she pointed with her fork, "and just talk myself poetry."

Jake reached out and took her hand.

She leaned against the chair, her eyes staring at the ceiling. When she turned back she seemed to him to have desire in her eyes. He went and sat with her, putting his arms round her shoulders. She laid her head on his hand and said, "No Jake. I want you but you belong to Rhosa."

"Rhosa left for America. I may never see her again."

"Rhosa still my friend." Jake stayed quiet for a while, suppressing the desire he had felt since he had first met her and which had grown more intense when she had asked him to go away together. Sensing what he was thinking, she said. "You understand?"

He smiled, "yes, I understand but it still takes a time for me to get used to the idea that I am alone with a desirable woman who wants me to treat her like a sister."

She stood up to clear the table, leaving Jake to think while she washed the things in the chipped enamel sink.

He waited for the clattering to stop then went to help her with the cupboards, which always stuck in damp weather. He was kneeling down, hammering with this fist at a stubborn door when she pulled him up beside her and put her arms round his neck.

"Dear man. I know how it hurt. I hurt too. All men I have been with, you are the one I hurt with most. I want you here." She stood back and put her hand on her heart. "I lie awake at night thinking about you. I have longing desperately. But I want you and Rhosa be together again and I cannot take you. So I lie there with

426

ache. I try to replace you. Go to bed with other men, some are nice but no one like you." To change the conversation, she turned quickly, walked to the conservatory and stared out at the storm driven lake.

When he had fixed the door on the cupboard and put the saucepans away, he walked in and stood beside her.

She was calmer now and said. "In Moscow I went in evenings to art school. They thought I painted good. While we here I want to paint again. Paint this view, sometime sun, sometime dark like now. Where we stopped this afternoon I walked to where that waterfall was falling over rocks. It looked so beautiful, like the Paul Lake painting you have in your office."

"That is a painting I am very fond of. Paul is an amazing painter. Tomorrow, I'll take you to the town, there is an art shop there, we can buy you paint and brushes and canvas," he said. "There is a nice pub there where they do a ploughman's lunch." He saw Marina frowning. "That's bread with cheese and pickle. That was all ploughmen could afford. We're out of the tourist season now, so we should be able to get a table. In the summer it is so crowded you can hardly move."

She was delighted with the art shop and with the young fellow who owned the place and who helped her choose the best brushes, paints and canvases.

As they drove back to the cottage, Jake said. "Nice young man, Sam, isn't he? He is an artist as well."

"I like him, he say he will show me lessons in painting."

As soon as they got into the cottage, she ran excitedly into the conservatory, laid out the canvas and started to sketch in the notepad she had bought. He left her alone while he read the newspaper and phoned his office with an idea for an article which had been spinning around his head since he had told her about the ploughman's life.

For the rest of the fortnight, he read and wrote while she painted. They would walk together often, wearing warm clothing against the weather which seemed to be set for almost continuous rain. Many times she would take the car and go to the art shop for what she called her lessons. One night, she did not return until late the following morning.

"It's your life, Marina and it's your holiday as well. I want you to do whatever you like," he said, when she apologised for leaving him all night.

"I will not be go town again," she said. "Sam drank much whisky, would not let me leave. It... not nice."

Jake saw how distraught she was. "Marina, you look as though you haven't slept at all. You go to your room. I'll make something for you and bring it up when you're in bed. I'll light the fire in your room so you'll be warm."

She was so overcome by his understanding that she rushed to him laid her head on his shoulder and burst into tears. When she had recovered enough, he sat her down in front of the fire and went to her room. In a few minutes he was back. "It'll soon be warm up there, I've lit the fire."

She gave Jake a kiss, held his hand and then went upstairs. He went into the tiny kitchen, poured out cereal for them both, made tea and took it up the tiny staircase. Marina had just finished undressing and was standing in front of the fire with nothing on. "Jake, you are such a kind, lovely man," she said as he put the breakfast things on the bedside table.

"Why are you still crying?" he asked.

In answer, she rushed to him and wound her arms and legs around him so that he almost fell over. "I am crying for lost love."

"Lost love for whom."

Marina did not reply but stared into Jake's eyes for so long that he began to feel self-conscious.

"Who?"

"For you," she said, "you must know how about you I think all day. When I wake and when I sleep it's you. Even when I am with others it is only of you in my mind." She took his hand and pulled him to the bed.

A log fell in the fire and a flame blazed into the chimney. An hour later the breakfast had been untouched and Marina was asleep. Jake left her bed and went downstairs to write.

It was late afternoon when he heard her crying and ran up the stairs to see what was wrong. The fire had died in the grate and the room was cold.

"What is it, Marina, why are you upset?"

For some long time she could not speak but then said, "Rhosa."

Jake frowned. "I don't understand."

"Rhosa is the close friend I ever had. Rhosa love you," she wept.

"I may never see her again. From what I read in the gossip columns, she has a lot of men taking her to parties." Jake said.

"Rhosa love you still, Jake, she has told me in emails many times. Also I love Rhosa; she kind to me, helped me to settle into London, found me a home to live, lent me money to pay the rent and introduced me to people who would be useful. It hurt that I sleep with her man. Hurt me and hurt her."

CHAPTER 42

As a journalist, Jake would meet and interview many people, providing a bridge between often warring factions between politics, art, commerce and other fields.

He had always got on well with people, would come away from interviews having made new friends and frequently would flirt with the women, some of whom were powerful in their fields. Some he would meet outside of business for varying lengths of time. Although pleasant for an evening, none excited any real interest.

A year passed during which time 'Future Politic' under his editorship became widely read and was a commercial success, but it would still have been financially advantageous for Harry to have put the money into another investment. More interested in social issues than in increasing his already considerable wealth, Jake found Harry to be what he had always wanted - an owner who gave Jake a free hand to decide content.

He would come into Jake's office, lean against his desk and ask Jake what he was working on, would nod while Jake explained and would then make approving comments. Sometimes he might ask if an emphasis could be changed but always he deferred to Jake's opinion.

Quietly they were fashioning a revolution. Increasingly what Future Politic said was being featured in the media and many readers, including politicians, were becoming convinced that the existing anachronistic and inefficient system of Government should be changed.

Jake should have been pleased but Firenze House was so pervaded with Rhosa's memory that he found he could not settle. He tried filling the place with partying people or dinner guests but even surrounding himself with journalist friends who spent evenings joking did not take his mind off her.

He considered selling and moving to somewhere where there would be no memory of her but it almost seemed that the portraits of Jacob and Mistry frowned at him when he harboured such thoughts.

In the gossip columns he read that Rhosa had made two films; the first, directed by Anthony Garden who now had a house in L.A., was a success and she had been nominated for an award. In the second, she seemed to have lost her way and the film failed to recoup its investment. He knew how much this would have depressed her and shortly after, he read rumours about her going into rehab.

Jake had received copies of both films from the studio that had made them, in the hope that he would review them favourably in Future Politic. In moments when he felt low, he would open a bottle of wine and play them. The first film entranced him but he was disappointed in the second one, the story was strong but Rhosa seemed lost.

After the second film had flopped, there were stories that the studio wanted to buy her out of her contract. Jake thought of writing to her but decided that the thousands of miles between them were too large a chasm to cross.

One evening he was at home alone, and had put on her first film in which she played a concert pianist stricken with a slowly progressing disease. The final scene where she collapsed while playing Chopin's Revolutionary was made more poignant by the standing ovation and cheering which the audience gave her as she was helped off stage.

The film was just finishing when he was interrupted by a knock. He stopped the recording with slight irritation and went to the door and almost collapsed with surprise to find Rhosa standing there.

"Rhosa," he said open-mouthed, "what are you doing here, you're supposed to be in L.A." She waited on the door step looking lost and apprehensive. For moments they stared at each other, each wondering what to say. Impulsively, Rhosa flung her arms around him as Jake held the door open for her to come in.

He sat her down in her usual chair.

"I've come to England and real people."

Her eyes wandered round the room with appreciation.

"This room with so many memories," she said. As she looked round at the familiar objects, she saw that the television was on and in front of the player was a DVD sleeve.

"Jake, why are you watching my film, 'Piano Symphony'?"

"I do occasionally." Jake nodded. "Let me get you a drink."

"Thank you, that thing you do with frothy vanilla would be lovely."

She stood in the doorway of the kitchen and said. "I've read everything you have written in 'Future Politic', I had it delivered to me in L.A. What you were writing needed saying, quite a few people I know in California now read it.

Waiting for words, she went to the breakfast bar and sat. Apprehensive and not sure of what to say without revealing the anguish in her heart, she asked, "how is the book coming along?"

He poured hot water into the pot and carried it to her.

When they were seated on separate chairs, he said. "The book... I put it aside."

"Jake, you didn't! Why did you do that?"

He served her the mug with its Mackintosh design which she had always liked, before answering "It was ours, Rhosa, not mine. It's just as we left it." Wanting to conceal his racing heart and do something which would appear relaxed and disinterested he filled his own mug and asked the question which had been on his lips since he had opened the door on her.

"What are you doing in England, Rhosa?" he said, "I had no idea."

She wanted to say 'because I missed you' but was still feeling her way and unsure how Jake would react, so said "If you want one word from the whole of the English language it is 'disillusionment'." She nodded. "Yes, that is the only word." She looked into Jake's eyes, trying to gauge what was going through his mind. "Can I talk? Do you want to hear."

"That's what I need, Rhosa."

"When I arrived in L.A. they gave me the whole works, even my own P.A. Seemed a nice girl, took me everywhere and introduced me to all the big names, even suggesting what I should say. She did everything and made sure I did all the PR people told me to do, made sure I heard all the gossip on anyone who was worth impressing and others whom it was best to avoid because they were passé. She made me aware that if I were seen with them, the papers would get the idea I was on the downward path with them. Amazing experience and at first it seemed like heaven to be so adored. I understood why the film industry is so successful.

The euphoria lasted about six months until one night when I was in my 'luxury' apartment; I woke up, lying there alone and in the dark. It hit me that they were role playing and they would have put the same effort into selling soap. I wondered if I was a person or a gift-wrapped commodity. Soap does exactly what they want whereas I started to answer back. The nice girl started to give me orders, orders that had come from my agent. 'You must do this, Rhosa otherwise...' I knew what they meant. I'd seen it happen, big names you don't hear of anymore destroyed with invented stories. There are always newspaper hacks queuing for a scoop. Give 'em a hint and it's in the headlines the next day."

"Michael Jackson?"

"I don't know the truth about him and I doubt that he ever did but his story was pure Hollywood. They made him an idol, got him dependent on drugs, stole from him and when he tried to get rid of those who took most of his money, they tore him to pieces. To them, he was just a trained monkey, except they would have been kinder to a monkey." Changing her mood, she said. "You'd never believe how tedious making a film is. Hundreds of people stand around waiting to be asked to carry out repetitive actions. The same with the actors, you might actually work ten minutes in a day but you have to be on call just for the moment the producer or director wants you." She sighed with exasperation.

"And all the time I was filming or doing anything, I missed you, Jake it was torment without you." She put her drink down and stood up to look at the portrait of Jacob D'Arcy. "And I missed him."

"Him? You missed a portrait?"

"Not the portrait in the frame so much as the echo he left. I am sure he still lives, directing our thoughts. There were times before I left when I sat here at night and I almost heard his voice saying the same things you say about the mendacity, deviousness and exploitation of those who govern our lives." She returned to her chair. "I wish I could have known him. Doesn't matter that I didn't because I was lucky enough to have spent time with you and I'm sure you're very alike in many ways."

As she drank, she said with a smile. "No luxurious biscuits, I see."

"If you'd told me you were coming, I'd have got some in to rival Armand's. Why didn't you ring?"

"Why?" she said, again looking apprehensive, "I could so easily have done couldn't I? I wondered many times and I've picked up the 'phone, begun to dial your number then put it down again. Sounds silly but… I was terrified. I am now, can't you see this cup shaking," she held her hand in front of her, "I 'phoned you the day after you walked out of the Square but couldn't get through to you. I came round to see you but you were out. It wasn't till months later that I met your friend, Charlie Farme. He was in L.A. working as a camera man and he told me you had gone to Paris. So we never said goodbye properly. You were a beast not letting me do that. I wanted to explain that my emotions were all over the place when we were in Grosvenor Square. You didn't know but it was the first day of my period, the pain was so bad, I wanted to lie down on the park bench. If I could have, I would have got inside your overcoat and slept surrounded by the warmth of your body."

"Why did we play such a stupid game, Jake? I've never regretted anything so much in my life. When I turned back to try to explain, you had gone. I tried to call you for days but you didn't answer, I fell over in the mud trying to run to you. By the time I got up you had gone. You left my life until today."

"When I was in L.A I saw you on television being interviewed about the mess the financial world is in. You had a banker sitting next to you. When you said that the actions was nothing more than a small thumb over a bleeding wound, he laughed but we all knew he thought you had no idea of the real issues. You were saying what they wanted to ignore but it's obvious to any honest person that you were dead right."

"I knew what I said would be unpopular. I saw the sneer from John Meddleton, he was the banker. If I had had the chance, I would have kicked him in the proverbial balls. Glossing over gaping holes is the common response of that type. The interviewer invited us to have a drink afterwards and, of course, Meddleton wanted to put the knife in again.

'You don't get it, do you, Jake? You can't accept how hard we are all working to get back to normality, can you?'

Jake grinned, "I almost vomited over him. 'Normality for you is your million quid bonus, your yacht, big house in the country and your glamorous wife. In your normality, have you ever been to one of those housing estates which I've heard you refer to as 'sinks'? Next time you crack open another bottle of bubbly because you are bored, think what you should be doing for those in poverty living in those sinks.'"

"Meddleton found he had to leave for a 'business' appointment. I smiled as he left because I know that his glamorous wife is not enough for him. When he is delayed by business, there are other arms he turns to for comfort."

"There are so many of that type in the film business."

"How long are you back here for?"

"I'm here, I'm not going back."

"You don't mean that you're not going to be making any more films?" he asked, desperately hoping she would say 'yes'.

She nodded. "It's funny I know, the one thing I always wanted was to make films and to be loved by my public. But even when I thought I wanted it so much, I knew that one thing the mind can't take is total adulation. We all need to be wanted but to be bathed in unthinking love is so unreal that it chokes off the supply of air to the brain and with it the stability we need."

"I was interviewed so many times just because I was a 'star'. I felt like saying, 'acting is only a small talent, it comes from an emptiness which the actor fills with the personalities of other characters. Once when I was on one of those 'gee yer wunnerful, Rhosa' television interviews where every question is saccharin sweet, I felt like saying to the unctuous interviewer. 'For God's sake you've said all this before and to every one you've interviewed, I am not marvellous. Let's get onto the real issues facing this affluent country. Like there are kids going hungry and having nothing more in their lives than crime and there are people unable to afford health care who decline unto death.' At the last interview I had, I said some of those things, phrasing them more delicately but not much because beforehand, they had plied me with too much drink at the reception. These things are scripted, they tell you the questions and what your response will be. The interviewer was completely thrown by what I said to him so obviously irritated he said 'Big subjects, Rhosa, we haven't got time here. Come back later.' Needless to say, they never had me back."

"Just part of the malaise we live in," Jake said. "We are expected to accept mendacity, get on with our lives and let others get on with theirs. That is the sickness in Capitalism; it ignores humanity for the sake of bottom line profit."

Rhosa nodded. "That sickness is an obscenity in the film industry. The honey words and the insincerity revolted me. 'Darling, how lovely you look, I loved you in that last picture.' They don't say the name because they have forgotten it and there are so many people they have to gush over that they'd need an encyclopaedic brain to remember every film. I once asked the female columnist, the possessor of silicone breasts and the wig of a teenage girl, which picture she meant. The answer said with a smile which only slightly concealed her embarrassment at not remembering was 'You know', and then suddenly 'Oh there's Eger Nolan, I must go and speak to him."

Rhosa watched Jake intently and finally said. "I missed all the things you stand for Jay. I wanted your ..." she shrugged her shoulders, "dependability. Over there the sun-streamed tide comes in and washes the sieved and cleaned perfect beach sand from beneath your feet. Nothing is real. I missed real and I missed you like hell."

"But why did you leave me such a note when you came to pick up your things?"

"If you had known the utter devastation I felt that you were not there when I came to pick them up. I didn't want to go, if you had been there and just said 'stay', I would have torn up the air ticket. I wrote just that short note because I was hysterical with grief, if I'd written more I would have broken down completely. I just had to leave the house that had brought us together, get in my car and drive away."

"Both of us were," he closed his eyes, "just stupid."

"Talk about writing a longer letter, what about you, you never wrote anything more than just a few lines at Christmas."

"I kept seeing photographs of you with other men. Seemed obvious you had got yourself settled and had forgotten all that we had together."

"Men! They were just adornments. Many times I didn't know who I would be going with but, the next day in the gossip magazines, there would be photographs of me and the man they had chosen. Sometimes he would be an unknown actor whom they were pushing. There would always be rumours of romance. My P.A. would then be bombarded with phone calls asking how long I had known him. It was her job to be slightly evasive and say she would have to check. Once someone I had never met but who claimed to be a friend gave an interview to the press saying I had always had a soft spot for the actor I had been with. I've even forgotten his name. It didn't matter, they were all vapid. I thought Anthony Garden was vain but he was only an infant. Those men would leave him for dead. Each hair had to be right; every photograph was vetted by them before anyone could use them. They would even ask my advice 'Do I look sexier in this shot than I do in this one? I'm not getting wrinkles around my eyes am I? Look that is a wrinkle, that bastard photographer, I told him to use his lights and he hasn't. It's a good picture otherwise - I must get that wrinkle air brushed out so we can use it.'"

"The studio wanted to keep me in the public eye so I had to go to parties they had selected, wear clothes they had chosen for me into which I was sewn before I was allowed out. Once during a two week break in filming I couldn't stop eating and I put on a few pounds. The following week they put a nurse with me who weighed everything I ate, locked the fridge - no, you can smile, Jake but there was literally a lock on the fridge. Took no more than a few days till I got back to my old weight. Only then was I allowed to go to parties." Rhosa laughed with Jake but without humour.

"It is their livelihood." Jake interrupted.

"Oh yes, I don't blame them for looking after their assets. They gave me the 'full treatment' and for a few weeks, I even began to believe my own publicity. But, you know, even when the limelight was shining and I was walking into a crowded reception full of people who were there just to see me. I just felt empty inside. I knew it was all flummery. I felt desperately lonely. It was a big effort not to scream out 'this is all nonsense, you don't care about me and you're all only here because your agents told you to' but I stopped myself. We, the cursed ones who have to display ourselves to get our fixes; can you imagine what it does to us. At the moment of total adulation we are filled with terror that it will all blow away. We crave success but the mind cannot take it, like in William Blake's 'Sick Rose', the invisible worm consumes innocence. I met a woman who had been Judy Garland's make-up artist. Even when she was making 'Wizard of Oz' she was fed coffee and slimming pills. When she became exhausted, they fed her stimulants. At night she was given barbiturates to make her sleep so she developed a drug addiction which led to a nervous breakdown and her early death."

"Then the last film I did brought me down to earth, no it was worse than that, it brought me down to the gutter. You may have heard."

"I read that you had to go into rehab. Was that true?"

"Not something I'm proud of. I've never been into drugs but I could have had them, as many and as often as I wanted. You know I had a weakness for alcohol. Over there it became just water like it was the necessary fuel to start the steam engine of the day. Without it I couldn't seem to function. Then one day a friend, the only real friend I had in that city of false friends, found me at the wheel of my car asleep. She'd been there herself and knew well enough what the problem was. She took me straight to her doctor and before I knew it, there I was staying in a villa with many other names you will have heard of. I had my own physician and a private room with a view looking out over the San Fernando Valley."

"They tell you you're cared for but you look around and you see famous faces but mingled with people who don't look right. These people try to befriend you. 'Talk to me Rhosa, I'm just someone who loves to listen.' I went onto the web to check on one, Julian Holroyd. I found he was a gossip columnist. Too clever to have a drink or drugs problem but he had a suite there, probably cost him $40,000 a month, but he could make a million from a good story." She shuddered at the memory. "You look around and wonder if there is

438

anyone you can trust and there is no one, they are all on the make. They build icons so that they can make money from their stories and then they destroy them and sell the story again. You wonder why you hear so much about Scientology and why so many big names are in it. It's because they will fight for you. They act like your insurance company. They are so wealthy that if a rumour is started, they will make sure it is shown to be a lie."

Her eyes met Jake's. "When I was in that place, I knew then that the only stability in my life was you, Jake. I desperately wanted to be with you. With thousands of miles between us I wrote a poem as a way of speaking to you. I meant to send it to you because you were the only one who would understand what I meant. I put it under my pillow one night after they had given me a sleeping draft. When I woke they must have found a crumpled piece of paper and thought it was just rubbish because it had gone. I never forgot it though and on the flight over I kept thinking about it and... you."

"Where is it?"

"It's not written down. I lost it once, I'll never lose it again. Do you want to hear it?"

"Please."

She stood up, walked to the other end of the large room and, facing the wall with her back to him so that her voice echoed, said

"When Stardom Comes

I am the beautiful, I am the blessed,
The obsessive and the bored
In public view, I exhibit
My so successful life
But when at home, I walk alone
Beautiful and blessed
So lovely and obsessed with life
But jaded and distressed
I stand apart in emptiness
Glam partners in my arms

439

> *The clothes I wear, designer best*
> *But no one lives inside.*
> *My mind has fear of solitude*
> *And all incessant talk*
> *Of happiness I claim to have*
> *Reflected in my smile*
> *But in the smile is loneliness*
> *And overpowering fear*
> *And when one day the curtain falls*
> *The womb I left calls back.*
> *But is no longer there."*

"You know, as I wrote it I couldn't get out of my mind the memory of Marilyn Monroe. Adored by millions but haunted by loneliness. After a party, she would return to her home where she had a white piano which she would play on until either the drink or the drugs would overcome her and she would sleep. Many times I felt like her. Publicly loved, privately despised." She folded her hands and stared at Jake, wanting to ask if she could come back but not daring to.

They both remained silent until Jake cleared his throat.

"How you suffered, Rhosa, I wish you had emailed me, you could have sent your poem."

"What would you have done?"

"I would have got on a plane to L.A."

"That's partly why I never did send it."

"How do you mean?"

"I wanted you to come without my asking you."

Jay went to sit beside her and wrapped his arms round her. They sat unmoving. "Oh, my dear," he said. "What fools we are."

Sensing her sadness, he said, "I'll go and do another drink, I need another and I guess you do after your journey. When did you fly in?"

"I'll make it. I can still find my way to the kitchen." She grinned, picked up the pot and went to the kitchen.

While she was away, Jake tried to read the newspaper she had taken out of her bag. Without thinking, he carried on with the crossword she had started. A moment later he realised with amusement that he had reverted to the old pattern where she would start a crossword, do all she was able to and then pass it to him to finish.

When she came back, this time with a plate of biscuits, she said. "I bought these for you when I came to pick up my things. They're the sort you like. You must not have seen them; they were in a tin in the cupboard, still in date."

"You never told me about them, you could have left them beside your note."

"I didn't know how long you would be and, knowing your tidiness, I put them away where I thought you'd see them." She laughed, offering the biscuits to him.

"My favourites too and they've been sitting there all that time, waiting for your return."

Rhosa sat down on the settee beside him and felt the warmth of his body through her dress. "You asked when I flew in," she said. "I've been here a week."

"Why have you waited so long, have you been busy?"

"Like I said, I was terrified. I sat in the hotel room looking at the 'phone stupidly hoping you would ring, although how could you know I was back or where I was? I've never suffered much with stage fright but I've got it now. Normally I know the script, how it starts and how it ends. This time I've just got blank pages." She looked over the top of her cup. "Can you take me back, or should I say, 'Will you take me back'. Or is another woman in your life? If there is, just say and I'll leave you now."

"Women - yes, several, but no woman, there has never been any, Rhosa." He held out his hand, she put her cup on the floor and went to sit on the carpet in front of him resting her head on his knee as Jake stroked her hair.

"I'm different Jay, not the Rhosa you knew at nineteen nor the Rhosa who left England last year, I think I am stronger and...more reliable. I don't touch alcohol and never will again." She squeezed his hand. "There will be no more late nights when I don't come back in time. I don't want to make any more films. I've reached the summit and I didn't like the view, it's strewn with the bodies of people who failed."

She sighed. "In those insane times the thing I wanted most was to talk with you. And never again to be expected to give only replies to an interviewer who just wanted me to say that I found living in L.A very exciting. If I'd hinted that I wanted to be in Firenze House to cook and clean, do the washing, ironing, shopping and pick up where we left writing the book, that would have been an admission of defeat, and defeat would not have been on their agenda."

She turned her head to look up at him. "Can I, Jay?"

"I'm not going to answer because anything I say would be trite. But there is a song by Eric Maschwitz, a man you will probably not have heard of but he has a complete novel in his lyrics. They've gone through my head every time I sat in this room and thought about you." He turned to the book shelves and brought down an ashtray with a cigarette stub in it. "You hardly ever smoked except when you were stressed. You must have put this here when you collected your things before you left for L.A. Your red lipstick is still on it. It made me think of the Maschwitz song.

'These Foolish Things'.

A cigarette that bears the lipstick traces.

An airline ticket to romantic places,

Oh how the ghost of you clings.

These foolish things remind me of you."

Rhosa squeezed his hand again. "I've got a suitcase packed in the car. Can I bring it in?"

Jake stood up. "I'll bring it in before you change your mind."

Rhosa passed him the car keys.

When he got back, staggering under the weight of the case, Rhosa said.

"There is a thing about a lost love by Susan Marr Spalding which so often went through my mind in the artificial life I was forced into when you and I were parted.

The whole world sings my song and I alone
Am silent: yet through my tears I sometimes say
To which of us doth greater joy belong?
He hath his love; but I – I have my song

I've never been a believer but sometimes when I was on my own in a hotel room, I'd think of it and ask God, any god if we could be together again."

"And now you're here." Jake smiled with intense pleasure.

"Remember the evening in the Festival Hall when the Czech pianist played Chopin and Rachmaninoff? He's there again tomorrow evening playing the same music. I've booked two tickets. I've also booked a table in the restaurant, by the window so we will see that wonderful view across the Thames. Will you come?"

"Tickets and a table," he smiled, "sounds as though you were pretty confident I'd be available and would be waiting here for you."

"Not confident," she put the car keys into her bag. "I thought booking them might act as a talisman." She looked at him apprehensively, "Will you come?"

"There is nowhere I would sooner be." He put down her case near the stairs, put his arms round her and said, "thank you for coming back Rhosa. Now I can start real life again."

That night in bed, Jake was drifting off when Rhosa said. "In L.A. I often thought about Jacob and Mistry. It would make a good film script, but there are some loose ends still."

"Mm," Jake mumbled, "are there?"

"Yes, like - did Mistry ever write anything in the diary about what she thought? Did she really die by drowning or was that a story to put pursuers off. And what about your white slave trader, Daniel Freidan. Did he steal those papers from Jennifer Williams? If he did why should he have done it? Why not just ask Jennifer? I'm sure she would have given him anything. And what happened to the Cardinal's jewels, are they still somewhere. I want to find answers to all those questions. We must search this house to see if there are more letters. We may even have to go to your Mr. Freidan and ask him a few questions."

She turned over to get his agreement. Heavy breathing came from Jake's side of the bed.

The next morning Rhosa was awake early. She left a note for Jake on the pillow which just said "I love being home with you, I'll be back soon", and went to get things from the shop.

When he woke, she was back laden with vegetables, meat, fruit juice, cereal, croissants, jam, butter, cold meats and a vanilla tea. "This tea was what I first had in Los Angeles. One of the few good things I found there."

"Aren't we going out tonight?" Jake said as he helped himself to breakfast.

She put her hand to her mouth. "Tomorrow night I meant."

When they had finished she said. "In a way I was sorry you had not done any more on your book, but in another sense, I'm pleased. I want to work on it with you. While I am clearing up, can you get me the opening where you are outlining your Alternative Democracy? I spoke with a publisher in California. He said you are right about political reform. It is what everyone wants to hear. He'd like to publish it."

Jake put his arms round her. She said as she bit his ear tenderly "Now that I am back home, I am going to write a novel about Jacob and Mistry, it's an amazing story."

THE END

EXTRACT FROM JAKE DEARSEY'S BOOK ON FUTURE CHANGE

This refers to the political system in Britain but all nations are the same, only the names need be changed.

CHAPTER 1

<u>COLLECTIVE DELUSION</u>

Colonel Drake discovered how to extract oil around 1859 and the world's economy has thrived on what seemed a limitless supply of cheap energy. This bounty which was laid down over millions of years will by the middle of this Century, be largely consumed in 200 years of mans' development. It is easy to forget that cheap has given all of us a standard of living enjoyed only by the wealthy of earlier eras.

Mankind's profligacy, greed and self-interest make it obvious that, without fundamental changes, we do not have a sustainable future. There have been half hearted attempts to concertedly reach agreement on the environment but what has the Kyoto Conference achieved? The answer is zilch. In 2009, we were prepared by our politicians for dramatic changes at the Copenhagen Summit. What did that summit achieve? Again zilch.

Everything we eat, drink, wear build or heat property with has been produced by consuming oil. Every time we get in our cars oil is consumed. So you cycle to work. That's very commendable but do you eat? Some estimates show that the food we eat contains very roughly about one tenth of the energy it took to produce. If we could eat oil instead of food, it would be more energy efficient. There is controversy about the amount of oil available and no one can yet predict how long it will be before oil becomes exhausted but by mid-century it will be in short supply. As with all other commodities as it runs out its price will rise. Underdeveloped countries will suffer first and will not be able to afford fertiliser to grow food or fossil fuels to cook it. The economies of wealthy nations will also be disrupted by inevitable price increases.

There are many examples of wasteful use of energy where, for instance, the same goods are being imported as are being exported. It is reported that the UK in one year alone, brought in 61,000 tonnes of chicken from Holland and exported 33,000 tonnes of chicken to Holland. Chicken tastes more or less the same from any country and there are not the climate differences which support the transportation of strawberries from say Morocco during winter when they can't be grown in Europe. The trade in many other products, pork, lamb, milk etc., with the same goods imported as exported is equally as stupid. This is not just illogical, it is unsustainable and can only exist as long as energy is affordable and available. It requires no great effort of imagination to see that huge quantities of oil and large amounts of climate changing carbon dioxide would be saved if nations rationalised the movement of products.

When eventually the world runs out of easily available oil, the crisis will affect every person in the world; never has this happened in the past. Before complete exhaustion, the oil rich nations will refuse to supply the rest of the world. History tells us that oil starved nations will then attack those who still have oil. The oft predicted World War 3 could be fought over oil, water, food or other declining resources.

Substantial reductions in our consumption of commodities to cope with the depredations that the twenty first century will subject us to are even now critically necessary. Governments talk about changing our use of declining resources but take no meaningful action. What holds back progress is simply a lack of political will.

Politicians are so comfortable that they fear the effect unpopular legislation will have on their careers. In the present regimes, the governing Party remains in office until the nation becomes so disillusioned that it votes another Party into power. The electorate is rarely enthusiastic about the Party policies but they have no alternatives. When a Party is elected, the 'mandate' which they claim to have received they consider gives them the right to adopt different policies from those in their manifestos.

As Fraser Nelson reports in the Daily Telegraph of January 2015, Parliament follows a cycle 'boldness in year one, a flurry of action in year two, a bit more in year three and then nothing much in year four as everyone prepares for a general election.' 'The cure for admiring the House of Commons is to switch on the Parliament Channel and witness a deserted chamber talking about non-issues.' Austin Mitchell, MP said 'MPs are coming into Westminster, pretending to do things when we are just electioneering and throwing custard pies at each other

Of major concern is that the system wastes the talents of those MPs and Ministers who have learned from being in office and, when they lose power become redundant. In 1997, Kenneth Clarke, the then chancellor, lost office but with the economy in a more stable state than it had been for years. The incoming Labour Government progressively wasted this resource by employing an ever greater number of people in the public sector thereby transforming them from private sector wealth producers into wealth consumers. Prime Minister Gordon Brown, could claim 'please sir, it wasn't me' by blaming the U.S. sub-prime fiasco as the cause of the credit crisis when it became evident that the claimed affluence of Britain was nothing more than a balloon inflated by borrowed money.

The word 'global' is constantly used by politicians even though they remain xenophobic in their actions. We need to accept that the thread that joins us is that we are human beings facing a common challenge. This should override all differences between us. We will survive only if we adopt long term solutions and forget the accident of birth which makes us French, English, German, Chinese, Moslems, Jews, Christians etc. Politicians are skilled at igniting the flames of hatred. Meet someone from a nation which we have been taught to despise and you will find they need friendship, enjoy humour, care for their children and want to be loved just like the rest of us.

We must become truly global and cease pursuing our own interests at the expense of other nations, races and religions. It may sound naively idealistic but our aim has to be to unite all nations, colours and creeds in an international endeavour for survival.

We accept that Governments claim success in transforming their countries when they can clearly be seen to be powerless against the tides of market forces. Economic activity, inflation, employment and all other measures of the health of a nation change on a global rather than a national basis. Measured in terms of Gross National Product and balance of payments, some nations are undoubtedly more successful than others. But, unless they are lucky to be able to control that precious commodity, oil, the economy of even the successful nations follows to a greater or lesser extent, the sinusoidal curve of other nations, sometimes lagging and sometimes leading.

Politicians claim that living standards have been improved by their efforts. The reality is that the major contributor to this has been science. Perhaps the most significant advance was nitrate fertilisers produced by the Haber Bosch process. Their availability stimulated massive progress in agriculture and provided the resource for the green revolution which has fed the world and reduced the cost of food production. It is claimed that over three billion of us are alive today because of this one development.

Unfortunately to produce nitrates sufficient to satisfy world needs requires more than one per cent of world's declining and increasingly more expensive energy. Increasing food production which will be needed for a rapidly growing population will become impossible.

Plants convert nitrogen from the air by the enzyme nitrogenase. Unless science can find a way to copy nature's nitrogenase on a commercial scale, many of the world's populations will die of starvation. Developments of this nature should be pursued globally and funded by politicians of all nations.

In 1265 when Simon de Montfort invited representatives from the various shires to 'parlez' and thereby set up Parliament in Britain, the nation was uneducated and unsophisticated. Similar systems have since become the foundation of all western societies but, as Dan Ilet of Greenbang has said, we are using an organization as a global tool when it was only meant for a feudal society. It has as its impetus, the notion that we, the general public are unable to make informed decisions so it gives us virtually no ability to change Government policy. We have undergone centuries of education since the founding of Parliament and we would be delighted to be asked to 'parley' before our leaders determine our future.

Parliament's role was to limit the actions of the King who had the power of life and death over his subjects and could break people as easily as snapping a dry twig.

The advancement of the interests of its members was the dominant motovation in the 13th Century, blatantly corrupt it remained so for many centuries. In the nineteenth century, it was ridiculed as 'Old Corruption'. In modern times, wrongdoing in Parliament is more covert. The term 'sleaze is now used to describe the exploitation by MPs of their expenses and other wrongdoing.

Long ago it became obvious that selecting a Monarch simply by heredity is not a guarantee of intelligence or ability and the Royal Family is now emasculated and without authority. Surrounded by outmoded customs and conventions it has become little more than a part of the entertainment industry. This is not to say that Royalty is redundant. The Monarchy gives Britain a stability which most of us recognise and there is little enthusiasm for its abolition.

Like Royalty, it is becoming increasingly apparent that Parliament is an anachronism. Because of outdated conventions, open debate is not possible and too much time is wasted in political infighting. MPs are not allowed to speak without catching the Speaker's eye. If they do get to speak, they have to use phrases such as 'My Right Honourable Friend' which we all know does not imply either respect or friendship. Backbenchers rarely introduce Bills in their own right. If they are fortunate to be given a chance, it is on a Friday afternoon when, as Zac Goldsmith says, most MPs are travelling to their own constituencies and any debate will inevitably be London-centric.

In earlier centuries broadcasting of new laws could take a long time. Today, via the media, information can be heard by listeners in fractions of a second anywhere in the world. The web allows us to debate issues more effectively than Parliament because we are not restricted by allegiance to an immutable Party Policy. Backbenchers frustrated by their ineffectiveness may be forced to resort to leaking stories to journalists.

Many of us are able to understand the tides in society and the economy better than those who are elected to represent us. Yet we tolerate a situation in which we are only allowed to put a cross on a piece of paper once every five years to set in motion a machine which we cannot influence.

It would be a matter of dismay to most of us to go to the visitors' gallery and to see the small number of Members who actually sit through the tedious charade that they call debating.to listen to a Parliamentary broadcast is sufficient to make thinking people despair. MPs express opposition to the other side's views by a bray, a snigger, a guffaw or loud shout. There is no room for subtlety in their speeches which are haunted by bogeymen in the other Parties and blessed by fairy princesses in their own Party. Of course, they are following the rules of the game which affects the lives of every one of us.

A dispassionate observer would interpret this as little more than a game where there are no winners but we who pour our taxes into Parliament are the losers.

Although Parliaments' role in making law could be superseded by modern communications, a debating platform where educated and informed people can analyse information, make intelligent decisions and deliver good law is necessary. That is what we voted for but we are subjected to the degrading spectacle where MPs score advantage by deriding each other. Debate in the House of Lords is less restricted by Party allegiances but we are concerned that contributing sufficient to Party coffers can buy an elevation to the Peerage. We also fail to understand how unelected Peers such as Lord Mandelsohn can be appointed to Ministerial positions without any consultation with the electorate.

Collective Delusion inhibits us from considering any alternative to the existing structure. We accept the charade that one party is seen by its members to be always right while its opponents are always wrong and ill informed. MPs only voice the truth when they are speaking 'off the record'. MinisterVince Cable, tricked by reporters of the Daily Telegraph into thinking he was talking to private individuals said that if he were pushed too far, he would bring down the Government. He would not say this in Parliament.

In any other human activity, there would inevitably be times when the other side had the best and most practical ideas but Party policy would not permit such flexibility.

A loud and headmasterly voice as adopted by Margaret Thatcher is valuable as is the ability to feign righteous indignation on behalf of the oppressed public. Honesty is considered a weakness and the system deliberately selects out those who voice their own opinions. There are certain phrases which all MPs use, such as 'too little too late' when the opposition refers to any action of the Government.

The laws Parliament passes are often so poorly thought out that they are seen as inadequate and requiring amendment. After endless debate, fox hunting was banned in 2005. The law was so badly engineered that even the police are unsure what they are meant to be enforcing. Why was the debate so prolonged, a cynic might say it was because the arguments were easily understood and therefore everyone had an opinion.

As Zac Goldsmith has said, Parliament is dysfunctional and, in the case of complex issues, most MPs having received no training have no understanding of what they are voting far and so MPs are little more than lobby fodder. To speak against the Government would be career suicide. On one occasion Zac Goldsmith asked for an explanation of what he was being asked to vote on and was given a two hundred and eighty nine page report written in gobbledegook. Bad law has given birth to a section of society directed at finding loopholes to, for instance, avoid paying taxes. In February 2011, the Regulatory Policy Committee found that 44% of proposals for reform in late 2010 were poorly conceived and had no analysis of costs or benefits.

The complexities of esoteric subjects such as chemicals and their toxicity either singly or combined will inevitably be poorly understood. It is amusing to speculate that if a backbencher demanded the prohibition of di-hydrogen oxide on the basis that it attacks everything can kill people in minutes and is poured into sewage systems by careless industries, the chemical could be banned. Mankind would then die out because di-hydrogen oxide is water.

Professor Tim Lang, advisor to the UK government on food policy was astonished that a cabinet minister felt that Britain does not need a farming industry because it is wealthy enough to buy in its food requirements. This is at a time when there is considerable pressure to reduce their carbon footprint by consuming locally grown food and our balance of payments deficit is frightening.

Why does Parliament not attract professionally trained minds in the fields of manufacturing, science, education, finance etc. The reason is not hard to find, there is a lot more to be earned in other enterprises. The man in charge of Manchester transport has been rewarded with four times the salary of the PM; the chief executive of the British Broadcasting Company earned about seven times the salary of the man who runs the country and many chief executives of small councils earn more that the PM.

So why do MPs enter the House? A major reason for becoming an MP is, of course a desire to serve the country but the Party structure inevitably suppresses this. Also, even when the media claim that MPs command as little respect as used car salesmen and estate agents, MPs still have status as individuals. The need for power is also a factor and if the route to power brings cabinet membership or the Prime Ministerial role, one becomes a candidate for a directorship of a major company. Lucrative speaking tours are a common route for ex-Ministers. Gordon Brown, whom some claim was the worst Prime Minister Britain had can now earn £tens of thousands for one speech; Tony Blair who has been called by Sir Christopher Foster, the worst Prime Minister since Lord North, has amassed a sizeable fortune and now has a foundation which earns £millions.

As Will Hutton states in 'Them and Us', 'politicians lord it over us, they dissimulate, they lie, we suffer them and patronise them. But they are to a large extent emasculated, fearful that they can be made or destroyed by the media. They owe favours to close supporters that have to be settled; they overpromise. They are prone to vanity and hubris.'

The so called 'prudency' of Gordon Brown took Britain to world leadership but not in a way the nation could feel proud of. At 328% of GDP, Britain has the largest consumer debt of any developed nation. The leaders who represent us and who make the laws by which our lives are directed should have had sufficient economic skills to foresee that their policies could only lead to financial disaster. The Coalition Government has pledged to reduce national debt but, in the life of this Parliament it will not be reduced but has been predicted by Liam Fergusson in the Daily Telegraph to double in size.

We tacitly accept the ridiculous situations in which Ministers with no experience are expected to be experts in Education, Industry, Environment etc. After often only a short period in office they are moved and are expected overnight to then become expert in other Departments. How many managers with important positions in industry or commerce could leave their responsibilities to someone who has inadequate knowledge? In 2010, the Institute For Government issued an unsurprising report which said that Ministers should undergo training. One ex Cabinet Minister is reported to have said that the largest thing he had run before being appointed was his constituency office, after becoming a Minister he had a staff of thousands and a budget running into billions. A response to this which is often heard is that civil servants advise the Minister. This means that either the Minister follows directions in which case the question what is a Minister's purpose must be asked or, alternatively civil servants advice is ignored and it has to be assumed that the Minister knows better than so called trained professionals. We expect that all other responsible positions such as judges, civil servants, teachers, doctors or administrators have to be trained and qualified for their positions. Yet those who set policies for these critically important sections of the community need have no qualifications.

We would never allow a lawyer to perform a surgical operation. Why then do lawyers decide on the resources that surgeons need or to constantly alter policies on education? In spite of the many changes which have been legislated over the past decades we still have education policies which deliver people ill equipped for the modern world

In April 1999, Deputy Prime Minister, John Prescott, stood in for Tony Blair. He was asked about the tax aimed at preventing wealthy people and companies avoiding taxation by keeping profits offshore and known as 'withholding tax'. Mr Prescott appeared not to have heard of the tax and thought that it referred to the poll tax introduced by Margaret Thatcher which had been widely unpopular, provoking violent riots and which many people had avoided paying. He said, 'As Secretary of State for the Environment, that disastrous poll tax is one that I constantly have to deal with. You should bear in mind, that we have now settled with the local authorities the most generous settlement they have ever received!'

Because, as is reported in the media, the Labour Government under Blair and Brown had only a superficial understanding of economics, it was beguiled by the illusion that growth in the financial industry represented increased production of real wealth. As Will Hutton points out in 'Them and Us', 'politicians find it hard to think beyond the next election. The electoral system and the centralization of the state inhibits long term policy making. By favouring the financial service industry, Labour reduced what in 1997 had been an 8 per cent increase in manufacturing output since1974 into a 2.7 percent reduction by 2009'

Mike Slade, the CEO of property developers, Helical Bar in the Daily Telegraph of September 30th 2011 stated that Grant Shapps, the housing minister did not understand how local authorities worked.

In his article in the Daily Telegraph of October 10th 2011, Roger Bootle emphasises the naivety of politicians, pointing out that Keynes highlighted the need in a depression to reduce taxes and increase spending but British Prime Minister David Cameron in his speech urged people to pay down their debts, thereby reducing purchases and spiraling the economy downwards.   Roger Bootle wondered if the speech was the result of complete economic illiteracy.

There is an argument that the function of Parliament is not only unnecessary, it gets in the way of progress. The nation seems to manage very well during the incredibly long recesses Parliament has voted for itself. Belgium, because of political in-fighting, frequently operates without a government.

We are repeatedly told that the system is 'democratic' but there is little democracy in a structure which allows the electorate only to choose between the policies of the three major Parties. Most of us would not choose either the candidates or the policies their Parties have devised. So undemocratic is this system that the only recourse of an aggrieved population is to riot. This is why we had students

454

committing criminal damage when their fees were dramatically increased. Since for most of us breaking the law is abhorrent and rarely fruitful we are left with the futile exercise of petitioning.

Collective Delusion is so pervasive that it inhibits us from even considering that there could be alternatives. We allow ourselves to be governed by people we would not select if we had real democracy. The arrangement does not give us any involvement in decisions even those as critical as declaring war. This was never more apparent than it was with Iraq or Afghanistan. Few of us could see any reason for these acts of aggression and we have been ashamed at the atrocities which have occurred. Quite apart from the appalling tragedy of so many families which have lost relatives, these wars are a significant contributor to the nation's obscene debt which will be handed on to our children and their children.

As soon as we have put our cross on our piece of paper and an election is concluded, we become disenfranchised. Ask anyone in this or any other country if they have confidence in their politicians and very few would answer 'yes'.

The committed will argue that we have access to our MPs and that it is their duty to make our views known. But how many of us can remember when our representative made a speech in the Commons. We so completely accept the impossibility of finding a platform for our views that we rarely speak to our M.P.s unless we have a serious problem and then it is usually because we have an individual grievance. It would be futile to ask a backbench M.P. to change the policy of the Prime Minister or his Cabinet. If we write to Cabinet Ministers we find that they are 'too busy' even to respond personally and in any case are unable to voice their own opinions because they must take account of the effect on their own careers. If they rock the boat they will be thrown out. When this happens, the party encourages them to resign on the pretext of a sudden attack of ill health or 'to pursue other interests'. In extreme cases they are sacked but the party machine which, fearing a debilitating scandal ensures that the P.M. writes them a private letter of praise which intriguingly maybe published in the newspapers sometimes even before it has been read by the recipient.

If a Minister has personal reservations about the way the Ministry was run before taking it over, it is considered unethical for this to be expressed. But if the Minister's party loses an election, every opportunity must be sought to denigrate the new Minister even though the retiring Minister's policies may not have been rescinded.

Consider one of the decisions of Tony Blair himself to continue with the Conservative Policy of building of the Millennium Dome even after grave doubts over its viability had been expressed by many specialists. Tony Blair wanted a 'beacon to the world'.

The UK National Audit Office calculated that the Dome and the New Millennium Experience Company had cost £789 million. The estimate at the time of conception of the dome was about £400 million. There was so little enthusiasm amongst the public that after it opened the visitor numbers were about half what had been expected. It is reported that Lord Falconer calculated that maintenance costs were £12 million a year. In 2002 all the exhibits were removed and the Chief Executive was discharged. AEG, an American company now rent it for a reported £6 million per annum. Entertainment is organised by O2, a Spanish company so profits from the Dome go overseas. A return of less than 1% to the taxpayer is hardly 'a beacon to the world'. In a commercial organisation, the instigator, Tony Blair would have been 'let go'.

It is incongruous that the status quo continues when its deficiencies are so glaringly obvious to us. Why is this? A prime reason is that we are apathetic and suffer from Collective Delusion.

Heather Brooke's 'The Silent State' illustrates that under the cloak of democratic security we are moving towards a secret police state. Our taxes are used to fund machinery which tracks and records all our activities. We could have a bad credit rating and never know about it until we go for a loan. Calls we make on mobile phones, every email we write, every time we visit the doctor or apply for a licence all these actions are recorded in a database and may be used but we are not allowed to discover what is contained in our personal records.

The lives of all of us are observed. Walk the streets of London and we may be recorded by film hundreds of times a day. But if we take photographs of the police or those who watch us we will be investigated. The inquisitiveness of the State is justified on the premise of protecting our security.

Heather Brooke applied under the Freedom of Information Act for details of the expenses claimed by MPs. She was told that it would cost too much to disclose how MPs were spending public money. She applied again and was told she could only ask for ten MPs' expenses. Before she received the information, a private members' bill was introduced quietly around Christmas time to exempt MPs from the Freedom of Information Act.

We the small minded and ill-educated electorate, could, of course not be expected to understand the complexities of legislation enacted by Parliament since it would obviously go over our heads. But in handing over control of our lives, we should at least be able to expect that MPs would act in our interests.

Listen to this from page 234 of 'The Silent State' for the sort of doublespeak which Orwell would have been proud of. 'When we write on behalf of constituents...we must be able to look them in the eye and say that in all circumstances what they tell us will not get out...It is like the relationship with a priest.' This is considered a sufficiently convincing argument to justify the exemption of MPs from their own law.

We had been told that there would be a 'recall' procedure which, if we lost confidence in our MP, would allow us to demand a bi-election. As Zac Goldsmith said at the RSA in January 2011, this has been quietly dropped.

An MP needs no qualifications nor do they have to be competent. The primary requirements are to be plausible and articulate. That happens also to be the prerequisite for confidence tricksters.

At each election, we are offered a policy which must last for five years. Generally the electorate is so disinterested in these policies that a large number do not vote in elections and the victorious Party is elected by a minority of the population. As little as one person in four of us may have voted for the Party in power.

The Parliamentary structure serves itself rather than the people it is supposed to represent. It sees its role is to bring in laws and that is just what it does even though they may be unnecessary and even harmful to the economy in suppressing enterprise. As reported in the Daily Mail of 27th March 2009 red tape introduced by Labour during its time in office cost firms £77 billion. The bill for the year 2008 alone was put at more than £10 billion, according to figures prepared for the British Chambers of Commerce.

Since 1997, there have been 3,000 new offences yet as far back as the Wilson Government, there was to be a bonfire of controls and John Major's Government claimed to reduce red tape. The Coalition Government has the declared intent that laws should be introduced only if other laws are rescinded. The implication is that the laws being scrapped were valueless; the obvious question then is why were they passed in the first place and do we need any more laws. As reported by Richard Fletcher in the Daily Telegraph of March 4th 2011, thirty new regulations were passed between September 2010 and March 2011 alone at time when Party policy is to reduce red tape. In the previous five years, Whitehall had published nineteen reviews into better regulations. The House is said to exhaust itself with late night sittings debating and passing laws, could it be that only by such means can it justify its existence.

If the machinery of Parliament had been effective, should we not over the last six hundred years have had sufficient debating time that our laws would by now be perfect apart from those applicable to modern technology?

The Political Parties can only survive if they have sponsors. In the case of the Labour Party the Trade Unions are major contributors and in the case of the Conservatives it is predominantly big business.

Will Hutton reports that Rupert Murdoch's purchase of The Times and Sunday Times was possible because Margaret Thatcher blocked its referral to the Monopolies and Mergers Commission and received News International's support for the rest of her time in office. When it became clear that New Labour would win the election in 1997, Tony Blair was summoned to Australia to meet Murdoch's top executives. Murdoch switched allegiance and New Labour dropped its plans to establish tough rules against cross-media ownership. Murdoch, invited several times to Downing St. was asked to come in by the back door, was it that David Cameron received the support of the Murdoch Press but did not want this publicised.

Is it not obvious that if a contributor making a donation can ensure that his interests become the policy of the elected Party then the rest of the community who have not the wealth to contribute will find their needs downgraded or ignored completely. Peter Oborne in the Daily Telegraph of 7th October 2011 commented on the many empty seats during the Prime Minister's speech at the Conservative conference, saying that the Conference is dominated by business lobbyists. They had left because the speech is the last and after that there will be no opportunity to meet and therefore influence Ministers so there would be no point in the lobbyists staying. The Conservative Party is influenced primarily by business interests because membership has dropped from three million in the 1950s to 177,000 in 2011. The results is that finance to run the Party has to be obtained from businesses. It is self-evident that businesses will only contribute if they thereby obtain favourable treatment. Peter Oborne and many other commentators state that the Conservative Government planning reforms have become a charter for property developers to rip up the countryside.

Is there not an inherent weakness in the way Parliament is structured which renders it excessively sensitive to the vagaries of the media, making Rupert Murdoch the strongest man in British Politics? The Press is unelected, is driven entirely by what sells newspapers which it does by spreading despair. In August 2011, alongside pictures of rioting in London showing buildings and cars being burnt, windows smashed and uncontrolled violence, the Daily Telegraph had as its headlines 'Carry on Looting'.

We all know that we are being manipulated but under the flawed systems we have, we are powerless to effect change. The uncomfortable link between politicians anxious to stay in power and press barons who control the routes to that power is an affront to every to a nation which has an inherent sense of fairness.

Parties in power manipulate economies to the detriment of the people. All the painful actions – increasing taxation and reducing national expenditure are undertaken by the party in power in the early years of a Government. This allows them to ease off, reduce taxation and increase spending in their final years. This was never more apparent than in the latter days of the Gordon Brown Government. Britain was massively in debt but the Prime Minister would not sanction his Chancellor's cuts in spending which were obviously necessary for the good of the economy.

The Gettysburg Principle

Do we need MPs? There is an alternative which could bring into reality, the oft-quoted intention of our leaders to give power back to the people. We might call the alternative the Gettysburg Principle after Lincoln's speech in which he called for government of the people by the people.

The Gettysburg Principle would change the situation in which we are given only the opportunity to vote for one of three Parties. What we need for the 21st Century is a government of professionals conversant with the complexities of the office they hold to provide us with efficient management of the economy, to produce maximum gain.

So we would have an educationalist as the Minister for Education, a trained physician as Minister of Health, an economist as the Chancellor of the Exchequer etc. Would not these people also make mistakes? Undoubtedly they would, they can be no more than fallible human beings but they would have a better understanding than the untrained minds of our present leaders. A committee composed of qualified representatives would prepare at least three different policies based on digital input from the electorate and their own judgement There would be no need for the enormously expensive elections we now have the electorate would vote by email mobile phones etc. on the policies which would then be administered by trained professionals who would have been selected because of their experience. If it was shown that they were not performing, they could be discharged. By an e-mechanism the electorate would be given opportunities to amend policies as world events changed. There would therefore be constant involvement and discussion by the public, knowing that they were able to effect change in policies which influence their lives and their wellbeing.

The Gettysburg Principle would be an advance on the present political structure because through modern methods of communication, it would be close to real democracy than has ever before been possible. By avoiding the expenditure of maintaining

Parliament, MPs salaries and expenses it would minimise cost and maximise efficiency.

Tax Simplification

The primary tool which Parliament uses to maintain its position is taxation. Society cannot function without effective tax collection machinery but the means by which tax is collected is very inefficient. We are all taxed many times over, if we deal only with the well- known taxes which come easily to mind, they are, P.A.Y.E., V.A.T. Car Purchase Tax, Fuel Tax, Road Fund Licence, Business Rates, Rates on our homes, National Health, Capital Gains Tax, Inheritance Tax, Stamp Duty. There are others and it is obvious that taxation takes too much of the nation's resources and in doing so suppresses enterprise.

Ibn Khaldun the mediaeval Muslim philosopher, Maynard Keynes and Professor Arthur Laffer developed what is now known as the Laffer Curve which demonstrated that reducing the level of taxation actually increases revenue and vice versa. In spite of this Chancellor Osborne increased Capital Gains Tax from 18% where it brought in £7.8bn to 28% where in 2011-12 it gathered £4.3bn and in 2012-13 it collected £3.9bn.

Efficiency of taxation can be measured as a 'Cost over Value Ratio' (COVR). As an ideal, a tax should cost nothing to collect. If people were honest (only an idealist would be naive enough to think they are) and calculated their tax correctly, sending it to the Revenue through the post at their own cost, that would represent an ideal and COVR could be calculated as roughly 100%. With the national and human character as it is, no one will pay an avoidable tax and many will want to conceal income and wealth if it attracts extra tax. We therefore need an army of tax inspectors who have powers which, in a democracy we find alarming. VAT and Inland Revenue inspectors can practice the methods of the KGB, invade premises and drag people from their beds in the early hours of the morning. In the name of tax collection, this is considered acceptable. The cost of all these inspectors, assessors, clerical officers, buildings, reams of paper, the time employed calculating our own tax is enormous. Hidden and un-quantified costs fall on companies in filling in forms, employing accountants, bookkeepers, VAT advisors and financial advisors which when added into the equation, could even result in some taxes costing the nation more to collect than the revenue they bring in. Even if we avoid buying anything and instead of owning a house, live in a tent in a forest to avoid rates and put our money into bank accounts we will pay tax on the interest and when the reaper comes, a huge chunk of any capital we have saved goes to pay inheritance tax.

Our complex and expensive taxation machinery needs reform and a simpler, more efficient process of collection. Any alternative needs to be cheap to run and be capable of reducing the army of tax collectors and advisors we have now. To do this we need to consider the sources of the tax these people collect?

All tax originates from businesses which produce profits and employ people to make things, farmers who grow food and importers who sell goods have to pay their employees a sufficient amount for them to have reasonable living standards. They also have to pay their employees an extra amount so that they, in turn can pay their own taxes. This direct and indirect taxation comes directly out of profits.

The proposed new means of gathering revenue for the exchequer would be to only take taxation from the wealth producers and not from their employees. The actual amount wealth producers pay in tax would decrease because COVR would be closer to 100%. Because of the simplicity and efficiency of collection, the savings over the existing machinery would mean that the Revenue would have a greater tax take. All forms of taxation except for that which would be applied to the wealth producers would be eliminated.

We, the electorate are disillusioned with the current political maelstrom. The Gettysburg Principle would provide a machinery to give us all a voice. In summary, the 21st Century will be so challenging that we need an alternative to the cumbersome and inefficient Parliamentary machine we have inherited. The current structure prevents MPs from acting in the best interests of the nation. The rising in the Ukraine, Egypt, Libya and other nations are just the visible evidence of a universal desire for freedom from suppression. The world is seeing a growing desire for real democracy, adopting the Gettysburg Principle of government and the COVR system of taxation would meet that need.

Along with politics, capitalism is in desperate need of reform.